Acclaim for Joy Williams's

The Quick and the Dead

"Beautifully written, profoundly strange, and fiercely mordant." —*The New Yorker*

"There is no writer in American better than Joy Williams at describing in fiction the evanescent state of mind of the contemporary female adolescent." —*Chicago Tribune*

"Poetic, disturbing yet very funny . . . the brilliantly controlled style [is] informed by a powerful spiritual vision." —*The Washington Post Book World*

"With a wry sense of gallows humor, Ms. Williams portrays a world where lines and guidelines are fast eroding. . . . It is a world many readers may well find disturbingly familiar." —*The Wall Street Journal*

"Weird and wonderful. . . . To read Joy Williams is to see everything with a disconcertingly clear peripheral vision." —*The Oregonian*

"An ambitious, sprawling novel . . . offering its own unique beauty and logic. From the beginning of *The Quick and the Dead*, we are reminded of why she's been compared to Céline and Flannery O'Connor." —*Bookforum*

"Hypnotic. . . . Williams' prose burns with a strange and captivating music."　　　　　　　　　*—Seattle Weekly*

"Each description, each riposte, each incident is like a little explosion. . . . A moral tale for a time of moral fuzziness."　　　　　　　　　—Rick Moody

"Vintage Williams—odd, funny, dark, heartbreaking, philosophical, and packed with the kind of detail, situations, and dialogue that can only come from her delightfully skewed and distinct fictional universe."
　　　　　　　　　—Austin Chronicle

"One-of-a-kind fiction. . . . There's no way to grasp all its dark, rich mysteries in a first reading, but I'm too scared to read it again."　　　　　　　　　—Bret Easton Ellis

"The bizarre is commonplace in Williams's world . . . but enormous pleasure awaits readers willing to enter."
　　　　　　　　　—The Plain Dealer

"Satirical, surreal. . . . A provocative depiction of a profane world without pathos."　　　　*—The Commercial Appeal*

"Joy Williams is a superb wordsmith."
　　　　　　　　　—The News & Observer

"*The Quick and the Dead* is an astonishing, thrilling thing: it's a two-read book, packed with sly humor and toughness, both masterful and freaky."
　　　　　　　　　—San Francisco Bay Guardian

Joy Williams

The Quick and the Dead

Joy Williams has received the Rea Award for the short story and the Strauss Living Award from the American Academy of Arts and Letters. *The Quick and the Dead* was a finalist for the Pulitzer Prize in 2000.

The
Quick
and the
Dead

The Quick and the Dead

Joy Williams

Vintage Contemporaries

Vintage Books

A Division of Random House, Inc.

New York

FIRST VINTAGE CONTEMPORARIES EDITION, JANUARY 2002

The Library of Congress has cataloged the Knopf edition as follows:
Williams, Joy.
The quick and the dead / Joy Williams.—1st ed.
p. cm.
ISBN 0-679-44646-X (alk. paper)
PS3573.I4496 Q53 2000
813'.54—dc21 00-034912

Vintage ISBN: 0-375-72764-7

Book design by Iris Weinstein

www.vintagebooks.com

Printed in the United States of America
10 9 8 7 6 5 4 3 2 1

And whatever is not God is nothing,
and ought to be accounted as nothing.
—THOMAS A. KEMPIS, The Imitation of Christ

Toward a place where
I could not find safety I went.
—YAQUI DEER SONG

Book
One

S O. YOU DON'T BELIEVE IN A FUTURE LIFE.
Then do we have the place for you!
You'd be home now if you lived here, as the old signs promised.
But first, a few questions. To determine if you qualify.

What is the difference between being not yet born and having lived, being now dead?

Don't use reason without imagination here.

A hare is the determinative sign defining the concept of being. Say you catch an actual hare of the desert and place a mirror to his nose; you will observe that a moist breath mark will appear on the glass. The moisture comes from the hare, though there is not a drop of moisture going into him. Does this disprove the axiom "Out of nothing, nothing comes"?

Do you consider the gulf between the material and spiritual worlds only apparent?

Don't worry about catching the hare.

Do you believe that what has been is also now and that what is to be has already been?

The dead have certain obligations. Is one of them to remember us?

Do you find that offensive?

Do you find the dead ridiculous? How about the dead finding the living ridiculous?

Nothing we do is inevitable, but everything we do is irreversible. How do you propose to remember that in time?

Which would you prefer to have your life compared to, wind or dust? Why?

Sorry.

I

The winter had not brought rain and there were no flowers, there would be no flowers. Still, the land in the spring of the year when Alice would turn sixteen could not be said to be suffering from drought. The desert knew no drought, really. Anything so habitual and prolonged was simply life—a life invisible and anticipatory. What was germinative would only remain so that spring. What was possible was neither dead nor alive. Relief had been promised, of course.

For more than a month now, after school, Alice had been caring for six-year-old fraternal twins, Jimmy and Jacky. They lived with their mother, who was away all day, cutting hair. Their father was off in another state, building submarines. Hair, submarines, it was disgusting, Alice thought. She did not find the children at all interesting. They cried frequently, indulged themselves in boring, interminable narratives, were sentimental and cruel, and when frustrated would bite. They had a pet rabbit that Alice feared for. She made them stop giving it baths all the time and tried to interest them in giving themselves baths, although in this she was not successful. She assisted them with special projects for school. It was never too early for investigative reporting. They should not be dissuaded by their teacher's discomfort; to discomfort teachers was one's duty. They were not too young to be informed about the evils of farm subsidies, monoculture, and overproduction. They should know, if only vaguely at first, about slaughterhouses. They shouldn't try to learn everything at once—they'd probably get discouraged—but they should know how things come into being, like ponies, say, and how they're taken out of being and made into handbags and coats. They should get a petition going to stop the lighting of athletic fields, since too much light obliterated the night sky. Excessive light was bad. On the other hand, some things perceived as bad were good. Wasps, for instance. They should not destroy the wasp nest they discovered in their garage with poisons because wasp-nest building was fun to watch in a time-lapse photography sort of way. They should marvel at the wasps' architectural abilities, their insect awareness of a supreme future structure they alone were capable of creating. Wasps were cool. The queens knew how to subsist in a state of cryogenic preservation in the wintertime. Jimmy and Jacky could get special credit for their understanding of wasps, agribusiness, slaughterhouses—just to name a few possibilities. She was willing to make learning interesting for them.

But she didn't help much with homework. Mostly the three of them just hung out. Little kids didn't instinctively know how to hang out, Alice was surprised to learn. Sometimes they'd walk down to the Goodwill store and see the kind of stuff people had wanted once but didn't want anymore. She usually didn't buy anything because she didn't believe in consumption, but once she bought a nun in a snow dome. The nun was only fifty cents because the snow had turned brown and clotted and fell in revolting clumps when you turned the thing upside down. What was a nun doing in one of those snow domes anyway? Alice had never seen anything like it. The twins had never seen anything like it either. But Goodwill was only good for once or twice a week. The rest of the time they'd sit around in these tiny plastic chairs the boys had in their junk-filled room and Alice would discuss things with them, chiefly environmental concerns. Alice liked talking about animals and excess packaging. She opened their small eyes to the world of drift nets, wetland mitigation, predator control, and overpopulation. She urged them to discuss the overpopulation problem with their mother. Sometimes their attention wandered. They had a bunk bed in their room, and they both slept on the bottom bunk. When they were seven, they'd be permitted to sleep on the top bunk. They could hardly wait.

Their mother hadn't paid Alice yet, and near the end of the second month Alice asked for her money.

"Yes, yes, sure," the mother said. "I have to go to the bank tomorrow. How about Saturday?"

She appeared Saturday morning at Alice's house in her big sloppy station wagon. Alice and her granny and poppa were sitting on the patio drinking coffee and watching the birds at the feeder. Actually, only Alice was watching the birds, since her granny and poppa were talking avidly about compost. Alice couldn't talk about compost so early in the morning, but they could. Compost was as munificent as God to them, just as interesting as God certainly. They said that the reason healthy plants repel pests is that they have such intense vibrations in the molecules of their cells. The higher the state of health, the higher the vibrations. Because pests' vibrations are on a much lower level, they receive a distinct shock when they come into contact with a healthy plant.

Why not? Alice thought.

Alice sauntered down to the station wagon, which was packed with luggage. "You taking a trip?" she asked.

"Didn't Jimmy and Jacky tell you? Oh, that's right, I swore them to secrecy. Let's go out and have some breakfast. I'll buy you a donut."

The mother gave Alice the creeps. She wore large, shapeless dresses she called her "jelly bags."

"I've had my breakfast," Alice said.

"I'd like to talk to you," the woman said. "Breakfast really isn't necessary. Why don't we go out to the state park—that's a nice ride."

Alice looked back at the patio, but her granny and poppa had gone inside. She shrugged and got into the car. Cars had never charmed her, and this one seemed particularly vile. They sped off to the park about fifteen miles away. The lovely, lovely mountains tumbled across the horizon.

The kids' mother moved one big arm and groped around in the back-seat. The car veered down the road, Alice staring stoically ahead, until she retrieved what she was after, a cocktail in a can. "Want a pop?" she said. Alice shook her head. "Sure?" the woman said. "It's mostly fruit juices."

I want . . . a scar, Alice thought. A scar that would send shivers up peoples' spines but would not elicit pity. She didn't want that kind of scar.

"Where are Jimmy and Jacky?" Alice finally said.

"With a babysitter."

Alice looked at her.

"I'm trying out somebody new just for the morning, then we're leaving. Back to the husband. We're going to be a family again."

"You owe me three hundred dollars," Alice said.

"I do? Those hours added up, didn't they?"

"Do you want a receipt for tax purposes?"

"I'd love a receipt," the mother said.

They entered the park. A small deceased animal was lying in the road, and the car ahead of them ran over it. They ran over it. A herd of men in fluorescent shorts jogged by.

"God, I hate this place," the woman said. She rummaged in the backseat for another pop.

"Why did we come here, then?"

"I mean the whole place, the state."

She turned abruptly into a parking lot. There were some benches and a few little structures for shade. She turned off the ignition and got out of the car. "Gotta tinkle," she said. Alice sat and gazed at the mountains. When you climbed, you'd move from cholla to juniper and pinyon, then to firs and aspens. Zero to eight thousand feet in forty miles. To live in a place where you could do something like that was sensational, like living exceptionally fast or living in two different bodies. The little animals of the desert didn't know that the little animals of the mountains, only moments away, even existed. Or the big animals the big animals for that matter.

Alice looked around the littered seat for paper and pencil to compose her bill, her legs sticking to the stinking vinyl of the car seat. She got out and stood in the shade. A tinkle, she thought. The awful woman was probably taking a dump. At last she and her jelly bag appeared. She had red hair today, though sometimes it was chestnut. She was a genius with hair color, there was no denying that.

"You know what keeps going through my head?" the woman said, "*DAK's incredible blowout price.* . . . We're getting a new stereo. Can't get it out of my head."

Alice handed her the bill she'd tallied. "It's in crayon, unfortunately, but I'm sure it will be acceptable. You could give me a check, though I'd prefer cash."

"That's what's going through your head, huh, like *DAK's incredible* blowout price?" The woman laughed and dropped the piece of paper to the ground. "If you think I'm paying you, you're crazy. Pervert. Bitch. You'd better watch out."

Alice looked at the piece of paper. What was wrong with it? It just lay there.

"My boys say you say the world would be better off without them. They say you killed a pony and a farmer and that you make them eat lettuce-and-rabbit-pellet sandwiches. They say you hate nuns and say not to flush the toilet every time when it's only yellow water. But it was the wasp nest that did it. I'm excessively susceptible to the stings of bees and wasps and could go into anaphylactic reaction and die. And they shrieked at me when I sprayed the damn thing. It was as big as a beer keg. They cursed me for destroying a thing that could have killed their own mother."

"Fatal anaphylactic reaction is actually rare," Alice said.

"Half the stuff they told me is even on the list."

"What list?" Alice said. Her voice sounded peculiar. *You could give me a check, though I'd prefer cash* kept sliding through her mind.

"The checklist of symptoms of satanic ritual abuse compiled by an after-midnight radio psychologist who's a nationally recognized authority on the subject. The list includes but is not limited to preoccupation with feces and death, questionable acting out, talk of mutilation and dismemberment, and fear of being normal and cooperative." She ticked them off on her fingers.

"Why, that's just stupid," Alice said.

"You're the one who's stupid, dumbass," the woman said, "thinking I'd pay for your time. I've got better things to do with my money."

"Jimmy and Jacky misinterpreted my remarks a little," Alice said. It was probably the hair and submarine emphasis in their background that made them somewhat wobbly in the comprehension department.

"You'd better watch it," the woman said. "Get away from me." Alice hadn't moved. "You'd better watch it," she said again, laughing, as she got into the station wagon. Then she drove away.

A black bird, a phainopepla, rocketed past and alighted on a trembling mesquite bush. Alice felt that the desert was looking at her, that it kept coming closer, incuriously. She stared into the distance, seeing it as something ticking, something about to arrive. A brief, ferocious wind came up and a Styrofoam cup sailed by and impaled itself upon an ocotillo. She started back toward the park's entrance, walking not along the road but through the desert itself. Cars and vans occasionally passed by. Tiny heads were what she saw, behind closed windows. She walked quickly, sometimes breaking into a run, through the gulleys and over the rocks, past the strange growths, all living their starved, difficult lives. Everything had hooks or thorns. Everything was saw-edged and spiny-pointed. Everything was defensive and fierce and determined to live. She liked this stuff. It all had a great deal of character. At the same time, it was here only because it had adapted to the circumstances, the external and extreme circumstances of its surroundings.

Plants were lucky because when they adapted it wasn't considered a compromise. It was more difficult for a human being, a girl.

She was never going to seek gainful employment again, that was for certain. She'd remain outside the public sector. She'd be an anarchist, she'd travel with jaguars. She was going to train herself to be totally irrational. She'd fall in love with a totally inappropriate person. She'd really work on it, but abandon would be involved as well. She'd have different names, a.k.a. Snake, a.k.a. Snow—no, that was juvenile. She wanted to be extraordinary, to possess a savage glitter.

She had curved back to the road and wasn't far from the entrance. The flattened brown animal was now but a rosy kiss on the pavement. She fingered the coins in her pocket. She'd get a soda and call her granny. She wished . . . she'd like to be one of those birds, those warblers that fly from Maine to Venezuela without water, food, or rest. The moment came when they wanted to be twenty-five hundred miles from the place they were and didn't know how else to do it.

She dialed from a phone outside the visitors' center. She wished she knew someone she could call illicitly.

"Poppa," she said. "Hi."

"Alicekins," her grandfather said faintly, "where are you?"

The Indians called what they heard on telephones whispering spirits. Whisper, whisper, said her poppa's blood, making its way through his head's arteries. Indians didn't overexplain matters—full and complete expression not being in accordance with Indian custom. Alice admired that.

"I'm baby-sitting, Poppa. I thought I told you."

There was an alarmed pause.

"Maybe I forgot to tell you, but I'm baby-sitting late. I won't be home for a while."

"We're fine. We're hanging in there."

"Of course you are, Poppa."

He hung up softly. He had certain phone mannerisms and this was one of them, breaking the connection gently, hoping it wouldn't be noticed.

Alice went into the visitors' center and entered the men's room just for the heck of it. She washed her hands and looked into the mirror. The assignment was to be . . . absolutely . . . expressionless. She stared at herself. She didn't look awake, was all. She'd get arrested if she went around looking like that. She pulled her hair down over her eyes and left. She hated mirrors.

She walked. An enormous grocery store appeared ahead, an outpost for the consumer cavalry. It was surrounded by ragged desert and sported large signs informing those who wanted to make something of themselves in this life that investment "pads" were available. Cows browsed the desert, token cows, hired to indicate a pre-pad tax category. A few miles later, the desert had vanished completely, the cows were no longer employed. She imagined what she would do to the woman's station wagon. She would work smoothly and calmly. She would pop the hood and remove the oil cap. Using a conveniently located hose, she would pour water into the filler hole and then top up the gas tank. She would find a can of brush cleaner in the garage and pour it into the radiator. She wouldn't do anything to the brakes for the little kids' sakes, but she would squirt glue all over the seats.

She was approaching House of Hubcaps, one of her favorite places. She paused and enjoyed the magnificent display of hubcaps. Great luminous wheels crowded the windows, reflecting and distorting everything in their cool, humped centers. They were like ghastly, intelligent, unmoored heads.

If the House of Hubcaps didn't have the hubcap you were searching for, it didn't exist.

She moved on, renewed, to Jimmy and Jacky's house. The hubcaps had refreshed her. They had cleared her mind. Vandalizing the station wagon would be too easy, too predictable, and by now far too premeditated. She should do something on a grander scale. She should attempt to liberate those children, those sour-smelling, sniveling, cautious little boys. All their mother had ever provided them with was good haircuts. She should free them from that corrupting presence, from the world of toots and jelly bags and poisonous sprays, but that would be kidnapping, and punishable, she believed, by death. Plus she didn't want Jimmy and Jacky.

The house was deserted. Cardboard cartons stuffed with clothes and broken toys were scattered about in the front yard, the word "Free" written on every one. The garage was empty. The rabbit hutch was empty save for a withered string bean. The rabbit was probably hopping around nearby, terrified. Or it might be hunched up somewhere in a narcosis of incomprehension at being hutchless. Or maybe the mother had boiled it and served it to the twins for lunch on a bun with some potato chips. Alice wouldn't put it past her.

Back at her own house, Alice got into her nightie and ate two cheese sandwiches and a bowl of spaghetti. Her granny and poppa sat in the living room watching Fury sleeping in his dog bed surrounded by his toys. Fury was named after the beautiful horse in the Bette Davis movie who is shot by Gary Merrill, who is pretending to all the world that he is Bette's husband. Bette Davis was her granny's favorite movie star. None of the new ones could hold a candle to her.

"Alicekins," her poppa said. "I'm so glad you're back. We have some questions for you."

"Good ones tonight," her granny said.

Alice made another cheese sandwich. She was not abstemious and ate like a stray, like a pound pet rescued at the eleventh hour.

"A woman goes to her doctor," her granny said, "and the doctor says she's got cancer of the liver and gives her three months to live. Cancer of the liver is a painful, horrible way to go and there's no way to beat it, the doctor says."

"Typical," her poppa said.

"What!" her granny said.

"Typical doctor." Her poppa took a Kleenex from a box on the table beside him and dug around in one of Fury's ears.

"Yes, well, she goes home and she and her son have a long talk and the son arranges it so that his handgun collection is at her disposal and she shoots herself. During the autopsy it comes out that she didn't have cancer of the liver at all."

"Just had a few pus pockets was all," her poppa said. He put the used Kleenex into his pocket without looking at it.

"So the question is, who's responsible for her death, the lady, the son, or the doctor?"

These kinds of problems always cheered Alice up. They weren't questions of ethics or logic, and the answer, under the circumstances, didn't matter anyway. She just loved them.

Corvus lost her parents to drowning close to the end of that peculiar spring. The phone rang at school, she was summoned to the office and was told the situation. It seemed unbelievable but was the case. They had driven down to the Mexican state of Sonora for their anniversary. They had been to the beach. They'd been swimming, sailing, even diving in the Gulf of California but had drowned coming back from Nogales on an off-ramp of I-10 during the first rainstorm of the year, just beyond one of those signs that say DO NOT ENTER WHEN FLOODED, signs the engineers claim (and continued to claim with tedious righteousness after the accident) are where they are for a reason. The last picture of Corvus and her mother and father together had been taken not long before in that same gritty border town, Nogales, with the burro on the tourist street, the timeless, tireless burro with the plywood sea and sunset behind him. Beyond the painted sea, people were living in cardboard packing crates with tin roofs held down by tires and old car batteries, beyond which a wasteland ran to the real sea, from which her parents had returned but never arrived. A frequent thought of Corvus: they had never arrived *back*. Still, she thought they'd probably laughed when they hit that sudden water, thinking they'd be through it in no time.

That burro picture was the worst, Alice thought.

She spent a lot of time at Corvus's house, a little adobe house with the practically required blue trim. Because the land had been grazed, there was nothing on the hardened earth but a few mesquite trees. An old Dodge truck sat in an otherwise empty corral, and there was a shining Airstream trailer, for it had been the policy of Corvus's parents to move every year. And there was a black-and-tan dog with a big head, for whom there was no one or nothing in this world but Corvus's mother. Not far away lived a neighbor whose name was Crimmins, and then no one for miles. The dog's name was Tommy.

Alice has no pictures. So she likes to look through the ones Corvus has. Corvus is culling them all the time, but the burro stays, and some other odd ones too, while some of Alice's personal favorites—ones that represent an ideal, ones that show a little baby, for instance, with a real mother and father looking at it so grave and thoughtful—just disappear. The photos are in a flat woven basket and Alice gently paws through them. Though there are fewer, there appear to be more too, as if there were another source for them somewhere in the house. She wonders if any ceremony is involved in the way Corvus handles the pictures. Corvus likes ceremony. The graveyard service was practically baroque in its ambition, even though no one else was there except a paid soloist and the minister. The stonecutter said he'd come but didn't. Alice had never heard a man with more excuses. When she and Corvus had gone to his shop the day before the burial to choose the stone, he had said, "I won't be able to do yours for seven months, minimum. I have a woman ahead of you who's catching up, putting new stones on all the family's graves, and that family goes back—golly, practically to John Wesley Powell. She's changing them all, totally into remodeling. She's got all these birds and wagon trains on them. That's the style now, color. One she wants is a World War Two fighter plane in one corner and in the other corner she wants a heart with initials entwined in it, a 'D' and a 'B.' I make these sketches, and she says, 'I keep seeing something else, I keep seeing something else . . .'"

"Isn't that bad luck, to change the stones?" Corvus asked.

"No, no, I'll tell you what bad luck is, it's getting involved with a rich mobster Papago. They're sentimental but ruthless. Ruthless. Their kids are cute as bugs, but they're ruthless too. If they don't like what you do"—he put his index finger between his eyes—"Bang. You're coyote kibble in some dry wash." The stonecutter was hunched and merry, the first to admit the difficulty of keeping up with death.

The minister had a remarkable basso profundo voice, and the whole service was runic and generic at once. When it was over, he clasped the two girls' hands and then patted Tommy. Tommy looked frightened.

"I can't believe none of your teachers came," Alice said.

"Our teachers," Corvus said. "Well, they didn't know my parents."

"What about relatives? Aren't there any relatives?"

"We're onlys."

Alice was an only too—well, partially, she guessed. Her situation was a bit complex.

"My granny and poppa should have come."

"It's all right, Alice."

"There must have been an address book we could have consulted."

"Alice," Corvus said, "there isn't anybody. Worry about something else. Look at all this grass. Do you think the mighty Colorado should be further diminished so that grass can grow to be mowed in desert graveyards?"

"I think it's nice what you did," Alice said. "This is nice. All the flowers. You did it nice."

"I don't know what I'm doing." Corvus was wearing a black dress of her mother's.

"You're doing it right," Alice said. "Those big caskets and the singer—you're doing it beautifully."

The girls huddled there beside the grave with Tommy. There was the sound of traffic. Meek, Alice thought. It makes you meek.

"Poor Tommy," Corvus said. "He's trying to think. You can see he's trying to think. Maybe I should have him put down, send him off with my mom."

"But you can't. You shouldn't do it now."

"No," Corvus said, rubbing the dog's bony head. "You'd never catch her now, would you, no matter how fast you went."

Alice was trying to think *dog*—the racing after that is dog. But then there was the staying and the waiting that was dog, too. "It will be good to have Tommy around," she said.

"You're supposed to pray when your heart is broken, to have it break completely so that you can begin anew," Corvus said.

Alice didn't consider that to be much of a prayer.

"I've been trying to think, too," Corvus said, "just like Tommy. It says in the Bible that death is the long home."

"Long?" Alice said. "As in *long*? What does that . . . that's kind of creepy, isn't it?"

"You're not afraid of death, are you, Alice? You just don't want to lose your personality." Corvus hugged her.

They stayed until it was twilight and the first star appeared. The desert dusk was lovely, even in this place, perhaps particularly in this place. The gates to the graveyard had been closed, and Alice got out of the truck to open them. As they got closer to the house, Tommy grew happier. He rode with his head out the window, his ears flying. The air was full and soft and whole, holding ever closer what he remembered in it. They passed Crimmins's, where a single light burned. The ground around his house had the look of cement and was enclosed by wire. The sunset was bathing the Airstream in a piercing light, but the adobe was subdued, prettily shadowed, its blue trim chalky, the marigolds Corvus's mother had planted massed like embers. Corvus slowly pulled up to the house, and Tommy leapt out to wait confidently at the door, panting, virtually grinning up at Corvus as she opened it.

The girls were going to eat everything in the refrigerator. It was Corvus's idea. There was mustard, jam, milk, and a melon. Oatmeal bread, salad dressing, onions and lemons, some spongy potatoes, three bottles of beer, a can of chocolate syrup, a jar of mayonnaise.

"I want to be sick," Corvus said, and they waited to be sick but were not. Finally Corvus was a little sick.

"I guess I could eat anything," Alice said apologetically.

Tommy lay quietly in front of the door, staring at it. This was the way she would return. When the door opened, she would come through it. They would greet each other as they always had. Then he would drink something and sleep.

The unpleasant feast had been finished and cleared away.

Alice said, "Sometimes I've thought the thing to do to these fast-food joints they build out in the desert—and those fancy places that serve veal—is to stage puke-ins. We go in, sit down, order, and throw up. Isn't that a good idea? But I just can't throw up."

"I think I'll take everything out of my mother's bureau," Corvus said, "and make a bed of her clothes for Tommy tonight."

"Don't do it all at once," Alice advised. "I'd put out just one piece at a time."

Corvus said, "In the house where my grandmother died, the night she died, her refrigerator put on a light in her living room."

"How did it do that?"

"My father explained it. He said it was the vibration of the refrigerator's motor turning on a loose switch on the lamp."

"What was it trying to *say*, I wonder."

"My grandmother was so proud of that refrigerator. She'd just bought it."

"I think that happens a lot," Alice said. "People buy a new refrigerator and something bad happens."

"My parents just bought that blanket," Corvus said, pointing to a Navajo Black Design blanket that hung on the wall. "See the way it is in the center, like the center of a spider's web? That's so the weaver's thoughts can escape the weaving when it's finished. So the mind won't get trapped in there."

"Did the Anglos think that up or the Indians?" Alice asked suspiciously. "It sounds like something an entrepreneur would come up with." But she wanted to be gracious and sympathetic, so she said, "It's nice that it means that."

"It doesn't mean anything," Corvus said. "It's just a way out of the process, an escape from completion."

Alice was relieved that she didn't have to embrace the design wholeheartedly. She was holding the basket of pictures in her lap and went back to examining them. She picked one up, smoothed back a curled edge, picked up another.

"You like those, don't you?" Corvus said. "I should give you the whole lot of them."

"Now, who's this?"

"That's my mother."

"It looks freezing out. Where were you living then? What's she holding?"

"That's Tommy as a puppy."

"He looks like, I don't know, a mitten or something."

"My father used to say that my mother raised Tommy from an egg."

"Who's this?"

"That's me."

"You're kidding. Really? It doesn't look at all like you."

"As a little kid."

"Really?" Alice insisted.

Corvus looked at the picture and laughed. "I don't know who that is," she said.

"And this?"

"She was my mother's best friend once. Darleen. When I was a baby she dropped me."

"I don't think I was ever dropped," Alice said. "It might explain a lot, though, had I been, I mean."

"She dropped me more than once, actually, each time in private. I knew and she knew, that was it. Then, when I was a little older, she saved my life. She saved me from drowning. But people saw us that time and it was pretty clear she'd instigated the drowning and saving me was just a way of absolving herself. My parents saw us from the shore. They were a long way off. She really had me out there."

"Do you think she was in love with your mother?" Alice asked. "Maybe she was in love with your mother." What a thing to say, Alice thought. Love's not that crooked. Though she suspected it might be.

"I remember her being with us pretty constantly. It was like she was a boarder or an aunt or my mother's stepsister."

"She didn't try to pass herself off as your godparent, did she?" Alice asked. "There is something so sinister about those people." They were unaccountable, shadowy figures, practically *bearded* in Alice's imagination, bearing peculiar half-priced gifts like peppermint foot cream or battery-operated lights you clipped onto books or socket-wrench sets. She'd never heard of an effective or efficient godparent. As liaisons went, they seemed to be pretty much failures.

"My mother never trusted anyone after that. Not even me. I felt that she didn't have much confidence in me. It's funny that this picture has survived all these years, isn't it?"

"Yes," Alice said. "I mean, no, not funny." What was sort of remarkable was that Corvus's parents had ended up the drowned ones. She chewed on the inside of her mouth to check thoughtless utterances. She should invent another habit since it was already sore. But you didn't invent habits, did you? Didn't they invent you?

"They got Tommy then—didn't they, Tommy?" The dog raised his head in polite acknowledgment, then lowered it with a sigh.

Alice looked at the photograph. She'd been holding it firmly, her thumbs at the woman's throat. She was blond and quite heavy, a real butter pat. "Are there other pictures of her around, or is this the only one?" She really thought this memento should be ditched.

"Whenever we were alone together, Darleen and I, she spoke to me in sort of a singing whisper. But in front of my parents she wouldn't whisper, she talked like anyone else. She didn't say anything out of the ordinary in front of my parents, she would look at me in the most normal way and then would look away again in an utterly natural manner, but when we were alone she'd say the most maliciously nonsensical things. She thought everything was grotesque. I was mesmerized by her."

"She sounds pornographic," Alice said. "She was, like, molesting your mind."

"She had me share her private world, all right," Corvus said. "And I soaked it all up, whatever it was that was in that whisper. People think innocence can soak up anything. That's what innocence is for. She never bored me, but when the time, in her opinion, came for me to vanish, I struggled. I struggled hard. Nothing in the whisper had prepared me for this. She had me scissored between her legs and she was turning, so it looked above the water like she was searching for me. The sea was calm, and where had I gone? And then she let me go. I popped up like a cork, too shocked to scream, and saw my father swimming toward me. He was a good swimmer, an excellent swimmer, and he'd almost reached me. My mother was floundering behind. She was trying to run through the water, to shovel it aside with her body. I noticed the marks the straps of her bathing suit had made on her flesh. The straps weren't aligned with the marks they'd made over the summer. I hadn't noticed that before, and I fell into detail then, the sweet, passing detail of the world. The next instant I was raised up, grasped beneath my arms, and Darleen said, 'Until again, Corvus. In this world or the next,' and she threw me toward my mother and my father."

"It's like you were being born," Alice said. "She was trying to take charge of you being born." She had quite crumpled the photograph by this time. She had wadded this woman—long overdue.

"That's when I had my first thought. I was five years old, probably a little late for first thoughts."

"I don't think that's late at all." Alice didn't want to ask her granny and poppa what her own had been and risk disappointment. They undoubtedly had it written down someplace.

"It was—There is a next world, but no one we know will be in it."

"That's *good* for five," Alice said. She wanted to ask her if she'd seen a kelpie when she was underwater. They were supposed to look like a horse, a little horse, and to warn you if you were about to be drowned or to assist in your drowning. She didn't know how it could do both, but that's what she'd read in some book that for a time had fallen into her possession.

But it wasn't appropriate to ask. Not shades nor ghosts nor apparitions should have a place at the table tonight.

"So what happened to her? Did she just walk out of the water and disappear?"

"She walked out of the water and across the beach and into the changing room, which was a large walled space without a roof. I'd always hated it. There were no private stalls inside, just an open area where women and girls changed into their bathing suits. The floor was dirt and the sky seemed always to be moving quickly overhead, and it frightened me. There were all ages and sizes in there, everyone quickly getting in and out of clothes, everyone awkward and hurried and pretty much silent, though not completely silent. The bodies seemed to be all one body, the differences only momentary, and this was horrible to me."

Alice put the crushed photograph into a bowl. She picked up a matchbook from Corvus's parents' considerable collection. There were hundreds of matchbooks, no two the same. "Never Settle, Always Select," her matchbook said. It advertised an indoor flea market in Gallup. She struck the match and stuffed it into the folds of the picture, but it went out.

Corvus smoothed the picture out and folded back the cover of another matchbook. She propped it open beneath the woman's face and when she lit one match, all the others flared.

"That's better," Alice said.

"My father carried me back to the beach and wrapped me in towels and then took me to the car. The car had been parked in the sun with its windows rolled up, and it felt delicious. My father held me in that warm car, and I'd never felt anything so delicious in my life up until then. My mother had gone to look for Darleen. She kept saying, 'I'm going to scratch her eyes out.'"

"I bet she would have, too." The phrase had always impressed Alice favorably, but she doubted that Corvus's mother was capable of such a thing. She had always considered Corvus's mother a genial person and had admired her bosom, which was nicely freckled. Corvus's father had been more difficult to gauge. He had studied to be a doctor but had had some sort of breakdown. He seemed strong, if unpredictable. He could have gone after this Darleen to her great detriment, though apparently he had not.

"My mother couldn't find her. We didn't even return to the house that night because my mother thought she'd come in and steal me, so we went to a motel. I'd never been in a motel before, and it seemed like a playhouse to me. My mother threw away my bathing suit and my flip-flops with the plastic starfish on the straps. She threw away all of the clothes of that day and bought me new ones. And we never saw Darleen again. We never talked about her."

"What a peculiar episode," Alice said.

"I have to go to school tomorrow," Corvus said.

"Oh, you do not!" Alice exclaimed. If ever there was an excuse, she thought. "Has the counselor gotten to you yet?"

"No, not yet. Oh, you mean in terms of career placement? She said physics."

"Physics?"

"I think her notes concerned someone else."

The counselor was supposed to assist the students with their college choices but also doubled in grief management, which made her sound to Alice like a dog handler, as though grief were something that could be taught the down-stay. There was no love lost between this counselor and

Alice, who thought she should stick to her smarmy recommendations and not be allowed to dabble in Corvus's life. She should be prevented from attempting to manage Corvus's grief. Maybe Alice could get a restraining order on her.

Tommy scrambled to his feet and stood trembling in the corner. The fur between his eyes was folded in a melancholy omega shape. He had dreamed, he had dreamed . . . it left him.

This was no place to be tonight for any of them, but this was the place they were.

Alice was in the Chilled-Out Pepper bookstore looking through a book on medicinal plants. She wanted to find something for Corvus's situation and her granny's diabetes and her poppa's gas as well as a little something for herself, something that would give her a little edge or obscure the edge she already had, she didn't know which.

She chewed her nails and read. Flecks of a once hopefully applied red nail polish fell onto the pages. Here was a plant fatal to sheep. Here was one that was good for honeymoon cystitis. Ugh, Alice thought. *Anil del Muerto* was good for sore gums and herpes blisters. Sunflower of the Dead. Of course, it smelled to high heaven. She couldn't find anything for Corvus. Whenever you went near the subject of sadness in these books, everything got a little vague, a little folkloric, a little picturesque. One book said that bathing in red-colored water could be comforting, a suggestion Alice found to be extremely irresponsible. Didn't red-colored water imply *veins,* practically? She decided on tronadora and prickly pear for her granny, silk tassel for her poppa, and anemone and passion-flower for herself. It was like putting together a Christmas list. Passion-flower actually was growing right at home, along with some gummy, noxious vines that the boys in the neighborhood who were on probation would come by for before their monthly drug tests. This vine, and the rather absent-minded access her granny and poppa gave the boys to it, was probably the reason why their house had not once been broken into, but Alice couldn't find it in the book. Passionflower, however, was described at length. According to early botanists, the three stigmas represented the Trinity, as well as the nails used on Christ's cross. The stamens were the five wounds, the tendrils were the scourges, the ten petals were the ten apostles, minus Judas and Peter, those old numbnuts, those betrayers. In an aggravated, irritable way Alice loved reading stuff like this, numerology stuff, this-means-that stuff, mystical correspondency stuff. But the passionflower tried so hard with its pinks and blues and purples, as though God would show off in such a strutty, obvious way. She was building up a real annoyance for the passionflower.

A woman at the checkout counter was making quite a fuss because a book she'd ordered had not yet arrived.

"It's *The Woman's Encyclopedia of Myths and Secrets,* and it was supposed to be in today. This is today! This is a gift to myself, and I—want—that—book!" She intended to read more about Coatlicue, the Aztec goddess who was supposed to be the protectress of lone women, of female outsiders who had powerful ideas and were therefore shunned. The would-be book buyer couldn't find enough about Coatlicue. She began knocking things over.

"Do I have to call the police?" the manager asked. "I'm going to call the police."

Alice continued to read through the medicinal plants book, trying to remember what she meant to recall about them. Sometimes she thought she really didn't know how to read. Things just went right through her as though they thought she didn't exist. Only recently her granny and poppa had been taking a quiz in a magazine that would tell you if you were likely to get Alzheimer's within four years. You chose ten objects and then someone hid them and you had to remember them all. Or you had to name as many items as possible in sixty seconds from some category, such as vegetables. Or someone read a list of twelve words and, ten minutes later, you had to repeat them. They all three had taken the tests, and Alice had been the only one who had failed. She had done particularly poorly on the word list. Even now the only word she could remember from it was *choice.*

"That's too bad, honey," her granny said. "This is not reassuring. You have a good chance of developing intellect-robbing dementia."

"I don't think you're supposed to give it to young people," her poppa said. "It's not a test for young people."

Thinking about the Alzheimer's debacle, Alice blushed. Another word on the list had been *dawn.* Maybe she just had delayed delayed recall.

She found herself reading "An insignificant bush, reaching modest height with insignificant leaves and flowers, its appearance is common and uninteresting." This was *Escoba de la Vibora,* or matchweed. Despite this insignificance it was respected, even revered, by those who used it. Good, Alice thought.

She was studying the book intently when a voice at her shoulder said, "Hi there."

Alice got her sunglasses out of her pocket and put them on.

"I didn't mean to startle you," the man said. He was wearing a suit and had exceptionally white teeth. Alice regarded him coolly from behind her sunglasses, which she wished weren't so smudged. Alice's intention was to make herself and to be nothing but the self she made, but the problem had always been where to begin. One should begin with a stranger, but strangers never paid any attention to Alice. But here was one and he was.

"It's just that you look to be about my daughter's age," he said.

"Is your daughter missing?" Alice asked. Although, of course, she could hardly care if she was.

"Why, no," the man said, laughing. "I don't believe so. My name is Carter Vineyard, and my daughter and I just moved here. She doesn't know anyone. I thought someone her own age could give her a call."

Alice looked at him. He was sophisticated-looking and sincere and had to be desperate, a little stupid, or intoxicated.

"You're about sixteen, aren't you?" Carter said. "Go to school?"

"The Marquise School," Alice said. "But it's almost over. A few more weeks."

"The Marquise School is where Annabel's going in the fall!" he exclaimed. "Isn't that a coincidence! It's an excellent school, isn't it?"

"Function in disaster. Finish in style," Alice said.

"Pardon?"

"The maxims of Marquise."

"Oh yes, indeed. Good," Carter said.

"The place is pretty vacuous, actually."

"Oh well, that's all right too, for a while, when you're young. You've got the energy to handle it. It's when you get older that vacuousness can really lay you low." He realized he sounded somewhat disoriented, but he was still puzzling over the maxims. They sounded good, but weren't they a bit terminal for an expensive boarding school?

"What's she like?" Alice asked.

"Who?"

"Your daughter."

Carter seemed unprepared for this question. "She's nice," he said. "Annabel is very nice. I have a picture of her." He took a wallet from his pocket.

Alice looked. "You can't tell much from a picture," she said, giving this girl the benefit of the doubt. "Who's this?" She pointed to another photograph of a woman in a tight white evening dress, laughing.

"That's my wife," Carter said. "That's Annabel's mother. She's dead."

"That proves my point exactly," Alice said excitedly. "Pictures, wow, there's no inkling in them of what's going to happen next."

"Hmmm," Carter said.

Alice feared she'd hurt his feelings. "Well, she was happy then, anyway," she said.

Carter put his wallet away. It was true that Ginger had been happy when that picture had been taken; she had been elated. Less than an hour later, still elated, she had demolished four cars in valet parking at a penalty of one hundred and fifty thousand dollars. ("If he thinks he has the only keys to our Mercedes, Carter, he's a fool. I would never have given that boy the only keys to the Mercedes.")

"Give me Annabel's number and I'll call her," Alice said, for the man seemed to have misplaced the reason he'd approached her in the first place.

Carter's face twitched. "Yes. Terrific." He extracted a pen and paper from his jacket in the elegant way some men have of producing these humble instruments.

"Do you have another girlfriend you could bring along?"

"I wouldn't right away," Alice said cautiously. Maybe a rapprochement with life could be made possible for Corvus by employing this Annabel person, or maybe not.

"I'm just wondering if I should find someone else as well. I was determined to do something about this today, get Annabel started." He gave a happy sigh. "I like it out here. People seem accessible."

He was a little nuts, Alice thought. She kind of liked him.

Outside, the *Woman's Encyclopedia of Myths and Secrets* person was crouched sobbing, in handcuffs, while a policeman watched her warily. "A work of reference ain't worth this, lady," he said.

Alice called Annabel and was immediately invited over to her house. It was in the foothills with a big pool and the city below and nothing behind but the hard, folded mountains still trying to conceal what they knew. The first impression Alice had of Annabel was that she was exceptionally tan. Annabel said her mother used to be able to tan like that, she loved tanning practically more than anything, but when she was forty-two, her skin stopped providing that service. It just wouldn't tan up for her anymore. She said that a friend of her mother's had told her that it was age and hormones and nothing could be done about it, and her mother had wept.

"Some people didn't know how to be friends," Alice said.

On the piano in the living room was a picture of Annabel's mother in a silver frame. She wasn't laughing in this picture.

Annabel made a spinach and fig and jicama salad for lunch, then she and Alice sat by the pool eating the salad and drinking seltzer water and chatting, tranquiling out on the trivial as some people do when they first meet and sometimes forever after. The area around the pool was intensely groomed desert vegetation. There was one of everything, but nothing was too tall except for three saguaros that clearly had just been purchased and were propped up with planks. Annabel confided that she thought saguaros were cute, the cutest things in the desert so far.

"This is a nice house," Alice mumbled.

"I like the airily articulated spaces," Annabel said.

Alice looked at her.

"That's one of Daddy's lines."

"But that Indian's a little tacky, isn't it?" The Indian sat in a bent willow chair, moodily gazing at the pool and the valley plain below. Alice had almost greeted him deferentially when she arrived. He was plastic, life-sized, dressed in a shirt and jeans and moccasins. His limbs were jointed, and his hair was braided. "I mean, when you think of the way we exterminated the Indian, the way we took his land and extinguished his spirit."

"Daddy says it's inferior taxidermy," Annabel said, nibbling on a fig. "It's just a dumb house present."

Alice followed the Indian's glum gaze. She told Annabel that deer often came down from the mountains and drowned in people's swimming pools and asked if that had happened here yet, and Annabel said, of course not, of course it hadn't happened. Alice said there were lots of robberies in the foothills and had they been broken into yet and Annabel said no, a million alarms would go off, the house was programmed to attack and behead the intruder practically. Alice told her about the Little Caesar Murderer, where the guy would get into the house, murder its inhabitants, then take a shower and send out for a pizza. Annabel seemed preoccupied.

"I should tell you," Annabel said. "I take these exercises, and sometimes they really work and I don't care about anything and I accept everything, but usually I'm very conscious of my body and I want to look pretty and have pretty things and be happy and open to new experiences and I want people to be interesting and fun and that's just the way I am." She twisted strands of her hair with her fingers and looked at the ends.

"What kind of exercises?" Alice asked. Near them, hummingbirds with the swollen bodies of mice hovered.

"Oh, you know, everything's in your *mind*. You just sit quietly and try to believe that. They're these exercises you do after someone you love has died. Someone figured them out, I bet he's a millionaire."

Alice must next have asked Annabel about her mother, the pale woman in the silver frame, for Annabel went on, formally and incoherently: It had not been long ago. She'd been struck by a car. Instantaneous, her flight to Heaven. There was something about a fish restaurant.

Alice, whose unevolved sense of compassion for her own kind had been more than once remarked upon, said, "A fish restaurant, here? Where do you find a fish restaurant around here?"

"She'd had four martinis and was mad at Daddy. She ran out of the restaurant onto the highway. It wasn't here, it was back home."

"I would absolutely refuse to go into any fish restaurant," Alice said. "Entire species of fish are being vacuumed out of the seas by the greed of commercial fishermen. People used to think fishermen were so cool, like truck drivers, but they're indiscriminate, avaricious bastards grossly subsidized by the government to empty the oceans."

Annabel gathered up her hair from the back of her neck, held it a moment, framing her pretty face, and let it drop.

"Do you know fish can talk?" Alice said. "They squeeze their swim bladders or gnash their teeth or rub some of their bones together. They produce sounds ranging from buzzes and clicks to yelps and sobs."

"I don't know what this has to do with my mother," Annabel said. "It just happened to be a fish restaurant."

"I've got this thing about fish," Alice admitted.

They were quiet for a moment, then Annabel asked, "Would you like to play cribbage? I could get out the cribbage board."

Alice had drifted off. She saw the noble swordfish rotting in the ghost net's raptorial web. Cribbage, what was cribbage? This Annabel was in deep denial. That swordfish was not swimming away. "No," she said, "let's just sit here."

"I love leisure time," Annabel said. "It's my favorite kind of time."

"Leisure follows the consumption pattern," Alice said, "and is managed by an industry that sells boredom-compensating commodities."

Annabel wished she had an emery board at that moment.

"Do you ever feel you're on parole?" Alice asked. "Not just locally but cosmically? And that's why you're not doing what you really want to do even when you think you're doing it?"

"Parole!" Annabel said. "Certainly not. I haven't done anything. Let's go for a swim. A swim is just a swim, isn't it? It's nothing you have to feel guilty about."

They swam. Annabel complimented Alice on her vigorous butterfly, even though she personally found the stroke unappealing. They bobbed and floated. Annabel talked about perfume. There was a perfume for practically every hour of the day. You had to be subtle but precise. At noon you would think you could go all out, but you couldn't; noon was tricky. She talked about travel. Annabel believed, and she believed this strongly, that when you went to another country you should always take little jars of bubbles for the children and little bars of soap for the adults and hand them out; it made for good relations, made those foreign people glad you were there. She talked about her sentiments and fears. She missed the flowers back east and the mizzle that accompanied the fog in from the sea. She sometimes worried about losing a limb—an arm—it would be awful. She didn't know where that worry had come from. She didn't even know anyone who had lost a limb. She talked about boys. She had slept with two boys; she was glad it hadn't been just one.

They got out of the pool, and Annabel offered to make lemonade, real lemonade with fresh lemons and raw sugar.

"You are aware, are you not," said Alice, "that American sugar is destroying the Everglades? Big Sugar is a wealthy powerful government-sponsored ecoterrorist that pollutes thousands of acres of one of the most remarkable ecosystems on the planet. Your little bag of sugar dooms hundreds of beautiful wading birds to death by phosphorus and heavy-metal poisoning. We should import our sugar from Cuba, kick the growers off the land around Lake Okeechobee, and—what are these!" A set of glasses on the cabana wet bar were colored in different patterns, stripes, and spots. Inside each was a scene of animals grazing or walking around, exotic animals such as zebras and leopards and giraffes, and on the glass was a circle with lines on it like the crosshairs of a rifle scope.

"I will not drink anything out of these disgusting glasses," she said. "Where do you get this stuff?"

"It was a house present," Annabel said. "Another house present."

"Your father has the worst friends," Alice said. "Where does he find these people?"

"I don't know, he just goes out and gets them!" Annabel poured Diet Pepsi into two plain glasses and hoped that not everyone she met out here would be as censorious as Alice.

C arter entered his bedroom with a terrible foreboding that Ginger would be there tonight. He undressed in the dark and slipped into bed. Almost immediately he heard a noise like someone rattling a newspaper. He turned on the lamp. Ginger was sitting in her little chintz-covered boudoir chair with an open newspaper raised to her face. She was close enough for him to read it himself, though he very much did not want to. There was a column on wine with an illustration depicting a nest in a tree. The nest contained a single egg that had broken open to reveal—well, it had hatched a wineglass, it was clear and birds with feet and wings but with the bodies of wine bottles were flying in to provide it with sustenance. That was repulsive, Carter thought. What edition was this?

"Carter," Ginger said, "do you remember at the club that day in the reading room, Jeannie Winters behind the paper? She said, 'One of my husbands just died,' and that was all. She didn't even put it down, she just went right on to the entertainment section. Wasn't that a scream? I thought—I would like to be able to do that." She lowered the paper. "But I never could, Carter, because I was wedded only to you. My life with you prevented me from being stylish like that."

Carter looked at her. "You seem rather deshabille tonight, my darling."

"While I loved you and all that, I would very much have liked to have gotten off a line as good as Jeannie Winters'. What do you mean, deshabille? It took a lot out of me coming here, and to this unfamiliar house. Why did you buy such an enormous house? And in the desert, thousands of miles from our home. I know what you're thinking, Carter."

"What?" he asked.

"You're thinking you'll keep moving around, farther and farther away, and I won't be able to find you."

Carter had always been grateful for his ability to conceal his thoughts from Ginger, but this, alarmingly, wasn't too far off the mark. Still, if you're not all-knowing when you're dead, very little makes any sense at all. *Very* little.

"I want to settle down for Annabel's sake, darling."

"What sort of future do you have, Carter? Really, think about it. You have a diminishing future, so why bother? You snore, you know."

"I do not snore," Carter said. "I have never snored."

"I used to think it was merely obnoxious, but it's undoubtedly sleep apnea, which is a potentially life-threatening disorder. You probably stop breathing hundreds of times each night, Carter."

"I do not snore," Carter said. "Darling, it's silly to argue about this. Tell me what it's like there, why don't you? Are odd stones in flannel rolled out to be adored?"

"Whatever gave you that idea?"

"I don't know. I've always rather had that notion."

"It's not like that at all, for godssakes," Ginger said. "That's the dumbest attempt at embodying the unspeakable I've ever heard."

"I misunderstand a great deal of what I think," Carter said.

"Speaking of stones, I wouldn't have minded one of my own. You could've inscribed upon it 'Here lies the victim of an unhappy marriage.' Nothing fancy, just to the point."

Carter felt warm, then cold, then warm again.

"You should be in bed by nine," Ginger said peevishly. "That's when the liver repairs itself, between the hours of nine and three. Your body turns to liver restoration during the hours of darkness. I see your liver at this moment, Carter—you may not believe me, but I do. It is yellow, knotty, and hard."

"Cut it out, Ginger," Carter said. "If you would. Please."

"You are a prime candidate for cirrhosis, you know. You don't have a hair on your chest. If you were a bit more . . . simian, you'd have a better chance."

"I didn't think you cared all that much about my liver, darling."

"You'll always be forever in my thoughts, Carter. When will you realize that? When?"

Carter shuddered.

"What are Annabel's plans for the summer?" Ginger inquired.

"She's just going to try and get her bearings out here, make some friends."

"I've never liked Annabel's friends. Do you know what will happen to Annabel? She'll grow up and then she'll die."

Carter was shocked for a moment. Though it wasn't a particularly radical comment, he felt the need to temper it nonetheless. "But she'll have had her own life, darling."

"Oh, you believe that," Ginger said irritably. "You'll believe anything."

"Annabel loves you, darling."

"Well, I certainly hope so. I hope she's not being encouraged to think that she idealized me inappropriately." She twisted a little pearl button on the bodice of her dress, kept twisting until it fell off. "Shit," she said.

Carter feared he'd find it on the floor in the morning and watched carefully as she placed the button in her pocket. She then spoke at length about the futility of existence and the vanity of all human effort and desire. Her monologues, if anything, seemed to be getting longer. Under ordinary circumstances, if people kept going on like this you'd tell them after a while to put up or shut up, but of course Ginger had put up. She had died.

She extended a narrow hand and pointed to his books, his ties, even his travel alarm from Tiffany's, one of his favorite things. "All this is unnecessary, Carter."

He didn't like the way she was eyeing the little clock. There had been incidents of destruction in the past. "Ginger, please don't break that."

"A *clock*, Carter? I mean, please. You're clinging to a *clock*?"

Carter covered the clock with his hand, where it ticked warmly.

"It crouches there watching the course of your life's disintegration. Its only function is to witness your decline."

"I like it," Carter said. "I like its lines."

"Time is circular, you fool. That's the whole point."

Carter resolutely held the little clock.

"Don't cling, Carter. I've come back to help you in these matters. You must commence the casting off of material things. Where are *my* things, incidentally? What have you done with my clothes?"

If he uttered the word *rummage,* she would murder him, despite the fact that it was a good churchy rummage to benefit . . . who was it? . . . Haitians, he believed. The clothes that had somehow managed to infiltrate the belongings they'd shipped out here had been donated to . . . he hadn't followed up on that transferal. He was silent.

"Your thoughts should be turning toward diminishment and cessation," Ginger mused. "Do you remember the last time I asked you to look at my vulva?"

He frowned.

"You wouldn't," Ginger said. "So Dennis Beebee finally looked."

Carter slowly recalled an awkward cocktail hour.

"Dennis said it was no longer rosily pink and plumply wrinkled," Ginger said.

Though that certainly didn't sound like Dennis Beebee, Carter was reluctantly remembering how Dennis had thrown his tie over his shoulder one evening for a better look at something.

"He said it was wan and smooth. Dennis Beebee was the last man to look at my vulva," Ginger said. "If anyone had foretold that at my birth, I would've laughed in his face. Nevertheless, he was a gentleman. It's strange, the turns life takes."

"Darling," Carter said sleepily.

"Have you lost weight?" Ginger said after a while.

"I don't think so. I've always been around a hundred and sixty."

"You look better. You haven't been losing weight for someone, have you?"

"Losing weight for someone?" He felt a chill run down his body, almost as though a hand was touching him.

"Your stomach looks much flatter. Carter, I swear, if I ever catch you in this bed with anybody, I'll give you both heart attacks."

Then she was gone. There was a peculiar smell. It wasn't unpleasant, but it was definitely not the smell of the promise of rain, a delightful smell and one he sorely missed out here. He looked at his little clock.

Alice's granny and poppa were discussing the superior hiding properties of certain paints when the cat from down the street seized a cactus wren studying a bit of broom straw on the patio. Zipper had carried off another victim.

"I hate that cat, I hate him!" her granny cried.

"Most black cats are noble and gentlemanly," her poppa said. "Zipper is not." As a young man, as a student, he'd kept cats and developed theories about them. Tortoiseshells were clever, docile, and tricky; whites were the fondest of society and tended to be delicate; black-and-whites did not trouble themselves unduly as to their duties as pets; and so on. Alice hoped he would not reiterate these opinions now. Alice made no distinctions, for she loathed all cats and had attempted to assassinate Zipper on several occasions.

"That Zipper makes me feel so old and helpless and foolish," her granny said.

Alice patted her hand. Her granny did look particularly helpless and old at the moment. Alice was astonished that she'd thought for so long that her granny and poppa were her mommy and dad. "Mommy, Mommy, Mommy," she'd squealed thousands of times in her life, right up until the fateful afternoon she got her menses. She was practicing lassoing. She had a nice rope and was capturing a statue of Saint Francis pretty regularly at twenty feet. The statue was cement and the size of a small child, with three intact cement birds on his shoulder and one missing one. All that remained of the gone one were claw lines etched into the folds of his robe. This was Alice's personal favorite.

She was coiling her rope when she felt it. It was like a roll of pennies sliding into her pants. Blood then coursed down her leg in a gay little rivulet. She ran into the house to tell Mommy, and events proceeded smoothly enough at first. Adequate information was provided, and Daddy was sent to the drugstore to get the proper paraphernalia. Then her mommy told her that though it had happened rather sooner than she'd expected Alice was *a woman* now and it seemed the proper moment to tell her that the situation was this: they were not her mommy and daddy but her granny and poppa. He whom she thought was her brother was her dad. Alice's mother had been a high school dropout who nonetheless had achieved some fame as Paula "The Flea" on a roller derby team called Hot Flash before her death in a small-plane crash.

The morning after this disclosure, her granny and poppa aged. The house grew small, cobwebs appeared, the plates crazed. Even Fury grew gray. Actually, Fury should have been the tip-off to the situation all along. The elderly always had dachshunds. Alice chastised herself for not having been more alert. But there had been nothing in her brother's behavior toward her that seemed unusual. He ignored her as, she believed, was the custom. He never looked at her directly but at a point somewhat beside her, and Alice had merely assumed he suffered from an unfortunate astigmatism that would embarrass him to acknowledge. Basically, she found him boring and shiftless, though she was impressed that he had his own apartment. When she learned that he was her father, his significance to her suffered even further. Then, his girlfriend, who loved sailboarding and hang gliding, who always seemed to be wearing a harness or a helmet, became his wife. Alice was repelled by her gaudiness, her powerful thighs, her straps and belts, the lurid colors of her shiny clothes. The newlyweds went off to Oregon, where the best winds in the world were said to blow on some hidden lake. They were going to buy land and develop the place. Wind would be their only commodity. *Commodity?* Alice hated these people.

She bore no grudge, however, toward her granny and poppa. They had done the best to save her, to provide her with a cozy life—a miscalculation, of course, but Alice appreciated the gesture. Deceit had kept them young whereas the truth had accelerated them practically into decrepitude. For two people who had led a life of deception for years, they seemed unanxious and remarkably trusting. But her brother was her father, and he didn't even care! That was perverse. He avoided her birth date, of course, but occasionally did send her greeting cards—unsigned, for he apparently feared liability. Alice hadn't had her period since the last time she'd practiced roping on Saint Francis, and that had been almost five years ago. She was gangly as a willet now, a misanthrope and disbeliever.

"Don't let that cat break your heart now, Mother," her poppa said to her granny. The three of them gazed at the softly fluttering breast feathers, all that remained of the wren, stuck in place by the ooze of trauma. "Why don't we make an excursion to the pet store and buy Fury some of those peanut butter cookies he fancies?" He turned to Alice and whispered, "Take her mind off that Zipper."

Alice would like to get a wrist-lock slingshot with a magnum-thrust band and a sure grip handle, and nail that Zipper once and for all.

"I think Fury suffers from sensory overload in that place," her granny said. "Too many radiant collars and educational toys. Too many bins of pig ears. Plus I think he was disturbed last time at seeing the corgi he thought he knew, waiting outside on that contraption." The contraption being a padded board with wheels on which the recently paralyzed rear legs of the elderly corgi lay. Inside, his mistress was being persuaded to purchase a puppy, a *bridge companion,* so that when the corgi's end came, she would be well on her way to solace.

"I don't think he actually knew that poor dog," Alice's poppa said. "But Fury tends to worry, Mother, you know he does."

They decided to leave him at home in his basket, the radio playing softly. Alice's granny got out her big sun umbrella, and they walked the few blocks to the shopping mall. In the pet store window was a sign:

WE'RE CLOSED TODAY OUT ACQUIRING NEW CRITTERS
ESPECIALLY FOR YOU.
REMEMBER! WE CAN GET YOU ANY CRITTER!

"Appalling," Alice said.

"They're expanding," her poppa marveled. "This place has changed since just last week. Look, that little pie parlor next door has turned into a Just for Feet store."

"They were such excellent pies," her granny said.

"That billiard parlor wasn't there before either, was it?" her poppa said. "Can't remember *what* was there, in fact."

"Care to shoot some pool?" her granny challenged.

"I wouldn't mind a little four-ball carom," her poppa said. "A little four-ball never hurt anybody." He winked at Alice. "Keeping her mind off Zipper," he said. They vanished into the merry gloom of the pool hall.

Alice wandered around to the back of the pet shop. She really didn't mean to enter, she just pressed against one of the doors and it gave a little. A flimsy chain dropped between the door and the jamb, and she popped it easily.

It was warm inside. She heard some rustling and chirping, the whistling hiss of the aquariums' aerators. This is Alice your savior, she thought. She smacked her knee painfully against a grooming table. Most of the cages were without residents, but somehow in an unpromising way. Had the proprietors sold all their captives, or had they just fled the city, one step ahead of their creditors at the breeding farms and puppy mills? The bins of barbecue-flavored pigs' ears remained. Alice didn't think Fury enjoyed those things at all, but rather hid them, sensitive as he was.

She filled up a shopping cart with some simpler life forms—lizards and toads, snakes and mice—and rolled it right back out through the door she'd popped. Society, as a rule, did not trouble anyone pushing a shopping cart. The further a cart was taken from the store where it belonged, the more deference was paid to the possibly unstable individual who had taken charge of it. Alice wanted to take the creatures back to her room and talk to them—debrief them, as it were—but when she drew near the house she saw that her granny and poppa had returned, pool playing having been less larky than they'd hoped. Alice took her refugees to a nearby wash instead and gravely liberated them, though they seemed to have little instinct for freedom. They had been considered food for too long and had undoubtedly seen too much.

've been thinking a lot about that last meal I had, Carter."

"I never went back there," he said firmly.

"That was surimi I ate, wasn't it. Why on earth did you let me eat surimi?"

"You didn't want to order what I ordered, darling. You never would."

"That's because you always ordered badly and wanted me to experience your miserable mistake. I caught on to that trick early in our marriage, Carter."

"I don't know what surimi is, Ginger."

"It's a fish paste, a disgusting fish paste that's then colored and fluffed up to make simulated seafood like simulated crab."

"Did you learn about it there?"

"Don't patronize me."

"Darling, I'm *not*—"

"You just pick information up here, in the course of things. I've been speaking to a fisherman."

"Not IXOUS himself!"

"Don't show off."

"IXOUS, darling. IXOUS! This is stupendous. Jesus Christ God's Son. The Savior!"

"I hate it when you show off that tiresome St. George's education."

"But this means that things fall into place after all. Why, this is good news indeed!"

"I don't know what you're so thrilled about," Ginger said. "This individual is from Louisiana. He only fished for sport. He was a real estate broker, one of those indefatigable, extroverted risk takers who fished to relax."

"That really got my heart to pounding," Carter admitted.

"He told me a little story. Sensitive men don't have to be violets, Carter. He had invented this little clamplike grill, but without any of those grill thingies on it, and when he caught a fish, he'd take it off the hook and put it in this device and he'd fillet it right there. Slice, flip over, slice. Two swift, economical movements and then back into the water with what was left of the fish. He never thought a thing about it, and neither did anyone else."

Whoa, Carter thought to his heart, which seemed determined to escape from his chest's ribbed stall.

"Except this one time, the fish just stayed there right by the boat, breathing through its gills and moving its tail even though it was just bones." Ginger paused. "And it looked at him."

"Looked?" Carter said.

"Yes, just stayed there and looked."

"What kind of fish was it?"

"A redfish, I think he said."

"Did it say anything?"

"Of course not. It just looked at him for the longest time. And then it sank from sight."

Carter could not hide his disappointment. Ginger was never going to get anywhere, wherever she was, if she just sat around shooting the breeze with some guy from Louisiana of all places. Sportsman's Paradise.

"Did he continue to fish after this incident?" Carter asked sourly.

"Not so much after that," Ginger said dreamily. But then she glared at Carter. "I don't know why I try to share anything with you, since you always miss the point. It wasn't an *incident*. It was a *moment,* a *meaning-ful* moment that changed his life."

"I don't mean to be crude, Ginger, but he's dead now, isn't he? His existence has been superannuated, right along with his meaningful moments."

"Don't think you're beyond being dead, Carter. You're not beyond being dead, not by a long shot."

"You know where I think you are, darling? I think you're in Purgatory!"

"Oh, for Chrissakes," she said crossly.

"Is there a mountain there? And a kindly curriculum?" Dante flooded thrillingly back. Dante Alighieri! And the room where Romance Languages was taught at St. George's; the smell of floor wax and the brightness of the boys' white shirts, light rippling against the walls and the snow falling, vanishing into the sea.

"You're back in that second-rate prep school, aren't you?" Ginger said. "Let me tell you what it's like here. I'll give you just a hint. If we see an ant heap, we don't think of it as an ant heap."

"No?"

"It's not an ant heap at all. That's the way it is here. It takes some getting used to."

Ginger was preparing to go. Carter could feel the grotesque gathering of resources this always entailed.

"I'll give you another hint too, Mr. Clueless," she said. "There isn't any mountain."

Alice couldn't decide between the wrist-lock slingshot and a BB air pistol. The latter would be more accurate at a distance, but she didn't want to leave a lot of spent ammunition all over the place. Something might eat it, a tortoise or a quail, so she settled on the slingshot. It's a beginning, she told Annabel. But it took her longer than she expected to master the weapon.

Annabel said, "I think maybe you shouldn't go after the ones wearing those little warning bells on their collars."

"Bells don't make any difference," Alice said.

"But it shows the owner's trying to be considerate," Annabel said.

Alice had a little folding shovel she carried in case her efforts were successful. Quickly the cat would disappear down a hole in the desert.

"Those signs on the phone poles are kind of getting to me, too," Annabel said. "Like Tina."

Tina is a member of the family. Please help!

"And Poco Bueno Trouble."

Poco Bueno Trouble needs his medicine!

"I don't know you very well, Alice, but I think killing a cat would be beneath you in many ways."

"Progressive social theories are beginning to consider murder a matter of little concern," Alice said. "Anyway, cats are false figures. People have them around so they don't have to address real animals."

"But a dog wouldn't be a real animal then either. What do you mean?"

They were out at Marquise School, and Alice was showing Annabel around. On a weekend afternoon, the place resembled a chic but deserted shopping center. There were fountain sculptures by gifted students, low, tasteful adobe buildings, old cottonwood and olive trees.

"If you love animals, you've got to love all animals," Annabel said stubbornly. "I had a dream last night, and you were in love with an animal. You introduced me to him. He was . . . well, he looked like a person, but I *knew*. Plus you said . . . I mean, you admitted it. I wasn't happy for you, but I pretended to be. Then I woke up."

"In my room I have a picture of a woman trysting with an octopus in a hotel room. Actually, it's more like a squid. A cross between the two. It's a great picture. The squid is sort of sitting in a chair, comforting her. Light streams through the window across the unmade bed."

"There's no picture like that," Annabel said.

"I look at it and think, Women are capable of anything."

"A woman thought that up, you mean," Annabel said. She couldn't believe this school didn't have boys, that she'd be going to a school without boys. Boys were nice, boys were normal. Alice was clearly not normal, even though she was, at present, all Annabel had—not counting Corvus, whom Annabel found difficult to think of as a friend, despite the fact that the three of them were frequently together, making up, in Alice's phrase, a not quite harmless-looking group. That was typical of Alice, wanting to appear not quite harmless. Annabel felt she had some insight into Alice; she wouldn't want much more. By the time school began, Annabel was hopeful that they would have gone their separate ways. She would meet new girls and make new friends, and she would nod pleasantly at Alice when she passed her in the hall. Her new friends would consider Alice unwaxed, uncombed, and unpleasantly intense, but Annabel would be kind. She would say, "Well, you know the situation at home is really quite strange" or "She actually is quite smart."

She would quietly defend Alice, but she would no longer associate with her. It would be such a relief to escape Alice's scrutiny. You couldn't even show her a simple catalog. Annabel had been ordering stunning stuff from this place in Idaho—cobalt-and-brown mustang twirling skirts and zigzag summer storm vests and liquid necklaces, all made possible by one or another of Carter's credit cards—and Alice hated the little catalog, was practically apoplectic over the manatee note cubes and the fake petroglyph rocks in velveteen pouches and the enameled plastic butterfly magnets, becoming particularly enraged over a photograph of a wolf offered for, Annabel thought, the quite reasonable price of seventy-five dollars.

"Listen to this!" Alice said. "'Half-hidden yet clearly curious, the wolf gazes out from the framed, double-matted print intently, forever watching from the woods. Protected behind clear acrylic.' Protected behind clear acrylic! That's the only place it is protected. Everywhere else it's trapped and poisoned and shot from planes and snowmobiles."

"These earrings on the next page are cute," Annabel said. "Don't you think they're—"

"This is despicable."

"But it's not. Look. See, right over the eight hundred number it says they give a portion of their profits for wildlife habitat preservation and that they'd like to give to all the worthy causes. See, right here?"

"You are not saving the earth by buying lizard earrings. And what does this mean? 'This whimsical duo in sterling silver has a mirthful attitude that's positively contagious.' What does that mean!"

"Why does it have to mean anything?" Annabel asked, pleased with the reasonableness of her retort. You just had to be sensible with Alice.

A lizard darted past, part of another lizard dangling from its mouth. It was all so bright and violent out here. Nothing had any subtlety, not even the light. "Alice?" Annabel called. "Where are you?" For, while she had been momentarily distracted by the cannibalistic ingestion in progress, Alice had vanished somewhere with that awful slingshot. The wind fluttered dryly at Annabel's face. She examined her toenails. They were perfect.

Walking, she passed through one courtyard into another. The school had a courtyard for each student, practically. It was ridiculous. Then she was in a sort of amphitheater that was set apart by two dozen or so ragged cypresses. Alice had said that they put on a lot of plays at Marquise. Annabel would try out for all the plays for she liked the dramatic arts. She saw a woman threading a rather uncertain passage among the stone benches. She was wearing a red dress and appeared to be very pregnant. She was too far away to say hi to, otherwise Annabel certainly would have said hi. She'd say, Oh, you're going to have a baby! Annabel wanted to have children, lots and lots of children. Eventually, of course.

Maybe she could have quadruplets. But there had to be something wrong with you first, didn't there? You couldn't have quadruplets all on your own; a lot of pharmaceutical assistance and scientific intervention was required. Dishes, there were those special kinds of dishes . . .

The woman hadn't noticed Annabel. Her head was lowered, and she was just going back and forth around the benches as though she were trying to flow around them in a terribly natural way. Annabel was now very much hoping that it wouldn't be necessary to say hi. If the woman started to have her baby and a foot or an arm started coming out, Annabel wouldn't know what to do. The woman continued to steer her big body around the benches. What if she were a homeless person and lived here? Annabel had never gone in for the fad of caring for the homeless, although Alice said there was a great deal to learn from them in the way of resourcefulness. They would come into Green Palms, the local nursing home, at lunchtime and pretend to be visitors helping their loved ones eat lunch and instead would eat the lunch themselves. The poor old souls would think they'd had their nourishment anyway. Could one be *too* resourceful? Annabel wondered. But this woman wasn't carrying cardboard. Didn't they always have cardboard with them? There wasn't a scrap of cardboard in sight.

The woman abruptly stopped and turned in Annabel's direction. Annabel quickly retreated, hurrying back to the succession of maddening courtyards. She found Alice sitting by a coyote sculpture, holding a bunch of weeds. A plaque explained that the sculpture had been made by Samantha Melby, class of 1997, from materials found in a nontoxic landfill. It was awfully good for someone their age, Annabel thought. This girl had a future.

"Do you know Samantha Melby?" she asked.

"Are you kidding?" Alice said. Samantha Melby had been voted by her classmates Most Likely to Succeed, whereas Alice had been nominated as most likely to be in charge of collecting bird carcasses on the shores of the Salton Sea.

Upon further inspection, Annabel saw that several condoms were stuck to the coyote's thrown-back head. The poor artist. Poor Samantha Melby. That was the problem with public art, it risked great ridicule.

"What are those?" she asked Alice, pointing at the weeds.

"I'm taking them back to look them up in my weed book."

Annabel smiled glassily at her. Sometimes Alice was like a child. She acted like a child and spoke like a child, and one could treat her as affably and falsely as a child.

"I like herbs," Annabel said. Her father had started an herb garden with the help of his new yard boy, Donald. Herbs weren't messy; they were contained in sunny little pots.

"They're okay," Alice granted. "There was that herb that Odysseus took to protect him from Circe's magic. It saved him from her enchantments while everybody else got turned into swine."

Annabel felt her brow wrinkling. "God, Alice, that was so long ago. It didn't even happen anyway, did it?"

Alice mused over her weeds, which had wilted dramatically in her hand.

"Is this school hard?" Annabel said. "I certainly hope not."

Alice shrugged.

"I hate Cs," Annabel said. "They practically make me nauseous."

"They don't grade here."

What a sensible grading policy! Annabel now sat quite contentedly in the uncomfortable sun, no longer feeling uneasy about the cats or the disquieting pregnant woman or her intentions to ditch Alice once school began. Her heart opened to Alice and to the simple justice of things, life's rightness, its essential fairness. Things just *were*. Or could *be*. "You're kidding!" she said delightedly.

"Yes," Alice said.

Annabel wanted to make Alice cry, just once. That was her goal, to bring tears to her eyes on some subject. Then she'd say, "I didn't mean it," and console her to the extent possible.

"You should have seen your tail drop!" Alice said.

"'You should have seen your tail drop.' I hate it when you say things like that. You sound retarded. Or like somebody's grandmother."

"My granny met my grandpa 'at the fair.' Do you know what that means? It means it was love at first sight."

The woman in the red dress entered their courtyard. She stood with her hands on her stomach and peered at the girls.

"Uh-oh," Alice said.

"What's the matter with you?" Annabel hissed. "Birth. There's nothing wrong with birth."

The woman came up to them. She was really not much older than they were. Her hair was a mazy mass of dark curls, and she had bright blank eyes. "Would you like to feel my tummy?" she asked Annabel.

"Oh no, thank you," Annabel said. "Thanks a lot. Really, that's very kind but not now? Not now," she said.

The woman smiled at her slowly and contemptuously.

"Hi, Candy," Alice said glumly.

The popping sound of rifles miles away rolled down the mountain. It wasn't robbery or homicide, rather the continuing subjugation and subtraction of nature in full swing.

"I lost my job," Candy said. "Teaching kindergarten. I never thought they'd fire me. I thought they'd be afraid of a lawsuit, but the kids got on my nerves the other day and I sent them all away. Just opened the door and told them to toddle homeward. A lot of those kids didn't even know where they lived, much to my surprise. Their parents think they're so smart, but they have zero survival skills. Social skills they have. They're polite and they share and they show sympathy and consideration, but has anyone evaluated the importance of social skills in a situation where one is faced with a stampeding mob or a knife-wielding lunatic? It makes me want to laugh."

But she was only smiling again at Annabel, contemptuously.

"When's it going to be, Candy?" Alice asked.

"Two weeks. They promised two weeks." The woman's hands seemed determined to grasp Annabel's own. They were small hands, the dimpled kind. They feinted about. "I am alone," she said to Annabel.

"What about the father?" Annabel heard herself saying. "The daddy of your baby should take an active interest."

"The daddy? You mean the perp?" Candy's smile had become more reserved. "But he's so busy. He's the bouncer at the White Shark, that neon country-and-western dance hall, he's the guy who patrols on the horse."

"Oh, I saw his picture in the paper!" Annabel exclaimed. "I thought he was so fly. That 'Acre of Dancin' and Romancin',' I'd love to go there."

Candy gaped at her.

"The cute ones sometimes try to take advantage," Annabel said uncomfortably.

"Who is this—this idiot?" Candy screamed. Then she spat, just missing Annabel's perfect toes, and moved heavily off, muttering.

"That is so disgusting," Annabel said. "What if that had hit my foot? What's wrong with her, anyway?"

"Candy's tale," Alice said.

"Yes, what is her *story*?" Annabel demanded, patting her toes.

"When she was seven months' pregnant, there wasn't a heartbeat anymore, but the doctors didn't want to do a cesarean or induce labor so she has to carry it around stillborn full-term and she's trying to make a new world cataclysmic situation out of it. The cycle has been broken, the web of life torn, dead world coming, et cetera . . ."

"Et cetera? You can't possibly be as cold and uncaring and unfeeling as you sound. That is the most wretched story I—"

". . . everything reversed, everything its opposite and out of order. Everything dead dead dead but continuing. She keeps trying to get the media involved. She wants to urge people not to make the event vulnerable to cult group misapplication, but of course no one wants to talk to her. Not even the cults are interested. She has potent materials to work with, but she lacks charisma."

Annabel wanted to go back to her own room, the peach-colored room that had been painted with the special brush in the special way that made simple wallboard resemble the finest linen. She wanted to lie down and put cucumber slices over her eyes.

"And that spitting, how far does she think she's going to get with that spitting?"

Annabel wanted to turn up the air-conditioning in her room as high as possible and curl up beneath a blanket. Annabel wondered if Alice was experiencing the same blotting up of the desert's colors, as though a giant gray sponge preceded them as they walked.

"That guy on the horse is such a jerk. He dumped her so fast. Don't go near him," Alice said. "He licks frogs to get high."

"Nobody would lick a frog," Annabel said without much conviction.

At the edge of the school grounds, a paper fluttered from a mock orange tree. It was a blurry picture of a cat with a little conical birthday hat on its head.

LOST WHITE CAT NAMED TU-TU.
TU-TU IS DEAF!

"Please, Alice."

"I am not responsible for Tu-Tu's disappearance."

"Oh, please please please," Annabel begged.

"I've never seen that cat before in my life." Alice looked into the cat's crazed photocopied gaze. Surely it had been the indignity of the hat that had caused Tu-Tu to seek a different life.

"Please," Annabel was saying, "promise me you won't kill cats for the time being."

Trying to make the world just and natural only makes it more unjust and more unnatural, Alice thought. "Okay," she said.

"I thought I was going to have a nervous breakdown for a second. Everything was pale, this blinding pale and . . . trembling. Is there any place around here we can get some bottled water?"

"Sure," Alice said.

"The kind that's treated by reverse osmosis and enhanced with minerals? That's the superior kind. You have to look on the label." After a while, she said, "That poor Candy."

"I think not being born is ecologically responsible," Alice said. She wasn't about to go all soft over Candy. "It has more sense than its mother."

8

Annabel wanted to commemorate her mother's birthday by having a nice dinner party for just the three of them, her mother and father and herself, with lamb chops and candles and some lovely dessert.

"I don't think this is a good idea," Carter said.

"I think some ritual restored to our lives would be nice, Daddy. I want to share some of my memories of Mommy with her. If you don't share memories, they'll disappear, and we're responsible for what we forget, Daddy."

Carter loved his daughter deeply, but the thought that she might be a little simple occurred to him frequently. Hadn't Ginger insisted on painting the entire second floor in the first trimester? Hadn't she persisted in those Bloody Marys at lunch?

"We'll remember her on her birthday," Annabel said determinedly. "We'll devote the whole dinner to her. If it works out, we'll extend it to other holidays. We'll set a place for Mommy and pour wine into her glass and put food on her plate."

Carter thought she was getting Ginger mixed up with Santa Claus. Each Christmas Eve they left some apples on the hearth for the reindeer. Plus a good strong belt of whiskey for Santa. Carter rubbed his face. "Are we really going to have lamb chops?" he asked.

Annabel nodded; it was her mother's favorite. Alice would kill her, of course, if she found out, but Alice didn't have to be informed of everything. She'd tell her they'd had pasta. Personally Annabel didn't see anything wrong with a lamb chop now and then.

"I'll take care of everything, Daddy."

Or perhaps, Carter mused, she had in mind that thing the Mexicans did. One day a year they gave the dead food and flowers and in general made a big fuss, so they'd stay put and wouldn't bother them all the other days of the year. Suddenly he became more interested. "What can I do to help, honey?" he asked.

"No gifts," Annabel said.

They dressed up and set the table nicely. At first it was a little strange, but the food was good. Annabel chattered away to Ginger about her new friends, looking fixedly at the empty chair. She told her about the pimple she'd found—she couldn't imagine where it had come from. She told her about the new Corvette Carter had bought.

"No, no," he said, "she won't approve of that." Annabel looked at him oddly, and he laughed.

Midway through the meal, Annabel began to cry.

"Oh, honey," Carter said.

"She's not here!" Annabel cried.

"She's probably not used to the house yet."

"I don't expect her to really be here, Daddy. That's not what I'm saying. That would be silly. I just don't feel she's listening to us. I don't feel her presence."

Where was she, for godssakes? Carter wondered.

"I miss her," Annabel said. "I wish we hadn't scattered the ashes. I thought the empty chair was going to be the best part, but it isn't." She quickly cleared the dishes from the table and disappeared into the kitchen.

Carter sat there. Really, Ginger, he thought, this is mean of you. To be a termagant is one thing, but where is your compassion?

"I miss her," Annabel called from the kitchen. "I miss her."

Carter believed this and was horrified. He had another glass of wine and wandered outside into a beautiful night, black and still. Couldn't make out a thing, actually, but he knew that all around him were Donald's admirable touches. Donald, the young gardener, had presented himself at the door just last week, offering his services, his landscaping services. Donald could move a rock and effect an improvement. Restless, Carter returned to the house, poured himself a nightcap, and got

...urned down the covers, put both pillows behind his
...ked open the Jack London.

...bel called out, "I'm going to deep condition my hair
... legs."

"Okay, honey."

"Good night, Daddy."

London had gotten Carter through many a long night. "There were
no mourners save a huge wolf-dog, to whom the taste of his master's
lash was still sweet," he read. This was the real stuff. Blood on the
snow. Sneering white silence. More blood. And no one cared. Nobody
cared, and there was no law. Blazing eyes, slavered fangs, and wretched-
ness. Oh, it was a maggot's life, a cosmos of death. But this was the
way things were. . . . Carter lowered the book, and shut his eyes. His
thoughts swung pleasantly to Donald. He was so tall. He had a face
smooth and guileless as a baby's and a thick mat of hair on his chest.
Carter would've loved to press his mouth against that salty, soft amazing pelt, but of course he wouldn't, absolutely not. He was an amusing
man, a lighthearted man, he wanted to be happy, not to make a fool of
himself.

He opened his eyes and flipped through the pages. "At the sound of
this, the cry of Life plunging down from Life's apex in the grip of death,
the full pack at Buck's heels raised a hell's chorus of delight." Carter
frowned and studied the book's cover. This shouldn't be included in a
collection of stories, it was part of *The Call of the Wild*. He was about to
turn off the light and think about Donald for just a tiny bit more when he
noticed Ginger perched at the foot of the bed. She was wearing a dress
he'd always disliked—a shapeless green rayon thing that you could see
right through.

"I always knew you were a faggot, Carter."

"Why, darling!" Carter said. "I don't understand. Why weren't you
here earlier?"

"What was that all about, anyway?"

"Annabel would have been thrilled."

"We never celebrated my birthdays, Carter, as you are well aware. But
it's your full-blown faggotry we're discussing here, not my age. And that

Donald character. Honestly, Carter, you are so common, so ordinary. That little scar on his cheek! And the way you speak to him. . . . 'This is all you have to remember,' Ginger said mincingly. 'Mozart's subject is pleasure, Beethoven's is joy, Wagner's an insatiable yearning, dissatisfied with all consummation.'"

Carter blushed; it was true they'd been discussing music.

"That scar's fake as a three-day tattoo."

"Someone dropped a pruning saw on him. He could have lost an eye."

"Well, I've lost everything, you idiot, and I'm not going to let you forget it. Why was I cremated? If I'd ever thought about it, I would have expressly instructed that there would be no cremation. And to scatter me where you did, in that sound. Some of the worst toxic polluters in New England dump everything they've got into that sound! I expected to be placed in a handsome vault. You know how I really pictured it? I pictured you going first, of course. And then when my turn came and I was lowered into our tomb, your skeleton arms would open to receive me."

She got that right out of Héloïse and Abélard, Carter thought, history's most tedious couple. He hoped Ginger wasn't going to start writing to him. "Darling, please," he said, "give it a rest." Dead for months and still complaining about his driving, the way he had to clear his throat sometimes, his tipping practices (twenty percent), which she considered excessive. He studied her. She looked the same, and she was glaring at him.

"You never liked my breasts. You never paid any attention to them."

"I disagree with you there, darling. I'm sorry to say I disagree with you categorically over that one. I love—I loved—your breasts, your silver breasts. Your pearlescent breasts."

"No, no, no," Ginger moaned. "You were a false alarm, and I answered it."

Carter's stomach hurt. Those lamb chops were down there thinking, What's happened to us now? Where . . . why, this is incomprehensible. . . . He closed his eyes, hoping Ginger might vanish, though this had not been effective in the past. She stayed and stayed, sometimes for hours, her masterly and intricate condemnation of him going on and on. Ginger was clearly, merely, a thought of his and could be replaced with another. Why couldn't he do that? Maybe he needed a little instruction along these lines, a little training. He opened his eyes. Ginger was still there.

"I don't understand," he said, "why you didn't show up when Annabel wanted you."

"Never, never will I. She'd flip out if I did."

"What is it you want, Ginger?" Carter asked. His stomach shrieked, then fell silent.

"I want you to acknowledge your responsibilities. You're a married man, and marriage is a sacrament. It is indissoluble. I'm mortified by this Donald business. Mortified. You've turned into an old queen, Carter. You look so silly when you're infatuated. Your eyes practically cross."

Suddenly, the bedroom door began shaking in its frame. The ties, hanging there on a hook, slumped to the floor. The door flew open, and Annabel stood yelling in full nightmare.

"Pieces—in all the corners. Small, but too big—little pieces—"

Ginger evaporated as Carter hurried toward his daughter. He wore enormous blue boxer shorts.

"Left-handed people die sooner," Annabel hollered, flailing out at him and hitting him in the mouth.

"Not true," he managed to say. "It isn't, no, none of it."

"Oh Daddy, I'm sorry." Annabel said. She went back to bed. Carter went to the kitchen and made another drink. He pushed ice under his lip, sliding it along his gum. Nobody he knew was left-handed. He put *Tristan and Isolde* on and sat in the dark. He loved *Tristan*. All meaning lay in the things its characters didn't do or say; everything vibrated within the stillness of the characters, poised for actions that they postponed indefinitely. Opera was wonderful, Carter thought happily. An art devoted to love and death and the cryptic alliance between them. An art devoted to the definition and interchangeability of the sexes, to madness and drink and blasphemy! The characters of opera obey neither moral nor social law, which was pretty much what he'd been telling Donald. He sat in the dark listening to everything happening darkly and invisibly. When it was over, he still sat there. He supposed he should have outgrown Wagner by now. He wanted to throw a party, fill the house with people. Use that piano. He'd been sold on the house because of the existent piano in the otherwise empty rooms. He'd never had a piano before. It had yet to be utilized for anything except to display Ginger's photograph and, more recently, Donald's weekly flower arrangement. Donald. He was such a talented young man. Carter was definitely going to throw a party, fill this place with some life.

9

Ray Webb was trying to sell shoes in Houston, Texas, universally acknowledged as this planet's place of penance. He knew no one. He hadn't a single friend. He hadn't had a friend since he was eight, actually—that little bald-headed girl in rehab had liked him—and now he was nineteen, drifting across the country, working, and stealing now and then. He wanted to be a waiter but was a little wobbly with the trays, and people didn't like watching his mouth as he reeled off the specials. He'd kept those jobs for about two minutes. If the little bald-headed girl came in for a pair of shoes, he wondered, would they recognize each other? Of course she wouldn't still be eight. They'd had some good talks once. Or rather, she had talked at him. He couldn't speak very well because of his stroke, which is why he was in rehab to begin with. The little bald-headed girl had been struck by lightning. She'd been out picking blueberries, skipping along from lovely high bush to lovely high bush, unaware of the darkening day, and *Whup!* Nine times out of ten she could guess how many pennies were in a person's pocket. Being struck by lightning had given her special powers.

Ray didn't drink or do drugs but various ischemic incidents had given him an eager, erratic nature and a variety of facial contortions that allowed permanent employment to elude him. He hated selling shoes. He wanted to sell boots, but the manager disliked him. Even so, Ray performed his office enthusiastically. After only a week he'd developed a patter he was proud of, even though the better it got, the more wary his customers became. He couldn't help that.

"You've got to take your time in selecting shoes," he began. "You have to choose the shoes for you. You don't want a shoe that's going to end up looking at you with reproach when you take it off at night, offended by all you did or didn't do. Some shoes just don't want to carry you through life. You can't tell this about them in a store—in stores they adopt a neutral air that makes choosing difficult. But our shoes' route is our life's course. Selecting them is an important decision."

"I'll have to think this over," his latest customer said.

He put a couple of pieces of gum in his mouth and went back to the storeroom.

The manager followed him. "You're not a drinker, huh?"

Ray looked at him, chewing. "I hate alcohol. I never touch it," he said thickly. "I have no respect for it."

"You sure have the personality of a drinker," the manager said. "It's like you're a dry drunk. It's weird."

Ray said nothing. He was enjoying his gum. The early stages of chewing always reminded him of the part of *In the Penal Colony* where they put the sugar-coated gag in the condemned man's mouth just before the immense tattooing machine starts needling him to death. It was his favorite story. He thought the machine was so cool, but no one wanted to talk to him about it. The image was somewhat sadistic he supposed, but mostly the ordeal was about enlightenment. Or about guilt, since man's guilt is never to be doubted. Kafka had wanted to be a waiter, too, in his own restaurant. Probably no one would have gone into the place. Ray wished he'd been an academic, but the opportunity had never come up.

"You annoy me," the manager was saying.

The exhilarating if disgusting sweetness of the gum was gone now. Ray looked around for a place to put the wad, where it might cause some unpleasantness.

The manager told him to check the boxes on the sale table. People would come in and fiddle around with the boxes, sometimes placing their old worn-out shoes in a box and walking out with a new pair. If it happened on your watch, you were docked several hours' pay. Several hours' pay for each instance of switched shoes. Ray gloomily examined a dozen boxes, three of which contained footwear not in its first youth. When had this happened? He must have been dreaming today.

The manager looked pleased. "I'm going for panda," he said. "No lunch break for you today." The manager loved Chinese food, believing it conferred upon him a sort of individuality.

Ray sat on a stool and thought about the little bald-headed girl. Something else had been wrong with her, too; being hit by lightning wasn't her only problem. She'd been on his mind a lot lately. She was sharing space with the monkey in his head, though the monkey still ruled. Ray started to fidget. Air potato sewer vine, he thought. This was not good. He made a circuit of his department, then peered around a partition at the boots. This was a different world, a man's world, though every bit as empty. He slipped around and into it and picked up a pair of blue snakeskin boots. He put a big black-brimmed hat on his head and picked up a leather bag with a shoulder strap. He pushed the boots into the bag, nobody there to stop him. He kept moving, out of the store and into the fat ventricle of the mall, moving quickly and feeling superb, as though slaloming through powdered snow.

He glided past the fetid food court, where he saw the manager pointing at the picture of a plate of food. That's how people ate these days. They pointed at pictures, then were served something indistinguishable from its portrayal. Ray's stomach growled. The little monkey in his head stretched full out beside an empty, dented dish. Ray didn't like it when the monkey just lay there like that, its poor hair barely covering its body. It made Ray afraid.

He slipped into a restroom right before the exit to the parking lot. The place was filthy and smelled strongly of pizza. He removed his sneakers and pulled on the magnificent snakeskin boots. They were a size too large, he'd have to get thicker socks. The hat was good, it fit better than the boots, though it called attention to his mouth, which the stroke had pulled down. Still, the hat made his mouth look potent, as if it were just about to express something important. With the hat, he looked like he and the world had some plans. He didn't know why he hadn't thought of a hat before. Good-bye Houston! He would miss only his sometime excursions to the Rothko Chapel, where he had made several shy attempts at surrendering to that artist's dark demands. Man's whole vision was held together with rabbit-skin glue, he'd been told.

The fat man was in Teepee Ten and Ray in Teepee Two. The sign on the highway said "Sleep in a Wigwam Tonight!" and Ray thought the man was going to go into cardiac arrest with excitement. He wanted to stand Ray to a night in a concrete teepee on old Route 66, the mother highway, and Ray said fine. He'd always taken for granted the bizarre impulses of others, particularly those who picked him up on life's long and winding road. He'd been hitching north for two days, and mostly people had food in their cars that they shared with him. The fat man had only a bag of tangerines. Ray didn't know they even made tangerines anymore. The fat man said he wouldn't buy him dinner, but he'd buy him breakfast in the morning.

In his teepee, Ray took a long, hot shower. He liked taking showers until the hot water ran out, but this hot water kept coming. It would not be thwarted. It was like it was challenging him or something. Finally he gave up. He stepped out and, since he couldn't find any towels, dried himself with a couple of washcloths. His feet had started to blister from the beautiful boots, and he tore a pillowcase into strips and wound and bound his feet. He felt as resourceful as the Cub Scout he had once been. He hoped all his cub mates were dead, the little bastards. They were always going on camping trips and catching chipmunks under pots and setting fire to them with white gas. They were always hanging around canals and shooting arrows into manatees, pretending they were whales. Once they'd even captured a Key deer by lobbing baseball bats and stunning it. This was in Florida, where a boy had to take part in a certain number of monstrous customs on his way to manhood.

Ray had never cared for Florida; he had been born in Washington State, but they'd moved, after his mother's third miscarriage, from a town where everyone had miscarriages, where the fish in the river were soft as bread, the trees warty with fungus, and half the dogs three-legged. It was one of those rugged American places, a remote, sad-ass, but plucky downwind town whose citizens were flawed and brave. He would never go back there, of course. It had probably been condemned by now anyway, the whole place buried underground in drums.

Ray lay naked on the bed, staring at his wrapped feet and feeling vaguely dismembered. They probably weren't dead at all, his cub mates. They probably had jobs in primate labs, hosing out the cages, keeping the electrodes clean, the suturing thread on hand, the trepanning saws sharp, the decerebration tools sterilized. When monkeys were taught to use sign language, they'd sign *Please. Please. Hello. Hello. Big Boy be good.* They bypassed the chitchat. *Help,* they'd sign. *Lonely. Cold. Michael good girl, good.*

Ray had been obsessed with lab animals since a creepy therapist had told him after his stroke that a little monkey had given his life so that Ray could get better. Ray hated therapists, the smiles, the loose white clothes, the cheeriness. They were all creepy. "Vivisection in controlled laboratory experiments results in better treatment for little victims like you," the therapist had said. "Don't let anyone ever tell you different. And now you've learned a new word today, haven't you? *Vivisection.* It's not a bad word." Well, fuck that, Ray had thought at the time, but he was afraid. The little monkey bothered him; he felt the little monkey hadn't wanted to be his friend. He'd given it a place in his head—by now its haunt of many years—but it still didn't want to be his friend.

"Ray?" the fat man whispered at the door to the teepee. Ray didn't move. He lay quietly on his bed, idly wondering what happened to that child who'd been raised by apes in Africa. Some farmers had found him near Lake Tanganyika and dragged him off, cleaned him up, dressed him in little Levi's and a flannel shirt, and put him in an orphanage. But he was too late for language, and he couldn't manage to open doors. Knobs and latches eluded him. The little kid was probably a grown fuddled man by now, longing to be groomed by loving hairy fingers.

"Ray?" the fat man said. "I know you're there. I like big wide tits. Do you like big wide tits?"

Ray's stomach was growling, and he was sure the fat man could hear it.

"You're such a disappointment, Ray," the fat man said.

Ray rolled over on his stomach and tried to go to sleep. He crushed the pillows against his ears. He'd heard that if you murdered someone when you were sleeping, you wouldn't be held responsible. You'd be acquitted in a court of law.

The next morning Ray found a coil of human excrement outside his door. He had to stop accepting rides from people who had peculiar agendas. He felt a rattling in his brain, a sound as though of something chained, knocking around an empty pan. It was midmorning. Ray had opened the door to see what time it was, as there were no windows in the teepees. The cement of the structure was curved backward from the door and painted in colored stripes to suggest blankets or skins. The day was clear and cold. The shit, actually, had begun to freeze. He saw a Chicano girl in a yellow windbreaker pushing a housekeeping cart toward him. She was accompanied by one of those strange, hairless dogs with small heads that the Indians once upon a time had raised to eat. This one was wearing a knitted sweater, its legs trembling from the cold. Still, the dog must dig being outside, Ray thought. Anyplace but the kitchen. He nudged the shit with the toe of his boot, then picked it up and lobbed it ten yards into one of the trashcans painted to look like a tom-tom. The girl looked at him with disdain.

"Are you leaving today?" she asked.

"Where would I go?" Ray said, but this failed to charm her.

"If you're staying, you've got to pay another fourteen dollars by eleven o'clock."

"Twenty-three hundred hours, huh?" Ray maintained his crooked smile, but she pushed past him, all bright coat and double-black hair, the dog vibrating at her side.

In less than an hour, Ray was out on the highway again. He was curious as to what his brain had in mind. It was very quiet. Tall, slender pines grew in ordered ranks along the road. They all had the same DNA. If one sickened, they all did. They harbored identical secrets and had limited careers. Even the ravens found them boring, the ravens particularly. Log trucks whipped by. He was in a national forest, Land of Many Uses. There was the febrile smell of laboring machines.

A pearl-colored Fleetwood Brougham swept past at terrific speed, then braked and fishtailed backward. Ray ran up to it, his boots whistling softly, and opened the huge door. The driver was small and wiry; her face looked damp and her eyes were dilated, and in Ray's opinion she'd stolen the car for sure. An open bag of blue corn chips was propped on the dash. He looked at it and felt weak. They drove in silence, Ray imagining pleading and weeping coming from the trunk. The driver abruptly turned on the tape deck.

After listening to it for a while, Ray determined that it was the most depressing music he'd ever heard.

"Hugo Wolf," she said reverently.

"It's really something," he said. "It makes you kind of want to tear your throat out."

"Wolf couldn't handle it," she said. "Mahler used to visit him in the mental hospital. Mahler could handle it and should be considered the lesser man for it. What do you think of Schumann?"

"Schumann," Ray said cautiously.

"One listens in vain," the driver screamed, "for anything extraordinary in Schumann's last works. They are simply weak!"

They passed burnt acres of land. The trees stood the same way they had before, stoically, in rows the same height, yet all were black. They thought they were still doing their job, but they weren't. Bleak, mad chords filled the Cadillac. Ray rubbed the left side of his mouth; its cold and rubbery feel always gave him comfort.

A dog was trotting across the charred land that did not go on forever. Ray could see the end ahead where it became green again.

The woman slammed on the brakes. "Look," she said, "a pet. We need a pet." She certainly was starting from scratch, Ray thought. The big car went into a squat body wallow as it made the turn.

"Look," Ray said, "this could end badly. I stopped once when I had a car. I saw a lost dog on a hot day trotting along just like this one, his tongue hanging out, no exit in sight. So I turn around, pull up behind him, get a water bottle out, fish around for some kind of dish, can't find one, was going to pour some in my hand for him. Get out, walk toward him, he tucks his tail between his legs and tears out into the highway where he's promptly chewed to pieces by the passing parade." He looked at her and nodded, assuring her that this was true. He recalled crouching there, his hand extended, in the same tiny blue flowers the dog had been trotting through.

"That's because you're a fucking loser, man," the driver said. She sped back, heaved the car around, and pulled off the macadam onto the crispy ground. The dog's ears went back, but he soldiered on, a little faster maybe. The woman got out. She was wearing a denim jacket covered with pins and glittering buttons over a dirty pair of peach-colored tights. She was a spooky little thing, Ray thought. He reached for the blue chips and stuffed as many as he could into his mouth. She stood there and clapped her hands the way his parents used to when they wanted a light to go on in the house . . . that's the kind of lights they had. His parents succumbed to gadgetry of all kinds. Ray put some chips into his coat pocket and kept chewing. The dog hurried onward, the woman walking and then running after it. Ray closed his eyes. There was the long shriek of a semi's air horn. He knew that he had to exit the car, that it would be unwise to remain in the funereal Fleetwood much longer.

The woman wrenched the door open. "You fuck, you loser!" she screamed. "How did you do that, you sick fuck?" Ray opened his eyes. Her own were dry but bloodshot. She possessed disturbing strength. His hat flew off as she removed him from the car and he stumbled onto the cinders and tore a hole in one knee of his jeans. More cinders rained on his bare head as the car scrambled away. He groped for his hat. The little monkey was climbing the walls in his head, making clear that it wanted out. Any avenue along the capillaries would do. There was an awful craving to get out. Ray didn't feel well. He ate a few more chips and touched the corner of his mouth for a while. It felt like the hooded towel he'd favored when he was a little kid with little rubbery animals on it from Noah's Ark. When he got up, he didn't look at the roadway but kept his eyes on the ground. A wallet was lying there, formerly belonging to one Merle Orleans, the poor bastard. The picture on the license showed a fellow who didn't have a clue that he'd bought his last Cadillac. Ray had found wallets before, sometimes in the darnedest places. With Merle's collection of credit cards, he could buy a used truck and some socks, definitely some socks, plus a warmer coat, and gloves. He had to get his own means of transportation and stop relying on the fickle grace of lunatics. Merle Orleans might very well be moving on into the afterlife. He didn't examine the face too closely as a matter of decorum.

In a few miles, Ray was long out of the burn and looking down into a valley. To his left was a runaway-truck ramp, where a semi lay wadded in loose gravel. He'd never seen one actually in use before. If you were a runaway-truck ramp, you probably had to wait a long time for some action. He assumed that this was the truck that had come between the gloomy chick in the Fleetwood and the pet of her desiring, and that she'd run the driver off the road. On the crumpled cab were dark silhou-ettes of animals—dogs, deer, birds—with lines drawn through rows of nine. What a fun-loving dude! Nothing was moving inside the cab. This was so almost morally acceptable, Ray thought. A police car was nearby, its lights pulsing.

"Oh dear," Ray said to the policeman, who ignored him.

Ray used Merle Orlean's plastic to buy himself a truck at a place called Gary's Beautiful Cars. The truck was matte gray with jacklights and chrome wheels and was an exception in Gary's lot, because most of his vehicles looked beat up and hard driven. Ray drove a hundred miles and then, at the urging of a large billboard, turned into the vast parking area of the Lariat Lounge.

The lounge itself was a rankly dim establishment illuminated only by a large TV. On the screen was a powerboat race, where some mishap had occurred and was being rebroadcast. A boat named *Recondita Armonia* had grazed and skimmed over *The Bat/Frank's Marine,* decapitating both the throttleman and the driver.

The bartender greeted Ray by saying, "You'd think that's just a helmet flying there, but there's a head inside."

"Wow," Ray said. "Where is this?"

"Earlier on, a guy did a classic skip-and-stuff and killed himself too, but they haven't been showing that one as much."

"Wow," Ray said again. "Where is this?"

The bartender looked at him.

"I mean, when?" Ray said, groping for the germane.

"Whatya wanna drink, pal?" the bartender said. "I don't got all day."

Ray ordered a beer. Though it wasn't very cold, he didn't want to men-tion it and further discredit himself in the bartender's eyes. You just couldn't walk into a bar; Ray was always forgetting that. Entering a bar took thought and preparation. The desired persona had to be determined, then assembled—in Ray's case, practically from scratch—and projected.

He gazed up at the screen, where the little helmet was tumbling over and over through the air. It's got to be Florida, he mused. That Easter-egg green water is definitely Floridian. He marveled for a moment about being here, thousands of miles away in Arizona, watching this balletic moment with hundreds of thousands of other people from coast to coast, all as one in the great world of human consciousness, observing and absorbing, all thinking pretty much the same thing: man's *brains* are still in that thing, probably saying *whoaa* and trying to cogitate this problem through . . .

He ordered another beer, which tasted just the slightest shade warmer than the first, then retreated with determined nonchalance into the establishment's other room. In here it was darker, and by error he seated himself directly beside the only other occupied table. Two men had been talking, and one of them pushed the curtain back from a filthy window so that more light fell upon the scene, a gaping desert light much disoriented at finding itself inside.

The men had been telling stories, and they waved Ray right in on the hearing of one, as though he'd been with them all the while, had departed only for a moment, and had now come back.

"So he spends Christmas Day in a motel room with my sixteen-year-old daughter."

"Jesus. Christmas Day."

"Disappeared right after the stockings. She came home that night, but it took me and my buddy until New Year's Eve to find him."

"You was always good friends, I recall."

"*Good* friends. No problem up to then between me and Modesto. My little girl can be a troublemaker sometimes, I'd be the first to admit it. So Modesto has this girlfriend he's crazy about, and she's got a little kid. It's Modesto's little kid. He's crazy about the both of them, but she's out of town for Christmas visiting her mother. She's in Bisbee. Her mother runs one of those cute-as-hell motels over there."

The man smiled at Ray, who couldn't help but wonder why they had befriended him.

"So I say to Modesto, when we found him, 'You've got a choice here, my friend.' We had him in his own truck. We was sitting on either side of him in his own truck. 'You got a choice,' I say. 'You can either watch your girlfriend and your little kid go down—and I mean *watch*, I mean *go down*—or you can eat these varmint pellets.'"

"Nahhhh!"

"Yes."

"Strychnine!"

"We had him outside his girlfriend's apartment. I mean, right outside. You could see the fucking mobile over the kid's crib. And I say, 'Take this, eat this, or else they die.'"

Ray gulped his beer. "Scared the shit out of him, huh?" he interjected.

"So the punk took it. He thought it was a movie or something. He thought he was exhibiting an ethical dimension."

"He might've thought it was an initiation or something," Ray said. Initiations were always a dark-before-dawn arrangement. Things usually got better afterward.

"So he swallows the damn stuff, and my buddy and I vacate the truck. Modesto sits there for a minute and then starts shooting all around the cab on his own accord in these convulsions. Banged himself all the hell up. Must've gone on for ten minutes."

"It wasn't really strychnine was it?" Ray said.

"Cops come eventually, and you know what they conclude? They conclude Modesto OD'd. They say he suicided."

"Cops are dumb around here, huh?" Ray said.

"That word 'initiation' is some word," the storyteller's companion said. "Don't hear a word like that every day."

"Man's trying to put himself in Modesto's shoes."

"Gotta be an asshole to want to be in them."

"Considering that Modesto convulsed himself right out of them, I'd have to agree with you. Those ten minutes were, well, they were beyond my wildest dreams of satisfaction," the man said contentedly.

Ray thought he'd better be on his way. He didn't even feel the need to finish his beer. At the same time, he thought he should buy a round for all concerned, though possibly that wasn't a great idea either.

"Like maybe you're imagining that Modesto's imagining he's being initiated into the No Fear club or something? Those assholes that have them banners across their windshields, those shade screens that say 'No Fear,' they belong to a club, right?"

"That is not my truck," Ray said.

"We saw you get out of it."

"It's not mine."

"Salaried pussies, they *lease* those vehicles."

"I stole it," Ray said.

"Ooh-hoo."

"I sure did." Ray wanted to appear a hardened criminal, but hip and friendly too. He pondered his exit line.

"You happen to know the Jesus prayer, wee-wee face?" the storyteller inquired.

Ray said nothing. His mouth seemed more insensate than usual.

"You just keep mumbling the ol' Jesus prayer, and it will wreak a little miracle on you."

"Wreak?" Ray dared. "I don't . . . what is it?"

"Lord Jesus Christ, Son of God, have mercy on me, a sinner."

"I don't know that."

"You just keep mumbling it"—the storyteller rolled his eyes and waggled his tongue in a rude portrayal of an idiot—"and mumbling and mumbling and you'll come to know that whatever happens to you is just something that happens. And what's even better is, you'll come to know that whatever you do to someone else is just something that happens too."

The other man stared at Ray's truck, absorbed in the flagrant breach of etiquette it represented.

"Adios, gentlemen," Ray said.

They gaped at him. "Adios?" they cried in unison.

"Don't die around here," the storyteller suggested warmly. "It will be utterly misconstrued."

Ray was already up and moving steadily through the bar, past the big-screen TV, now focused on *Recondita Armonia* in the dry pits. There wasn't a mark on her.

Even with a considerable number of partying people, the house was in no way crowded. Carter supposed it was a bit large for his and Annabel's needs, but they'd always lived in large houses. Anything under twelve thousand square feet Ginger had considered a hut. In their marriage's prime, they had needed various rooms into which to retreat after quarrels had reached their towering crest. As a matter of fact, whenever they had bought a house (and they had moved frequently during Ginger's spate on earth) one of their requirements had been rooms that served no other purpose. But though Carter had paid top dollar for this place, it lacked what could be considered a post-altercation crawl space. This pleased him, for any place that intimated a way of life other than the one he had shared with Ginger was a pearl beyond price.

He had toyed with various themes for this evening's party but finally decided just to let the champagne flow and see what happened. He did suggest dressy. Carter loved dressy. He himself was never more relaxed than in a dinner jacket. There was something about a dinner jacket that was so relaxing, it just took you a million miles away.

Annabel was wearing her alpaca swing coat and her beaded chiffon skirt, two of her most fabulous things. Alice was wearing houndstooth slacks from Goodwill and a clean T-shirt with no railing message on it. Though Annabel had forced a little makeup on her, she'd rubbed most of it off. "You looked so sultry," Annabel complained. "Well, maybe not sultry, but that cherry chocolate lipstick looked good on you. Effects can be achieved, Alice, you just have to experiment." Corvus wore an unexceptional white sundress, but what she wore hardly elicited notice; it was the intrigue of her face, the sleekness of her dark hair. All three of them were motherless. Annabel thought they should have more in common than they did.

There was the civilized, slapping sound of martinis being made.

Carter found himself enjoying the company of several young men. "Now, for Wagner," he was saying, "opera was a political creed and spiritual gospel; its aims were revolution and salvation. He wanted to *transfigure* the lives of those who heard his work." The fine young men were attentive to these sentiments.

About a hundred guests were present. Carter had found them here and there. Ginger had never liked his friends, so he'd gotten into the habit of making new ones readily. Back east, Ginger had actually been instrumental in getting one of his nicest friends deported to the horribly infelicitous country of his birth, a place where everyone spoke a different dialect and murderous fights broke out over the slightest misunderstanding. His friend had previously managed to inadvertently insult a number of his countrymen, and Carter feared that the homecoming had not been a pleasant one.

"You know," one of the young men was saying to Carter, "Wolf House is only a few days' drive from here, in Sonoma. If you're a London fan, you have to see it. It was his dream house, in the works for years, and it burnt to the ground the night before he was to move in."

"I *do* want to see Wolf House," Carter said. He had an empathy for structural decay on a grand and brooding scale, generally a bad tendency in an architect. Hadn't the disaster in this case been the architect's fault—a great writer's dream thwarted on the telluric level by a faulty venting design? It made him glad he had never truly practiced his profession.

Donald discreetly turned Carter's attention to the rising moon, which had rolled past the mountain's corner like an immense cruise ship.

Corvus was quiet as always quiet, though taking everything in, Annabel suspected. She would hate to be the kind of person who had to take everything in all the time. Corvus made her feel like a merry little insect or something, though she wasn't at all snobbish or supercilious. She had perfect skin, almost translucent, and sometimes Annabel would just gape at it. There were dog hairs on that white sundress, though, she noticed pityingly.

Alice was sitting on a couch watching a man in a tuxedo play the piano. A woman in a silk jumpsuit sat beside him on the bench, and Alice looked at them sulkily. The woman began to sing. She didn't have a bad voice, she was confident and playful. Alice bit her nails, dragging them out of her mouth on occasion for inspection. The woman was singing witty lyrics in a light, assured voice, and the man in the tuxedo grinned at her, a cigarette hanging out of his mouth, his hands flying over the keys.

"Alice, what are you thinking about?" she heard Annabel ask. "You're all scrunched up! Do you want some hummus?" She extended some on a cracker.

"I can't eat," Alice said.

Annabel looked at her respectfully.

"I . . . he . . . they just won't let him out early. We keep hoping they'll let him out early." The reason she didn't date, Alice had explained, was that she already had a boyfriend, who unfortunately was away in prison.

"It's too bad you have to think about parole all the time," Annabel said.

Alice wished she'd never invented this absentee boyfriend.

"But I don't think prison's anything to be ashamed about," Annabel said. "It's something lots of people have to just get behind them."

What was he in jail for anyway? Alice wondered. Nothing good.

"I'm sure he doesn't even belong in prison," Annabel said. "I knew a boy back home, he was piloting his dad's motorboat at night and he hit a buoy and killed two of his friends and they sent him to prison. He was there a whole year, and he didn't belong there at all."

Alice looked at her.

"Well, he was a nice boy, I mean. Basically. And they'd all been drinking—even the dead ones. What's yours look like, you've never told me. I don't picture him as being particularly cute . . . more compelling-looking."

"It's difficult to describe someone you love," Alice said.

"So he's really going to be in there forever, or what? That's a big responsibility for you. They want them to feel remorse, is the thing. He should profess remorse."

"Annabel," Alice said, "I don't want to discuss it."

"I *understand*," Annabel said.

Now the singer was embracing the man in the tuxedo, giving him a big kiss on the side of the head. Then she slid gracefully off the piano bench and joined the party. The man sat with his back to the girls, not doing anything for a moment. Then he lit another cigarette.

Alice heard a woman say, "Before I start writing I feel affectionate, interested, and frustrated. In that order. Afterwards I feel relieved, disgusted, and confused. Sometimes I don't think it's worth it."

"What kind of poems do you write?" someone asked.

This soiree was sort of out of it, Alice thought.

The man in the tuxedo turned toward her. "What would you like to hear, darling?" he asked.

I'd like to hear you moaning in ecstasy in bed, Alice thought, startling herself. Men did that, didn't they? She gave him a smile and felt her lip snag on her tooth the way Fury's did sometimes after he yawned and her poppa would have to reach down and unhook it.

"Without the guidance of request, I always play 'I Get a Kick Out of You.'" After he finished, he came over and sat between them.

"The woman who was singing with you," Alice croaked. "Is she your lover?"

Annabel giggled. She had never seen Alice behave like this.

"There are certain women," the man in the tuxedo said, "who love men like myself. They're fascinated with us, we're a challenge to them. Do you suppose he'd fuck me? they wonder. Do you think he could do it?"

"Really?" Alice said.

"That is the case," the man said.

"Some people are so shallow, " Alice said.

"Some people are *tremendously* shallow," Annabel said. "I knew a boy back home who, if someone he didn't like told him something he thought was dumb, he'd laugh in a noblesse oblige fashion and then he'd look at someone he liked and shrug and say 'Noblesse oblige.'"

"Have you ever had a man, darling?" the man asked Annabel.

"A few experiments," she said. "They were actually just boys. Sort of. Back home." The piano player was sort of disgusting. Leave it to Alice to be enchanted.

"Do you always wear a tuxedo?" Alice asked.

"Always," he said. "Never without it. In church you can't see it for the robe."

"Church?" Alice exclaimed, troubled.

"God is the net. We are the creatures within the net."

"Oh, that's kind of pretty, I think," Annabel said. But then she didn't think it sounded pretty at all.

"You need to see the net for it to work," he said. "It's not enough to be in it. We have to be conscious of it over and over again."

"We make our own net," Alice said. She couldn't believe he was a churchgoer. She'd have to work her way around that.

"But we don't make it out of that marvelous light stuff," he said. "We make those ugly, hard, crude, clangoring links."

"You really go to church?" Alice asked.

"I play the hymns. They pay me for it, though I would do it for nothing. I find church very sexy. I love Protestants."

"Then you don't believe it?"

"Believe what, darling?"

"It just arouses you?"

Annabel gave an alarmed, piercing laugh.

" 'I fled him down the nights and down the days/I fled him down the arches of the years/I fled him down the labyrinthine ways of my own mind/and in the midst of tears I hid from him,' dah dah dah dah. 'From those strong feet that followed, followed after . . . ,' " the man in the tuxedo chanted, his eyes half shut. "The minister loves the old mystics. I think he's going to have a nervous breakdown any Sunday now. Expectation runs high." He seemed to notice Corvus for the first time, and he smiled at her and bowed a little.

"Well," Alice said, "God's not my owner."

"You must like cats," he said.

"Cats?" Alice said.

"The chosen allies of womankind."

"Would anyone like a beverage?" Annabel said.

"Cats are accustomed to making their own decisions and implementing them out of their owner's sight."

"I don't care for cats at all," Alice said.

"Coffee perhaps?" Annabel persisted.

"No coffee for me, darling," the piano player said. "I drink coffee at night, and I have bad dreams—headless, one-eyed men with their mouths in their armpits wanting you-know-what from me and such."

Annabel never told her dreams since the time she had asked her mother if she wanted to hear about one that in Annabel's opinion was particularly artful and mysterious. "I dreamed . . . ," Annabel had begun. "I dreamed I was in Hell," her mother interrupted, pretending those were the words Annabel was about to speak. It was nine in the morning and her mother was having a screwdriver and a cookie.

"Would you like some ice water?" Alice asked.

"Ice water would be fabulous," he said, "but hold the ice."

She went off happily for the water. Obtaining the simple element in a glass required intensive negotiations with the bartender.

"Plastic relies on an unrenewable resource," Alice complained. "It's not truly recyclable, and the petroleum involved requires extensive use of toxics in manufacture. Plus it's the largest trash contaminant of the oceans. As a caterer, you should be aware of this and set a better example."

"Who invited you, might I ask?" the bartender said.

She eventually returned with something acceptable.

"This is a perfect glass of water," the man in the tuxedo said.

They watched him drink it, the muscles in his neck moving.

"What were we talking about?" Annabel said. "Oh, church . . ."

He put down the empty glass. "I take most of my meals on a church plate," he said. "That is, a plate with the representation of my church's building upon it. It's my only plate." He looked at them piously. "I have very little."

"I'd love to see it," Alice said.

"Words don't express our thoughts very well, do they, darling?" he said.

"I've always thought that was true!" Alice agreed. "Who came up with the idea they could? Some sort of control freak."

"She meant the plate, I think," Annabel said.

The man in the tuxedo giggled richly.

"Thank you, Annabel," Alice said.

Fretfully, Annabel got up and wandered off to see what her father was doing. He was speaking to a young man whose very long blond hair and pale cream-colored clothes made him look rather like a palomino.

"Our marriage was a mutual solitude, as the French say," Carter was saying.

"Oh, Daddy," Annabel sighed. She went outside feeling as ethereal and misplaced as her mother. One of her mind exercises was to choose a star, pretend it was Ginger, and confide in it. She looked up and began, "I'm unhappy, Mommy. There's nothing to do out here except cocktail parties and nature." Even as she spoke, she heard a scuffling in the desert just beyond the pool's walls, followed by an inhuman cry and a preoccupied silence.

"You wouldn't like it out here either, Mommy," Annabel continued. "You wouldn't tolerate it for more than five minutes." She didn't know what to tell her mother. Nothing sounded right to her. She certainly wasn't going near the Big Sister debacle. To fill up some time, Annabel had offered to become a Big Sister. Her Little Sister came over to the house, and all she wanted to talk about was Girls' Ranch. The worst thing about staying there was that they gave you hair conditioner only once a week. Plus the shampoo wasn't the hydrating kind with natural humectants, and every girl in there had bleached hair and needed follicle nourishment. Annabel commiserated with her about this at length. Little Sister was an exceedingly shy and clumsy child, spilling a full glass of tomato juice all over the piano. This so humiliated her that she called her taxi-driver boyfriend, who arrived and drove her away before Annabel had been a Big Sister for even forty-five minutes. Later it was discovered that she'd keyed Carter's Corvette, stuffed bananas down all the toilets, and stolen a bottle of Patrón. "She certainly knew her tequilas," Alice had said.

Annabel started over with another star. "Mommy, if you were me . . ."

A massive object hurtled over the wall and into the swimming pool. It was the size of a motorcycle, thrashing darkly. She screamed, and it churned through the water, extinguishing the little floating candles, cracking hard against the ladder, entangling itself in the temperature duck. It sank, then struggled heavily upward. Two black nostrils stared like empty eyes.

Carter strode out with several young men, all with drinks in hand.

"Mr. Vineyard," Donald said, "it's a deer." He jogged to the garage, where all the tools hung within their chalked-up outlines, rakes and hammers, hoses and shears. When one was taken away to be used, it looked, as far as the garage was concerned, as though it had died.

Everyone had straggled out by now. "I can't watch this," the poet said, then added, "If it breaks its leg, what you have to do is call the fire department."

Donald ran back with a garden hose. "We'll make a sling, perhaps we can haul it out that way." Carter quite unexpectedly jumped into the pool. "Oh no, Mr. Vineyard," Donald cried, "you could be struck!" Shouting, Carter's young friends followed him in, hesitating only to kick off their shoes and remove their jackets. "Rodeo!" one yelled. The deer was sinking once again, flattening out somewhat like a carpet. The young men in their billowing shirts seemed disturbingly sexual to Annabel as they grasped parts of the animal and pushed it toward the steps, laughing and grunting, leaving behind them a wake of plastic cups and lime wedges. The deer struggled out, slid sideways, and fell back with a scrabbling crackle of hooves against the tile. Annabel was sure she saw blood in the water. Her inviting limpid pool had been transmogrified into something rank and exclusive. The animal, tipped upright on the steps once again, heaved itself from the water and in one wobbly leap vanished over the wall into the desert whence it had come. Carter's jacket was sliced straight through; his hands were torn. The young men, too, had suffered varying degrees of damage to their clothing, which seemed to delight them. They all climbed out in high spirits, hugging and punching one another.

Donald brought an armful of large white towels from the poolhouse. "You're a nice man, Mr. Vineyard," he told Carter earnestly. "A new soul in my opinion." He dabbed at Carter's head with a towel.

Alice was standing beside the piano player, with whom she had become quite smitten.

"What a macabre environmental event," he said.

"Now you know what I was talking about," Alice said to Annabel.

"What do you mean, 'Now I know'? I don't know anything! This doesn't happen every time a deer falls into a swimming pool, does it?"

Annabel wanted someone to turn off the pool light. Where was the stupid switch! The water looked murky and was still rocking against the sides of the pool. And the deer or someone had chipped her favorite decorative tile, a little mermaid with starfish on her breasts. Half of her gentle little face was gone, and who could fix that! No one could.

Alice followed the piano player back into the house and watched him as he smoked. "You're too much for me, kid," he finally said. "You've got the look of the pilgrim all over you."

"That's my friend," she said. "Look, my boyfriend's on death row, so I can't do anything with you, really. We can't have an actual love affair because of him, okay, so I just want to hang out."

"I love it," he said.

"I just want to run with you."

"I don't run, dear. Goodness."

"I don't mean jogging. Not that."

They looked at each other in amazement.

He ground out his cigarette and lit another. "What did he do?"

"What?"

"To get there."

"Oh! It was a crime of passion."

"I love prisoners," he said, blowing smoke. "Tell me though, honey, are you jammy or minty?"

"I—I don't know what you mean."

"Straight or queer."

"I'm not either one."

"You know what they say," he said, tapping his fingers on his knee, "When the two shall be one and the without as the within and the male with the female, neither male nor female, that's when the party begins." He laughed without opening his mouth.

A car started up in the driveway, its headlights turning the bats in their threaded flight above to silver.

"This particular party's almost over, thank God," he said.

"You're not leaving, are you?" Alice said. "Where are you going, where do you live?"

"You're a saucy one. I live in a room, a dirty little room. You can't see it. I'm at that time in my life when temptations abound."

"Do they have shapes, your temptations?" Alice asked. More people were leaving the party.

"They have the shape of intemperate tendencies, honey."

"You can call me by my name," Alice said. "It's Alice."

"But I don't want to, honey."

"What's your name?"

"Sherwin."

"It isn't!"

"I've spoiled everything again," he sighed. "I always do." He ground out another cigarette in the brimming ashtray. "Does that ashtray spook you?" he asked. "Sometimes they can be very spooky. Sometimes I just smoke and look at the ashtray and think, What will have happened by the time it's full? And just when I feel I'm about to understand what the ashtray is, at the same time, with a certain wonder and even fear, I feel I've never understood it and I don't understand anything." He widened his eyes.

She didn't care about ashtrays. An ashtray could never perturb her like that. She simply wanted, if he ever looked away, to take one of the cigarettes he'd smoked, crushed remnant of his pleasure and need, put it into her pocket, and keep it. She wished he'd say her name.

"Alice?" he said.

11

Ray felt he was pushing his luck with Merle Orlean's credit line. Stealing without a weapon was fun, but it made a man less virile and flexible after a time. So he decided to settle down for a few weeks. There were mountains all around this town, sort of pretty, and it was warmer than where he'd been. This was serious heat, and Ray liked heat. He got a job at an Indian crafts shop, Morning Star Trader, by answering an ad in the newspaper. "I have experience in sales," he told the owner. Morning Star Trader claimed they sold old pawn but didn't. Anyone seriously into old pawn wouldn't be caught dead in this place. Besides, where did this old pawn keep coming from? Ray didn't believe in old pawn. He scarcely believed in history. The shop sold inconsequential jewelry, greeting cards, kachinas, sand paintings, and fetishes. There was also a table offering Mexican *calacas:* Here were the skeletons at the vanity table, getting married, discovering infidelities, playing instruments, feeding the birds, at the beach. Great stocking stuffers, or put them in bunny's basket at Easter time. But the public needed no urging in this regard, thinking the *calacas* hilarious. The *calacas* flew out of there.

What took more skill was the field wherein Ray shone, the selling of the fetishes, those tiny animals carved from bone or stone. "It's all bullshit," the owner had told him, "but all bullshit is relative, you know what I'm saying?" Ray did. He admired the owner, who trusted him and was never around. Ray pushed the little objects as telepathic and life-enriching. The manner that had failed him in the selling of shoes worked brilliantly here. Through a little research he'd learned that it had once been very weird with the Zunis and their fetishes, which originally had been consulted for success in hunting or to prevent sickness and defeat.

The fetishes lived in special jars, where they ate and breathed and their power was contained. They were frequently washed in blood and feathers and scrubbed with pieces of hide, and repulsive objects such as human eardrums were often attached to them. They were sticky and rank from the cornmeal they were fed. Zuni beliefs were complicated and covered every known dilemma. The men had to be careful, and the women had to be even more careful than the men, because there were more things they could do wrong, such as not washing the scalps properly or failing to keep the scalp jar in good order. They had scalp jars all over the place. If a woman's husband died—undoubtedly because of some screwup by the wife—she was obliged to mourn for a full year. At the end of the year she was supposed to have intercourse with a stranger, to whom she must present a gift he would then destroy. That part was sort of cool, Ray thought, but the custom had probably been suppressed along with so many intriguing traditions in this secular age. After awhile, the Zunis started to make things up and connections became imprecise. Their cruddy innocent world collapsed.

In the shop, he pushed the fetishes solely as honest messengers from the world within, quiet helpful inner voices. As the customer peered into the locked glass case, Ray would begin, "The one you're attracted to first is usually the one for you—it has something to say to you. The right one has a subtle yet powerful draw."

He would leave them for a moment to ponder this, then return. They were usually older women. Morning Star Trader wasn't that great a place to meet girls. They seldom went for badger or snake; mostly wolf or bear would get the nod. If they weren't at all serious, they would ask to see toad, possibly gila monster. These were the knickknack sort. Seldom did eagle impress them, perhaps being too close emblematically to that out-of-fashion colonial effect once so popular in the overpopulated and spiritually malnourished Northeast, a region from which many of his customers had recently fled. Eagle's power had been compromised.

If they seemed hesitant, Ray would ask, "Do you wish to hold one in your hand?" He peddled the fetishes as focusing powers, as channelers with the ability to lead one away from puzzlement and distress. His odd face—suggesting, as it did, fate—only seemed to help. "If you're responsive, they can be very useful," he would say quietly, though sometimes he'd get wound up and suggest that mole could help in strengthening the immune system or that falcon enhanced one's communication with a pet. But mostly he supported the big vague picture.

He had suffered only one return in two weeks working at the store, from a woman he'd encouraged to go off with mountain lion. The lions weren't moving. Ray felt it was because their carver insisted on making their shoulders too big and their heads too small; things looked screwed up. He'd told the woman that this particular fetish protected the traveler. He didn't know why he had come up with that angle—little monkey messing up his wave—but it turned out this was precisely what the woman wanted to hear, and she took two to double-dip their assistance. By the end of the day she was back, the engine block on her Buick having cracked before she'd even gotten home.

"Car travel isn't real traveling," Ray said. He could barely enlarge on this before he was forced to admit that the store did not provide cash refunds. He was about to suggest she consult white wolf to remind her of the transitoriness of events, but she threw the fetishes—still wrapped in tissue, not even out of the bag—at him and left. He was replacing them in the case when another customer came in, a moody-looking girl in dusty black. Ray felt composed; he'd pocketed seventy dollars on the mountain lions, and the store still had them. When he began his riff, the girl looked shocked.

"Please," Alice said, "you're polluting this for me."

"Well, fine," Ray said.

"Give me a break."

He made an ironic bow and went over to the *calacas* table. There were the skeletons at the mirror, at the typewriter, taking photographs of one another, walking their little skeleton dogs, in the bath. He had a headache. The little monkey was dragging a useless limb across the inside of his head, mopping inside it with its soft floppy arm. This was how his headaches were: neither piercing nor pounding, they were just the little monkey's nerve-dead arm swinging back and forth. He wanted to close up, go back to his room, have a beer, get the monkey comfortable and count the money he'd saved. The windfall with the lions had really kicked his savings up. He wanted to buy some gear and find some wilderness and camp out for a while. He'd already lifted a pretty decent backpack from an unlocked car. Astonishing how many cars remained unlocked in this day and age. But he had a ways to go before he'd outfitted himself properly. "Sometimes in the wilderness you have to rely more on your equipment than yourself," as the ads said.

"Have to close up in a few minutes," he called to the girl.

Alice was crouched in front of the case, her fingers pressed against the glass. Then she stood up and rested her arms on the top, still looking.

"Don't lean on that," he called. "It could break, easy." His mouth inadvertently broke into a grimace, for the little monkey had stopped with the sweeping and sort of lost its balance and stumbled, as it often did. Once, when Ray was ten, he'd gone to a psychiatrist and tried to describe this sensation. "It's like it slips sometimes and falls through glass—thin, thin glass like ice, and levels and levels of it . . ." he'd ventured.

"That's sex, son," the doctor said warmly. "That's puberty. That's your hormones talking."

"Sex?" Ray said.

"I've heard sex described that way a thousand times," the psychiatrist said. "Let me tell you something about girls while we're having this conversation. Girls have hair down there. It can come as a shock to the uninformed."

Young Ray felt like telling him that to reduce any mysterious feeling to the sexual was to grievously mutilate its true relevance. He had told him in the only way he could at ten. He'd told him to fuck off. And he hadn't mentioned the little monkey to anyone since, not that this had quieted it down or consoled it any.

"You're determined to break that, aren't you?" Ray snapped at Alice. He picked up a bottle of Windex and a roll of towels and made a great show of cleaning the glass while she stood there.

"I'd like to see that one," Alice said.

"Raven," he said. "That's a hundred and eight dollars."

"I still want to see it."

Reluctantly, he removed it from the case. He wanted her to assume that she shouldn't, at that price, expect to hold it herself. "This one is associated with transformational powers. As a confident—"

Alice looked at him—and not at his mouth, either, where most people got stuck. "Even though they're made by people just out to make a buck, you shouldn't mess with their abilities like you do." She snatched the raven carving from his hand and turned it over. "Why does it say eighteen dollars?"

"Whoops," he said. "Guess my eyes get tired at the end of the day." There was an unpleasant silence. "If it's a gift, you can get that price off with a little bit of nail polish remover. I think the great transformer is money, you know what I mean? It can turn into anything. It's practically alive, man," he said, excited by his insight.

Alice studied it, ran her grimy thumb across it.

"Why don't you take it?" Ray said suddenly. "Just take it, I'm giving it to you." He liked doing this, saying the exact opposite of what he really felt, being nice to people he disliked. To be unnatural and spontaneous, to create confusion and unease, was satisfying. He thought of the little monkey doing what he shouldn't be able to do, *seeing* through those sewn-shut lids, nudging a peanut with that insensate limb, arguing in a persuasive language never heard before against protracted and untimely death. "Say 'Thank you,'" Ray prompted.

"I won't accept it." The fetish made a little click as she set it down on the glass. "It's not for my friend. I mean, it was supposed to be for her, but it isn't. I think you've defiled this whole case," she added.

"I was only joking," Ray said. "Why would I give you something for nothing?"

The moment she left, the little monkey recommenced its dragging, stricken circuit in his head.

12

Carter had bought some satin sheets in the hope they might help him sleep.

Ginger sat in the chair by the empty vanity table. "So how did your day go?" she asked.

Carter looked longingly at the sheets. "Well, the Wilsons are in town, dear, and I had dinner with them. They're on their way to the Four Corners area for their anniversary. Twenty-five years!" A quarter of a century, with considerable help from the Percodan tablets prescribed after they'd thrown out their backs when the club car in which they'd been riding had been struck by a slow-moving freight. They had never taken a train anywhere again and instead zipped about the country first-class on airplanes, whacked out of their minds. They were great fun to be around.

"I hope, for their sake, they don't run into any mice," Ginger said. "The mice up there make dust that's virulent. A person breathes it in, gets a headache—then Curtain! Dead within twenty-four hours."

"A mouse makes a—?"

"Oh, I'm giving you the short version, for godssakes. Why go on and on about things?"

Carter was silent.

"So tell those tiresome people they'd better watch out. What did you talk about at dinner?"

Didn't she know this? "Jazz and palms, mostly," Carter said. "Those people really know their palms. They don't just toss around the common names, either. No sugar, jelly, or Madagascar for them."

"So?" Ginger said, looking at him intently.

"Madagascar is somewhat of a general term."

"I heard a very nice thing about the people of Madagascar. They used to bury dolphins who washed up on beaches in their own graveyards."

"Really!" Carter said, charmed.

"But they don't do it anymore."

Carter sucked on a Tic Tac.

"Do you know that one Christmas season Pat Wilson corrected me as to who was Joseph in our crèche display?"

"I don't recall that." Carter did remember the crèche, though, very well. They'd bought it in Venice the winter before Annabel arrived, and again there was that phenomenon that always thrilled him: snow falling into water. The memory threw his thoughts into a cold twilight. He lay on the bed with a sense of restless paralysis.

"I've never forgiven her. She said that my Joseph figure, the figure I'd placed in the Joseph position, was clearly a shepherd and belonged back with the sheep. And she moved it!"

"Well, she's off to the Four Corners now," Carter said vaguely.

"Appointment with mousie," Ginger said.

After a few moments, Carter unobtrusively switched on the television. They were culling elephants somewhere in Africa. The terrified herd shrank back from two small men with machine guns. "Ginger!" he cried, "what have you done to the channel?" He groped for the changer but couldn't find it. On the screen, a wet human palm displayed a slippery elephant fetus; a finger jiggled the tiny trunk, arranged the tiny legs. Carter at last located the changer, and now black ghetto youths with remarkable hair were ambling around an open coffin, fluttering their hands above the corpse's placid face in some bizarre ritual of respect.

"See how nasty it all is," Ginger said. "Nasty, nasty. Come with me, Carter. Come to where I am." She raised her arms.

She meant the gesture to be inviting, he was certain. "But what about Annabel?" he said. "She's still just a child, and there's no one to take care of her."

"Annabel? She'll get along. Children stay children for far too long. Annabel will be fine. You're not raising her properly anyway, what with those soirees you're always hostessing. It's humiliating the way you're all a-bubble around those young men. And that *one* man . . ."

"Which one is that?"

Ginger made a ghastly face. "The hireling."

"The piano player?" Carter said. "He's a wonderful piano player."

"You don't understand, do you? Never have, never will. You can be so obtuse. But I used to love you so much! I loved you so much I even tried to walk around the house the way you did. It made me feel less lonely."

He should kiss her, he thought, but the distance between them was so great and he was so tired. Too, he'd be insane to kiss her.

13

A t school, a little more than a week after her parents' funeral, there was another call for Corvus.

"This is your neighbor, John," the voice said. "Your dog is barking."

"I'll be home by two," Corvus said.

"It's howling. I can hear it through my closed windows. What's going on?" He sounded reasonable.

"He's in the house," Corvus said. "He's not outside."

"I'm a mile away. It starts up the minute you leave in the morning."

"I'm sorry."

"What's it need, water or something? Food? What's its favorite food? Or maybe it needs its mouth wired shut."

"What?" she whispered.

"Anything I can do," neighbor John said.

"I'm at school now," Corvus said. "I'll be home by two. That's only an hour from now."

"What is it you're saying, babe?"

"The dog, Tommy, he misses my mother." She was shocked she'd said this. She was ashamed. The words were hopeless, nobody wanted them.

"Then somebody should tell your mother to get her goddamn ass back home and do whatever she does to keep that dog from howling." He hung up.

Corvus turned to the secretary seated behind her office desk. The woman's child was standing in a playpen regarding Corvus with disfavor. She was too old for a playpen, but it had been arranged that the secretary could bring her in once a week.

"Your mommy and daddy are dead," the child said. "I don't like you, you smell funny."

"Melissa!" the secretary said. "Now, what did I tell you! That is very, very naughty, Melissa. Corvus, dear, is everything all right?"

"I have to go home." She hurried outside. The windows in the truck were down, and though she'd wedged a cardboard liner behind the windshield, the temperature inside was still over a hundred degrees. The steering wheel and seats were scalding.

"Death is normal, Melissa," the secretary was saying back in her office. "Death happens sometimes."

"I don't know what it *is*." The child stamped her feet.

It took twenty minutes. It always took twenty minutes. She drove through the outskirts of the city and into the bladed desert and beyond, through empty ranchland. Hawks lay in sandy furrows, their beaks open, in the shadeless noon. She passed John Crimmins's. Her own house was at a distance it might take four minutes to run to. She bounced over the cattle guard Tommy was afraid of and up to the house. Above two metal chairs on the porch, a wind chime tinkled from a beam.

Tommy was standing just inside the door. He wagged his tail once and peered past her, then turned and went to a coat lying in the corner. He curled up on it, his chin resting on the worn corduroy collar of her mother's coat.

"Tommy," Corvus said. He wagged his tail once more but didn't look at her. The house was cool and quiet, the curtains were drawn. She took some ice cubes from the freezer and, holding one in each hand, ran them across her face and through her hair. Ants crawled through Tommy's dishes on the kitchen floor. She threw his food out and scrubbed the bowls clean. She would get padlocks for all the doors. She would get Tommy a comrade dog. She would get a third dog, a fierce one, to protect them both.

She drank a glass of water and put fresh food in his bowl, but he could not be coaxed to eat it. After a while he got up and walked through all the rooms quietly, without making a sound: a ghost dog. Corvus hadn't heard him howl since the night of the funeral, the night Alice had been here. He lay down again on the coat, his expectancy dimmed. Just before dark she took her father's binoculars out to the porch and looked through them at John Crimmins's. Two lights were on, soft as the lantern lights her mother liked to use at suppertime. She put Tommy in the truck and drove to a grocery store, where she bought fried chicken. Then she drove to the Hohokam Drive-In, pulling in next to a woman whose large horned lizard sprawled next to her on the crown of the seat. Corvus smiled, but the woman just stared at her. What was the connection, after all, between taking a dog to the movies and taking a horned lizard? There wasn't any.

She fed Tommy little pieces of greasy chicken until only bones were left in the bag. It was going to be all right. On the screen, love was having its difficulties, its reversals, but it persevered or at least metamorphosed. Tommy sat in the front seat, looking through the windshield at the big screen. Everything was going to be all right. Corvus gave him a big smacking kiss on his muzzle the way her mother used to. She tried to imagine that she was her mother and that she was Tommy, too. Though the moment was willed and racking, it came close to comfort. Then it drew back.

That night, Tommy made no sound. He slept on her mother's coat in the hallway. In the morning she went to school, but before her first class had ended she was summoned to the office by a phone call.

"It seems to be that importunate man again," the secretary said. The playpen had been removed. She had at her side, instead, a steaming cup of coffee and a round, glistening pastry.

"Hello!" John Crimmins said. "This is your neighbor, John. I want you to hear this. It's what I'm being forced to hear."

Corvus heard Tommy's mournful howling, which sounded as though he were there with John Crimmins, right beside him.

"Where is he?" Corvus said.

"He's not with *me*, kid. What would I want with him? I choose my friends carefully. I taped this earlier from my doorway and I'm still tap- ing it. It's pathetic, isn't it?"

Tommy's song rose and fell, ran, twisted, then rose again. She would put him in the Airstream, hitch it to the truck, and drive farther into the desert. Or she could go the other way, deeper into town, for as the town sprawled outward, it abandoned its old developments. She could pull into the parking lots of the Tortoise, the Desert Aire, the La Siesta, resorts where the rooms had been razed and all that was left were the signs, awaiting the right collector, and empty pools the size of railway cars. She could camp on the pavement of any number of defunct shopping malls. She could live anywhere.

The connection was severed.

"Isn't there always a third time?" the secretary said. "But next time I'll tell him I'm calling the police. At first I thought it was an emergency, of course, but what kind of emergency could it be now?" She became flustered. "I won't allow that person to reach you again, dear," she said more diplomatically. After Corvus left, she frowned at the baked good from which she'd taken a nibble, baffled as to why she had once again fallen for the one with the undesirable cheese.

For the first time Corvus wondered what she would do with all the days ahead. It was as though she'd been unconscious and had just now awakened to terrific pain and uncertainty. Once more she sped homeward, but when she reached John Crimmins's she stopped and cut the engine. She could hear Tommy's voice faintly in the air, but it seemed contained, as though in some heart's chamber. She sat in the truck for a long time, looking at the house, and then got out. She rapped on the door, but there was no answer. She waited on the porch listening to Tommy's thin wail, a reminder of the emptiness at the heart of everything. She waited through what would have been the Anzai Culture, through Shakespeare and lunch and philosophy. Waiting, she felt John Crimmins on the other side of the door, waiting, too. In front of the house was a water spigot on a pipe. A drop of water would slowly form and drop into a ragged, shallow, cement depression on the bony earth. Sometimes she raised her eyes and traveled the distance between the two houses. She pretended that her mother was home. Her father was away—he would be back, his absence wasn't unusual, he was expected soon—but her mother was there, reading the book she'd begun, absorbed, a little mystified. Corvus rested the back of her head on John Crimmins's door and forgot why she was waiting. A car raced by, and an arm flung a bottle from the window. It shattered and lay sparkling. Good as buried, she thought. Good as buried.

She got into the truck and drove home.

Again he was just inside, the sound of the truck coming over the cattle guard having stilled him with its possibility. He peered past her as before, then gazed at her sympathetically, for she was not who she should be. She put Tommy in the truck and drove to the Airstream, backing in close to the blocks on which the tongue lay propped. They'd had the trailer for years, but Corvus hadn't been in it for a while. When she was little, she had pretended it was a space station where she could communicate in elaborate, time-consuming ways with aliens. Saintly, they did no evil things, were about a yard tall, and looked like owls. Corvus could not move the tongue of the trailer alone, not one inch. Alice was strong, she could help her tomorrow.

In the morning she decided to take Tommy with her to school. She would tie him to an olive tree next to the truck. She would take some of her mother's sweaters for him to lie on. He watched as she made herself ready. He lay on the coat, gnawing at one paw, which was raw from his gnawing and licking. Corvus drank a little coffee from her mother's favorite cup—a white teacup with lilacs painted within—then rinsed it and placed it carefully on the drainboard.

"C'mon, Tommy." He stood and walked stiffly toward her. "C'mon, you're coming along today." She heard the growl on her skin, as if it hadn't even come from him. He stood heavily in front of her, all obdurate weight, looking at her steadily and brightly. He didn't growl again; that part was over. He returned wearily to the coat. Corvus took a blouse from her mother's closet and crumpled it up by his head like a fresh dressing for a wound. He smelled hot and sour, there was a moist crust beneath one eye. She rubbed it off, then took a dog brush and ran it across his coat. She shut the windows and turned on the swamp cooler and the radio. "Liberation can come," a voice ranted, "only through the destruction of the world of phenomena. . . ." She turned the dial forward and back, tears in her eyes. The devil had been spotted at the casino on the Yaqui reservation. He was good-looking, and each slot machine disgorged hundreds of coins when he passed by. She settled on a band of static and left.

In school she learned that the American Indian had discovered the zero prior to its discovery in India. She learned about the significance of

landscape in medieval art. Flat country meant the most; it denoted apoc-
alyptic end. School was unreal to her, the books, the papers she wrote
crowded with slanting script, her hand upon the papers, writing. She
envied Tommy his utter animal sadness. He was complete in it, he could
not be made separate from it. The air felt electric though there were no
clouds, no sign of freshening change. Still she felt the snap in what was
like a current trembling thickly through everything that was that day. But
it was all so distant from her, the moment and her presence in it. She felt
it would be this way from now on.

Tommy had always been afraid of the cattle guard, of the meaty empty
smell of the pipes. The truck, once more, lurched and rattled over it,
toward home. The long home, Corvus thought. The door was open, a
window broken. Tommy was on the porch. He was so long that his tail
almost reached the floor. She could still see the brush marks on his fur.

The rope was white and new, and it was knotted tightly around the
beam with the other end tied around the porch railing. Her mother's
coat had been dragged partway across the floor. It had been a comfortable house, plates and chairs, a deep sofa, lamps and books, the pretty
things of home. She went to the kitchen and pulled open the drawer that
held the knives. There were a number of them. She had thought she
could use everything up. She would empty everything familiar to her of
its purpose. She would keep the house and finish school, and slowly her
life would be used up. Through diligence, she would come to the end of
the past. That had been her plan, but now there was nothing. She was
seeing nothing, looking at the drawer of knives.

From a distance there was the sound of coyotes calling. Her father
had always quoted Huxley—"A Trio for Ghoul and Two Damned
Souls"—when the coyotes called. They stopped.

She went to the stove and blew out the pilot lights. As a child she had
always been fascinated with those beguiling darting lights of dancing
blue. She opened the oven door and, sliding out the broiler plate, blew
out that small light as well. She smelled the threads of gas. She could die,
too. The obviousness of the choice gave her a peculiar swift delight. It

was correct. It was enchanting, really. But she did not want to die so enchantingly, so obviously correctly. She wanted, instead, to die slowly, day by meaningless day, unenchanted, bitterly meaninglessly aware.

There was a gallon of kerosene that her parents had used for the outside lamps. She laid it down in ribbony whorls throughout the house, then went out to the truck. A jerry can of gas was strapped down in the bed because the fuel gauge was broken. The speedometer cable was broken as well. You never knew how fast you were going or how far you could go. She circled the house spilling the gas, then backed the truck across the cattle guard to the road. She had to go back into the house for the matches. She brought the bowl outside and went through seven worn books, a match per book, before one of them lit. "Reasonably Priced Banquets," it said just above the striking zone.

At first nothing burned. The flame flared and smoldered with a certain knotted energy. Then it gathered, as though with an intake of breath, and it began, the flames lapping out and licking the jellylike pads of the cactus, the marigolds, the steps, the fur of the hanging dog. The wren's nest in the eaves popped softly. Then the heat found the grassy core and with a boom and another three more, like the sounds of shotguns striking down owls at dusk, it was all burning, the pictures and tables and clocks, the Indian blanket with its canny exit for the mind, all of it, her mother's things, her father's.

Corvus saw owls falling. This was how she felt it. Her own soul witnessed it in this way, their great soft falling, the *imago ignota* of their alien faces.

Book
Two

G OOD MORNING MR./MS.
You have been deemed a candidate by Physician/Family/Staff
for the Terminally Ill Program, and therefore the following
comforts and electives will be denied to you beginning at 3 a.m.
this day and extending into any remaining future. Television,
oxygen, antibiotics, cookies, batteries, cooling waters, green
pastures, and heretofore merciful acts of providence whether
deserved or undeserved. Any peaceful dark that comports itself
as den, lair, sanctuary, or refuge. Freedom from fear. Any acts
of grace except those that passeth understanding. Podiatric care.
Dental care. Donuts with jelly. Eyeglasses. Excursions. Any exercises to discourage muscle atrophy. That stupid little hard ball
that we encouraged and encouraged and encouraged you to
squeeze and you never would will be taken away. All wishing,
hoping, and desiring. Ice in a cup to crunch. Key chains. For
the ladies, hats. Remaining to you is any comfort available from
dreams. We do not suggest attempting to dream of starting
over. Do not dream of the first kiss or the one who will have been
the love of your life. Avoid specifics in terms of the beauty of lightning, meadows, eyes, the touch of certain hands. Avoid those old

constructions—the nesting box made of cedar, the bookcase mortised with pegs, the child's swing so easily made at the time. We suggest, rather, of dreaming of smaller balls within larger ones, of blue air liquid, of small shining clouds, of rhizomes. Dream of rhizomes if you can.

14

Alice wanted very much to harass, torture, and, with any luck at all, destroy John Crimmins, but she had to find him first for he had disappeared immediately after the fire. There were already new tenants in the house he'd rented, a blameless couple with a pet peahen named Attila. The blameless couple annoyed Alice, ignorant as they were of John Crimmins's whereabouts, unknowing of Tommy or his end, blithely incurious about the charred plot of land to the south. Should not sickening cruelty leave its impressions upon the surroundings? Should not a repulsive act taint the very air?

"I understand why you burned your house down," she said to Corvus. They were sitting in the Airstream, which they had towed into Alice's side yard. "It's like the Navajos used to burn their hogans down if someone died in it, isn't that so? Then the Anglos taught them to stop doing this, so if they had a sick baby, say, who just got sicker and sicker? They'd put it outside the house so they wouldn't have to burn it down when the baby died." The telling of this story had held more promise in its inception; it had been meant actually to comfort and confirm. But as with so many of Alice's utterances, it had veered from the confirm-and-comfort path.

"I think you did the right thing, Corvus, that's all I meant," Alice said. "I think you always do."

Corvus said nothing, and Alice began talking again about John Crimmins, how they would go about finding him. Alice knew there were methods by which an appealing, appropriate-looking person could get any information desired on anyone else, and she vowed to transform herself into such a person, if necessary, to see that John Crimmins met his punishment.

"I'd like to shake those people up," she said. "How can they not know anything?"

The place had been broom swept, the blameless couple said, which was all that real estate law required. They aspired to become real estate agents themselves someday. The place had actually been quite clean when they took occupancy.

"I want to find him and drive him crazy," Alice said.

"You're driving me crazy," Corvus said.

"Well, that would be . . . you'd be the wrong person." I will never let you be crazy, Alice thought. She felt the stronger of the two for an instant and was frightened. But the instant passed, both the feeling stronger and the fear of it.

Corvus could not assimilate his act into her life, so she placed him out-side the way she thought about her life. Doing this was going to make her sick, Alice believed, though the idea that things that happened to you weren't your life was sort of interesting. Corvus didn't believe John Crimmins's power was legitimate. She never talked about him, never accompanied Alice in her musings as to what he had done before and what he would do next.

"A person like him," Alice said, "just can't slip back into civilized society."

"Why not?" Corvus said.

"He'll feel remorse eventually and jump off a building," Alice said hopefully.

"No, he won't."

"Tommy'll come back to haunt him," Alice said, though she didn't really believe this. Tommy, hung, then burned to the bone, would, instead, be racing after Corvus's mother, never arriving at her side for-ever, released too late by the cruel facilitator, John Crimmins.

15

Ginger's manifestation startled Carter for it was in the sober hour, that practically canonical hour before the first cocktail of the evening.

"Darling!" he said. "Isn't there anything to do there?"

"No," she said, "nothing to do. Working, sexing, resting, thinking—you can't do any of it."

Sexing? Carter thought. That was so depressing.

"Go ahead," she said impatiently, "make your drink."

He took special care with this one.

"How does it taste?"

"It doesn't taste all that good, actually. Ginger, you're making me nervous."

"Do you remember how you ruined our honeymoon, Carter?"

Like pushing a rope, he thought. No, no, that had been later. "So," he said, "how are you?" He took another swallow.

"I feel as though I've taxied away from the gate but haven't taken off yet. There's this unconscionable delay."

"Oh my," Carter said. "We both know what that feels like. That flight to London—"

"I think it may be something you're doing."

"Me?" Carter said. "But I'm not doing anything out of the ordinary, darling. Everything is very everydayish here."

She rubbed her bare arms as though chilled. The gesture gave Carter goose bumps. "You believe I'm preventing you from, ah, 'taking off'?"

"You were always suppressing me, Carter, always holding me back."

"You have to stop thinking about me, Ginger. You have to take the next step." He looked at his ice cubes. There wasn't anything around them.

"Let's not argue again tonight, Carter," Ginger said. "Let's be friends. I'd like to give you something, a little gift."

This discomposed him utterly.

"It's not like that, Carter. Where would I get a gift? Use your head! It's advice, some advice. When we were together there was always this, this . . . haunting insufficiency."

"That's not advice, Ginger," he ventured to say.

"I'm not through!" she snarled. "*Won't* you let me finish a sentence!"

How had he summoned her here, how, how? She was right. He must be doing something. What innocent thought or haphazard reflection was bringing her back so vividly all the time? She was his personal maenad. Maybe he was listening to too much opera. A frenzied woman who coupled marriage with carnage in a twisted rite was practically a definition of opera. This was Ginger to a T.

"You can't make me suffer anymore, Ginger."

"Ha," she said.

At least they weren't trapped in a car together, hurtling down some highway. He gave the ice cubes some more whiskey.

"My advice is . . ." She paused. "Imagine renewing our vows, Carter, you and I. People do it all the time, all sorts of people. And what do they do before they renew their vows? They remember the happy times. The wonderful things. The bright, not the black. I am your wife and spiritual partner. I want you to come to the threshold again. Remember when we were on the threshold of marriage and all you knew was love and hope?"

He silently resisted this interpretation of his complex feelings at that time.

"I want you to see me in that light again," she said. "You're not seeing me in the right light. And that's why I'm unable to 'take off,' as you so crassly put it."

He protested this mutely.

"What's the matter with you?" she snapped. "You know, I almost went into intensive care that night. I debated whether to go into intensive care on the ride in the ambulance, and then I thought about all the unpleasantness that would entail and decided against it. I never thought you were going to carry on like this, Carter. I should've chosen intensive care. You would've had your hands full then, all right."

"You could decide?" Carter said. "It really was up to you?"

"You make me regret everything I do."

She was truly expert at this, Carter thought.

"That was a big choice I made, and now you're making me question it."

No, he couldn't possibly assure her that she had done the right thing. He was trapped. "I wish you'd give me the chance to miss you," he said tentatively. "I think you'd be pleased."

"How would you do that?" she demanded. "I'll tell you how. You'd remember happy times, or you'd anticipate happy times and wish I were there to share them with you. You're putting the cart before the horse. No, I think I'll keep coming back until this thing is resolved." She was scratching her neck in that nervous way she had. It really was the cocktail hour now, well into it. "Do you have any of those little snacks I like, those spicy snacks?"

He tried to behave as though he did but just couldn't lay his hands on them. They'd always given him heartburn, he hated them.

"Doesn't *Donald* like them?" she said venomously. "What's he doing tonight, out hand-pollinating something?"

The thought of Donald fluffed Carter up a bit. "Donald—" he began.

"Oh, I don't want to talk about him," Ginger said. "I want to talk about me, about us, Carter, about the potential we still have together."

"There's no need to be jealous of Donald, darling," Carter said. "He's a caring and serious boy, a student of Buddhism. I actually think he could help you, Ginger."

"Slow fat white dudes studying Buddhism make me sick."

"Donald isn't fat," Carter protested. Ginger had always been overly conscious of weight.

"I can just hear him. 'It's only death, Ginger. Everything is fine.' I wish people like that would shut up. Does he say, 'Thank you, Illusion,' every time he manages to overcome some piddling obstacle in his silly life? 'Thank you, Illusion, thank you . . .'" she minced.

Had she been eavesdropping on Donald? Or were Buddhists—WASP Buddhists, in any case—wandering around in the unthere there just as unfulfilled as Ginger?

"You've always hated women, Carter. You showed it in so many little ways. You never used the ellipsoidal or elliptical form in your work, not once. It was so obvious, the efforts you made not to employ the oval form. You don't even like horse racing. Most men, real men, like horse racing, but not you. The shape of the track was too feminine for you, too frightening."

"Wagering has never appealed to me, darling. I have never wagered. Gambling is a disease." Horse racing actually did repell him—those thousands of pounds of caroming flesh, bodies all treated with Lasix to keep the blood circulating inside where it belonged. Didn't want that blood flying around the track on its own.

"A disease! Like drinking, you mean? Like infertility? You're such a sap."

"Infertility?" Carter said. "I didn't know that was a disease."

"They're fighting to make infertility a disease so insurance companies will have to pick up the tab."

Pick up the tab? Ginger's language was beginning to fall off. Why was she keeping abreast of current trends, anyway? It didn't seem necessary.

"The things you people fight for," she sneered.

She was sounding more and more reactionary, Carter thought. Though one couldn't expect the dead to be big fans of progress. He wasn't fighting for anything, certainly not disease, if that's what she was accusing him of. If anything he was fighting to stay awake, even though he'd scarcely finished his second drink. Staying awake was Donald's most recent recommendation—arrived at, of course, by way of the Buddha. According to Donald, when some fellow inquired as to how in the dickens men were supposed to conduct themselves with women, the Buddha had first replied, "Don't see them." Fine, fine, in Carter's present predicament, that should've been more than sufficient; but then the fellow had persisted, good for him, and said, "But if we *do* see them, what are we to do?" and the Buddha had answered, "Stay awake."

Carter widened his eyes, and Ginger became, if anything, bigger.

"You should know something," she said. "Annabel is not your child. She's Charge Peabody's daughter."

"Oh stop it, Ginger." Charge Peabody was a stellar twit, a real tosspot. Ambassador to three countries. He'd drunk himself right into the grave.

"Have him exhumed. DNA testing will prove it."

"I'm not exhuming him, Ginger."

"Legally his child. She could make a little money off his estate. Dig him up! I should think you'd want to get this straightened out."

Carter darkened his drink. A nice brunette drink. She would never call it a night now, he knew. For her the night was just beginning. There was morning knowledge and evening knowledge—there always had been—and he was going to get an earful.

16

Alice roamed the mountain trails in the coolness of early morning. The wilderness was less than an hour's walk away, which wasn't right, of course, but that's the way the world was now, available. She trotted along the trails, her eyes picking up bones. Her eyes were good at bones: lizard jaw, webby coyote skull, the winged eye sockets of the jackrabbit, tiny mice feet encased in owl droppings. She never moved them from their resting spots, she never collected. There was a hummingbird impaled on a barrel cactus, flung there by a momentary wind, a dust devil. Above the pierced and iridescent body, a bright yellow flower bloomed. That's what Alice liked about the desert, its constant, relentless conflict with itself. The desert was unexpectedly beautiful and horrible at once. She wished she could interest Sherwin in it, but he professed a distaste for nature, however peculiar its forms. She was running this morning to burn off some energy, so that when she saw him in his own apartment—he had actually invited her there, he had actually said cumawn over if you wanna—she'd be a little worn out and not say immature things or much at all.

Alice heard a motorbike's whine and saw dust rising. Bikes were banned because they stressed the bighorns, though some people argued that there were no bighorns left. They had seen them once but not for a while. Alice had never seen one. The bike was tossing itself down the mountain in brief airborne flights. The bike was yellow and the biker wore black and they looked hinged together, the man and the machine. Waggling and snapping, the thing bore down. She stepped off the path into an outcropping of broken rock and picked up the first large stone she could hold in one hand, for she was not going to let him pass without protest.

Sherwin lived above a statuary shop. The neighborhood was a little odd; it looked as though it catered to particular whims, but it was quiet now and empty, all those whims apparently catching their breath.

"So here it is, now you see it," Sherwin said. "The room of monstrous legend. You want something to eat?"

"Where shall I sit?" Alice said. "Is it all right if I sit on the bed?"

"Sure," he said. "So how are you?"

"What are all those statues down there?" There was a dachshund one foot high and five feet long. Maybe her granny and poppa would like it. On the other hand, maybe they wouldn't. It might seem a bit cemeterian.

"Did you see Neit, the one with the veil? I like her. A friend of mine's got a deposit on her, though. Anything with a veil, he goes for."

"Neit?"

"Greatest of the Egyptian goddesses. She has written on her 'I am everything which has been, is, and will be and no mortal has yet lifted my veil.' Or words to that effect."

"I didn't see her," Alice admitted. She was embarrassed that she'd been drawn to such a carefree object as the dachshund.

"I gotta have something to eat," he said, and started frying bacon in a pan. The room soon filled with smoke and smell.

"That food had a face," Alice said.

He built two ghastly sandwiches and quickly ate them.

"My grandmother pours the grease in an empty coffee can," Alice said. "I don't think you're supposed to pour it down the sink."

"Yeah?" Sherwin said. "Would you like a piece of pie?"

"When you're here, are you always eating?" Alice asked. "I usually eat a lot too."

He put a white pie box beside her on the bed. The pie was half gone; it resembled lemon meringue. He sawed off a piece for himself with a spoon and ate it walking around.

"Nothing even working on a nostalgic plane out there," he said pointing out at the street. "If you look out a window and can't even grub a little nostalgia out of the busy view, you've hit bottom."

Alice looked at him happily.

"Your friend Corvus," he said, "I think I have her figured out. She's living in order to disappear. Nietzsche said that. Are you going to remember that?"

"No." Alice didn't want to think about Corvus now.

He laughed. "I think your friend is capable of something drastic."

"I'm capable of something drastic too."

"You want to do something, all right. You want to be a seminal figure. But what do you want to do right now? You wanna go out and get something to eat?"

"Can't we just stay here?"

"You want a glass of water or something?"

"Would it be a perfect glass of water?" Alice asked slyly.

"Water is so mysterious, I love it. It can't get wet. It's exempt because that's what it *is*. I just love that about water. You can't think like that for too long, though; it's like one of those alive thoughts. You think, Agghhh, it's *alive*."

Alice imagined being by herself and then a man who looked like him arriving. They would lick each other's hands, they would bury their faces in each other's hair.

"If I was a gay boy your age, same eyes, same mouth, same old raunch, you wouldn't be interested," he said. "When I was sixteen, I wanted to be known for the lowness of my morals and the highness of my mind. I've been meaning to ask, do you have the same dreams as your mother?"

"No!"

"I've heard that happens. Girls and their mothers."

Alice's mouth began to hurt again, taking her out of his room and her happiness. She ran her tongue over the loose tooth. It seemed very loose. Throwing a rock at the man on the motorbike had not been a gesture without consequences. He had skidded around and back toward her, taken his helmet off so she could get a good look at his stupid face, and walloped her with it. She had moved back so it hadn't connected the way he intended, but the visor had still clipped her. Sherwin probably thought she'd bruised her mouth herself, for a more interesting look. That's what she would've thought. She used to do that when she was younger. Take a piece of skin beneath her eyes, say, and give it a good twist so she'd look intriguing. But she hadn't done that for years.

He sat down beside her on the bed. She was wearing jeans and a baby blue T-shirt that said "Thank you for not breeding." She stopped tonguing her tooth.

"I love you," she said cautiously.

"I love you too."

This disappointed her.

"Words are just noise, Alice," he assured her. "Language is just making noise." He nibbled at the side of her face, making tiny grunts of pleasure.

The tooth had freed itself. She held her hand to her mouth as discreetly as possible and maneuvered the tooth into it. She swallowed blood, murmuring. He drew back and saw specks of frothy blood on her T-shirt.

"I lost my tooth." She opened her hand. The large, white tooth seemed almost voodooesque. She didn't like looking at it and wondered how dentists made it through the day.

"You're still losing your teeth?" Sherwin asked. "You're younger than I thought." He was, however, nonplussed. He had a greedy body and a wayward mind, but this was slightly more than he could handle this afternoon. He watched her go into his bathroom, cupping the tooth in her hand, her jeans loose over her flat little ass. He heard water running into the sink, then it stopped and he heard her taking an admirable piss.

When she came out, he said, "You piss like a horse, Alice. It sounds great."

"Oh, thanks," Alice said distractedly. She had wrapped the tooth in a piece of toilet paper and put it in her pocket. She had folded another piece of paper into the oozing socket. She supposed she should go home. Maybe when she had some money she'd get a gold replacement with an emblem on it, maybe a scorpion, but that's what nose rings did, she didn't want to be considered a nose ring. Every time she thought of something, it seemed it had already been a trend for hundreds if not thousands of people for some time. What if there weren't any new thoughts? You drifted around until you bumped into something that had been there all the while, then you attached yourself to it because you had to attach yourself to something. A stupid tooth had fallen out and she felt outworn, undone, but maybe that's how a tooth falling out was supposed to make you feel, maybe that's just the way a tooth falling out operated.

"You've got an awful lot of prescription drugs in there from veterinarians," she noted.

"I'm a werewolf," Sherwin said. "Which explains the tuxedos. But mostly it's that I don't know any writing doctors. I don't mean to appear curious, Alice, I don't want you to think the less of me, but why are your teeth falling out?"

She considered her strategy. She wouldn't tell him. She would be mysterious, alluring. "I don't know," she said.

"Were you in an accident?"

Her actions would be ravishing and unfathomable.

"Did someone hit you?"

She told him everything. It no longer seemed like an experience she'd had.

"Don't pick a cause, Alice, they're all so inconvenient. Differences of opinion have been known to occur."

"The mountain is off-limits to motorized vehicles. It's a rule."

"He could've had a gun."

"Oh, he did. He waved it around." He'd told her that he could rape her as well but he wouldn't, she was too ugly. "You're not too ugly!" Annabel would protest when told and then appear perplexed.

"Don't engage yourself," Sherwin said. "That's the key to everything. Don't traffic in social responsibility."

"I don't want to be socially responsible at all," Alice said. She wanted him to be dark, the things he said to be dark. She didn't want advice or for him ever to be helpful.

"Look, honey, if you believe in the utter value of the individual, you've got to devalue the rest of the world."

"No, you don't."

"Yes, it's necessary. It just follows."

"It hurts to talk," Alice said.

He crushed some ice and wrapped it in a rag. "That underwear is perfectly clean, I assure you," he said.

"How do I look?" Alice asked. "Do I look okay?"

"One seeks in vain among debased superlatives." He pressed the ice against her jaw, then shrugged. "It's too late for this. Do you feel nostalgic yet?"

Through the cold she could smell nicotine on his stained fingertips.

"That guy had a job before you environmentalists took it away. Now he has nothing to do but ride his bike, his only treasure, then go home at night to terrorize his children and beat his wife. Spousal abuse is directly linked to environmental regulation. It can be stamped out only by stamping out nature—not human nature, the other one. That alone will provide jobs and stop the breakdown of the American family."

Alice reluctantly dragged her tongue from the tantalizing vacancy. "Can you see it when I smile?"

"You should forgive him, for starters. Forgiveness is cool."

"Forgiveness is optional," Alice said. "Sometimes it's not appropriate at all."

"Forgiveness is complicated, you'd like it."

"I'm not a complicated person." It was as though he were talking about Corvus again.

"You ever watch that television show, *Ricky and Romulus*? Every Tuesday five to five-thirty? One's a paraplegic black guy, and the other's the white guy who crippled him in a robbery. Black guy says, 'I have forgiven you, I am in the living process of forgiving you, I want to help you get employment, an apartment, a high school diploma, I want to help you get clean, I want to pay off your credit card debts.' Romulus is a good guy. Can only move his lips and eyebrows. Looks like a big gray melon sitting in a chair. Ricky, on the other hand, is a skinny, jittery, hyped-up, drug-addled flamboyance cursing and bawling 'Lemme alone, I've served my time, I've paid my debt to society, I don't want your skanky forgiveness, get off my ass, I wish you were dead, man.' They go at each other for fifteen minutes and then viewers call in with supporting arguments. It's a remarkable program."

"How can it be on every Tuesday?"

"They've been on for over a year now. The quality of mercy is an inexhaustible subject."

Alice thought that their first time alone together had gone well. Well, fairly well. When she got back home she asked her granny and poppa about *Ricky and Romulus*. Did it exist? She stood in darkness just around the corner from them, worrying about the havoc her tooth would wreak on their small savings.

"I don't watch that," her granny said. "It's like those wrestling programs. There's something insincere about it. If we're free Tuesday five to five-thirty," her granny said, "we're usually tuned into *Women Betrayed by Companion Animals*. Some of those stories can make your hair stand on end."

No lights were shining in the Airstream. Alice slipped into her room, which she thought of as the kind of room where somebody who someday would do something cataclysmic would spend her formative years. The only decoration was the picture of the woman and the octopus. Alice loved this picture and had studied its every nuance. She undressed, and as she was pulling her T-shirt over her head, the tooth fell to the floor. She picked it up and almost put it beneath her pillow. When she had been a little kid, of course, teeth had dutifully turned into cold hard cash, in one of the perverse and jolly customs perpetrated on little kids. A classic capitalistic consumer ploy, designed to wean you away at an early age from healthy horror and sensible dismay to greedy, deluded, sunny expectancy. The idea that there was some spirit out there who paid for teeth—what was it constructing anyway? What was its problem?

She got into bed and waited for sleep. She liked waiting for sleep. It wasn't like waiting at all.

She reflected on the octopus, as she did most nights, so intelligent and shy but extending itself, as it were, moving out of its solitary nature, unoctopuslike, impossibly in love. She had always related more to the octopus than the woman, although the woman had to be fairly interesting to find herself in this situation. An octopus could brood and plan for

the future, that was known, everybody knew that, and it was undoubtedly brooding and planning at the very moment depicted, while the
woman looked as though she had given up. The octopus, so bright and
solitary and weird, was giving the situation its full attention, whereas the
woman knew that it was suffocating and being poisoned by its blood-
stream just by being in the room with her, and that brooding and planning wouldn't help at all. The difference in attitude was what made the
situation tragic.

17

C orvus chose to volunteer once a week at the nursing home, Green Palms, and the first Thursday Alice and Annabel went too. They were accepted and acknowledged much like the dogs, Tiffany and Helen, who made their rounds on Fridays.

A green van transporting a few gloomy cleaning ladies and a manic, moonfaced physical therapist picked them up and took them out into the foothills, where Green Palms was concealed in a magnificent riparian area. Nothing was supposed to be built here, but the developers had won approval by making the nursing home the cornerstone of their resort package. Green Palms was state-of-the-art End of the Trail. In an act of conceptual brilliance, it was tastefully concealed from the resort's supper clubs, ballrooms, pools, gymnasiums, and stables; a glimpse of it could be afforded from the golf course, but from the more expensive suites it was invisible, and from a distance it could not be seen at all. The van wound its way slowly up narrow roads and through a number of guard-house gates, which opened in recognition of a decal on the windshield.

"I wish we lived in a gated community," Annabel said. "I mean, the strangest people come up sometimes and say they're lost, and Daddy believes them."

"Gated communities should be unconstitutional," Alice said.

Then they were there. *The palm at the end of the mind,* Alice thought when they arrived, a line from a poem she'd read at school. The teacher had spoiled it for her somewhat by saying that the poet, according to his notebooks, had considered another line for that slot. *The alp at the end of the street.* She could hardly imagine anyone getting to the palm at the end of the mind via the alp at the end of the street, but the ability to do so, she thought, was what this place was all about. They were all solipsists in Green Palms, all heroes and heroines of their own vanishing consciousness.

Corvus suggested that Alice and Annabel think of the people here as already being dead, which meant that visiting with them and doing little things like rubbing cream into their hands or spraying a pleasant scent on their pillows was something very special.

Annabel protested this.

"That seems awfully extreme," Alice admitted.

"When you're with them, have a picture in your mind of yourself drinking from a glass," Corvus said. "And picture the glass as already being broken, shattered."

Annabel had never seen Corvus so . . . animated, if you could call it that.

Inside, Alice was given a Mr. Barlow and a Very Brucie and an Ottolie. Annabel was assigned to a Mrs. Fresnet. "Oh, that's that inexpensive champagne," she said. "Is she part of that champagne empire?"

"Do Mrs. Fresnet, and then we'll see about you," a nurse's aide said.

Corvus was directed to a waiting room where a number of residents were waiting for a marimba player who'd failed to show up. It had been an hour now. "You're going to be a terrific disappointment to them," the aide said, "but you'd be doing staff a big favor."

Annabel was looking at something crumpled standing in the hallway, saying "A nice soft peach" over and over. People hobbled and eddied around her. It was a little crumpled man, and he had been saying "A nice soft peach" for about ten minutes now. She approached Mrs. Fresnet's room with dread.

Alice went to Mr. Barlow's room first. Mr. Barlow had been a professional gardener—the master gardener, actually, in Washington's Floral Library—who couldn't care less now about his tulips, or any tulips: the Mary Poppins, the Dreaming Maid, the White Triumphator, the Queen of Night. Alice couldn't get much out of Mr. Barlow, who just stared at her with glittering eyes. Very Brucie was better. He still had some odds and ends to relate. In his youth, he said, he had been handsome and reckless, and the wild things he had done had been referred to as "very Brucie." He had a barely viable roommate whose presence didn't bother him at all. The only difficulty was when the man's son visited, which put a strain on everyone. The son, a bald, florid man in a tight gray suit, had visited intensively in recent weeks, playing the "Rosa Mystica" at his father's bedside on a small tape recorder. The "Rosa Mystica" was supposed to be unbind-and-assist music, but the father didn't die and the son stopped coming. Alice wondered if the tape she'd seen in the parking lot that very morning—broken and unraveled, smashed, really, it appeared to have been run over or stomped on—was the same. No way to know for a certainty.

The air in Green Palms felt restrained. There was a sense that salvation was being deliberately, cruelly withheld. And there was a speechless concurrence that it was hardly significant that in their lives the birthday presents had been purchased, the weeding done, the letter written, the windows washed, or the preburial contract sensibly arranged. And if, with some effort, they could recall the affairs that had been consummated, the roads taken, the languages mastered, the queer meals eaten in foreign lands, of what lasting consequence was that? This had been the destination all the while. Having been a good householder, having run a tight ship, having fought the good fight, whatever, it mattered not at all. Alice pushed Very Brucie in his silent shiny chair around the hallways, her hands trembling a little. She was here because of Corvus.

Mrs. Fresnet, who, as far as Annabel could ascertain, was *not* of the Fresnet empire, was worrying that her "Do not revive" form was not on file. Annabel went to the office to inquire and came back with a copy of it. Mrs. Fresnet took the form and studied it, then smiled at Annabel. "What am I supposed to do with this?"

"Isn't this what you wanted?" Annabel asked, smiling back. "For your peace of mind?"

"But this is a copy," Mrs. Fresnet said, "not the real thing. The only real thing they give you in here is custard." She opened her mouth wide, and Annabel was afraid she was going to let out a corker of a scream, but Mrs. Fresnet slowly closed her mouth again. "I have fifteen dollars in my account that can be withdrawn weekly for personal hygiene, and I want you to withdraw that fifteen dollars and keep it. It's yours. Then I want you to get me out of here and drive me away, out in the desert into the sun-steeped scene of a bigger, darker world."

It couldn't be sun-steeped and dark at the same time, Annabel thought, but you had to give these people some latitude. "I can't," she said. "I don't have a license to drive. I don't have a car."

"When I was your age, I was more resourceful," Mrs. Fresnet said. Then she opened her mouth again and gave an ear-splitting, sustained scream. Annabel ran out of the room to the nurse's station, where the same glum aide was presiding.

"She feels better after she does that," the aide said. "Then she asks for some cup custard, and you're supposed to get the cup custard and sit there while she eats it, which will take, in your perception, forever."

"Please tell my friends I'll be waiting for them in the van," Annabel said.

"The van's not out there now."

"I'll wait for them in the place the van's supposed to be when it's there," Annabel said. She was never coming inside this place again.

Alice had advanced to Ottolie, who resembled an iguana. She sat in her chair, wrapped in an iguana-colored shawl, and didn't acknowledge Alice for some time.

"I never sleep, you know," Ottolie finally said. "Never. Someone sleeps for me. She lives in Nebraska."

"That's great!" Alice said.

"Aksarben. That's where I get a lot of my people. You have to learn how to delegate tasks."

"I love your name," Alice said. "It's such a pretty name. Could you spell it for me?" Alice had picked up a brochure at the desk that said visitors should engage the residents in simple recall.

"I've changed my name." Ottolie slowly blinked her eyes. "When I was a little girl traveling with my parents, their name was Wright. Mr. and Mrs. Wright. We all had a horse named Tony. Tony the horse. Have you ever had to bury a horse? It's a heck of a dilemma. You need your father to do it. They're the ones who do it best. Mothers are no good for that situation. Do you know what might happen to you tomorrow? You could fall or be pushed. You could be the result of a random bullet." She leaned toward Alice with the details. "Somebody celebrating his baby daughter's birthday, firing a gun into the air. You happened to be in the vicinity. Wasn't intended for you, was meant to fall harmlessly to earth, but it ended up on your plate anyway. Or mercury could leak through your gloves. Say you were conducting an experiment with a type of mercury that had no known relevance to anything and it splashed on your skin and there you'd be, six months down the road, rotting from the inside out. You'd say to yourself, Why was I fooling around?"

A nurse walked by Ottolie's room and waved.

"Every person who dies in here," Ottolie confided, "is the victim of one of those bitches relieving their sexual tension. They strangle us, and it relieves their sexual tension. I'm sure you don't know anything about sexual tension—you're too skinny—but these nurses have it."

Another nurse passed by.

"That one's the worst," Ottolie said.

They both regarded the empty doorway and the wedge of waxed corridor beyond. Actually, Alice did have some suspicions about the nurses. In a book she'd been reading about nurses' experiences in Vietnam she had come across one nurse's account of goober contests. The nurse was working in a ward where no one ever got better, no one. They were all just boys in there, none of them much older than twenty, and they were all comatose and mostly limbless and the nurses would upon occasion, usually national holidays, place them in competition with one another. Bets were taken, money changed hands. The nurses would prop them all up in bed and arrange the beds in a row. Each nurse had a boy and each would clean out her boy's tracheotomy hole at the same moment and the boys would involuntarily shoot out these big balls of phlegm, sometimes a considerable distance. The nurse recounted that she had had a hard time adjusting when she returned home, which was of little surprise to Alice. The boys who had shot the goobers were long dead, and the girl nurses were old women now, recalling their youth.

Alice decided against sharing the nurse's tale with Ottolie, who was still formulating another tomorrow for Alice.

"You could be making a sandwich and accidentally set yourself on fire. Do you know how to make a sandwich? You have to preheat the oven to three hundred degrees."

Corvus appeared in the doorway. Ottolie smiled at her and said, "I think you're someone else."

"It's time for me to go, Ottolie," Alice said.

"You know when I knew I was a goner?" Ottolie said, "I was about to explain the mountains to a friend. I was about to say, 'There are the Mustang and the Whetstone Ranges, then, less sharply cut, are the Rincons and Tanque Verde, while soft in the distance loom the noble Santa Catalinas.' I was about to raise my arm and grandly indicate but I could not raise my arm. I'd forgotten how it was you caused your arm to be raised."

"I'm sorry, I have to go now," Alice said. "I'll see you next week."

"On the other side of the valley are the Mules, the Dragoons, the Winchesters, and the distant wild Galiuros." Ottolie pursed her lips. "The distant wild Galiuros," she called, as if to someone.

As Alice and Corvus were leaving, they passed a lady bent almost double creeping down the hallway, gripping her walker. She was making up her grocery list. "Flour, yeast, raisins," she said. "Tea, eggs, grits. A good broom. A *good* broom . . ."

18

C arter came into the living room and saw the three girls sitting on the sofa.

"So, what are you plotting today?" he said merrily. He felt exceptional after an uneasy week. Donald had encouraged him to go on a fast where he drank nothing but water and ate only a kind of clay, and he felt exhilarated if somewhat weak. The black scorpioid toxins that had appeared in the toilet bowl were—well he didn't want to dwell on them, but they were damn impressive. Appalling, of course, but now he could understand the quiet pride people could take in the purification of their intestinal tract. He felt wonderful and was quite unaware that he looked haggard and unwell.

Alice looked up at him, startled. Her face was mobile and expressive, and what he saw on it now was dismay and random guilt. She would not do well in a police lineup.

"Mr. Vineyard," she said.

"Hi," Carter said, thinking he should start over. They all were looking at him in astonishment. Madness is flight, he always thought when he saw Corvus, such a curious name, though lovely. He'd never understood why Ginger had insisted on the awkward name, Annabel, for their bundle of issue. It brought to mind a dairy.

He looked at his dear Annabel. "Honey," he said, "I didn't mean to interrupt."

"Are you all right, Daddy?"

"I'm *fine*," Carter crowed. Thank God for Donald and his clay. And Ginger hadn't visited him for the last several nights. Maybe she was actually . . . gone. He was cautiously optimistic. The last time she'd shown up, she kept asking, "Do you think I have pretty eyes?" but he'd had the wit not to look at them, into them, whatever. Her eyes had never been particularly pretty, though he would've been out of his mind to have said so. They were normal eyes, he recalled, in no way transfixing.

"We were thinking of going on a camping trip," Annabel said, "and I was saying I could make a soufflé but—"

Carter frowned. "A soufflé?"

"—but Alice said just hard-boiled eggs."

"Isn't it too hot to go camping? Though I don't mean to block any tendency toward enthusiasm."

"It's more of a retreat," Alice said.

"You're awfully young for retreats," Carter said.

"Daddy," Annabel said, "we are not children."

"I'd be afraid of the bears."

"Oh, Daddy."

"I would."

"Bears were extirpated from this area," Alice said, "more than fifty years ago."

"In my reading the other day, I came across this line by John Muir," Carter said. "'Bears are not companions of men but tenderly loved children of God.'" He directed this to Alice. He liked old Alice.

"What utter crap," Alice said.

"He was a fine man," Carter protested. "He began the American conservation movement."

"I hate people who talk like that," Alice said. "It mixes everything up."

"He wrote a very nice book about a dog," Carter persisted. "*Stickeen.*"

Alice was unimpressed. Corvus looked at him and smiled.

"Do you have a dog?" Carter asked.

"No," Corvus said. For an instant he gazed openly at her face, which didn't seem quite human to him. Or rather, it *was* human but one that most humans didn't happen to have. That was preposterous, of course. Suddenly he felt a bit wobbly. What he needed was a big milk shake.

"I should get you all library cards," he said, trying to shake off what seemed to him a curious numbness. "Wouldn't you all like your own library card? Many a summer hour was made delightful to me through books as a boy."

"That was then, Daddy," Annabel said.

"Well, yes," Carter said.

"This is now."

He was reluctant to admit it. He sat down opposite them but, eliciting looks of disappointment, bounded to his feet again. "I didn't mean to interrupt your deliberations."

"Here comes Donald," Annabel said. "He just drove up."

Donald! In his little lotus white car. Carter's heart soared. At the same time, he thought he glimpsed a vulture rising on voluptuary wings from the swimming pool, where it had been hunched, drinking. Remarkable, the things that came to drink. Sad, somehow. He excused himself and hurried out to greet Donald, to direct or be directed in their labors together.

"Is he still the gardener?" Alice asked.

"Of course he's still the gardener. What do you mean?" Annabel was looking at the hiking boots she'd just bought for this expedition. Never in her life had she encountered anything so totally without charm.

"Well, there doesn't seem much left to do around here. It all looks pretty nice."

"Some people get very involved in gardening, Alice. It can become a lifelong obsession. Sometimes they just move rocks around together. Donald is a big believer in fighting ass . . . acid—God, what is that word?"

"*Acedia*," Corvus said.

"That's right! You are so good, Corvus. You could go on *Jeopardy* or something. It means sloth, right?"

"It means more like experiencing the moment as an oppressive weight. It means listlessness of spirit." Corvus pushed a fallen wing of black hair behind her ear.

Annabel didn't know what else to do, so she smiled generously. "Well, he's got Daddy moving those rocks, all right."

Alice was inquiring as to what Carter's occupation actually was.

"He was trained to design things. Not office buildings or skyscrapers but other stuff. Not houses or furniture either, exactly. He was trained to make use of *space*, Alice. But he never did. I guess he and Mommy just wanted to relax. He was asked to design a zoo once. He had some wonderful ideas for it. It was in Newark and had a tropical rain forest wing. It had mold and microbes and everything. Plus one of those quetzal birds. I remember because I asked for one of its feathers after it died. But I never got one, or if I did I can't remember what happened to it. But it really was a good zoo. There was an elephant there who painted pictures with her trunk. Watercolors. You could buy them."

"They made an elephant paint watercolors?"

"She liked it, I think. But they weren't very good."

"This was your father's idea, to make an elephant paint watercolors?"

"Oh no, she'd always painted. She'd been at the old zoo for a long time and she'd been painting there too."

"Zoos are prisons, Annabel."

"But that's just the point. Daddy wanted to make it more pleasant. His idea was to build invisible walls or something so nothing would know it was in prison."

"'Invisible walls'? What do you think an invisible wall is?" Alice demanded.

"Alice, stop hounding me! She's hounding me again," she said to Corvus. She'd heard you could marginalize people by abstracting them in their presence, referring to them to another as though they weren't there. It was a social skill she wished she were better at. It didn't work at all with Alice.

"What did the quetzal do? Fly into the invisible wall? Was your father upset when it died? Did he feel he had blood on his hands?"

"Of course not. It could've died of old age as far as anyone knew. It just died. Really, you know what you inspire people to do, Alice? Lie. You inspire them to lie. You ask a question and then you get so annoyed when you hear the answer—"

"All answers are annoying," Alice said.

"My father never designed a zoo, all right? He never did!"

"Did he ever design one of those special rooms in airports where people are escorted to hear the news about plane crashes?"

Annabel looked at her.

"*Will anyone waiting for the arrival of Flight 501 please go immediately to the Privacy Lounge,*" Alice intoned. "I wonder what those rooms are like. Do they use them for anything else, or is it all set up for that one specific purpose?"

"You are so heartless," Annabel said.

"I bet you won't find any invisible walls in one of those places."

"If your granny and poppa went down in a place crash, you'd be upset."

"They haven't flown in years. It hurts their sinuses. I'd be upset," Alice said.

"And what about that stupid Sherwin? If flaming Sherwin went down in flames, you'd be upset."

"I don't know, actually," Alice said.

"He is so disturbing. I hate the way he looks at you, it's such a disturbing look."

"Yeah, well, I don't mind that so much."

"He looks at Corvus in a disturbing way too, I think."

"That's because Corvus is so cool," Alice said lightly.

Corvus shook her head and laughed.

"There's no way you could have a loving, fulfilling relationship with him," Annabel was saying. "Plus he's way old."

"He's twenty-six. That's not even ten years older."

"He is *lying*," Annabel yelped. "See, you just bring that out in people. You know what I think of when I see him looking at you? I think 'white slavery.' 'White slavery,'" she repeated a little uncertainly. "I think he'd use you to set up a situation for himself. You'd get men for him somehow. You'd be together, which would look weird of course, but that would intrigue certain men he wouldn't be able to get otherwise with those repugnant looks of his."

We could be two on a party, Sherwin had said to Alice, *you and me*.

"Those people are so jaded, you know, it's hard to know what they really think," Annabel continued. "Do you ever ask him what he feels? I bet he says, 'I don't feel anything.' I think he's shy and lonely and used to getting stuff even if it's not exactly what he wanted. It's not just the bad skin. One time I had a crush on a football player with bad skin. But he was a football player. And there was a boy who had a limp I liked. One leg was a little bit shorter than the other, but otherwise he was adorable and very, very popular. Sometimes being a little imperfect is interesting, only Sherwin isn't just imperfect, he's . . . they don't even like women. They think we're fish or something, they—"

"Fish?"

"Yes, they call us fish, Alice, they have no respect at all."

Two on a party, and when the party ends you'll still have a life ahead of you. There'd still be time for another life, he'd said.

"I wouldn't even consider friendship with him, if I were you."

"I don't," Alice said. She *had* lost the tiniest bit of interest in Sherwin in recent days, however reluctant she was to admit it. She'd discovered she wasn't interested in the human mystery. It was the nonhuman mystery that held, if not exactly promise, at least the clues, though they weren't exactly clues either, and Sherwin with his "You wanna be my girl pupil? You wanna be my Eustochium?" was getting on her nerves. Sherwin, she was beginning to realize, represented the human mystery in one of its most convoluted and self-conscious forms. He said when he left this place, he'd send for her, send her a ticket. *Would she join him there?*

"If you got a free ticket to somewhere, would you take it?" Alice asked.

"Oh, I would," Annabel said. "My God. Out of here? No question."

"I don't think I would," Corvus said.

Living in that Airstream had made her even odder, Annabel thought, but she wasn't surprised that Corvus wouldn't accept a free ticket. She'd insist on making her own ticket, out of flattened thorns or something. And it wouldn't even get her anywhere! Not really. Not to like Rome, say, or Paris.

"I know this is just an imaginary ticket," Annabel said, "just a 'what if,' but are you really going to stay around here forever, Corvus? Won't Social Services get on your case or something?"

Alice said, "Annabel—"

"Well, I'm just being sensible."

"Who wanted to make a soufflé on the camping trip?" Alice demanded.

"I mean, the first thing Daddy and I did when my mother died was, we just *fled*. All our stuff was shipped out afterwards, even Mommy's stuff, which dismayed Daddy, he thought he'd left very specific instructions. I was a little upset at first because we fled like *thieves*, practically, but now I realize a person can't just continue to adapt to certain sorrowful locales. If I had to keep driving past that restaurant on my way someplace, over and over that spot on the road, I—"

"Annabel," Alice said, "when we go on our retreat, we're not going to talk so much."

"Oh, it's fine when you're talking," Annabel said. "And why do you keep calling it a retreat? That sounds so moody. Why don't we just commune with nature? Isn't that what people are supposed to do when they go camping?"

"We'll put a mattress in the back of Corvus's truck and drive as far as we can on one of those fire trails. We'll spend the first night in the truck, then we'll hike all day and come back to the truck at night. We'll try to find that little waterfall." Like the bighorn, Alice had never seen the little waterfall, while others claimed they had.

"I'll bet there's trash around it," Annabel said. "Those things are just magnets for people's trash. But nature doesn't care. We'll be communing with uncaring nature." Oh, Alice sometimes made her feel so foul. "I hope we're not going tomorrow," she said crossly. "I have things to do tomorrow."

"Alice and I are at Green Palms tomorrow," Corvus said.

Annabel would never enter that place again. Her mother would say, "If I had to be buried like that, I'd rather not die." She said it after every funeral she and Carter went to. Her poor mother! She had loved getting dressed up and going to funerals and saying funny, awful things about everyone afterward.

She looked outside. Carter and Donald were in bathing trunks and lying side by side on bright blue pool mats. The two of them were not moving rocks at all.

19

Ray had considered carrying a fetish with him, but number one, he didn't believe in them—he'd seen the carvers bring them in by the gunnysack, like pecans—and number two, his little monkey was fetish enough for anybody. The little monkey had been quiet lately, maybe because it dug the flute music that was always playing in the store. Ray would be grateful, extremely grateful, if he didn't have to worry about it all the time. The monkey might finally be settling down, perhaps even realizing that it and Ray were one, that this had been the purpose of its sacrifice. Theirs was not a symbiotic relationship, though. The little monkey never had any opinions of its own; say Ray had a girl someday, he didn't think the little monkey would have an opinion about that. Ray could hardly say, "So what do you think?" He just wanted it not to be distraught. He wanted it to be conscious and not distraught, was that too much to ask? If it were unconscious, or rather if Ray became unconscious of it, matters would be worse. It's the stuff you're unaware of that kills you.

Regarding his camping gear, Ray had been canny. He'd ordered a tent, some fancy freeze-dried food, and binoculars from a catalog, received the delivery, and then denied he had, having signed for it in invisible ink. What stuff he'd learned in Cub Scouts! He might as well have gone to grifter school. He'd picked up a lot in those prestroke days. He wished there'd been more of them.

Besides scamming some of the larger items, he'd indulged himself by purchasing a few things as well, such as a knife and compass. He bought a walking stick with the knob carved into the shape of a grizzly's head (Grizz = hunter, nature's pharmacist) though he liked the brown bear's stick better (power, adaptability) because it followed more naturally the whorls and ways of the wood. But he ended up with the Grizz. Who knew the dynamic behind the purchasing impulse, anyway? If he knew that, he could be hired anywhere; he'd be paid for simply not talking to the competition. He bought a snakebite kit that looked a little Mickey Mouse to him (Mouse = servility, conformity), but at least it was a contingency that had been packaged. Seeing as how there wasn't an antidote to everything, it behooved you to grab whatever you could.

It was his first solo trek, though he truthfully couldn't consider it a trek: he would never be more than twenty miles from something, some ranch or working mine or trapline shack. He had maps. Still, if it wasn't a trek itself it might lead to one, and then another, and then the trek would become a true and endless one. There'd be secret knowledge. Fulfillment. He'd come back just to prepare to go out again to remote, empty, and beautiful places where self and sanity had no more meaning than the wind dropping at nightfall. He'd experience the no meaning and he'd feel entire, not all chopped up the way he felt now. The little monkey knew about these things, it knew about the validity of no meaning. Ray gave it credit for that, the little monkey had suffered, and it knew. It existed in no temporal future. The past, the light that shone externally upon it, even when the eyes of monitors and data crunchers had wearied of it, shone still.

Ray was at the ranger station the moment it opened, his stomach burning from too much coffee. The ranger was taking his time displaying a grouping of pop-up books to their best advantage. He pulled the tab on the elf owl lurching out of the saguaro. He pulled the tab on the jackrabbit hightailing it away from the hawk. He pulled the tab on the bobcat swiping at a butterfly.

"I could use a little help with this map here," Ray said. Rangers peddling merchandise—it wasn't right. It was supposed to be a dangerous occupation, and here he was fiddling around with kiddie books. The nameplate above his pocket read "Darling."

The ranger ambled over to where Ray stood. Ray spread out the map and told him his plans. The ranger blinked at him, seemingly unimpressed. "You in good health?"

"Hey," Ray said.

"My mother, when she had her stroke, her face pulled down just so." He tugged at his own lip.

"What the hey," Ray said.

The ranger shrugged. "Here's a pretty hike for the time you got. Two days in, a day there, two days out. You take the West Fork Trail four miles into Harold's Canyon, follow that until its junction with Scorpion Flat, take a right on Bitter Biscuit Trail about six miles until it tops out at Bless Your Heart Peak. If you come across the cairn with the red paint on it, you've gone too far, that's the conjunction of Pig Root and Bill Bustard Trail. . . . There's a birders' cabin there."

Ray snatched his map back. Man made him not want any instruction whatsoever. What kind of idleness was it, naming everything like that? He and Darling did not part on the friendliest of terms. Ray lunged up West Fork Trail at a trot and six hours later didn't know where he was. But that was fine with him. That was fine.

On the afternoon of his second day he came across the birders' cabin. He consulted his map. Maybe they'd moved it. The cabin was locked and the windows were shuttered. The lock was a long cylindrical one with letters instead of numbers on the falls. Ray spun "GONE BIRDING," and it sprang open. People were so transparent, he thought, so suspicious and simplistic and coy. He dropped his pack on the porch, then took off his hat and rubbed his sweaty hair vigorously with both hands. Inside the cabin was neat and had the civilizing touch of womankind, of avid, affluent, educated female birders. It must be nice to come up here, spot the rare birdies on their nests, listen to their songs. Ray knew nothing about birds. There was some dove that said *who cooks for you-all,* that was about all he knew. Of course the dove didn't really say that, he knew that too.

The large, open room was filled with bunks and tables, and along the back wall was a glass case filled with avian specimens. The method here was to collect the whole package: mom and dad, nest, eggs, nestlings in various stages of growth. Ray was head-to-head with some type of flycatcher here. Nest made of the midribs of mesquite leaves, quail feathers, and thatch, the tag read, and bound with insect threads. "A unique domed cradle of particular artistry." "That's true," Ray said aloud. The eggs were dappled, all lavender and red. "Clutch," Ray said. The word just came to him. There was a sudden sizzle in the back of his skull as though a seam were running down it. Of the smallest nestling, the tag's comment read, "This newly hatched youngster looks little different from the worm it was being fed." "Where would we be without that valuable insight?" Ray remarked loudly. He picked up one of the adult birds; it was dry and light as a piece of popcorn. This was a little weird, he thought, bordering on the indecent. How would the birders like to have their skulls made into bird feeders? Put it in their wills, show a real dedication to their lifelong hobby. Ray would suggest it to them. He found a pen in a drawer along with lined data sheets. "Fetched another set!" was scrawled on one. A sadistic activity, bird counting. Ray pressed the pen down, but his intention was dissolving like mist. He pressed harder, but the pen didn't move. Then it made a few quick, unsatisfactory marks. Ray looked up, chastised. There were dried flowers in a vase, a big framed photograph of laughing people in khaki and floppy hats. He had wished harm upon them, had contrived to insult them, his own kind. He had the sensation that the back of his head was splitting open, little fingers curling and pressing the folds of matter back. He looked at what he'd written. His handwriting . . . he should exercise more caution with it. Discouraging. He found his hat and pulled it carefully onto his head. The hat and the headache got along, he'd found.

He left the cabin without closing it up and gathered up his pack and stick. His fleeting equanimity toward the birders had vanished. He picked up the lock and threw it quite a distance. "Go birding in Hell!" he yelled. His own shout cheered him. He struck off toward the west, where already the crescent moon was visible, and made a careless camp just before dark. He ate two candy bars, then lay flat on a blanket and stared up at the wheeling heavens. They were really tearing around tonight. Birds meant . . . they *meant* freedom, that's what had gotten him so upset back there. But at the same time, birds were different from what they were supposed to mean. The wings of a bird were in fact its forelimbs. When you got on the road of thinking about anything for too long, you just had to turn back, had to turn back.

At dawn, Ray was up and hiking. By ten o'clock, he still hadn't come across anybody. What, did they name these stupid trails and then never set foot on them again? He was looking through his binoculars at an abandoned mine-shaft hole. There was the ore cart. He glassed the canyon wall, then idled down through the dense brush, clinging close to a winding dry wash. Among the tans and rounded greens he saw a pile of white, which he determined after a moment was a bighorn sheep. If it had been raised and released by Fish and Wildlife personnel, it had to be dumb as a post. Then he determined that it was too immobile even for the activity of dumb rumination, that it was, indeed, dead. He hastened toward it. It was a ram and only recently dead. As an animal, it had been compact and efficient and powerful, but it didn't have a clue what it was up to now. It was meat, nascent square cut, chops, riblets, and shank, right out of his mother's *The Joy of Cooking*. But of course people didn't eat these things, they resourced out the head and horns. Though the horns were small, a determined Zuni could still get scores of fetishes out of them.

The ram didn't look as if it had been shot, it had just damn died. In Ray's opinion, this was a transplant. Transplants were addled as a rule, they could never really shake the tranquilizers. The condors being made in California could drown in a puddle. Ray wanted the ram, wanted to report it to that dickhead, Darling. He took off his pack and managed to pick the animal up and heave it onto his shoulders. Clutching its legs, he staggered a few steps before he rolled it back onto the ground. Then he dug out the compass and map and absorbed himself in their arcane projections. He knew where he was. A direct route back would make his trek look like a scalene triangle. He couldn't make it to the ranger's station before dark, but he'd be there by the next morning. Ray rooted the nonessentials out of his pack—why the heck had he brought cologne?—and clipped a ditty bag to his belt. He glanced at the pricey gear he was leaving behind and saw it for what it was: pilferage, vain pilferage. The walking stick looked downright foppish. Ray felt he'd already gained some inner knowledge on this trip. What was important now was getting the ram out; it was giving a shape to his trek, just like the angle of return. Yeah, he'd be packing out a bighorn!

After a few hours, Ray was suspecting that the beauty of the scalene triangle was an illusion of exuberant misperception. Maybe the shortest distance between two points didn't exist in nature. He'd tied the ram to his back at one point to steady it, but when he slipped and fell he'd just about had his ear knocked off by a hoof. He looked with disfavor at the steep arroyo; like every damn one of them, it was just something to scrabble down, then scrabble up again. He was trying to drink less water when he rested, devoting himself to tweezering out cactus spines. Some larval life-form that had commenced work on the ram's belly had gotten under his shirt, or maybe that was his imagination. He felt as if he'd been transporting live coals. After tweezing out everything he could reach, he heaved the ram up onto his shoulders once again and it fell familiarly into place. Still, the weight immediately began to affect him. He should gut the thing out, but that would be a diminishment of his coming triumph. He took a few crablike steps over the shale, then skidded into a partial fall for twenty feet. The next time he fell twenty feet, he passed out and dreamed of lemonade, of the way they used to make it from ants back in his cubby days. He was popping big-headed ants into the water per instruction of the cub master, who was saying, "These are of the soldier caste, and their heads are huge and swollen so that they may more effectively block the nest entrance." . . . Explanations weren't what were essential now, though, Ray thought, it was the thirst that was important. He dreamed of thirst.

20

State investigators were prowling the halls of Green Palms trying to determine if the poor old souls were being served greyhound in their ground meat dishes. It had been discovered that the little kids at Jiminy Cricket Day Care had been eating greyhound tacos all that month and already were showing severe emotional and behavioral problems simply by being told about it, problems that were now expected to persist well into their teens and possibly beyond. But no proof was found that the old people had been gumming down racing dogs. The elderly inmates, their blood flow slowed to a trickle as it labored up to and around their brains, did not, in fact, give the possibility much credence.

"Doesn't taste much like greyhound to me," Elmer said. "It doesn't taste *fast*."

"For most inhabitants of modern industrialized nations," Alice said, "the principal contact with other species does take place at the dinner table."

"I won a hundred and fifty bucks once on a horse named Miss Whirl, which was the closest I've been to the animal kingdom," Elmer said. "Not to disagree with you, kid."

"This your granpa?" the investigator asked Alice.

"Sure he is," Elmer said.

"I'd shoot myself before I ended up in a place like this," the investigator confided. "My girlfriend's interning at Mercy, and you know what they call folks like this there—the ones always clogging up the ER? They call 'em crocks and fogies. They call 'em snags, rounders, shoppers, and crud."

Alice didn't much care for this investigator.

"Is this the closest we're going to get?" Elmer said. "This ground-up greyhound you have to take by spoon? For months I've been begging them for an injection. Smash the testicles of a young dog, I say, pass it through filter paper, inject via the leg, and *bingo*—the diminution of the function of one's sexual glands will be reversed! One will feel physically improved!"

She didn't like Elmer either.

The investigator gave a thick chortle, a sort of wet gurgle in which Alice detected the birth of his own cardiovascular problems and irreversible mental decline. She hoped.

She walked down the hall, peeking into the rooms. Sleeping, sleeping, sleeping. She paused at Annie's, for she was not sleeping but sitting upright in her chair, watching the six bird feeders—tray, oval, and tubular—that hung at her window and to which no birds came, principally because they hung within rather than without, Annie not trusting the space beyond, a patio occupied by an immense cooling and heating system that serviced the entire floor. Annie had been the subject of some discussion ever since her daughter had brought her husband's ashes over and placed them in the bottom of her bureau. Annie had not been told that her husband of fifty-seven years had died, since Green Palms frowned on such information being imparted. What was the point when grief was not germane, when it could not be comprehended or withstood? Here only the moment existed. Annie gave no sign that she inferred that her husband rested near her in the third drawer, the one she'd never used much, even when the handsome bureau had resided in the bedroom of the yellow farmhouse in the orange grove they had tended. Annie and her husband had known those trees, the peculiarities and pedigree of each, their yield, the ones the cardinals favored.

"Let them be together, they want to be together," the daughter had said, dropping off the ashes. She felt badly about allowing her father to starve himself to death in the sensible efficiency she'd found for him after selling the grove against his wishes.

His ashes were packed in a box made of orangewood. Everyone who passed Annie's room could smell the insistent fragrance. There had been a little shop on the highway side of the grove where Annie and her husband had sold bags of oranges and orange perfume and orange wine, orange blossom honey and boxes made of orangewood with a mirror inserted within the lid. This was one of those.

The staff was quietly observing Annie's reactions, but she hadn't had any. The orange was definitely making all the effort. Annie was one of the dear ones, the sweetie pies, still neat and continent and mild, but a wolf or a goose would have sensed and then grieved the loss of its mate more than Annie had, a limpet would've detected something missing. If specific compounds could create little dead islands in the brain, could annihilate the glowing shade-wracked jungle of caring and desire and delight and flatten it all to a sunbaked crust over which not even the most primitive thought crept or left a track, of what possible use was anything that happened to a person in this life? It made the staff wonder, even at $6.50 an hour. And although what they knew about neurofibrillary tangles and neuron-secreting chemicals could be fit onto the tip of a pencil, it made them pause as they prepared to go home with a rose and a piece of sheet cake, for visitors were forever bringing sheet cakes and roses to this place. But quickly there was no time for wondering, for the meal had to be made, the bills paid, the child's drawing appreciated, that crayoned drawing of the spiderweb that looked like the sun.

Alice lingered, chewing on her fingers, thinking about Tommy and all the stories she'd read about grieving creatures, the faithful hounds that wouldn't depart the hospital steps, the dock, the bar, the bier where the object of their ardor had last been seen. Animals were prescient, determined psychics, insistent in their speechless warnings, their final spectral farewells. Weren't they always showing up at their loved one's office in the next town scratching and whining, their silky coats mussed, their ghostly eyes beseeching, when in fact they lay in the street miles away, crushed by a speeding car? Weren't they always howling and carrying on at the very moment the daughter away at college was being introduced to the serial killer, when the son was skidding into the head-on crash, when the master was breathing his last in intensive care? Weren't they always wagging their tail in some dead beloved's garden at something that wasn't there? And here was Annie, who hadn't experienced the slightest discomfort when her husband died of starvation, the last thing to see his stomach a bit of oatmeal. They hadn't spent a night apart in fifty-seven years before she'd dropped that teacup, the lustrous leaves of the orange trees quaking above her, the dropping of a teacup the death visitant, the beginning of the end for many of the female inhabitants of Green Palms. Here now was Annie, blue eyes widely alert, alert to nothing, watching those empty feeding stations. The world was all a mare's nest to Annie. There was no sign, she gave no sign. There was not the thinnest spirit wire of connection in that room. There was nothing.

Orange labored in a void.

21

Carter appreciated the constellations. There was the summer Triangle high in the sky. There were the wings of Aquila and Cygnus. Just before midnight the ringing phone had awakened him, but he'd decided to let the machine get it. Let the machine get it, he thought. But then he had grown curious and loped into the other room and pushed the message button.

"Granpa's coming home from the nursing home tomorrow," a woman's flat voice said. "It's the business office's doing. They're turning him over to us, barks and whistles and all."

She seemed to be calling from a take-out restaurant. "Triple bacon and jalapeño number fourteen's getting cold here!" someone bawled.

"Any suggestions?" the voice paused.

"Twenty-one up, twenty-three—"

"I know you're there, you dirty bugger. You'd better pick up . . ."

Carter returned to the bedroom. His Hermès fox-and-hen tie lay on the floor. He was sure he'd put it away. Was Ginger showing up when he wasn't even in the room? Was she distracting him with wrong numbers, the voices of unfamiliars, so she could do something unpleasant? There were impossible phenomena like Ginger, and then there were even more impossible phenomena of a higher and more disturbing order than Ginger. He examined the tie, which appeared unharmed. He hung it carefully on a rack with its more somber companions.

He turned off the lights and resumed gazing at the stars through the enormous windows. It was really quite a nice house, Carter thought. The evening was quiet. Then there was the unmistakable sound of someone mangling his mailbox at the end of the driveway with a baseball bat.

Through the silken air he heard it clearly—a dozen lurid wallops followed by the screech of a car's tires. Then silence again.

"Daddy?" whispered Annabel at the door. "Daddy, can I come in?" He opened the door to the hall, but Annabel wasn't there.

"Honey?" he said.

She simply wasn't there. She was in her own neat and fragrant room sleeping, dreaming she was in a department store buying gloves, long, white, elbow-length gloves with three tiny pearl buttons at the wrist. Her mother was the salesperson and was performing in that capacity with aloof professionalism. Down aisles heaped with goods Annabel drifted— all head, as is the custom in dreams, more consciousness than head, really, with the sense she was *behind* her head, it being a mask of sorts that fit around her like airy rubber. Then it was no longer a store but a beach. She and her parents had prepared a picnic, and her mother was putting up the beach umbrella while her father was laying out the plaid blanket and mixing up the Dark and Stormys in the brightly colored aluminum cups. It was a lovely deserted white sand beach with soft grasses and less than the usual amount of garbage discarded from ships destined for distant, unexotic lands. Her father was proceeding efficiently, having already provided Annabel with her favorite cup filled with cranberry juice and well into sampling his own rum and ginger beer, but her mother seemed to be having some difficulty arranging herself. She kept jamming the umbrella pole into the sand, but the point would not set properly. The tip proved to be covered with shell and yolk, which at first glance didn't present itself as such but which, as her mother continued to stab and root about and raise and plunge the pole again and again, became more adamantly shell and yolk. Ginger had selected a sea turtle's nest for their umbrella site and had scrambled its leathery contents to a briny batter.

Annabel woke up, displeased.

What made the dream particularly unpleasant was that this picnic had indeed occurred, more or less, and unfortunately had degenerated in a similar manner. Annabel had never had a dream so redundant.

22

orvus, Corvus. They kept calling her name. He didn't know the names of the other two. One was very pretty, and the other one, who didn't even remember him, was just a madwoman. How could she totally not remember him? There was something not right about her.

"'Corvus,'" he said. "Doesn't that mean raven?"

He didn't think she was going to speak, but then she said, "It's a constellation too."

"Oh yeah, where is it?"

"It's by Virgo to the south."

Despite himself, he looked up into the heavens. It was still a clear day.

"You found me," he said modestly, "but why did you tie me up?"

The ram was arranged with its head on a boulder, facing Ray. The rest of it was covered with dirt and brush—or had he sawed off the head, as he'd dreamed of doing to quicken his passage? "Where's my hat?" He might as well have been addressing the ram for all the response he got.

"You know," he said, "night's going to happen, and we're going to be attacked by something attracted to that. We are."

"You killed the only thing around here, I think," Annabel said. "We haven't seen anything, not even one of those little things that look like chipmunks."

"You think I killed that? I did not kill that!" These antihunting, antilife freaks, you had to handle them with care. "I found it, I was trying to salvage it. I don't even have a gun, so how could I have killed it? And even if I had, I would've had a perfect right to. People do kill these things, you know, they've killed oodles of them."

"Oodles?" Annabel laughed.

"Hey, yeah." Ray was a little encouraged.

"Bighorn hunting has been restricted for years," Alice said. "Last year it was eliminated." She had arranged two little hummocks of green twigs on either side of the ram's head.

Ray went back to talking to the pretty one. She was wearing a short shiny red jacket that looked expensive. The other two were dressed like bums. "I have my suspicions concerning the Fish and Wildlife Department," he said. "I think they've been meddling with natural law, you know? I just found this thing. You're dealing with practically a nonevent here. I just happened upon it, I swear."

"Wherever you go, there you are," the pretty one said, and smiled.

"It's 'Wherever you go, be there,'" Alice said. "Wow, Annabel."

Ray was sitting on a mat of prickly pear cactus and couldn't move without getting spiked. He wouldn't mind seeing Ranger Darling right about now. These girls would get a scolding! The best thing about his situation was that he wasn't lost. If they would just go away and leave him alone, he'd rally. But there were worse things than being lost. When you were lost, all you had to do was relax and not panic. Being lost was an overrated problem. Ray drifted off. The pretty one, Annabel, was defending her version of the being there business to the crazy one, maintaining that what she'd said was close enough. It was just before dusk. Then there would be dusk. Then night. Day again. The little deaths—*las muertes chiquitas*—then the big one. It was all practice. Ray stared at the animal thing. With the girls on either side of it, the scene was a perversion of the pictures in the hunting mags where beaming guys and the now and then gal in chocolate-chip camouflage posed with the recently acquired dead. The dead looked relaxed and still handsome but as though they didn't quite get the occasion. Present, but a world apart from the hoopla. The living looked happy, not that their joy made much sense if examined on a deeper level. He wondered if animals had a sense of *las muertes chiquitas* too. What had he been thinking when he'd picked that thing up!

"You've been talking and talking over there," Annabel said.

"I must be nervous," Ray said. "You-all haven't really hurt anyone before, have you?"

"No," Alice said. "You're our practice object."

"But you're not going to hurt me," Ray said.

"We're just going to leave you here," Corvus said.

"Alice wants you to know the thing you've hurt by turning into it—in your mind," Annabel explained. "Then you'll think in a different way and be a better person."

"The time to do that was before," Ray protested. "It's putrefying now, everything's falling apart in there now, it's not going to work."

"What's not going to work?" Alice said.

Ray didn't feel so good. He could feel the little monkey's heart beating wetly beneath its gray skin. The little monkey had stretched its whole scrawny length flat out against him and was wordlessly expressing its situation. It, too, was not lost. It had undergone unnecessary surgery, had painfully recovered from it, had been killed piece by piece and disposed of part by part, and this had been its orbit of eternal occurrence, suffered over and over again. But now it was falling from orbit, it was tensing to bail. The relationship with Ray was drawing to a close, and the little monkey couldn't care less. But Ray cared. Which he attempted urgently to express, because if the little monkey went, so went Ray. The depth of his sigh surprised him.

"Is this the worst thing you've ever done?" Alice was asking him.

"I didn't do anything!" Ray wasn't going to tell her about the time he'd tried to shoot an apple off a dog's head with a pellet gun. It had been that little creep Rocky's idea, but Rocky could be very persuasive. "Sit," Rocky had said to the dog, some stray. Almost any dog would sit if you said sit; it was weird, as if they all were tuned to a martyr's deliverance. He had missed the apple by a mile and was fortunate not to have hit the dog, the dog at that moment being so relative to the apple.

"I don't feel good," he admitted. His legs and wrists hurt from being tied in what wasn't even a proper knot. He knew proper knots from his Cubby days. And this wasn't one of them. The little monkey was dragging its long self around Ray's tightening head again.

"Do you want some aspirin?" Annabel asked.

"Annabel," Alice said, "let him not feel good if he wants."

Ray believed that if he'd been traveling with a dog none of this would have happened. One of those hybrid wolf pups he'd seen advertised. He'd get a major collar for it, made of heavy, rippling, silver threads, the stuff knights hung around their necks to protect them from arrows.

"I always carry aspirin," Annabel said. "I have a silver pillbox I keep them in."

"Annabel," Alice said, "who taught you to be friendly to everybody you meet?"

It's breeding, maybe, Ray thought grimly, being brought up properly, and where were you brought up, Alice, he'd like to ask, in penitentiary day care? They had no weapons, as far as he knew—God, keep weapons out of the hands of women!—and at best a pretty muzzy agenda. He hoped they weren't into disinterested malice, but girls weren't as a rule, were they?

Annabel popped an aspirin into his mouth.

"Could I have about a half a dozen more?" Ray asked. "And some water?" There was something vaguely quasi-religious to this, even sexual—not at this exact moment, of course, but possibly in a future moment. Three chicks and an American male, bondage and threat, great lawless fun just waiting for the unexpected spark. Three flowerpots waiting for his seed. He was at their mercy *and* their service. He could do it! He just had to coast out this headache, keep being congenial. I'm shy but I'm hung like a horse, that was the implication he wanted to project. He wanted to shine as a hostage.

But his head felt frail, almost transparent, with the ghostly little monkey now shrunk into a corner. And the monkey was transparent, too, and he could see within it an even smaller monkey. This was a first, the monkey within the monkey within.

"I don't think he's well," Annabel said. "He doesn't look well."

He wouldn't admit he was subject to collapse. He was a stroker, and strokers never admit. When he recovered from the first one, he said the prettiest things. The words he could pluck out of air positively shimmered! He was a poet, a walking *I Ching*. It was beautiful.

How's that pancake taste, son? Good?

Burning driftwood indigo!

Want to go for a ride in the car with me, son? I have to get some bread and Modess.

The dilatory are unfortunate even if strong!

But the second episode made him angry and mean. The pretty words left and shitfuckfart arrived, knocking on everyone's door, the answer to every query. He snarled and flailed in a cave with greasy walls. The world existed to be cursed. Then that passed too, and he cried at everything. When he saw a brimming trash can in the street, when he saw his mother put on lipstick, when someone shook cereal into a bowl. He cried when he slept. Anything would get him started except for another person's tears. When his mother started to bawl, Ray dried right up. He couldn't help it, in fact, her tears made him laugh. Clearly, he was placing her under a lot of stress with his random reactions to the varied sampler that was his stroke, or strokes, warmly referred to by his therapists as TIAs, which made the attacks, the *incidents,* sound modest and unassuming, little wavelets washing prettily over his own personal cell system rather than brain-sucking riptides.

Yet throughout all this buffeting change the little monkey stayed with him and Ray appreciated its fidelity. He also appreciated that it wasn't a beagle or a bunny, plenty of which also ended up in labs, and he'd have to be insane if he had a bunny or a beagle in his head. The monkey was an acknowledgment and example of science's beneficial uses. The monkey was a little scary, maybe, but it wasn't *insane.* Ray felt it to be naturally intelligent, rather like himself, and similarly unhappy as well.

When, after a few months, the uncontrollable crying stopped, Ray hit the road. He took the money from his father's fat, worn wallet, the very sight of which would've set him to sobbing only a short time before, and cleaned out the silver from the sideboard for hock. Good heavy stuff, it was a service for twelve that was seldom used, which sort of hurt Ray's feelings since it might have provided some style to the banal and unsavory antistroke diet they all choked down night after night at the kitchen table. What was that pattern called? Winnower. No, it couldn't have been called Winnower . . .

He was drooling a little, as though in sleep. He twisted his shoulder forward and rubbed it against his chin.

"Why do you have to have a silver box for aspirin?" Alice was saying. "Why?"

"It's from Tiffany's," Annabel said, "and I love it. I love the inessentials. I wouldn't want a life without them." She looked at Ray and smiled.

He made an effort to smile back but didn't think he'd done it. Maybe they were lezzies, he thought, trekking, mountaineering lezzies and not little flowerpots at all.

"My arms are feeling numb," he said. "Honest to God. This is tied too tight or something."

"It's scarcely tied at all," Corvus said.

"Corvus," he mumbled. He liked saying her name. "Corvus, you've got a beautiful name, man, it's as fine as Pythagoras."

Geometry. Ray had loved geometry before his stroke. He'd had an aptitude for it. Angles, lines, everything sharp and clean. He'd really gotten it. And Pythagoras was so stellar. When Ray was a kid, even before he knew he loved geometry, he'd read one of those big-print kids' books about heroes—he could see it clearly, its cover was golden—and there was Pythagoras in a flowing robe, and he'd read that Pythagoras thought that in a previous existence he'd been a bush, which was such a stellar thing to admit to thinking.

"Say something else to me, Corvus," Ray said. "You're the sensible one here."

But it was Alice who spoke: "We have to go soon. You have an opportunity to discuss a hunting ethic before we do." She was fiddling with a knife and fork. For an instant he was anxious that she would poke it into his thigh and begin to carve, then he saw that instead it was a stick she kept snapping ever smaller. Ray rubbed his mouth with his sleeve again. "I have no hunting ethic."

"That's my point," Alice said. "That's very clear to me."

I know you from before, he wanted to say, but he said, "The problem is with transients. Transients," he said emphatically. "The problem is with transients and the *chandelier*. They don't know about the chandelier until too late. No, no. Sorry. They know about the chandelier, but they don't know it's going to go *out*." These three chicks were going to murder him, he thought, but he would talk them out of it. He had built the foundation and now was raising the great structure of his thought. "Whereas in the case of the monkey, the monkey can warm itself by a fire, but it can't feed a fire, it would never think to feed the fire, but it can take comfort from it. But with the chandelier, everyone knows about the chandelier whether they think about it or not. Everybody—the animals—beneath the chandelier we're all aware of it together!" Ray felt close to tears. Even the little monkey. Once . . . it had dazzled.

Alice looked at him. He was as mute as the poor old bighorn. "Why don't you say something?" she demanded.

Meanwhile, Ray was giving it everything he had. Human beings have language, they are not defenseless. The little monkey slumped in the corner of his head, only its big black eyes seeming alive. It wasn't impressed by the story of the chandelier. The little monkey was going to renounce all attachment to him, all concern and function, trust and faith. Monkey as Lord, it was just letting him go.

The air was cooling, and the sky unravelling, turning a bizarre peach color.

"Corvus," Ray said. But he couldn't really see her, his view blocked by the sheep, which was staring at him maliciously. And the smell was terrible, although it didn't seem to be coming from as far away as the sheep. It was closer to home, actually, something burning through his own heart's ventricles, boiling in the fluid-filled cavities of his brain.

"Feed the flock of slaughter," he said. How long had the three of them been gone? They *were* gone, he suddenly realized, but they'd made havoc of him. His mind was a sloshing, brimming bowl, and the little monkey was dabbling about in it with long cold fingers, trying to rehabilitate and refresh itself maybe, trying to acquire the strength to go on. That was good, Ray thought distantly. It wasn't letting him go. His whole head felt like a split coconut, and the little monkey was dabbling around in the spilt thin milk of it. Once Ray had seen a man open a coconut with a machete and had not empathized with it at the time, but now he could—the unliving meat with no plan for itself. His mother protested that the coconut had been opened in a dangerous fashion. The man was large, with a deep dirty tan and a shark tooth wrapped in string around his neck, and he wore a green hat of woven fronds. This was in Florida, a tourist thing, a man opening coconuts outside an open-air aquarium with a sign before each murky pen:

NO WHISTLING OR CLAPPING
NO BABY TALK

He remembered running, prepreprimanded among the dark pools.

The monkey continued to push its little hands around Ray's mind. Ray felt less pain than discomfort, he felt sleepy and softly mauled. Then he became aware that he was swinging his hands from side to side behind him and could touch the end of the rope with his fingers. And then he was free. His hands flopped loose. He dragged them in front of him, rubbed his arms. He was trembling. He wanted to stand up but sensed a considerable gulf between thinking about moving and moving. He rubbed his hands on his knees. I wanted to do that, he thought. He looked at them, he watched his hands cupping his knees. But this isn't the way getting up is done, it's done some other way. He pushed his hands down his legs to his boots. The animal grinned at him beneath its curved and broken horns. But I appear unhurt, Ray thought after a time. "Sawdust," he said, which was horrible for him to hear, for "sawdust" wasn't the correct word—very seldom the correct word in practically any circumstance.

Ray had always considered himself one balls-to-the-wall puppy. He had thrown himself into the life he'd been given with ardor, *ardor*, yes, and now he wasn't even walking upright but just crawling on the ground, creeping over it with no more sense than a snake. His left arm was useless, and his left leg, although possessing more feeling, seemed ambivalent about committing itself to Ray's purpose. Ray felt no more than a simulacrum of himself humping and rolling and scrabbling down the trail. He knew it was the trail, close to where he'd begun, because it stank and he could see the prints of many soles in the dust. He knew he was alone because he couldn't feel the little monkey anymore. The little monkey had bailed. He hadn't entrusted Ray with the packing of the parachute. The little animal—which when new is always holy and unceasing but which in Ray's case, it's true, was maimed and neglected and could not be comforted—had finally flown. Ray crept, panting, along the pointed ground. He knew his life had changed.

23

Corvus drove; Alice, as the thinnest, was in the middle. "That was so unsatisfactory," Alice said. She had yearned blindly for the onto-logical parry and thrust and was disheartened that this, this *victim,* she thought dismissively, had been incapable of it. What was wrong with his mouth, anyway? He looked like a crybaby.

Annabel had been afraid for a moment that she'd lost her silver pill-box after giving that boy the aspirin, but here it was again, thank heaven. Always a bridesmaid, never a bride, she was thinking, and didn't know why. They never said, Always a best man, never a groom. This one she could never visualize as a groom, as anybody's groom. What had Alice wanted with him? She just hadn't thought the moment through, which was so typical of Alice. Some sort of frontier savagery thing, that was the closest Annabel could come to describing her behavior sometimes, but she wasn't really savage or even malicious; it was just that if you weren't rebutting her preposterous sentiments every minute, you'd find your-self—well, not mesmerized, Alice was no mesmerizer, but dismantled or something. Annabel frequently found herself speechless before such blind momentum. Back home, Annabel had played little parts in theater productions, not school ones but civic ones, and she'd been valued, she'd been told she had talent. She had even been in a commercial once—all she'd had to do was look at a package of chewing gum with delight—but out here she felt like a kind of supernumerary.

"I don't think we should go out so much," Annabel said. "You're never going to get me to go camping again."

"We never *went* camping," Alice said.

"That was no hunter, either," Annabel said. "Please don't delude your-self."

"He was sort of pupal, wasn't he?" Alice realized that he hadn't killed the animal, but this didn't concern her overmuch. Evil must be repaid, and not necessarily to the one who'd done the deed. You had to grab whoever was available and annoying and see what came of it, although in this case it hadn't been much. He had been irritatingly familiar, as though they'd conducted uncompleted business sometime in the past.

"Pupal?" Annabel said. "He was far from cute, but he wasn't that disgusting."

"I think you can only do bad things," Corvus said, "if you forget you're going to die."

"Oh," Annabel said. Corvus made her nervous. How fast were they going, anyway? The Dodge's speedometer was broken, as well as the gas gauge. The truck was a death trap, and this hair, this Tommy's hair, was always floating around inside. I would have this vacuumed, she thought, in the most thorough way.

"Remembering you're going to die lets you do bad things," Alice said. "Besides, what we did wasn't bad. We revived him. Lying there with that poor tormented thing all wrapped around him, he could've suffocated." She had seen her first bighorn, but then again, she hadn't.

Corvus's hands, green in the dashboard's light, purled across the wheel. The saguaros waved them on, but at a four-way stop, they paused. Music screamed from a car to the left. *Liar fuckin liar ah'm gonna squash you like an insect.* The car sped off to the horrid gaieties of town.

"We're about to reenter," Corvus said, "the steak and lobster world."

"I used to love four-way stops as a little kid," Alice said. "They just fascinated me. I'd kneel in the backseat in awe. I thought it was proof that adults knew what they were doing."

"We should have listened to him more," Corvus said. "He was talking in some lost language."

"I didn't hear him say much of anything," Alice said. "As an experiment, he wasn't very complex."

"As experiments, we're all complex," Corvus said.

Annabel did not consider herself an experiment. She was Annabel née Vineyard, and she was going to do her best to pretend that this year, when it was over, had never occurred.

"Because we're made for both this life and another one," Corvus said. "At the same time we have to regard as one this life, the next life, and the life between."

"The life between?" Annabel exclaimed. "Is that like a so-called life?" That's where I am, she thought. They passed a large billboard advertising vasectomy reversal services.

"That guy wasn't up to this kind of thinking," Alice said.

Who is? Annabel thought.

They pulled into a service station. Corvus gassed up the truck while Alice cleaned the windshield. She liked the overlapping, dissolving lines the squeegee made. Annabel went inside and looked at the magazines. *Your Prom* looked fascinating. She took it over to the checkout line and stood behind a man with an immense fistula on the back of his neck. It had a little black hole in the center of it as though he were in the habit of trying to locate it with a pin or a pen. What if eternity was like this? Standing behind a huge fistula in an unmoving checkout line with the last copy of *Your Prom* magazine. She moved over to the other line, but here the customer ahead of her was wearing what appeared to be one of her mother's suits. She was almost absolutely sure it was her mother's suit, the cranberry-colored one with the big buttons. The woman was much too large for the suit.

Annabel hurried outside. Dozens of people were gathered beneath the moth-crazed lights, smoking and idly staring. Everything was so busy and ugly, Annabel thought, so *inconclusive.* She saw Corvus and Alice in the truck, gazing out the windshield at the roiling backdrop. Of course Alice hadn't cleaned the glass completely, she'd missed whole areas as she always did.

Annabel squeezed in beside them on the truck's bench seat as some boys walked by and squinted at them appraisingly. What if the three of them ran into that boy again, Annabel wondered, the one they'd tied up? He didn't seem the kind of boy who would hold a grudge, who'd report or identify them or anything, but it would still be awkward. What would anyone *say*? Had Alice foreseen such a contingency? No, of course not. She didn't know about Alice—or even about Corvus, who in her opinion had been rendered practically abnormal by sorrow—but if she ever saw that boy again, she would just *die*.

ickey was baby-sitting his own child, Mallick, which means "king." That had been Loretta's idea, he'd had nothing to say about it; she'd gotten to the birth certificate form first, and after seventy-two hours any changes cost fifty bucks, so Mallick it was. The kid was almost two years old now, but Hickey still hadn't adjusted to the name and didn't think he ever would. King, for Chrissakes. He and the kid were driving around after supper. They'd been bacheloring it for three days now, Loretta being off in Minnesota at a wolf howl.

"It's so beautiful, Hickey," she'd said when she called to tell him what time to pick her up at the airport. "Hundreds of people all out there silent beneath the stars, you can hear a pin drop, and then the wolves howl and when they're through, everyone cries, 'Thank you, thank you!' and we all applaud. The applause is just thunderous. It's thrilling."

He didn't want to hear about it. He and King had pointedly not been invited on this expedition. Every four months Loretta would leave them for a weekend and go off and do some damn thing involving crowds. Loretta loved crowds. Hickey was more solitary by nature, as he believed was King, with whom, as yet, he had forged no bond.

King sat in his padded car seat studying the scenery as though he found it vaguely inadmissible. Even dressed in lumpish toddler clothes, he had an annoyingly aristocratic air about him. Sometimes Hickey meanly called him Miss Me, which perturbed King not at all.

Also in the car this evening, holding marijuana smoke carefully in his lungs, was Hickey's friend Kevin, whose lady had left him a week before.

"It was a simple thing," Kevin had told him. "You know how it started? It started she looks at me one morning, I'm having my beer, and she says, 'You know how you spell woman, Kevin? It's "w-o-m-y-n." That's how you spell woman, you lazy ugly worthless freak.' And she was gone. She'd always wanted to open a bakery in Belize, and I suspect she's down there this very moment. I used to say to her, 'What kind of ambition is that, running a bakery in Belize? I have more ambition than that.'"

Kevin had once published a book of saguaro photographs in which the cacti said funny things befitting their incongruent natures. It was something you'd read sitting on the can. Then he'd published a sequel in which they said additional funny things, but this hadn't proved as successful. Hickey told him he was belaboring the concept.

"Sometimes I wish Loretta would just leave for good," Hickey said, "instead of this once-every-four-months thing. Then I could get on with my life." He looked at his son and nodded significantly. King ignored him.

"You'd miss her if it was permanent. I miss my lady's sweet buns bad. Maybe I should go down there, get a job in a dive shop, fill air tanks or something. Work my way back into her affection."

"That's dangerous work," Hickey said. "What if you fucked up and somebody's down there at seventy feet sucking bad air? You'd get sued." Hickey feared the legal process although he'd never been in a courtroom, never even been called for jury duty. But he had courtroom dreams in which he stood before a robed female who was about to disclose something to him in catastrophic detail.

"You've got to know the *kairos,* Hickey," Kevin said somberly. He extinguished the roach stub with his fingers and swallowed it.

"What the hell is that?" Hickey said.

"Opportunity. You've got to know when opportunity presents itself. You've got to be able to recognize it. Like I saw opportunity in these cactus once. I saw economic possibilities, whereas most people wouldn't necessarily. Now I hate them."

"I hate 'em, too," Hickey said. "What the hell time is it, do you know?"

"Time is a provisional thing," Kevin said. "Hours are an opportunity for human action, nothing more. Do you mind if I light up another joint?"

"Just don't blow it on King. His mother'll smell it."

"Let's stop and get out," Kevin said. "What say, King, you talkin' yet?"

"Nah, he's not talking. I was trying to get him to start while Loretta was away—would've made her feel bad, teach her she just can't take off like she does because things happen, little milestones that come but once."

They passed a *descanso*, a white wooden cross wreathed with faded ribbon, the name of the unlucky decedent spelled out in nails. King, clutching a mouthed rusk in one small hand, gave it a furry look. Hickey downshifted and continued until it was out of sight before stopping. The men got out, but King sat firm.

"Has he smiled yet?" Kevin asked.

"Well, yeah. But he don't smile much," Hickey admitted.

"Good-looking boy, though," Kevin said doubtfully. They passed the joint back and forth. Two shallow arroyos veered down on them in a green V. He wasn't about to ask if he and Loretta had ever thought of having King checked out. Hickey seemed in a bad mood. And he was in a bad mood too. The saguaros were looking at him as though he cut quite the comic figure out there. It used to be he felt intimate with the giant cacti when he smoked, but now he just wanted to fuck the loony things over. And they were so goddamn big, which Kevin had never found amusing, sensitive as he was to being five feet five and three-quarters without the augmenting lifts in his cowboy boots. When his girlfriend had still been fond of him, she had reassured him by saying that Kant had been only five feet tall and nonetheless a large and successful thinker. Kevin had checked out a synopsis of the shrimp philosopher's work from the Bookmobile, but little Immanuel seemed pretty dated to him, as well as being confused, a waffler, in fact. That is, did he believe in God, personal freedom, and immortality, or not?

The saguaros, their arms upraised in mock horror, looked as if they were about to fall over from laughing at him.

"Who said paranoia is having all the facts?"

"Hell if I know." Hickey was brooding about the sort of relationship he and King would have when his son grew up. King might try to kill him; he could see them squaring off in the messy living room. Or King wouldn't make the attempt himself, he'd think he was too damn smart for that, he'd *hire* someone to slip into his own father's home in the middle of the night to dispatch him. Loretta wouldn't be there, of course. She'd be conveniently absent in some crowd, thousands of witnesses attesting to her presence, and King would have his flunky alibiers lined up, too; but Hickey wasn't going to allow this to happen, no he wasn't. He'd survive, and then he and King would have themselves a little talk.

"Somebody said it," Kevin said.

Then again, maybe he and King would never have their little talk. It could happen. And his life would just be Endure and Evade, over and over. That would be the rhythm of his years. That would be the judgment.

In the truck King sat more or less contentedly, though missing the throaty burble of his father's Floatmaster muffler—a pleasure that, he knew from experience, would recur once they were on the road again. The sound of the Floatmaster was to King the anthem of the gods.

"You got your shotgun?" Kevin inquired.

"'Course. Got both of 'em."

"Let's shoot up some saguaros. Look at the arms on that one." He pointed to a configuration that was annoyingly cosmic.

"Let's make 'er dance," Hickey agreed glumly. He went to the truck and removed the guns from beneath a Mexican blanket behind the seats. He hadn't shot up a sag for some time. "We got to move out a ways. King don't like loud noise."

"He's a sensitive, good-looking boy but you don't want him getting too sensitive," Kevin advised.

"Sometimes I think King and I don't share a common atmosphere," Hickey said, heartfelt. "And Loretta encourages that."

"Paranoia's having all the facts," Kevin said, sincere. He'd like to carve that on his goddamn hearthstone.

Shooting felt good. Joy consists in this, after all, the increase of one's power. They walked as though reconnoitering dangerous territory, firing, the green cortex of the cacti spraying like splashed water through the air. Kevin chewed off an enormous branching arm with a half dozen shots and it crashed, wetly splintering, on the ground.

"One of these damn things can kill a man if it falls on him," Kevin said.

Hickey expressed indignation, although in fact he was feeling better, happy even. The air felt good out here, sort of supple and kind, and he was happy to get away from King's watchful supereminent gaze. He popped some chain-fruit cholla.

Kevin was feeling better too. He lightly hammered a cactus that appeared to be appealing comically for pardon, but it was just fooling around, it was saying, "Life's a bitch and then you die," which was why Kevin had had trouble selling his second edition of *Cactus Talk*. It all sounded like exceedingly familiar shit.

A plane flew high above them in the perfect sky—Loretta's plane, no doubt, right on time, dropping down from the north. After Hickey picked her up at the airport, she would want to be taken out to dinner for Indian food from India, a place where people shat and bathed in the same river and worshiped cows. She would have a little pimple on her nose, which always happened when she traveled. She would talk about the wonderful people she'd met. People were nothing special. Didn't she realize there were five and a half billion people in the world, how could any one of them be special? Think about it, Loretta, for Chrissakes! He hated Indian food. Endure, evade, Hickey mused, firing. He and Kevin were walking farther and farther from the truck and tiny judgmental King. Since their targets weren't moving at all, they were delighted to see an object fluttering and seething toward them in the twilight. Hickey really couldn't tell what it was. All push and sprawl, it was so smudged that he couldn't make the damned thing out. He couldn't even tell if it was humping toward them or sidling away.

"How do you interpret that, Kevin?" he yelled. But Kevin was firing, having already interpreted it as something inanimate but in motion, inanimate but confident in its effortless ability to succeed without ever having to be alive, an ability that perturbed Kevin. He emptied his shotgun under the pretext of a duty honorably discharged. And Hickey fired too. He had the better gun—his daddy's, with the shaggy-legged hawk in full plummet etched upon the breach.

Ray didn't even have the opportunity to see his old friend Pythagoras in the flowing white robes, holding an animal to his mouth to catch his dying breath, for Pythagoras believed that only animals perpetuate spirit. Ray didn't have the comforting chance to see that. His self merely scattered. Into the lacuna.

25

The television was on again. A startled bull with a ring through its immense nostrils stood in a river. Piranha swirled about. The bull turned gray like a block of chalk, then transparent, and then it was a skeleton, floating away.

Ginger, Ginger, Carter thought, then unplugged the television, turned the screen to the wall, and draped his bathrobe over it.

"Did you buy that stock I've been telling you about?" she asked.

"I have not," Carter said. He decided he was going to be matter-of-fact tonight. No more, no less. Ginger had been urging him to buy a particular stock, insisting upon it, though she'd never shown much interest in the market in the past.

"This is how people get ahead, Carter, through insider information. I'm giving you a tip."

"Cyberstocks are very tricky, darling. The market's still sorting itself out."

"Aren't you interested in how I know?" she said.

"I wish we'd done this together before," Carter said. "It would've been fun, but under the circumstances I—" Could Ginger have put on a few pounds? Impossible, Carter thought. But there was no doubt about it, she had become a little hippy.

"What are you looking at?" she snapped.

"Thinking," he said, "just thinking."

"It's going to be instant gratification with this stock, I assure you."

"People who want instant gratification get clobbered by the market. This sounds very similar to the biotechnology craze just a few—"

"Don't try to educate me, Carter. I can't believe you still have a long-term horizon."

Long-term horizon? She certainly had been talking to someone. "Why not?" he asked cautiously.

"Have you rearranged this room?" Ginger demanded. "You have, haven't you? You've done something with the mirror."

He looked guiltily at the mirror, which Donald had moved only a few days before. "You never should have a mirror that reflects your image in bed, Mr. Vineyard," Donald had told him. "A mirror that reflects your body while sleeping causes unnatural dream states and a weakening of physical vitality."

Carter got a kick out of Donald calling him Mr. Vineyard. It was getting to be a little joke between them.

"The entire room looks different," Ginger said, annoyed. "Is it that dolt Donald's doing? You'll be hanging crystals in the windows next! You'll be putting baskets filled with feathers in the corner." Her wide hips moved her fluidly from one side of the room to the other while she ranted about Donald. She was looking astonishingly well nourished, Carter thought with dismay. She wasn't fading away at all.

"You've moved the lights around as well! It's much dimmer in here."

Donald had told Carter that due to overbright bulbs, the bedroom was an extraordinarily unstable environment.

"Have you ever heard of *bagua*, darling?" Carter ventured. "*Feng shui?*"

"I cannot believe this!"

Empty vessels make the most noise, Carter thought. Maybe this is what that meant.

"It's just an idea," he said, trying to be conciliatory.

"I know what it is, for godssakes, and it's an *Oriental* idea. Carter, you're becoming a flake. You were always dull and predictable and rational and money-oriented, and to hear you now—well, it's pathetic."

"My journey has changed," Carter said, "as has yours." He felt a little giddy talking to Ginger like this. Butting heads, as it were.

"Do you intend to marry Donald?" she said.

"Why would Donald want to get married?" He hastened to add, "What a preposterous notion."

"Has he suggested a hot-air balloon ride yet?"

"No," Carter said. Skimming over the desert peaks and valleys in a colorfully patterned balloon with Donald . . . the idea had come up. Casting off at dawn. Elevating with the rising sun. Champagne, a few silly sandwiches. Maybe on his birthday.

Ginger pulled her hair around in front of her face in a vaguely familiar gesture and peered at the ends. "I'm letting my hair grow," she said. "Don't you love it?"

Carter put his head in his hands.

"Passion was never your forte," Ginger went on. "Your member was adequate, but your lovemaking lacked élan. Admit it, Carter. You preferred making money."

"Darling, it's so late," Carter said from behind his hands. "Isn't it late?"

"Why don't you look at your little clock?" she suggested.

Carter looked around the room, which Donald had quite transformed. Where was the clock? Ginger was taking exceptional satisfaction in its absence. His minor losses and setbacks clearly won her complete approval. Ginger was mean, she was so mean. She was aggressive, destructive, and bored, a pyramid of seemingly indestructible neuroses. No way was he going to buy that stock. He would stand firm on this one, appeal to her snobbishness. Did she want to use the opportunity she'd been given, in what was a stunning reversal of nature's laws—to indulge in common necromancy? If only she'd make some friends there. Surely the dead had their fascinations. But Ginger hadn't been at all interested in or moved by the dead even when she was alive.

"Carter?" she resumed. "Do you know what I'd like for Christmas?"

That was a hard one.

"Don't look at me all agley like that, Carter."

"I was considering giving Annabel some pearl earrings," he said.

"Annabel . . ." Ginger said. "Oh, *Annabel*. I hope you're not planning on giving her *my* pearl earrings."

"She'd treasure them, darling," he said without much hope.

"Don't even think about it." Ginger seemed to be examining her hair again.

"Christmas is quite a ways off," Carter said. "It's summer here. It was one hundred ten degrees here today."

"'*Here?*'" she scoffed. "I'm quite aware of where you are, Carter, and it doesn't impress me one bit. In any case, Christmas will be upon you before you know it, and what I want for Christmas is you."

"Me?"

"You're so tedious tonight, Carter. So self-absorbed. What do you think I'd want—a rosebush?" She laughed unpleasantly. "People who think they can get away with planting a goddamn memorial rosebush are beneath our contempt."

"You shouldn't want anything now, darling, least of all me."

"You're a shadow of what you used to be, Carter, it's true. We both have to admit it."

"Darling, I'm simply going to have to say good night now." He was in a panic of exhaustion.

"Darling," she said. "Darling, darling, darling, darling. You're wearing the goddamn word out. I wish I'd had a bodyguard. He could've gone to restaurants with us and had sense enough to recommend shell steaks and yogurt with peaches to soak up all the booze we drank. If the place didn't have shell steaks and yogurt with peaches, he would've escorted us elsewhere. He would've been forthright, with a big sunny grin. He'd wear blue suits unabashedly. He'd be strong. He'd instinctively know what I needed. He'd be protective and adept—"

Ginger was working herself up to quite a pitch. Then there was a queasy retinal flash and she was gone.

Carter wandered out to the kitchen. He recalled a friend of his who claimed his wife had left him after the doctor had changed her anti-depression medicine. That's all it took. Why hadn't Ginger's doctor been more enterprising? He wondered if he should tell Donald about Ginger. The only thing the young man knew was that she was dead, which normally would have been enough. Should he confide in Donald? He could see the boy's handsome, thrillingly unresponsive face. Donald might say, "Consider, Mr. Vineyard . . ." Donald frequently prefaced the laying out of parameters in this manner. *Consider.* What a remarkable, elegant word, Carter thought, the way Donald said it. He poured himself a drink.

26

Sherwin was eating lunch at one of his favorite neighborhood establishments. The building had been conceived as a bank, but the bank had failed. Now it was a restaurant whose intentions were difficult to determine. He and Alice were sitting in an enclosed patio that once had offered the convenience of a drive-up window. A striped awning hugged the area, altering the hue of flesh and food alike. Each table had a card propped among the condiments (the ketchup looked quite green) stating YOU'RE NOT GOING COLOR-BLIND! OUR NEW AWNING CAUSES THIS EFFECT! PEACE!" Sherwin was eating pasta primavera. Oil glistened on his chin. Alice, opposite him, hadn't said anything for some minutes.

"You ever notice that I got a glass eye?" Sherwin asked.

"No," Alice said.

"Pretty interesting, huh?"

"No," Alice said. "You don't have a glass eye. Both of them move."

"That's because it's on a coral fragment. There's a real piece of coral back there that the muscles are attached to, so it can swing around a little bit. A little piece of coral from America's only living reef tract off Marathon, Florida."

"You can't take coral in the Florida Keys," Alice said. "It's a crime. A felony."

"A felony!" Sherwin said.

"A misdemeanor, then. It should be a felony."

"My God, she'd deprive me of an eye."

"If you don't have an eye and you put in something that looks like an eye, it doesn't seem like the you I know. The you I know would want a big hole behind dark glasses, or you'd want an eye that looked like a tattooed egg."

Sherwin grinned at her. "Surely you didn't say a tattooed egg."

"One of those eggs, you know, it starts with an *F*."

"Fabergé."

"Right. Fabergé."

Sherwin stopped grinning. He looked down at his plate and pushed it away, then picked up a cigarette he'd left burning in the ashtray.

"Coral is alive, you know," Alice said fretfully. "The coral reef is like an underwater forest, and a variety of marine life depends on—"

"I'm ordering some buffalo wings and sweet potato fries. The sweet potato fries are good here, you want some?"

"Why do they call them buffalo wings?"

"The term is supposed to connote whimsical fantasy, Alice."

"That is *so* offensive. In less than a hundred years, Americans reduced the quintessential animal of the continent by ninety-nine-point-nine percent. Only twenty-three remained when—"

"Alice, have some fries."

"Do you know that more than forty percent of our food has been genetically altered?" she said wearily, then gazed at the iced tea before her. Everything was big in this place, enormous. There must have been a quart of it in a disgusting pink plastic glass.

When had she fallen out of love with him? Sherwin wondered. For about two weeks, he could've asked her to do anything and she would've. That was love, wasn't it? He'd thought he had all the time in the world to decide what to do with her. She'd amused him, repelled him. Women had always repelled him, they were whiskered slits, irresponsible, barbaric, they'd eat you alive. In dreams, he'd embrace a woman and turn into a pillar of blood.

"So when did you stop being crazy about me?"

Alice blushed. "I'm crazy about you. Why did you say you have a glass eye when you don't?"

"I was just making conversation," Sherwin said. "But since you're not crazy about me anymore, why don't you tell me what you wanted from me in the first place?"

"I don't want anything from you," Alice said. "I just wanted to be with you, like now." She looked around at their surroundings, at the two loud women sitting nearby. They had poured sugar on their food so they wouldn't eat anymore.

"So I went out to get the blower fixed," one was saying. "It's under warranty and they've moved—there's an arrow on the door that says 'Moved two miles down the road'—so I drive two miles down the road and there's this hacienda-style house, though modest, with a tile roof and a center courtyard, and I go in to pick up the goddamn blower which has been nothing but trouble and I say, 'What is this, a house?' and they say, 'This is Tarzan Zambini's house!' and I say, 'Who the hell is Tarzan Zambini?' and it turns out he was a lion tamer with the circus and he retired out here with his lions and they lived on one side of the house and Tarzan lived on the other and there was a swimming pool between them and the lions would swim in the pool, they loved it, but Tarzan had to move out and give up his lions when the highway went through. There he was out in the middle of nowhere with his lions, and comes progress's inexorable wheel to slice his spread in half, and now there are these stupid lawn mowers where the lions used to play."

"Where'd Tarzan move to?"

"I think he just passed on. Where's a person going to move to if he's used to having lions? Most garden apartments that are affordable and safe, who'd accept an odd old fellow like Tarzan? Probably wouldn't even let him have a clothesline."

"I hate to differ with you, Vivian," her friend said, "but they'd allow him a clothesline if it weren't visible from the street."

Alice was ambivalent about the fate of Tarzan Zambini. Was it deserved or not?

The wings had arrived with the sweet potato fries. Sherwin was wearing his tuxedo. His fingers were greasy. Watching him had given Alice much pleasure in the past, but now she felt nothing. Would she forever be an empty onlooker at the feast of life? She shook her iced tea, and it spilled a little. She ate some bread.

"That's a famous painting," Sherwin said.

A wall was devoted to the glaring thing. "Famous?"

"It's a reproduction of a famous painting. *The Icebergs.*"

"I like it," Alice acknowledged, "but I don't think it belongs here. It doesn't seem suitable decor. It's like the owner's too cheap for air-conditioning. Not that I approve of air-conditioning."

"You know why you like it? Because there aren't any people in it. There's a funny story about the painting. See the tiny little mast in the corner?"

"There's food on it, I think." The work had not escaped spillage.

"That's the crow's nest from a wrecked ship. The artist's name was Church, a famous landscape painter a century ago, but when he exhibited *The Icebergs,* no one exclaimed over it. The reaction was so reserved that Church lugged the painting back to his studio and painted in that tiny little smashed-up crow's nest to give it a little human dimension, see what I'm saying? Like, man was here, even though he was destroyed, he got to see this cold, immense, monumental thing and was ennobled by his very inconsequentiality before it."

"Did they like it any better after he put the wreck in it?" It was the smallest of corrections, Alice noted.

"The public? No, flotsam and jetsam didn't do it for them. Flotsam and jetsam just reminded them of their own paltry selves, that they were tramps and drifters and vagrants in this life, nothing more. The public hated the painting. Church was crushed. Frederic Edwin Church. Of the luminist school." He regarded Alice thoughtfully. She was sexless but troubling. He wanted to go away and then send for her, that's what he wanted. He wanted to leave and have her follow. We are in exile here. We are strangers and pilgrims in this place. Two on a party, a solitude of two. He wanted to twist her to him.

"Note the cruciform shape," Sherwin said. "It's a very persistent symbol. The symbol of symbols. The cross represents a way out; it moves, renews, implies further voyaging. But Church used it cynically. The painting disappeared. It got lost for one hundred and sixteen years. Then it was found. In some stairwell at a school for bad boys."

"Why not bad girls?" Alice said. She was listening to a story that wasn't true, maybe, a story that could still be altered. Annabel had told her not to encourage him by believing him.

Sherwin laughed. "Bad girls! They would've torn it apart with their long, painted nails. They would've wanted to see it burn. It was a kind providence that kept it out of the bad girls' school."

"Well, what did the bad boys do to it?"

"They didn't harm it, except for one bad boy who signed it."

"That's nice!" Alice exclaimed. "What happened to him?"

"Forget him, he's dead by now. Don't you want to belong to me?"

Alice took a swallow of her iced tea. It tasted like the smell in Fury's ears. Some of these herbal teas went too far.

The waiter came up. "Impossible to sleep, impossible to stay awake," he said. "You want anything else? A nice mud pie?"

"Maybe my wife does," Sherwin said.

The waiter looked at her, amused. Alice reddened and shook her head.

"Naw, that's it then." Sherwin took a twenty-dollar bill out of his wallet and gave it to the man, who wore white clinging plastic gloves.

"Have a nice remainder of the rest of your life," the waiter said. "Gotta cough." He turned away.

Sherwin shook his head. "The last act begins inauspiciously."

"I don't get this place," Alice said.

"That's because you're a child of the dominant culture."

"I'm nobody's child," Alice said.

"We won't come here anymore."

"Good."

"Sometimes I prefer the haunts of criminals, but sometimes I like to avoid them too."

Alice glanced at the two women. They were sprinkling more sugar on their food just to make sure. Tarzan Zambini had been dismissed.

"No criminals patronize this place," Alice said.

"Just you and me."

"I wish," Alice said fervently.

Outside, a man in harlequin rags was screaming at the empty street, declaiming against a world that cared a great deal less than he imagined.

"Yeah," Sherwin said, "you and me."

Alice nibbled more bread.

"What are you going to do about that tooth?"

"I'm getting an oral implant," she said guiltily.

"You'll be tracked down through your teeth. You won't be able to call your life your own."

"I don't have a Social Security number," Alice said.

"I thought you were going to unhinge things. You don't need perfect teeth for that."

"I never even had a cavity before," Alice said.

"Soon you'll be getting bone-density scans. Time goes by like this." He snapped his long fingers. "But still, I want to confess something to you. I never intended to live this long. You want to cuddle with me in a bathtub?"

It didn't sound wholesome. "Sure," Alice said. "But you don't have a bathtub." She remembered that there was no tub where he lived; instead, a shower stall of that somewhat flexible consistency.

"You know anyone with a tub?" Sherwin lit another cigarette, and his hand shook a little. He'd tried it before. There were names for people like him. Attempters. Parasuicides. He preferred Attempter. If you were successful, you were called a Completer, although they avoided the word *successful*. He'd known guys . . . Larry, a Completer if ever there was one. He'd gone out in the most beautiful leather coat. None of them had known he even owned such a thing. It was unborn calf, or some buttery, ineffable creature. Larry had employed pills and Absolut, and what a presentation their Larry had made: fresh haircut, pedicure, a dash of glitter on his eyelids, Purcell playing over and over on his distinguished audio system. *Cave, Cave, Dominus videt* . . . Larry had actually thought God was watching!

"How about your friend Corvus? She got a tub we could borrow? She's always seemed mystical and pessimistic to me. It's an intriguing combination."

"You and Corvus should never ever meet," Alice said.

"What do you mean? We've met."

"You can't talk to her this way, the way we're talking, this I-love-you stuff, this words-are-just-noise stuff, this bathtub stuff."

"You know to what I allude," Sherwin said. "This is wonderful for me."

"You're kind of like a disease," Alice said sincerely, "an immunizing disease, which I like. But Corvus, no, no, no."

"An immunizing disease," Sherwin said.

"Corvus is . . . I don't want you to talk about Corvus." She stood up. "I want to go."

The horrible waiter reappeared, seemingly transfixed by the sight of them together. Sherwin looked at *The Icebergs* on the way out. There was something on it, Alice had been right, not food itself but the stains of food. The crow's nest really was a nice touch—a little desperate, of course, but Sherwin had always found the shape of a cross to be pleasing. The cross was the symbolic image of death, a death distinguished from mere biological anonymity, a death surrounded by an aura of hope and uncertainty.

Out in the street, the man in the harlequin clothes was screaming, "The word *God* shits some people's minds!"

"The word would be *shut*," Sherwin said to him mildly. "Don't you mean *shuts*?"

Emily Bliss Pickless lived with her mother, whose most recent boyfriend was a man named John Crimmins. They had met at a gun range, where Emily's mother met most of her boyfriends, although she made herself a rule of never double-dipping them. Emily's mother thought this John Crimmins was "darkly intelligent." Emily did not share this opinion, but she didn't mind him. When he wasn't around, she didn't miss him either.

The first thing he told Emily in confidence was that he might be the Son of God. "It's a hypothesis I'm checking out," he said. "I got the same initials, don't I?" He grinned at her. He thought Emily was as dumb as is.

"I could never be the Son of God," Emily said, not caring much.

"No, you couldn't," John Crimmins agreed.

He had many things he didn't like, whole lists of them, and urged Emily to be equally discriminatory in her life, though he warned her against adopting his particulars. Emily didn't like him enough to adopt his particulars. J.C. didn't like mayonnaise, dogs, or beer in cans.

"Why don't you like dogs?" Emily had asked.

"Do you know anything about the Son of God?"

"Not much," Emily admitted.

"He was nailed to a cross of wood and left to die hanging in the air."

"Well, I know that," Emily said. "Everyone knows that." To most people, it was the most compelling part of the story. She also had heard that he had *come back,* been *resurrected,* which she found extremely revolting, repugnant, and impossible.

"What else do you know?" J.C. demanded. He was sitting hunched over the breakfast table watching some cereal turn the milk blue. Her mother was still asleep.

In the first few weeks of their acquaintance, Emily had pretended that she didn't know how to read. She'd ask him what signs said, billboards, magazine covers, newspaper headlines, and the like, and he'd always render them incorrectly. He'd change only one word sometimes but often entirely alter the meaning. They'd amused themselves each in their own way in this manner, for some time. Emily didn't think he'd ever caught on.

"Nothing else," Emily said. "I forget." You had to act dumb around adults, otherwise there was no point in being around them at all.

"When the Son of God died, there wasn't any of him left to bury. Even his bones disappeared. Every last scrap of him vanished. Do you know the whys and wherefores of that?"

Emily shook her head ever so slowly back and forth. Her mother lacked all discrimination when it came to men.

"The dogs took everything. The dogs that were always hanging around crucifixions. The crucified hung there as food for dogs, grim pickings for dogs. The reason the Son of God disappeared from the tomb was that he was never in the tomb, he was in the bellies of dogs. And to this day, you know, a dog will eat you. If you're in a room with a starving dog and you're powerless for some reason or another, he'll eat you."

"Not if he likes you, he won't," Emily offered.

"*Likes* you," J.C. snorted. "Even if he *loves* you, he will."

Emily's mother walked into the kitchen. She looked at Emily as if she didn't know how she had gotten there for an instant, but then she looked pleased. Though her mother loved her dearly, this was a way she often looked at her after the separation of some hours, particularly night's hours. Emily didn't mind it much, feeling like a little flower that had just come up to everyone's surprise.

"Another thing that I don't like," J.C. went on, "is other people's soaps."

"You haven't been using my duck and chick soap, have you?" Emily had her own tinctured soap, which she didn't like using as their distinctive shapes would be blurred if she did. Because of this reluctance, Emily's person was always somewhat soiled. "Mom, don't let him use my soap."

"J.C. wouldn't touch your soap, honey," her mother said, and yawned.

J.C. and Emily watched her yawn hugely. Emily was worried that one day her jaw would lock open like a sprung door, and there they'd be: her mother wouldn't be able to work, and Emily pictured them wandering around in rags, begging, a little veil over her mother's mouth to keep people from pitching coins in and keep the bugs out.

"I hate watching you wake up," J.C. said. "Woke up you're a fine, delightful, good-looking woman, but your waking up is a process I don't believe any man should be subjected to."

Holding her hands in front of her mouth and still yawning, her mother retreated back into the bedroom.

"She should take medicine or something for that," J.C. said.

"So is that the only reason you don't like dogs?"

"Isn't that enough of a reason? I'm telling you something historically accurate. Dogs have been getting away with too much for too long."

"Have you ever bitten anyone?" Emily asked. "I wish I could bite someone whenever I felt like it."

"You look like a biter," J.C. said. "You feel like biting me?"

But Emily demurred.

"Come on, come on." The arm J.C. extended had black hairs growing on it up to the elbow, where they abruptly stopped. "Not everyone would allow you this opportunity."

Emily continued to demur, suspecting that if she did sink her teeth into his arm, he'd swat her across the room and right into the boneyard. She had things to do in this life, although she was unsure as to what they were.

28

W e must see things we do not see now," Nurse Daisy would say off and on throughout the day, "and not see things we see now." Alice was assisting the nurse in the bathing of poor Fred Fallow, who weighed close to 350 pounds and had to be hoisted into the tub via block and tackle. Her duties were to scrub him with a long wandlike stick.

"I always think when I do this," Nurse Daisy said, operating the lift, "of a dolphin being moved to its new home in an aquarium. I saw a picture of it in a magazine once. How you doing there, good boy? How's the warm water feel on the old bottom, Freddie? How's it feel on the old tush?"

Freddie gave a piercing, strangulated cry.

"Upsy, downsy, back and forth, looking good, Freddie," Nurse Daisy crooned as she feathered the gears and swished Freddie back and forth through the water. "Isn't water a remarkable element? It's exempt from getting wet. It's as exempt from getting wet as God is exempt from the passion of love."

"I've heard that," Alice said, working the brush. "The first half anyway, somewhere." Sherwin, probably, who admired exemptions in general.

"I wouldn't be surprised," Nurse Daisy said. "Thoughts are infusorial."

When she had first made the nurse's acquaintance, Alice wondered why she wasn't working in rehabilitation since she was so strong and tireless in exhorting her lumpen charges, but each time Alice assisted her, it became clearer why she wasn't. Nurse Daisy had more grim homilies about a bland, absentminded God than Alice had ever heard, and she poured them enthusiastically into the ears of those without hope. God had the maternal instincts of an alligator in regard to its spawn, was

Nurse Daisy's opinion. By effort and good works ye are not saved. It was hopeless to struggle, hopeless to strive. We live and die like little seeds that come to nothing.

She swished the moaning Freddie back and forth while Alice daubed worriedly at his back with the brush. The nurse was stout and sallow with a melodious voice, and hair the softness of concertina wire. Nurse Daisy did not cohere—her personal characteristics were at once pronounced and very much at odds with one another. There was even the possibility that she actually believed she loved the hapless souls gathered beneath her cold and comfortless wing.

Alice had a little theory about the soul that she was somewhat loath to share, as certain of her theories had been discredited in the past. For example, when Alice was a child, she had believed the sex of a baby was determined by the one who'd tried hardest in the making of love; girls were made by women who *concentrated,* and boys when the woman wasn't quite paying attention. Concerning the soul, she had tentatively concluded that when someone ended up in this waxed and fluorescent way station that was Green Palms, his or her soul was still searching for the treasure meant for it alone. But the search had gone on just a shade too long. The soul didn't know where it was, only that it was in the place where the treasure meant for it alone would never manifest itself. As a tentative conclusion, Alice had to admit this wasn't much, and there were several large issues it didn't address at all. Still, there had to be an explanation as to why some people ended up being tenured to death for so long without being dead.

"Birth is the cause of death," Nurse Daisy liked to say, which is why they didn't allow her to fill out the death certificates either, although she once had scribbled, "The set trap never tires of waiting," and, since no one could decipher her handwriting, it sailed on through.

Nurse Daisy dragged and bobbled Freddie around in the tub. "Makes you feel like a little baby, doesn't it, Freddie? Dawdling and dandling in here with all your life before you, which is why you can't remember it." She turned to Alice, "More suds, dear, please."

Alice hauled in the brush and foamed it up with a bar of Ivory. She had been unsuccessful in her attempts to convince Nurse Daisy to eschew the use of Ivory.

"They test all their products on animals," Alice had told her. "I could provide you with some very disturbing and convincing brochures."

"Ivory soap is the madeleine of our country's innocence," Nurse Daisy said. "No one can resist the evocative smell of Ivory on a bit of clothing or human skin, most exquisitely on bed linen. The smell draws one toward trees and earth, silken dough rising, rain in the early morning. The numbing weight of infrastructure, franchises, seven hundred channels—all is lifted from us with its purifying scent." She fluttered her small, coarse hands Heavenward.

"Ivory soap's parent company is responsible for the death of fifty thousand animals annually," Alice said.

"Our capacity to do evil has nothing to do with our innocence," Nurse Daisy said. "Honestly, dear, sometimes you sound as though you just fell off the turnip truck." She gave Freddie a quick two dunks. "Whoopsie and whoopsie! Peekaboo! Here you are again!"

When Alice had first started coming here, Freddie would say, "I want to go *hoooome,*" just like they all did, but he didn't say it anymore. The management explained to Corvus and Alice that the residents didn't really want to go home, they just wanted things to be the same as they once had been. The distinction had to be made. Home didn't have anything to do with it, they assured Alice and Corvus.

"Where's your friend today?" Nurse Daisy asked.

"Which one?" she said.

"The only one you have. When I was your age, I only had one friend, too. We were girls together."

"She's assisting Nurse Cormac," Alice said.

"Nurse Cormac was born with a wimple. I hate her pious guts. No balls. Timidest person I ever met. Feckless do-gooder. Simpleton." She spoke without excitement.

Alice daubed Freddie unhappily. He was very old, inert, massive, and alive.

"You ever drown anyone doing this?" Alice said.

"Would they allow me to continue if I had?" She reeled Freddie in a bit.

"Well, I don't know," Alice said. "Don't you think he's clean enough now?"

Nurse Daisy pretended to look at a watch on her wrist, although Alice had never seen her wear one. "Still possible for your circle to close today, Freddie. Still some time left in the day for the circle to do the right thing. But the circle closes in its own good time, doesn't it, Freddie? Can't rush your secession into dust, the evaporation of your little droplet above the sea . . ." She had hoisted Freddie up and away from the tub and was keeping him more or less upright on a padded vinyl trolley. "Towels, please, dear," she said to Alice.

With relief, Alice swaddled Freddie up. A soapy smell rose from his pale, globe-shaped head. Innocence. Incomprehension.

"There's my little bunny," Nurse Daisy said.

Someone screamed, and Alice blinked.

"Nothing serious," Nurse Daisy said. "I know my screams."

Alice frowned.

"You think I'm adding a teeny tiny bit to their suffering, don't you?" the nurse said. "But no one consciously suffers here. That's the tragedy of this place. All this remarkably calibrated suffering and not a bit of consciousness involved."

Nurse Daisy dried Freddie and dressed him in a blue sweatshirt ("*Iowa Hawkeyes* today, Freddie"), a diaper and red sweatpants. She regarded her handiwork with a very complicated expression, an expression Nurse Cormac couldn't have achieved if it had been painted on her. She stroked Freddie's vigorously rampant eyebrows flat with her finger. The flesh around her simple gold wedding band was swollen. She should have that thing cut off and enlarged, Alice thought.

"Do you go home to a husband?" Alice inquired. She couldn't imagine.

"I'm sure your own story is far more intriguing. Do you get credits for coming here? Points?"

"I don't think so," Alice said.

"Complicado, our impulses. The tubies, dear, for Freddie's feet."

Alice ripped open a fresh package of tube socks. She knelt and pulled the white socks over the large feet, which were sadly warm, and bloused the sweatpants over them. Secreted beneath his skin just below the breastbone was a battery that kept his weary heart beating wantonly. It had been implanted when the subject of his future was still coming up. A majority of the tenants of Green Palms were so implanted. Nurse Daisy called the apparatus the Devil's little lamb. She called the socks toddling tubies for negotiating the chasm—the chasm, as Alice understood it, being the divide between life and death, although in this place the chasm had shrunk to a crack, even less than a crack, a crease, something technical and maladroit that people here couldn't manage to fall into.

Freddie had a daughter who came to visit, and she was sixty-six, but Alice hadn't seen her for a while.

They wheeled Freddie out of the scrub room into the main corridor, then down to an enclosed patio where they deposited him with three silent, similarly swaddled denizens. The patio faced the arbor where the employee of the month was entitled to park. All month a dented car painted with flowers, childish pansies, and petunias had been parked there. It belonged to Nurse Cormac, who frequently was awarded this honor.

"No daisies, you'll notice," Nurse Daisy said, "a quite conscious omission."

"You ever get to park your car in that slot?" Alice asked.

Nurse Daisy ignored this absurdity, though she did snort softly through her delicate nostrils, another anomaly on her blocky, unbalanced face. The repertoire, if not the mobility, of her features seemed endless.

They both studied the small, optimistic, reliable car. A wooden fish, with which Nurse Cormac was known to be well pleased, carved in the Holy Land, dangled from the rearview mirror. It had been rendered in an abstract rather than classical manner. The only other explanation for the artist's banal vision was that it wasn't a fish at all.

They turned and walked back along the corridor, the smells of supper, creamed, minced, mashed, and pattied, preceding them.

"If we don't take our time about it," Nurse Daisy said, "we can still bathe Hattie." Hattie used to be a beauty from Philadelphia with a lovely voice, but now, wrinkled, mute, and weighing scarcely more than a boom box, she was here. The body was but a foolish thing, Nurse Daisy liked to assure her, nothing but a counterpart, a substitute, a saboteur, a fraud, and a thief. Unremarkably, her words never soothed. If Nurse Cormac was known for assuring everyone she touched with her cool hands that the Lord Jesus would appear to them in the manner that would enable them to see Him most clearly, in the form they would most recognize, a personalized, monogrammed, shaped-to-order savior for the end of each distinctive life, Nurse Daisy tirelessly projected an unambitious unimaginative Death, who showed up wearily and never on time.

A toilet flushed. Someone howled, "I want to go *hoooome.*"

"Do you know what position Freddie used to hold? He was an important man, a good man. It's no secret. Let me tell you. He influenced thousands of lives in this state."

"What difference does it make?" Alice said.

"So you think that reality is the present, is that what you think?"

This was the most remarkable query Alice had ever heard. She wasn't going near this one. But she said, "Reality's no present," something her poppa might say but hadn't to her knowledge. She wondered where Nurse Daisy went after work. She imagined her home to be a thorny, unwelcoming wattle.

"Ho ho," she said. "Very good. Present as in 'gift.' Up for assisting me with Hattie?" She believed that Alice was not among her anonymous accusers, the names of which were legion.

In fact, Alice wasn't one of them, but still the woman wore her out. She blushed and lied. "My friends and I are going to a movie."

"In my day," Nurse Daisy said, "when you went to a movie, just as you were settling in and the lights had gone out, a film personality would appear on the screen appealing for funds for some worthy cause promoting human health or longevity. A disease that required eradication— some part of the Devil's work that needed to be stamped out. Do you believe that disease and death are the Devil's work?"

"I do not."

"The Devil is Jesus' brother. Throw that up to Nurse Cormac sometime, she'll go through the roof. Do you know anything about electricity?"

Charged particles manifesting themselves as attraction and repulsion, Alice thought mechanically, though she knew that for the nurse this explanation would hardly suffice.

"Negative electricity is as good as positive electricity," Nurse Daisy instructed. "It's all electricity."

Alice thought with discomfort about her oftentimes casual use of electrical products.

"Let's return to the movie I was speaking about—or rather, as it was in my day, the pitch before the movie. A film star would appear, and the star would appeal to you directly, look right into your eyes. He would acknowledge your presence before him. And he would talk about this or that disease or viral calamity or genetic injustice and his words would be interspersed with the images of all manner of humankind struggling to be well, and he would thank you in advance for opening up your heart. Then the lights would go on, and individuals would pass through the aisles soliciting donations. People would dig into their pockets and purses and give to fight the evil afflicting others. There was something about the lights and the rows upon rows of strangers and the waiting for the movie that would make every person give, not a single one abstaining."

"I would've abstained," Alice said.

"Your quarter would have paid for a monkey, your dime for a rabbit, your nickel for a mouse to help researchers find cures."

"What!" Alice yelped. "You didn't give, did you? You left the movie in protest, didn't you?"

"You were able to do so much good for a quarter in those days. They made it easier for you than they do today. Today it's harder to make a person feel guilty. You know the man who blew up the building and killed one hundred sixty people? His sister said he's not guilty even if he did do it. His sister said, 'He's not a monster.' She remembered happy times together. They played Clue. On their parents' birthday they would make them breakfast and serve it to them in bed. How did that All-American ritual get started, do you think? It's always seemed quite unwholesome to me. To serve your parents breakfast in bed on their birthdays? I'd bet anything you never did it."

They had reached the nurse's station, where the nurses were chatting about the previous evening, when two residents on the same floor had died within ten minutes.

"That happens so often," one said. "Months go by, then out of the blue, one gets taken. Then another one."

"You think It thinks, Well, as long as I'm *here*," the other nurse said a little giddily. She was regarding a plate of cookies as though it were all a matter of selection when clearly it was not, the cookies being identical as far as Alice could tell, round and brown with colored sprinkles. They looked desperate, as if baked by someone in despair. Most of the gifts or goods in Green Palms exhibited that aura. When the nurse finally selected one, she had to move others to get at it. She took her first bite just as wizened Wilson Greer II rolled up in his wheelchair.

"Is that the *balut*, ladies? Share the *balut*, for Christ's sweet sakes! No hoarding!" He extended bony fingers toward the plate. Wilson had it in his head that any treat people gathered around was unhatched duck embryos still in the shell, something he'd discovered in the Philippines prior to becoming a guest of the emperor and participating in the Bataan Death March. There wasn't anyone on the floor who didn't associate water being sucked down a drain with Wilson's aural memory of the sound of his best friend and fellow officer Colonel Rodney Wren being bayoneted on the road. There wasn't anyone who had been around Wilson more than five minutes who didn't have the catchy ditty

> *Here's to the Battling Bastards of Bataan*
> *No poppa, no momma, no Uncle Sam*
> *No aunts, no sisters, no cousins, no nieces*
> *No rifles, no guns or artillery pieces*
> *And nobody gives a damn . . .*

rollicking around their brains, insistent as any show tune.

"You're not eating that correctly," the hoary warrior told the nurse. "You have to make a little hole in it, suck out the broth, then peel the shell slowww-ly and eat the yolk and the chick. It's best before the beak and feathers appear, but sometimes you can't be choosy, you know?"

People began to drift away. "You call yourselves *balut*?" Wilson said to the cookies. "You're no good!"

Alice palmed three cookies off the plate and attempted to swallow them quietly.

"You know they've committed psychosurgery on me," Wilson said. "They buried sensitive electrodes deep within my brain, which allows my brain waves to be sent via a two-way radio to a central computer.

Whenever I have an urge they consider inappropriate, the computer sends back a message of its own, inhibiting me. The computer blocks my attitude to just about everything. I don't know which way is up. I don't know my ass from my elbow. My inner compass lies dead. My Indian guide has left me."

Alice looked at him helplessly. A nurse pushed against the back of the wheelchair and said, "C'mon, Wilson, din-din time."

"Bitch, cunt, whore," he said. "Filthy phantom animal."

"Goodness," the nurse said cheerfully, running the wheelchair casually into the wall. The jarring silenced him.

Alice understood exactly what he meant about losing his Indian guide. It was the worst thing. They were supposed to stay with you always, but that was only if events went as anticipated, which they seldom did. But an Indian guide would never lead you here unless he was a particularly resentful one. Your *nagual*—your guardian spirit—wouldn't lead you here either.

Corvus was coming out of the library, where the well made their attempts to relate to the unwell. The library was designed to look like a tasteful room in a private club. Light fell warmly from beneath orange shades. There were oils of Montana's mighty Missouri River before the power plants got their hands on it. A few little upper-class knickknacks. Books behind leaded glass. But the leather-looking chairs were actually upholstered in vinyl, so bodily leaks could be wiped off in a jiffy; and beyond the draped windows waited the white ambulances with their silent sirens that never sounded on their passage to the undertaker, that moved softly down the highway, softly, when employed. Alice had seen them go.

"I saw your friend the piano player," Corvus said. "Is he performing in the rec room, do you think, or is he visiting someone?"

Alice didn't want to see Sherwin in this place; in fact, she didn't want to come across him in most places. Someone laid a frail hand on hers. It was a hand belonging to a tiny old man. "What meat mollifies the howl of famished shades?" he said, patting her as though these words were his gift to her. Let her do with them as she wished. Alice had been in Green Palms long enough to know now that when they said "meat," they didn't mean "meat." Even a month ago, if the tiny old man had come up to her and asked, "What meat mollifies the howl of famished shades?" she would've recused herself on the basis of her vegetarianism, but no more. Words didn't even mean their opposite here—they could mean anything. The tiny old man shuffled away.

The rec room was near a long windowless area with a door at either end. Alice looked in the first door and saw nothing, just the fish tank with its glittering grottos. The fish looked as though they didn't know what they were doing here either.

She walked down the corridor, past the wall covered with children's drawings. Alice believed that encouraging young children in the arts gave them the false assurance of interpretation. Their artwork was forever being displayed at Green Palms, although the children themselves rarely made an appearance. When they did, they were met with bafflement, even hostility, by the residents. Alice looked in the second door.

"Isn't that him?" Corvus asked.

Alice saw no resemblance between the shabby man in the windbreaker and Sherwin, whom she had found so unfathomable and thrilling. This man looked . . . hazy.

"No?" Corvus said. "Well, he's got to be his double-walker then."

You couldn't tell from the double-walker's expression whether he'd been visiting with someone or was just about to. Usually you could tell.

"Call his name," Corvus said. "I bet he'll raise his head and look at you."

"I will *not*," Alice said.

"Call another name and I bet he won't."

The windbreaker was a dreary green that Annabel would probably call *fern, ugh.* He had the demeanor of someone who had to determine every day how to present himself, someone who was holding himself together with the greatest effort, who was exhausted by it and taking a rest from his labors now.

"Absolutely no resemblance," Alice pronounced.

"How would you describe him, then? Describe the differences."

"I wouldn't know where to begin," Alice said. "It just isn't him at all."

"And though to anyone other than yourself the likeness would be quite uncanny, you don't feel drawn to him or touched by him?"

"No!" This reminded Alice of Nurse Daisy's "We must see things we do not see and not see things we do see." It was too much to remember, and she didn't think it was a desirable thing to do anyway. She didn't want to do it, and she didn't want Corvus to do it either. Was this what Corvus was doing? The man in the green windbreaker was no more than a wraith of Sherwin, a visitor here, a stranger. He didn't acknowledge them. He seemed, as they say, lost in thought.

"He's got protuberant eyes. That's supposed to mean a person has a good memory. Does he have a good memory?"

"No, I don't think so. You mean a past? I don't think he has any past at all. Let's go. I don't do as well in this place as you do."

"I spent all afternoon with Merry Mendoza," Corvus said. "Merry Mendoza thought that a fly in the courtyard was her sister Julia come back to life. Not every fly out there was Julia, of course. Merry could differentiate. And could reflect quite unsentimentally on flies in general. It's easier to kill a fly than save it, she told me, because some flies aren't nobody. But still, say you do save a fly, she said. For example, it's inside and it's struggling to get out but the window's shut and it's buzzing against the glass, so you try to catch it between your fingers or, better yet, cup it in your hands because it's not nice between your fingers, it's wet, so you cup it in one hand and open the window with the other and release it and the fly's out there thinking, I want to do something for that person, but then it begins to think, Be realistic, what can you do?"

Alice didn't think it was healthy to discuss flies all afternoon. She studied the children's drawings. Apparently it was a traveling exhibition that had originated in the Wildlife Museum and would continue on, after it had been sufficiently absorbed by the geriatrics, to the state university library. Alice realized that the drawings were meant to depict animals, most of which resembled airplanes or cars. A child named Cedric had printed over a rectangle of dirty white, "The skin under a polar bear is black. Polar bears in fack are individuals of color." Cedric had received an A over a B+ for his efforts, the lesser grade possibly because he had misspelled fact. He had also written a short letter of appreciation to the museum itself. "I really enjoyed all the different animals. I hope you got some more the next time I come." The Wildlife Museum had been erected almost a decade before, and Alice and her little classmates—all then the same age the fawning Cedric was at present—had been given a free tour. She bitterly recalled her docility, her naïveté, her credulity, her utter lack of judgment. In a too-big dress and red cowgirl boots she stood tittering with her group, awed and irreverent at once. She had felt a giddy self-satisfaction, she remembered, looking at the animals.

They were hollow, she'd learned, all the children had learned, utterly hollow. It was possible to make them lighter and lighter, and they were being made lighter and lighter. A child could hold one aloft. Each year through grade school she went back—*Mark your calendar, children!*— but grew suspicious. This hollowness wasn't such a good thing, she decided, this lightness, nor was the darkness behind the drains that had become their eyes. And they were not beautiful, they were not, this way. She felt not duped but a subject of attempted neutralization. They were your other. Guardant. *Nagual.* But you were being taught not to know them, not to recognize them. They were semblances wretched and unassimilatable.

She also remembered an egg. It was in the museum's BIRD OF PARADISE display. It was convivially child-sized, and "What you can do" was printed on it above a small creased hole like an infant's mouth, through which you could drop coins to purchase a hectare of rain forest, or prairie, or marsh and save it from vanishing. Had Alice put her tooth money in? She doubted it.

"Don't forget my aortic valve replacement," a frail man called after them as they left. He was exceedingly frail, even for this place. Of course, no one got replacements for anything after they'd checked into Green Palms. The opportunity for replacement was past.

Corvus headed not toward the green van but toward the little spring where they sometimes watched the animals drink at the end of the day. It was a modest font and modestly it lay upon the earth, a suggestion of water really. Along the path to it, Alice saw a baby's filthy pacifier tipped insouciantly against a flower the name of which she did not know. Vexed, she climbed after the pacifier and kicked it farther. Corvus walked on.

She often went without speaking, but this felt different to Alice. Had she disappointed Corvus, perhaps terminally? *I don't do as well in this place as you do.* Anyplace. No place. She grabbed the skin between her eyes and twisted. Stupid, stupid, she whispered. She wondered what that boy was thinking now. That had been miles away, and she certainly didn't expect to come across him anywhere around here, although she did believe their paths would cross again someday. Boys got over things, even a thing like that. By now the experience probably seemed like a total illusion to him. Alice liked to think that she and Corvus and Annabel would do it again. They would bring justice with no mercy, randomly. It had to be random, otherwise it would seem bourgeois. And it would be just boys and men at first, until they'd perfected the craft. Maybe they'd even grab that Cedric. The first time had been messy, no craft at all. If he had been a girl, she'd be claiming for years to whomever would listen that she hadn't gotten over it, would never get over it. The girl, had she been him, would have nightmares, problems with intimacy, a failure to connect, an inability to express feelings. Boys were better about such things, Alice had to begrudgingly admit.

The day was commencing its delicate dying in the sky. It was still early and therefore skunk time at the spring. The other animals always conceded to the skunk at first, but not forever, just at the beginning; and this, as the skunk comprehended it, deliciously, uniquely once more, was the beginning of the beginning of the night. The girls sat, leaning against the exposed roots of a cottonwood tree. Two mule deer arrived with their preposterous ears. Jackrabbit. Fox. Corvus's silence felt soothing again, and Alice rocked in it a little. The sun slipped away and still they sat in silence. When it was almost too dark to see, they went down the trail they had only recently ascended.

29

Mom, if J.C. moves in here, I'm moving out," Emily said.

"Don't be silly," her mother said. "He's not moving in, he has his own place. He used to live in the country, but now he has a little bungalow in town." She was changing the vacuum cleaner bag, the swollen, filled one dribbling dirt on the floor. Emily thought it would be appropriate for her mother to say, "Don't be silly, you can't move out, you're eight years old. You are my little bunny, my little bear, my little moonslip. You need your mommy to take care of you. You need your mommy to put fresh sheets on the bed, pour you milk, buy you notebooks and pencils and such, buy you new white sneakers. . . ." But her mother said no such thing. She struggled with the vacuum bag, which continued to spill dense gray matter over the already grubby floorboards. Emily had heard that some people, when they died, turned into something like this, bones and all, but she didn't believe it. How could you believe something like that?

"You're supposed to change that when it's no more than two-thirds full," she said. "Otherwise, you'll damage the machine. Stewart, my colleague at school, the one who's retarded and likes to vacuum, he told me that."

"You don't have colleagues, you have classmates," her mother said. "Where does all this shit come from? Take it out to the garbage can for me, Emily."

Emily carried the item out with a measured, exaggerated step. In case anyone was watching, it was best to appear that you were involved in a matter requiring great skill. A single enormous container, much taller than Emily, served the needs of the alley. She never understood why her mother often failed to take in the whole picture—in this case, how could Emily accomplish the task with which she was presented when she was only four feet high?

People weren't supposed to place dangerous materials in the container, but its enormity encouraged laissez-faire. People were not supposed to put batteries in it or pesticides or paints or used oil, but people did, they did. Emily knew her own mother was guilty in that regard. She'd turn her in to the authorities, except she doubted they would know what to do with her. You were supposed to wait! You were supposed to keep your unwanted lifestyle toxins until Amnesty Day, which she'd attended twice in her brief life. Responsible people drove their cars in a solemn procession to an unnaturally smooth, dome-shaped hill out by the interstate highway. Attendants in white plastic suits and red gloves accepted the toxins and placed them in long container trucks. No one smiled. No one said thank you. Somebody once tried to dispose of a newborn baby, but someone else heard it crying and piping in a bag and that had almost been the end of Amnesty Day. You had to be careful what you called things because some people would just take advantage. People were too literal. Someone brought a bald eagle, a bald eagle utterly entire, shot straight through its big yellow eyeballs with an arrow. The eagle didn't cause that much of a fuss, however, whereas some hundred people had come out of the woodwork wanting to adopt the infant. The reason a child was so popular simply because he had been plucked out of a dump eluded Emily.

She placed the bag of vacuumed dust by the great imposing cart's wheels, pretending she was propitiating it. Not that it had ever given her anything, but she couldn't help but have hope in waiting. Her colleagues at school were always telling about the wonderful items they found. One girl, Lucy, had found a parakeet and brought it home, and now it sang and looked at itself in the mirror and had only colored comics on the floor of its cage and everything.

Emily returned to the house with strides as long as her short legs could provide, still highly aware of being observed. Houses only looked empty. They were never empty.

Her mother was noisily banging the vacuum cleaner into corners.

"It doesn't seem to be doing the job, does it?" Emily noted.

Her mother turned it off. "J.C.'s coming over for supper, honey. Try to be nice."

"What are we going to have to eat?"

"Presentation is more important to J.C. than the food itself. Isn't that interesting? When he told me that, I thought: That's an interesting way to deal with the food problem." Emily's mother's archenemy was the recreational calorie.

"So what are we going to have?" Emily asked.

"Something . . . flamboyant," her mother said.

"You're not going to try and masquerade cow again, are you?" Emily said. "You know neither J.C. nor I eat cow. You're always trying to slip me cow. From when I was a little baby."

"You'd never know it was cow," her mother said. "Oh, I'm just kidding. I'm making raspberry chocolate cake."

"I don't think that's adequate for supper," Emily said. "I think I need more nourishment than that."

"You are such an old lady, Emily, honestly."

"I'm not receiving adequate nourishment. I want to be tall—a little over seven feet tall."

"I know you don't care for it when I'm frank, Emily, but you're not going to be tall. Your father wasn't tall. He wasn't stupid, but there was one thing about him and that was that he was short, quite exceedingly short. I'm not saying he was malformed, honey, just short."

Her father, over the years, had gotten progressively smaller. He was shrinking fast, though he'd been holding at jockey size for the last month or so.

"We've got to have more than cake for supper," Emily said.

"Stained-glass faux veal loaf," her mother said. "How does that sound for tonight? Fresh colorful seasonal vegetables providing the stained-glass effect."

Emily knew her gullibility was being tested again and wished her mother would respect her intelligence. Most likely it would just be another bean-and-burrito night from Food for Here and There. Emily would be required to ride down for the burritos, risking her life on a bicycle path dominated by Rollerblading women pushing tricycled hooded strollers containing the next generation, women who would hesitate or veer for no one. Her mother would serve the burritos on plastic plates. Lately she'd been pouring J.C.'s beer into a glass for him and she didn't put the milk carton on the table anymore. That was about it for presentation.

"Mom, do you know bats eat bats sometimes?"

Her mother scratched her on top of the head as though she were a pet. Indeed, though hardly freakish, Emily was about pet size.

"You've got so much sand in your hair! What do you do, just pour it on your head?"

Sometimes she did. Personally, she liked the feel of it.

J.C. arrived in new jeans, baby blue ropers, and a tight snap-button shirt. Emily thought he looked ridiculous.

"Hiya, Pickless," he said, rubbing her head. "Jesus, what you got on your head?"

"Oh, I know . . ." her mother began.

"You want me to wash your head?" J.C. asked.

"No," Emily replied.

"Why, I think that's very nice of J.C.," her mother said. "Why don't you let him wash your hair? You don't have anything else to do."

J.C. washed her hair in the kitchen sink while her mother watched. He was very good at it. The water was the proper temperature, and he didn't use too much soap.

"You got an interesting head," J.C. said. "You should get it read sometime. I couldn't do it, I'll admit. I'm not about to tell you I could when I won't, but there are those who can. You could even shave your head, and you'd still look okay."

Emily kept her own counsel.

Her mother was looking at J.C. admiringly. "This is so nice of you, J.C.," she said.

"I like washing hair," he said. "It was a hard discovery to make, but I made it." He dried her hair roughly and then began to brush it out.

"Don't yank my scalp off," Emily said.

"Not in the kitchen, maybe," her mother said.

"You got any beer?" J.C. asked.

"Oh, I don't!" her mother cried. "I meant to get beer. I'll go get some."

"I guess I should've brought my own," J.C. said sourly.

After Emily's mother drove off, he brushed out Emily's hair as she sat in a lawn chair in the backyard. The brush made its way to the snaggled ends, meeting considerable resistance. A tangled bundle of Emily's hair flew westward. "That just snapped right off," J.C. noted. "You got the hair of an unhealthy person. If you decide not to opt for the shaved skull look, I predict you'll be looking at a wig shortly down the line."

"I don't care," Emily said. "You become what you are."

An hour before sunset, already the mountains were adopting their hooded, secretive glaze. The sky beyond them had the hyacinthine hue of deep Heaven. Emily had never liked this time of day and made considerable effort to find some inane but absorbing pursuit to see her way through it. Something about a sunset demanded an assessment of one's hours. What had she done today? She hadn't even learned how to blow her nose. Her mother had a wish list concerning Emily, and the mechanics of nose blowing had been featured on it for some time. It would be on that disheartening list again tomorrow.

"It sure is going to be a pretty evening," J.C. said.

She grunted.

"You don't take to the end of the day kindly?" J.C. said. "I had a wife once, hated the end of the day. Picked an argument every sunset. The prettier the sunset, the worse she'd get. She'd be spitting spiders. She was okay otherwise, but a pretty sunset would just set her off. I think it was a fear of the passing of time. She resented it."

"Sunsets do kind of bother me," Emily admitted. "You can watch them, but they don't need you. Even when you're not watching them, you know they don't need you."

"If there's one thing that don't require you, it's a sunset," J.C. agreed.

"But you think they do," Emily said, warming to the discussion. "You think you've got to watch them and say, 'Oh, it's so beautiful.'" She'd rather propitiate a Dumpster.

"I was married to that woman for six days," J.C. said. "The worst six days of my life. We were taking our honeymoon in this old seaside house, and each night the sun would go down and bathe us in refulgent glory and she'd start her quarrel. We'd quarrel all night, and in the day we wouldn't speak to one another. We'd read. The house had only one book, and we were both reading it. She'd gotten to it first and so she'd read a chapter, then she'd tear it out and give it to me and then I'd read it. It was about this Japanese doctor who invented the first anesthetic back in 1805 and his wife and his mother were always arguing and their daughter who was around your age dies of a cold and the wife goes blind after she insists that he try out his anesthetic on her instead of all the dogs he'd been experimenting on so she could share in his fame. Dogs were tottering around half dead through the whole goddamn book. They all had names like Mafutsu and Ostugi and Miru, because they were Japanese dogs. Couldn't keep 'em straight."

"Don't tell me any more dog stories," Emily said.

"I vowed never to marry again."

"That's good," Emily said.

He pulled her head sideways with the brush and kept it there. "You don't care for me much, do you? But you'd better get used to me because I'm going to be around. What do you think about that?"

Emily felt that a truthful reply would not be in her best interests.

"I do not know the dog stories to which you refer when you say 'any more.' I never told you any dog stories."

This was more than Emily could bear. "You have," she said.

He yanked her head down farther and she wondered if there was a possibility of it just snapping off. She didn't know how it was attached to her neck in the first place.

"It's not for you to make the judgment," J.C. said, "as to whether you've heard a dog story from me."

Emily tried to think a happy thought. She was driving with her mother toward the mountains. Tarantulas were crossing the road, waving their furry arms, and vultures were roosting in the cardon cactus. All was right with the world. She was drinking sweet syrup from those tiny waxy bottles, then chewing on the wax just this side of being sick.

J.C. hung his face down close to hers. She could smell toothpaste. Then he straightened, pushed her head up again, and resumed brushing. "We all got our dark side," he said. "Sometimes we like to take it out for a walk, sometimes we don't."

Emily would have liked further elucidation on this point, though not from him.

"I could make you like me," J.C. simpered. "It would be easy. Like, all I'd have to suggest to you is that we build a tarantula town together, and I'd have you eating out of the palm of my hand."

Emily was shocked. Could he have had an awareness of her happy thought? Despite herself, she was intrigued. An entire town of tarantulas with different careers and objectives and modes of entertainment? "You would not," she said, comforting herself with the suspicion that he lacked genuine knowledge concerning this tarantula town.

The brush descended and stalled, each time a little farther.

"I had a buddy once worked in a morgue, combing out people's hair. He got a kick out of it, gave them all the bells and whistles, every one."

"What's a morgue?" Emily asked. "Is it like a jail?"

"It sure is!" He sounded so delighted that Emily knew she had erred deeply.

"He doesn't do that anymore, though," J.C. said. "He does something else now. He's late, my buddy is. He doesn't show up anymore. Do you know what it means to be late? If I say 'My late buddy,' you know what that means?"

Emily was silent. J.C. was having a hell of a time. "Whoops," he said, "there goes the brush. All those snags of yours broke it."

Emily put her hand against her head. It felt peculiar, like a piece of slick cloth. She thought it had lost some diameter. Her ears rang a little.

"You don't necessarily look better, but you do look different," J.C. said. "You want to bite me now? I'm giving you another crack at this. You're still not scared of me, are you? You do this to anybody else, and you'd be medicated up to your eyeballs. You'd be wearing a collar that would give you a shock every time you had a freaky thought." J.C. rolled up the sleeve of his shirt.

His arm looked just as unappetizing to Emily as it ever had. She guessed that wanting to be a biter wasn't the same thing as being given the chance to bite.

"You can do anything you want in this world," J.C. said.

"No, you can't," Emily said modestly.

"Why, sure you can. And if you don't you'll never know the consequences. You won't be leading any kind of life at all. Of course, some consequences are better than others."

"You can't do anything you want," she insisted.

"Yes, you can! You just need an authorization card. You know how to read yet?"

"No," Emily said quickly, trying to look aggrieved. She was hoping he'd put his hand on some reading material and pretend he was trying to teach her. His mean-spiritedness in this fascinated her.

"Your mother must be starting to worry about you in that regard." J.C. rolled the sleeve of his shirt down and took a wallet out of his pocket. The wallet was black and worn and folded over on itself, an ugly thing. He paged through some cards before extracting one. "Right here is my authorization to do anything I want."

It was a card from a department store. Apparently if J.C. bought ten items of underwear at different times he'd get an additional item of underwear free. This included the purchase of pajamas. He was six down and had four to go. Someone had used a paper punch to tick off his purchases. "You only get ten permits?" Emily inquired.

"Then you get another card. But it's harder to get authorization for the second card." He looked at her expectantly, then put the card back in his wallet. "You're kind of an inert child, aren't you?" he said. "I'm glad I don't have any kids." He had felt somewhat tenderly toward her a moment ago but was getting more impatient by the instant. "I don't like kids."

"I thought it was dogs you didn't like."

"I got that out of my system," J.C. said. "Now I don't care about them one way or another. I'm in balance regarding dogs."

Her mother returned with the beer, looking flushed and pretty. "Oh, I *hurried*," she said.

J.C. took a ring off his belt loop that had a few keys on it and a tiny bottle opener. He opened one of the bottles and took a long swallow. Then he opened another and handed it to Emily's mother. She smiled at him. "Nature's most perfect food," J.C. said, and took another swallow.

"Have you two had a nice time together?" her mother asked. "Oh, honey, your hair looks marvelous."

"Best I could do with the material at hand," J.C. said.

Emily wandered off into the yard. She crouched down for a thimbleful of sand, and was about to sprinkle it on her head but stopped short, remembering she was already under suspicion for this act.

The yard had big clumps of dead-as-doornail bushes lying all over the place, acting like bushes though they weren't even rooted into the ground anymore. There was that marble she liked to leave there. The tiny perfume bottle to which she always professed delighted surprise. The lizard's perfectly round hole.

Emily patrolled the perimeter. Beyond the chain-link fence, Ruth the Neighbor's yard was perfectly green with grass. Ruth was applying something to it with a machine the shape of a child's doll carriage. There was a drum in it, and the drum rotated and threw out just the proper amount of poison, corrective, simplifier, whatever it was. Ruth wore a paper mask over the lower part of her face. She was balding, and her remaining hair was an unconvincing black. Ruth was the one who took Emily to the Amnesty Days. The next Day was on the autumnal equinox, quite a way in the future, and Ruth thought it was quite the mistake, for most people were suspicious of equinoxes—believing them to be unorthodox, even pagan—and participation might be low. Emily didn't know what pagan was. Possibly she might like to be one. But what she really wanted was to be a triggerman, or a poet. She did not want to work in sales.

She looked at her mother and J.C. together, a discomforting sight, and trying to coax up another happy thought, selected the train one. Trains passed through town four times a day, and Emily would ofttimes bicycle down to see them. There wasn't a station, just a Dairy Queen and a small park practically paved with long red Dairy Queen spoons. Three of the trains would stop and people would get on and off, but the fourth train just tore on past, whistles wailing, and Emily particularly admired this one.

30

Dick and Dinah Webb sat behind their ten-foot cement-block privacy wall having tea. Two fainting goats, an ostrich, a kangaroo, and an assortment of pigs, ducks, and turkeys dabbled and milled around them. At the moment Dinah did not realize she was in Florida. She was in Africa, still puzzling over something a guide had explained to her years ago.

"When elephants can get beneath the bark and into the wood of the baobob tree, it's just like chocolate cake to them. That's what he said. Now, chocolate cake—what could that mean?"

The goats were playing on a little hill that Dick had built for them. Otherwise they showed no sign of being aware of the Webbs' existence.

"He was an idiot," Dick said. "Too smug by half."

"What's the other tree the elephants liked?"

"The speck-boom," Dick said with satisfaction. As far as he was concerned, this was the best part of the day. Their conversations varied but were always ones they'd had before. Once great tourists, they now were pretty much confined to their property because of Dinah's arthritis.

"The branches and stems had the puffy appearance of the arms of a doll," Dinah said.

"Beyond weird," Dick agreed.

"I'd like to have one of those trees. Do you think we could get a seedling or something?"

"A cutting?" Dick said.

"Could we, old sweetness?"

"I'm sure."

"But where would we get the elephants?" Dinah laughed girlishly.

Her gruesomely contorted hands rose a little, then fell back into her lap. Suddenly she wasn't in Africa anymore—the terrifying sunrises, the thick beaks of the birds, the gazelles floating through the air. She had loved the sliver of green in the fierce bone white of the thorn tree. But now she was unwell and in Florida. But where was that? Florida could be anyplace, which had always been one of Florida's problems.

A bell was ringing, which signified a visitor at the gate.

"I hope that's not you-know-who," Dinah said. Louise, a friend, frequently dropped by. She had Parkinson's disease but had money too, and she'd paid thirty thousand dollars to have a fetal-tissue implant. A slender tube had been inserted into Louise's skull and fetal cells dripped onto her brain. She was a big fan of the operation, and it was all she ever wanted to talk about.

"Or it may be Won-Yee," Dick said. "Is this Won-Yee's day?"

Twice a week, a Chinese acupuncturist put needles in Dinah's ankles. This is where the garbage gets taken out, he always said. These are the garbage trucks collecting the garbage. Though she liked the needles, the metaphor was getting on her nerves and giving her shingles. She would give anything for it not to be Won-Yee.

Most likely it was just another passerby complaining about the wall. "Eyesore, eyesore, eyesore" or "If someone comes home one night a little muddled and runs into this he will surely kill himself and you could be sued. It don't matter if you got the permit from the county. You could be sued and sued good" or "When you going to stucco the damn thing?" Usually they just stuffed anonymous messages into the mailbox, but sometimes they rang the bell before disappearing. Many were the objects the outside world tried to lob over the wall as well, but because of its height, most fell backward—to Dick's satisfaction—onto the public way. Still, one of the ducks had been struck on the head with a bottle, and once the kangaroo had almost choked to death when it tried to swallow a small spray can of Slo-Cum.

Dick Webb loved his wall, which had been up almost a year. The footers went down four feet, and maybe for its birthday he would put a lot of jagged colored glass on top. Before the wall, their grassy yard had run neatly trimmed to the curb, and there had been concrete animals instead of live ones. He had constructed them himself, having always worked in the medium, as it was, being a concrete finisher by trade. He loved casting the statuary, stippling, swirling, and molding the lifesize animals to Dinah's specifications. But people would bust them up or cart them off while they were sleeping, so he'd built the wall. The idea had come to him in totality one morning while he sat with his glass of grapefruit juice and his cafard, his life a shade, Dinah weeping at the kitchen sink where she was soaking her poor hands in salt, hands that she believed would surely be the death of her. He saw the wall, the whole concept, and set out to build it at once. The real animals had been Dinah's idea, he couldn't take credit for that. God knows where she got them. People were always excessing animals.

The bell kept jangling shrilly at the gate. Dick hiked up his trousers and headed toward it.

"Don't let it be Won-Yee, dear," Dinah said.

A deputy sheriff was standing there gazing up at the wall. He took off his hat. "Is this the family home of Ray Webb?"

"No," Dick said. What had their boy done now! He must have some syndrome besides his ill health. He was always doing something.

"You are not Mr. Webb *pater*?" the deputy said and frowned. He was just trying it out, that word. In his experience, any word that put more distance between himself and the individual he was dealing with was backup assistance.

"I am not," Dick Webb said.

The deputy put his hat back on again. "Do you have any idea where the Webbs live? I have some unfortunate news for the Webb family."

Dick lowered his voice for added sincerity. "I don't," he said. He wouldn't dream of troubling Dinah with this. For one thing, it would take so long to explain who Ray was—he had never been an easy concept to grasp—and when she did make the connection—her son, her only child, her troubled boy!—she would get upset. He could see her eyes tearing up, her poor hands paddling the air. Unfortunate news. That could very well mean you-know-what, Dick thought. Before long the deputy would return with verification that he was indeed Webb *pater*. He and Dinah would have to leave before that happened, get someone in to take care of the animals, go someplace that couldn't be simulated in the backyard—Antarctica, maybe. They'd take a cruise . . .

"We're renting," Dick said as an afterthought. "Just moved in yesterday."

The deputy looked doubtful. "Why would you want to live behind this thing?"

"Was it Bobby, dear?" Dinah asked when Dick returned. The kangaroo was sitting, as was its wont, with its head in her lap.

"Bobby?" Who was Bobby? Dick felt a little tired. "No, it was Won-Yee."

"Oh my, I just don't feel like having the garbage taken out today."

"It's all right, I sent him away."

"Oh, thank you, dear. You're my precious terror, my old precious terror, that's what you are." She gazed at him fondly.

Got to move on now, Dick thought. Get those tickets. Death is not failure, son! If indeed Death was what the deputy had been implying. Death is but a night between two days. Death is the Radiant Coat. Or perhaps Ray himself had offered the Radiant Coat to someone. You never knew about that boy. Had he once thrown an ax at his mother? No, of course not. It must have slipped from his hands at the kindling stump. Had he cursed him, his own father? No, never.

"Dear?" Dinah said, concerned.

"How about some aurora borealis?" Dick offered. "We'll take a cruise and see the ice shelves calving their icebergs. Dawn at night. Penguins." He might have gone too far with the penguins. They might be in just the opposite place.

"Why, dear," Dinah said, "that would be lovely."

Book
Three

ADMISSION.
You are Here.
Enjoy.

They seem expectant still, though they have already walked within the Riddle, not this day but long before. They walked within the instant that is Death's Riddle, and many moments later were reconstituted here, placed in the hollow liturgical court of this black garden. They roam no wilderness. There is no wilderness. It preceded them into the hands of man.

This is Eden turned hex backwards, where they have been resurrected into an air-conditioned hum. Belief in resurrection was the butt of pagan jest. The difficulties, the logistics of it . . . better to see dust as both more and less than dust and be finished with it. But here, in this place, the work was done hygienically and to scale, though the problem of the soul remains and is all the greater because their life had been their soul and was extinguished with them. Here the heavens are false, as is the very rock. The water is glittering real but slakes no thirst. From an egg (a debated touch)—a large hinged egg not centrally located—come the sounds of the morning when desired and the sounds of the evening when appropriate: the murmurs and cries, the preparation. Over everything, a dimness that does not quite touch them, but hovers instead like those angels who are unable to tell whether they move among the living or the dead.

31

Carter had started thinking of the girls as the Three Fates. He didn't know why this image should have lingered in his mind, except that he was a classical sort of fellow. Contrary to the popular visualization, he had never seen those ladies as decrepit, tottering old crones but as irrational, merciless, impatient maidens. How did they all get along? They seemed so different. One spun, one measured, one cut. The only name of the three he could remember was Atropos, the Inflexible, which was definitely Alice. He thought of his dear Annabel as the spinner—good-hearted, a little unaware of what she was doing—and quiet Corvus as the measuring one. Alice was amusing; she'd be quite the zealot if she survived her adolescence. Corvus was tragic but allowed no gesture of condolence. She was utterly uncommunicative with him, though she did smile pleasantly if cornered. She lived in the protectorate of suffering.

He let all three of them have the run of the house, but they didn't really seem to do anything, other than in his imagination, spin, allot, and snip. What were the *names* of the other two? He should look it up or ask Donald. Donald was such a student. While he was at it, he'd ask him the name of the Furies too, why not? They could look up the information together. He carved a light little image in his mind of Donald's earnest blond head bending over a sourcebook . . . together . . . learning . . . their breaths lightly mingling. . . . Carter shook himself violently and surveyed his surroundings cautiously. No one there. The girls were in the kitchen, burning something; toast, it smelled like. The Furies, also, were three in number, though not so differentiated. The *Dirae*, the Terrible Ones, but they were well meaning in their way, weren't they? They just wanted to set things right. They didn't live on Earth, but they visited it a lot. Like Ginger. He was surprised she hadn't shown up one night with a whip of scorpions. Then he'd know what he was dealing with! An old myth. Irrelevant. Ginger was . . . irrelevant.

No, she wasn't, he thought. He yawned and looked moodily at his large bare feet. He had to get a good night's sleep soon. Take a bath before retiring, Ginger advised. Don't dry off, just climb dripping between the sheets. Your body, attempting to protect itself, will expend energy, making you sleepy. What she wanted, of course, was for him to contract pneumonia.

In late morning, it was one hundred fourteen degrees. What was he doing here? The heat made him long for a cool New England murky. His hair felt recently boiled. He had the groggys as well, most familiar-feeling groggys. Shouldn't drop another touch, really, beginning today. In the kitchen he saw that the girls had cleaned him out of fresh fruits again, except for two pomegranates withering in a wire basket. What was the impulse behind buying these things? In thousands of house-holds pomegranates crouched wizened on counters. Other fruits were all taken, even plums, but pomegranates were always left. There was something shady and unsatisfying and reproachful about them. They weren't provocative like an orange, compassionate like an apple, weren't straightforward like a pear. When he got his shoes on, he was going to toss them out in the desert for the little foxes. Then he saw a note: "Daddy, we made you a fruit shake. It's in the fridge." Carter was touched. It tasted delicious, too. He finished off the entire blenderful and regarded the pomegranates with more equanimity. Let them be what they were. What was the harm?

The girls were outside, lying under a couple of pool umbrellas. The Moirai—Daughters of Night provided with shears, the Destinies who spun the fatal thread. They didn't seem to be conversing with one another. Young, their whole lives before them, or pretty much. Gracious, it looked hot out there! Sometimes he thought that if he could just get through this summer, everything would open up.

Carter emptied ice cubes into a bowl, added water, and immersed a fresh dish towel in it. He carried it into the living room and sat on the sofa, tipping back his head and laying the cold cloth across his eyes. Donald had suggested tapas sex.

He had.

"Tapas!" Carter had cried. He thought they were those small, warm, oily appetizers served in Spanish bars. At least that's what they'd been in the days when he and Ginger were roaming around over there, watching those stupid bullfights, throwing the cushions in indignation, driving fast and gaily through the sharply edged Castilian landscape. He had wanted to go north to Montserrat, where Wagner's genius had placed the Grail, but they had never made it, he couldn't recall why. It hadn't been Ginger's fault, he was almost certain; they hadn't quarreled so much in those days, hadn't disagreed about every last thing, their innocent wishes had been more synchronized. Still, they had never made it to Montserrat, huge rock reared high in the clouds.

Back then, she had called him her stroke oar.

He pushed the cloth through the ice. "What!" he had cried. "Sex tapas?" Evidently—as Donald had quietly explained it—it was a union between two individuals wherein the sex organs are used, only not in a conventional manner. Sexual energy is controlled with *intense* concentration as it rises to a climax, the orgasm is experienced in the *head,* and the sexual fluid is reabsorbed *back* into the system, giving the individual extra energy. Physical desire is conquered in the same instant that it is fulfilled. It sounded quite refined the way Donald described it.

Carter stirred slightly against the cushions. He liked the idea of sex conquering physical desire—inappropriate physical desire, it might be argued—at the same time that it satisfied it. It sounded like a resourceful, streamlined process, not exactly fun but thoughtful and mature.

When Carter had politely inquired if Donald had ever attempted this unconventional sex before, the boy had softly expressed himself in the negative. Not that it mattered, of course, Carter said, but he guessed what he was asking was, if it went badly—well he supposed there was no way it could go *badly* but if it turned out more *conventionally* than they might have wished—would Donald be disappointed, would he think less of himself, less of Carter, less of both of them together for it? Because that would be . . . that would be unfortunate, because Carter was fond of Donald, very fond.

Who was that guy, Carter wondered, sprawled upon the pillows, who spent eternity up to his neck in water, parched with a thirst that could never be assuaged because every time he bent his head to drink, the water fled away leaving the ground all around him parched and dry? He felt a little like that guy. Frustrated.

He was in a mythical state of mind this morning—sinister punishments, great opposing armies clanging around in his head, visions of boyish sport. He groped in the bowl for an ice cube and put it in his mouth. He was willing to give this tapas sex a try, he had told Donald, though maybe they should put it on hold just for the moment. He'd been sober when he said these things just as Donald was leaving for the day, which was only yesterday; it was only when he was alone, which was only last night, that the nice brown drinks kept topping themselves up, producing the debilitation of the moment. He lay there chewing ice, a cool cloth over his eyes, thinking dartingly of Donald—those dazzlingly clean T-shirts he wore, that little pursed gash on his clear face that drew the eye right down into it . . . Carter groaned. They should try it out, but *where*? Not in this house. He could see Ginger capering around as they tried to concentrate. He wondered what it entailed—far more than just hauling out the old hose, he would imagine—but he'd been so excited that he hadn't pressed for details.

"I don't want to be a careerist," Alice said. "A career, no thanks."

"I certainly don't want one either," Annabel said. She was almost out of avocado body butter again, she could scarcely fathom how this had happened. "There's nothing special about not wanting a career." Alice thought she was so idiosyncratic. "Having a career has never preoccupied me. I want to—God—live a little, at the very least."

Corvus lay between them like some creature in hibernation, though not curled. Annabel would protest, and she would protest loudly, if Corvus were lying curled in the classic fetal position of the inarguably depressed. She was spending too much time at Green Palms, that unscrupulous place from which emanated foul tales that just got worse and worse. That poor Mrs. McKenney, who kept a ten-dollar bill under her pillow to tip the girl who would have to wash her up after she died, had been robbed. She checked on that ten-dollar bill a hundred times a day, and someone had managed to swipe it while she was sleeping. It had been an employee, of course, a member of the rotating staff. Everyone kept rotating and rotating, they were there, then they weren't there, then they were back again and you thought there was some schedule to it just before they were gone for good. The only ones who seemed even semipermanent—practically there since inception, which hadn't been all that long, though the residents must have felt it comprised their entire lives—were those two nurses, one of whom was a total fright. Corvus shouldn't involve herself so much in that place. Why didn't anyone ever tell Corvus anything? Like, you must do this or you mustn't do that? Corvus was throwing herself against a wall over at Green Palms. And Annabel thought that no matter how brave you were, if you just kept throwing yourself against a wall, what was the use?

"Corvus," she said, "would you like the last of this body butter?"

Corvus opened her eyes. "No, thanks," she said.

Annabel smiled at her. "It's important to keep your skin moisturized."

Corvus closed her eyes again.

"I don't want to be part of a control group," Alice was saying. "You know, when doctors give people placebos and other people medicine that might help them, I don't think that's ethical. I don't want a placebo, and I don't want the other stuff either. I want to be free."

A hot breeze raised the scalloped edges of the pool umbrellas. It sounded like wavelets lapping far away. Corvus was making it sound like this, against any will she could muster not to: it was the sound of water filling her ears, the memory of the water her mother's friend had offered. An early call to chaos and calamity, to the other side. But she had survived that moment and was now surviving sorrow.

There was something shameful about surviving sorrow. You were corrupted. She was corrupted. She was no good anymore. She was inauthentic, apocryphal. She wanted to be a seeker and to travel further and further. But after sorrow, such traveling is not a climbing but a sinking to a depth leached of light at which you are unfit to endure. And yet you endure there.

"Corvus?"

She didn't open her eyes, just breathed in, breathed out. She'd had her own brief career as a lobbyist in the arcade for the still-living dead. She had wished to restore them to some success. She had talked and talked to them, projecting herself without words. She had clasped their worn, warm hands. They had thought her a fool. She needed to tamp herself down now, tamp herself down, measure out her breaths until they were gone. No one had to know she was doing it.

"Although sometimes people can get better if the placebos are administered in an enthusiastic way," Alice said. "I don't know, it's a complex issue. I don't want to be indifferent to anything, I don't want to think of anything as inevitable."

"Things are inevitable," Annabel said. "Lots of things just are."

"I don't want to be"—Alice wasn't sure about this—"credulous? But maybe I do."

"You've really got us in a state of suspense here." Annabel looked irritably at her stomach—flat, though not so flat as she'd like. Beaded with perspiration and oil, it looked pretty good, she thought, though utterly wasted on present company. She hoped she could hold on to her good skin, not hold on to it literally of course, but an awareness of the importance of proper maintenance, which she had, must surely give her an advantage over girls who didn't give it a second thought. A phone rang. It was never for her. No one even knew she existed up here, out in the desert in this stupid house.

"You can still see the moon," Alice said. "I like it when you can still see the moon in a daytime sky."

Corvus opened her eyes, moved her eyes without moving her head, breathed in, breathed out, tamping herself down into that leached and lightless depth. She saw the moon, almost empty, standing hollow. Her mother's friend had always pointed such a moon out to her. It appears that way because it's carrying the dead, she'd told Corvus in her quick, low, gay voice. The moon is killing itself from carrying so many dead; you can expect to hear something strange when the moon lies like that. How had her mother happened to have as a friend such a Lilith? How had they met? For that matter, how had her parents met? She had never been told. She would never be told now. The hair of our heads will be like clouds when we die, her mother's friend had said, your hair and mine and that of everyone we love and hate. I don't hate anybody, Corvus had said. Like clouds, this woman said, when we become as clouds.

Carter hung up the phone. He and Donald had planned a most satisfactory evening for themselves, although that ambitious union Donald had in mind was still on hold. They were going to hear a string quartet downtown—opera companies never came within miles of this burg—after which they would enjoy a late supper. He felt better. Everything seemed fresher now, even though he was still uncertain about how precisely to proceed. "Should I order cyanide," he sang, "or order champagne?" He should throw another party soon. Get that piano player back.

lice's granny and poppa were looking at a puzzle in the funny papers, a block of wavy, unfocused multicolored lines. They would bring the page close to their faces, then push it slowly back.

"I see it," her poppa said.

"I see it, too," her granny said. "Why don't you try it, Alice?"

Alice studied it, crossing her eyes even. She wanted to be the kind of person who could see things that weren't initially or even necessarily there, wanted the surprise of seeing the other something that was in everything, its hidden nimbus, its romance. "I don't see anything," she said. She felt hot with disappointment, as though in this simple optic failure she had failed the challenge of life.

"You don't see the kayak?" her poppa asked.

"Kayak!" Alice said. "All it is is a kayak?"

"When I was a girl, it was Jesus opening his eyes," her granny admitted. "These big heavy-lidded eyes, and they'd just slide slowly open and bore right into you."

"Didn't have to explain, just proclaim," her poppa said. "That's the way it was in those days."

"Why bother, if it's only a kayak!"

"Don't get so upset, honey. Go get Corvus. See if she can spot the kayak."

"She's sleeping," Alice said.

"That young woman sleeps too much," her granny said. "I wish there was something we could do for her."

"A locked heart is difficult to unlock," her poppa said. "We're giving her shelter for the moment, that's the important thing. Shelter is what she needs right now."

He cleared the table of the Sunday papers, and put out the supper things. They were having tortilla soup and coffee cake tonight. They had their favorites frequently.

"Do you know they're raising pigs now for their organs alone?" her poppa said. "No more bacon or those barbecued ears that Fury likes. They'll be too valuable for that."

"I think Fury buries them directly, to tell you the truth," her granny said.

"Seeing animals as food is so primitive," Alice said.

"That's what they're saying. This is more civilized. Pigs will be bred for hearts and valves adequate for transplanting into needy humankind."

"That is so wicked," Alice said.

"If you needed a kidney," her poppa asked, "would you accept one from a guinea pig just to tide you over?"

"Certainly not," she said.

"A guinea pig kidney wouldn't do Alice any good," her granny protested. "It would be far too small." She was more down to earth than her poppa, who sometimes just liked to stir things up.

"Animal donors are the future," he said. "I can see the first pig on the cover of *Time*. The pig prior to the selfless donation of his heart to the president."

"*Time*, that rag," her granny said. "Well, I think it's unfortunate. What will happen to children's books? What will become of the classics? Remember your favorite, Alice? It was *Charlotte's Web*."

"'No one was with her when she died,'" Alice said, her mouth full of coffee cake.

"What's that?" her granny inquired.

Alice swallowed. "No one was with Charlotte when she died. That's how it ends."

"It couldn't have ended like that, I'm sure," her granny said, troubled. "That must be the next-to-the-last chapter."

"What interests me about this xenograft craze," her poppa persisted, "is that it shows people have found it's enough for them to live in this world. They just want to keep on living. That's where knowledge and the march of science has brought us. Right back to square one." He coughed and tapped his chest with his fist, a piece of cake having gone down the wrong way.

"What is 'xeno'?" Alice asked. "Was that the name of the pig?"

"Xeno, from the Greek. It means 'stranger.' Know your roots and prefixes, and you'll find the world more accessible, Alice."

"There's a lot I don't want to know," she argued. "There's a superfluity of knowledge. Most of it is useless. I choose not to know." She blushed. When she had said something similar to this to Sherwin, he'd said, "You want to turn from civilization into a starlit darkness, don't you, darling?"

"Don't you worry about that C in school," her poppa said. "There's always next year. And I don't want you worrying about that kayak either."

Alice, blushing, ate her soup. A.k.a. Xeno, fiercely ate.

"I prefer news to knowledge," her granny said. "I suppose because I'm getting along."

"Talking about the news—" her poppa began.

"You know what this lady said to me at Green Palms?" Alice said. "She said, 'Talking about tossing puppies back and forth,' as though I'd been talking about tossing puppies back and forth."

Her granny and poppa looked at her. Fury was looking at the wand on the window blind tremble so slightly. He didn't know why it did that.

"What did she say next?" her granny said.

"She didn't say anything next."

"The reason people in those places seldom show resentment or complain about their situation," her poppa said, "is because of a lack of continuity in their thinking."

"Talking about the news," her granny said, "did you hear about the woman in Detroit? Wanted a baby, stole one. Nothing unusual about that. Thing was, it was her girlfriend's baby and the girlfriend hadn't had it yet. Two girlfriends sitting around one night drinking wine and worse, and this woman gets it in her head that she wants that girlfriend's baby and she just carves it right out of her, just scoops it right out like you would a melon, with some implement she found in the kitchen."

"The Motor City," her poppa said.

"It's not called that anymore," her granny said. "Anyway, woman went

back to her own place with the baby, but she got arrested shortly thereafter. It was discovered that the idea hadn't popped into her head suddenly at all, it was premeditated. She had a complete layette she'd
purchased days before. Baby in question found to be perfectly fine."

"I have something to contribute," Alice's poppa said. "Did you hear
about the old gentleman who shot his wife and their aviary of cockatoos,
then entertained some recovering addict who was trying to get her life
back together by going door to door selling some sort of cleaner?"

"What kind of addict?" her granny said.

"Smack, I believe."

"What do you mean, *entertained*?" Alice asked.

"Provided her with a cup of tea. He was just about to do himself
in when the addict knocked on the door to relate her tale of self-
improvement. His name is . . . I can't remember his name. Eighty-six
years of age."

"Poor soul," her granny said.

"Wife was ailing. Old gentleman was ailing. He was afraid that they'd
deteriorate completely and their feathered companions would end up at
the dump."

"That's where they would've ended up, too, if proper arrangements
hadn't been made beforehand. Course, that's where they'll end up
now anyway." Her granny cut them all another sliver of cake. "I bet that
addict hustled right back to the needle after that experience."

"Shot all his loved ones with a rifle right here, in our community. Then
did you hear about the two hunters who shot a man crawling down one
of our mountains? They thought he was a game animal and just blew him
away at dusk, thought he was something else entirely. A case of mistaken
identity. They said that dusk confused them."

"It makes you feel we're all living in some darkened dream," her
granny said.

It was sad when people tried to control the future by killing
everything they cared about, Alice thought. Still, the future was a dangerous place. That's what made it the future. But how could you shoot a
cockatoo with a rifle? That wasn't really appropriate. Her poppa must
have heard that one wrong.

After supper they turned on the television. The best thing about the set, in Alice's opinion, was the panther lamp on top of it. The panther had a little chain around its neck that had engrossed Alice for long minutes as a child. She had fiddled and fiddled with that chain. She wondered what she'd been imagining.

"This is a rerun," her granny announced.

"I haven't seen it before," her poppa said.

"You most certainly have." Her granny tapped the screen. "All these women here, they've eaten their mothers' ashes. That's what they have in common."

They were an earnest assemblage, heavy, for the most part, in big-collared dresses. Some had taken just a taste before the internment, others were gradually consuming the entire box. They cited their mistrust of authority, their desire to take responsibility for their own grief, their determination to wrest control from the middleman.

"It's coming back to me now," her poppa said. "They talk about that pilot in California, at the end of it, the one who was supposed to be scattering ashes over the Pacific at the behest of families and was instead stockpiling them in one of those franchised Cubby-Holes."

"Saving on airplane fuel, I guess," her granny said. "Found two thousand boxes of cremains in one of those storage lockers. Been getting away with it for years."

"That one," her poppa recalled, "two in from the left . . . camera doesn't pay much attention to her, but she's the one who found out she'd been working her way through the wrong ashes after an investigation uncovered gross carelessness at the crematorium."

"It's a rerun," her granny said. "We've seen it all before."

33

What are you reading now?" Ginger asked.

He put the book on the night table and carefully placed on the open pages a heavy strip of leather with his initials embossed upon it. It was a gift from Donald. Carter couldn't imagine how he'd ever marked his place before. It reminded him of a cestus, that leather contrivance Roman boxers used to wear around their hands.

Ginger seemed a little twitchy, the way she used to behave when she had the Smirnoff flu. Surely she couldn't have taken up that business again.

"Reading is so inconsequential, Carter."

"I enjoy it, darling."

"You'll be shocked when you realize exactly how inconsequential."

"I was reading about Darwin and just came across a charming anecdote. When he took his child to the zoo and they looked into the cage of a sleeping hippopotamus, the little boy said, 'Daddy, that bird is dead.'" Carter chuckled.

"And you find that funny?"

Ginger found very few things amusing. People falling, slipping, or sprawling inadvertently used to make her laugh, but that was about it. Once Carter had pitched forward at breakfast in an attempt to avoid dribbling some honey from an English muffin onto his shirt front, an event that had put Ginger in a sparkling mood for the rest of the morning. Had she thought he was having a heart attack? In any case, she'd found it quite funny.

She moistened the tip of her finger with her tongue and smoothed her eyebrows. At least that's what it looked like she was doing. "There's a woman here who saw herself before she died," she said. "Her exact double."

"Really?" Carter said. This sounded rather gossipy, and Ginger had never been one for gossip. Carter did not know if this signified a promising development or not. Was she settling in there?

"Yup," Ginger said. "Her exact double. Rooting through the sale panty bin in an outlet store."

Carter picked up the bookmark, which was lobbed and weighted at both ends. Maybe he'd get Donald a belt for his birthday next month. A belt was a good idea. A belt for one thing, absolutely.

"Don't we look all a-bubble," Ginger snarled. "Thinking of *Donald* again?"

"Jealousy is a base emotion, Ginger, it's not good for you."

"Not good for me! You haven't once thought about what was good for me, ever since I died. You're not even grieving, for godssakes. You didn't even lower the flag back in Connecticut. Not even for one measly month did you lower it."

"Darling," Carter said. "People feel sad, they *grieve,* because when someone they love dies, this person, this loved person, is no longer to be seen. But in our situation, our unusual situation, I do see you. You're very much seen by me, which makes it impossible to give you the grieving that's very much your due." He offered one of his most sincere smiles.

"Don't you feel badly about the flag?"

"You have to be in politics or something, don't you? So I thought."

"You infuriate me."

"It never occurred to me that you would want the flag lowered, Ginger. What do you think about what I just said, darling?"

Ginger said nothing.

He should recite Lucretius to her, a tantalizing punishment. "Cease thy whinings, know no care." You are dead, Ginger, dead! Give up! The intentions of the man's words, exactly. "Nor can one wretched be who hath no being!" Not that she seemed wretched, exactly; she was merely, as in life, making him so. Where was *On the Nature of Things,* anyway? A little book whose dark blue cover was warped a bit from getting tangled up in a damp beach towel once. He was beginning to misplace everything.

"I'm going into the other room," Carter said.

"The other room is crowded," Ginger said. "I believe Annabel's in there with those girlfriends of hers. Girls who haven't enjoyed the advantages Annabel has, Carter. I don't know why you allow her to associate with them."

"You can come along if you'd like," Carter said slyly. She had never shown up outside the bedroom. He'd always attributed her appearance to a certain relaxation of his defenses, those moments of unfixed reverie before sleep that, when she got her teeth in them, morphed into detumescence and dismay.

"You're not going to walk out on me, Carter."

"Come along, then," Carter turned, too quickly perhaps, and suddenly had a dreadful headache. He wondered if he could make it to the door. But with the headache came a quickening sense of urgency about his untenable situation.

"Headache?" Ginger suggested. "Didn't you used to have headaches as a little boy? That gradually increased in frequency and severity until they were pronounced incurable by a number of doctors? And then they went away. Isn't that right?"

"Ginger, you simply have to stop talking for a moment, darling, please," Carter said, crouched in awe before this headache, a Visigoth of a headache, a Cat tractor of a headache, a sucking tornadic funnel of one.

"I'm surprised you weren't asthmatic as well. Like half those teacakes at St. George's."

He couldn't hear her now over the roaring in his head. Then the pain receded, ebbed like a wave sliding back with a slight hiss from the beach it had darkened.

"Couldn't find your bolt-hole for a minute, could you? Always good to know where your bolt-hole is when things get overwhelming, when there seems to be no escape," Ginger said complacently.

What was a *bolt-hole*, for heaven's sake? She was palling about with Australians, Louisiana fisherfolk, and women who went to discount stores for their underwear. If this had been an ordinary party, she would have made Carter take her home long ago. Did Cole Porter and William Blake have their own area or something? He supposed they might. There might be some multisectional partitioning of the Beyond. Why not?

"When you can't find your little bolt-hole," Ginger said, "you can find yourself being ripped apart by unhappy circumstances."

These were, of course, unhappy circumstances, Carter thought. Strange and unhappy and peculiar circumstances.

He opened the door. There was a long carpeted hallway, then the living room, where the three girls lounged. Petals from white roses had fallen prettily over the piano.

"Would you mind helping me find something, girls? I'm looking for a book, a little book."

"Are you sleepwalking, Daddy?" Annabel asked.

"Why no, no. I thought I'd just come out for a small nightcap and ask you girls this question." To ask that they come into the bedroom was probably improper. He should wait until daytime. But Ginger never showed up in the daytime.

He went to the refrigerator and pushed a glass against the ice dispenser's tongue. Radiant ice in long fingers crashed down. He thought of the icicles on the eaves of the buildings at St. George's. Never had there been such splendid icicles. The boys had broken them off and fought with them on frigid winter mornings. There had been some pretty amazing injuries, but they'd laughed them off in the full throat of boyish exuberance. He had been thinking about St. George's a lot lately. He wondered if he should move somewhere where there would be ice again. He missed ice, superior ice. He poured scotch into his glass, and everything became less interesting in many ways.

He returned to the girls. "I can't reach something in my room. I was hoping you could help me."

"You're taller than any of us, though, Daddy," Annabel noted. "Are you sure you're not sleepwalking?"

Her comment seemed strange to him; maybe he didn't need this drink. He swallowed it anyway.

"What were you-all talking about?" he said. "I could hear your voices."

"We were talking about Mommy, Daddy, and how none of us has a mother. I was saying how Mommy used to clean up after my throw-up— I was always throwing up, remember?—and there was a little bronze bell by my bed and Mommy would always come when I rang it and she always let me put out the candles after dinner with one of those little candle snuffers. One was a silver cone and one was a little beehive and I was trying to remember other things because it was my turn. Alice didn't want her turn."

"Well, those are very pleasant things to remember, honey," Carter said. Ginger had never allowed Annabel to put out the candles and in fact hadn't spoken to the child for an entire week when somehow the beehive candle snuffer had found its way into the play yard and Annabel had flattened it with her tricycle. As far as the throw-ups, Carter did recall stuffing a number of towels into the washing machine one winter season, but mostly a psychiatrist had dealt with the situation.

"Would you girls come into my room for a moment?" he said. "Just a moment."

But of course Ginger wasn't there. What had she done to his mind! She'd taken part of it and was gnawing on it like a sandwich. He saw what the girls saw as they looked around the room, his rumpled bed, the scattered books, the empty glass beneath the lamp, the rings the glass had made. The room was decidedly giving the wrong impression.

Beyond the large window a coyote sauntered by with the neighbor's Siamese cat in its jaws. Only Alice saw it.

"What's out there!" Carter exclaimed.

But Alice wouldn't say, for Annabel's sake, although she couldn't conceal her interested approval.

Oh, the stubborn girl, Carter thought.

The coyote paused to rearrange the cat in its jaws, and Alice discreetly pulled the blinds.

"I was thinking of clearing out of this room, cleaning it out," Carter said. "What do you think?"

"Daddy, it's after midnight," Annabel noted. "And you just changed this room around last week."

"I was thinking of doing a little more to it, like tearing it down completely. Just whacking it off from the rest of the house."

"You could put in a wildlife pool," Alice suggested.

"Yes!" Carter said. "Then maybe they'd stop using our pool. Do you think they'd honor the distinction?" Carter was all for making distinctions. If Ginger would just make a distinction or two, principally between the requirements of the dead and the needs of the living . . . but Ginger's mind, or whatever it was, made no distinctions, although a certain sloppiness was occurring in her style, a worrisome blurring of boundaries. She had used the phrase "Your ass is grass" the other evening, for one thing. How could one's ass be grass? One's days, of course, that was another matter entirely. However bibulous Ginger had been before, when she was alive, she had always been viciously articulate. She had always been witty and destructively unique. But he half expected her to scream, "I'm gonna smack your butt!" any evening now, or "Get your butt over here!" like an overextended toddler-laden woman in some shopping mall. It would be sad, really, if Ginger were reduced to screaming "Oh, my God!" over everything.

"A wildlife pool would be a great idea," Alice said. "Just knock this whole room down."

"Daddy, you can't be serious!" Annabel said.

The girls stood around him, a puzzled triad. The Three Fates plying their ghastly shears, although only one did that. Atropos . . . Atropos . . . What were the others named? Klotho! He was cheered to remember. Klotho. But on the last one he still drew a blank.

"So many books in here," Corvus mused.

"Yes, I like to read," Carter said. "Sometimes I read all night. Please, take any you'd like."

But of course she wouldn't. The girl wanted nothing, he could see it in her eyes. It must be fearful to want nothing; it wasn't as fulfilling as it sounded. She must feel sickeningly hobbled all the time. Yet she didn't look anxious, any more than she looked indifferent.

"What can't you reach, Daddy?" Annabel said.

The liquor had been spreading nicely through Carter, but it had now—and he couldn't pretend otherwise—stopped. He continued to watch Corvus as though she were about to do something startling or inspirational. He realized he was holding his breath, then began thinking of Ginger again. They say that with people who die suddenly, you should

tell them right away they're dead or there'll be trouble and misunder-
standings on both sides. But he had apprised Ginger of the fact immediately, he was sure of it. Oh, that dreadful night, they'd both been tanked,
and after the accident there had been all this discussion about the
restaurant having dumped grease on the highway in the past, getting rid
of it in the middle of the night, and causing accidents, but none, before
this, fatal. Grease, grease, grease—that's all anyone was talking about
with the ambulance still wailing in the distance. And that stupid sign
pulsating over everything: THEY'RE TOO BIG TO BE SHRIMP. The evening
was preposterous. Really, Carter couldn't blame Ginger for not taking it
seriously.

He was in a sort of trance, during which the girls had discreetly left.
Carter felt shaken. It was as though he had invited them all in to watch
him be sick. He feared he would no longer enjoy quite the same stature
in the house, that of the carefree but intelligent and reliable adult, someone who could be expected to be reading sensibly and artfully in his
room at night yet could nevertheless be counted on should an emergency arise, someone who knew how to spend money and still had a
future. Of course there had been the deer-in-the-swimming-pool incident, but that had been an exceptional evening. His liver hurt.

He went into the bathroom and shaved carefully. By now it was after
two o'clock. The hours between two and dawn were like a gift that only a
few unwrapped, a puzzling, luminous gift. He pushed the pillows up
against the headboard, lay down, and stared straight ahead. What did
those girls do all night? He should know, he should be more responsible,
offer more guidance, but he was just a drunk widower in love with a yard
boy. He got up and pulled the blinds back. The dark shuddered, as
though he'd interrupted it.

He got back into bed. He wished he could write or paint, that he possessed some small talent. To race through the night with a pen! But writing makes everything clearer and worse at once, that is, when it wasn't
making everything appear worse without clarifying it. That was the problem with writing.

All was quiet. There was no Ginger, not even a pneumatic one. Isn't
that the way Paul suggests the dead are resurrected? Pneumatically?
The thought of Ginger being pumped up by the whispering breath of a

caring supreme being discouraged him. What a carnival everything was, one big lurid carnival. He sighed and turned on the television. "I'm going to kill you," one half-naked person was saying to another, "but I'll refrain from eating you because of your rank." They seemed to be Druids, meeting in some sacred grove. But did Druids talk like that? He was certain Ginger was doing something to his television. The magnetism of inharmony. He turned everything off and gazed fretfully into the dark.

34

The Wildlife Museum had been built around the same time as Green Palms by a man named Stumpp, who had shot more than a thousand big game animals and now wanted to share some of the more magnificent specimens with the general public in exchange for an enormous tax write-off. They were all Stumpp's animals, brought down by his own plump hand in Africa and Alaska back when those places were truly their selves. Africa at this point in time particularly broke Stumpp's heart, crawling with people as it was. All those scrawny humans crouching in the dust. He wouldn't go to Africa anymore. Let them have what was left; he'd partaken of it when it had been glorious. Stumpp wasn't one of those trophy hunters who went on and on anecdotally about the beasts he'd shot. He couldn't recall each and every incident, not even most of them, but he felt warmly toward all his animals. None of them had given him any problems, not like some of the humans in the cities over there, who would just as soon cut your throat if you didn't give them coins for whatever nonsense they were offering you— nails or screws or Chiclets or the like.

The Wildlife Museum was built to resemble Harlech Castle in Wales. Its original design had included a moat in which Stumpp had planned to place several sharks, but this idea had been scuttled by a candy-assed county commission. But Stumpp was glad he hadn't sued on the sharks' behalf. They would have been alive, for one thing, which would have compromised the integrity of his establishment, and they undoubtedly would've been harassed by the schoolchildren on whom the museum depended for much of its revenue. The kids would have been chucking everything down at those sharks: last year's laptops, trumpets, baseballs. The sharks would've been sitting ducks for those kids. So there was no moat. Instead, in front of the castle, were the typical parking designations, the stenciled collection of circles and lines that in developed countries announced that the place was sacred to the halt and the lame, that while they might be wobbly on their pins and had to cart themselves around in rolling chairs like packages, they still had rights of access and could be interested in things, in this case the dead of other species looking beautiful. The rear of the museum butted up against thirty thousand acres of National Monument land and was all glass and splashily lit, so it was quite conceivable that animals wandering down their trails at night could look in and witness perfection, not that they'd know it, of course.

In fact, Stumpp was a little bored with his museum. The *Hwyl!* was gone. It was stuffing the project down everyone's throat that had been fun. And he was tired of dealing with taxidermists, a vain and surly lot insulted when it was suggested that they were little more than upholsterers. Not one of them had any balls, in his opinion—real balls. They all thought they were artists, yet you couldn't really tell one's work from another's. There was a limit to what was possible in making an animal look alive that wasn't. He was down to one in-house taxidermist now, a mop-up man.

Stumpp was a West Virginia boy, who as far as he was concerned had been born at the age of fourteen, when he got interested in buying and selling gold coins. As he liked to say, and did say to guides and gofers from Mozambique to the Brooks Range, you could spend your life like a damn goat staring out a crooked door through the rain at the mud, or you could spend it some other way. Life was what you made of it or, rather, what you made of your perception of it. Stumpp had dumped gold early and been equally prescient in the timing of his other interests and acquisitions. Most recently, with minor effort, he was doing extremely well in the arenas of gene research and embryo cryopreservation. Shooting megafauna had always been just for relaxation.

But he hadn't been able to relax lately, and it was beginning to trouble him, as was the smell of shit he was detecting everywhere—not strong, but faintly pervasive. Ignoring it took effort, exhaustive effort of an intense mental sort. Did he have to become a goddamn yogi to escape the smell of shit? Nobody else smelled it, and he'd stopped asking. Not that it was a conversation stopper. Stumpp found that in good bars, hotel bars, say, where a martini cost ten dollars and arrived in a glass with the surface diameter of a goldfish bowl, people would accept this observation convivially, women in particular. Stumpp had a lot of respect for women and judged them to be more perspicacious than men.

"I can't believe a man like you is having this . . . ahh, problem," his last redhead said. "You seem *radioactive* with belief in yourself, which I find very attractive."

But it had been a while since his last redhead, since he'd been flattered by any beautiful woman. These days were different days. There was something technical about them, undistinctive. You couldn't tell the scientists from the vandals. You could order viruses through the mail—pathogens, toxins, what have you. A clever schoolchild could wipe out all the bees in a meadow during recess. They were breeding rhinos with no horns to make them less desirable. Couldn't even get your goddamn rhino anymore. One of the companies he'd invested in was churning out genetically identical sheep. He stood to make millions, but what sort of real pleasure could be wrested from making money off genetically identical sheep? Where were bravery and singularity and radioactive charisma? Ever since the completion of the museum, Stumpp had felt himself in decline. It was as though he were descending some kind of goddamned terraced path with the smell of shit on a rising wind at his back. For it was at his back, giving lie to the sentimental saw that a wind at one's back was to one's advantage. The way Stumpp felt it, the wind was serving the interests of those yet unborn. Sometimes he even imagined it speaking, in the manner of an obnoxious junior high school coach: "Let's give everyone a chance here, let's allow everyone a crack at it." . . . He should probably pull his money out of all that human egg research. But his money was making so much money. A tough call, money or mental health. Investing in the future had its psychological drawbacks. His money had even spread into oocyte banking. Eggs were being harvested from aborted fetuses. It was getting a little out of hand, those crazy scientists horsing around and having more fun than they had at Alamogordo, supercooling this and flash-freezing that. The lights go out these days, some power grid fails, and it's not just your digital clock that gets scrambled and your freezer food that needs to be tossed, you could lose whole families, potential waiting families, nonexistent, sure, in theory, but with every right to exist. Everything that didn't exist had the right to, was the new thinking—made an end run around the ethicists with that one—and although such notions would make money, particularly if you got in on the ground floor, Stumpp was ego sophisticated enough to see trouble ahead. Stumpp's own parents (gone now) had been unexceptional in the extreme, but at least they'd had the grace to get him in the proper way. "It was in a rowboat, Stumppie," his mother said. "I knew it at the time. It was like BINGO . . . my body knew." At least they'd had the happiness of the old thrust and heave, the unexpected yaw. But these days it was all assisted fertilization, micromanipulation, people in different rooms. The joys of sex were irrelevant in the present climate, or so it seemed to Stumpp. His own old bean hadn't seen much action lately.

The egg business was driving him crazy. He was thinking too much about it. He'd pull out of eggs. See if that tempered the wind at his back.

Sometimes he'd come to the museum of an evening, entering through the gift shop with all its trinkets. Signs of the Wild, ossified turds (utterly without odor), did well here—the kids loved them, but they'd get the shock of their lives if they tried shoplifting them. The whole shop was wired, everything had to go through the scanner. Little bags of sand— Own a Piece of the Sahara, Own a Piece of the Sonoran Desert—little cheesy books on habitat, videos of animals dangerous to man, tapes of sounds, night sounds, prerain sounds, postrain sounds, everything was tacked. Absolutely nothing could be taken without paying for the damn thing.

Stumpp disliked the gift shop. He'd never bought a gift for anyone in his life; it was one of his remarkable features. But it was necessary to pass through his gift shop, which he would do, scowling, in order to get into the Wildebeest Lounge, where he would mix himself a martini before entering the Great Hall to see his old friends, the animals.

The bears and big cats were in one room. Cheetahs by the baker's dozen. No biggie, that. Common as pins now that the secret of their breeding code had been cracked. Takes two males to impregnate. Interesting, but not supremely interesting. It was their nonretractable claws that were sort of spellbinding. In another room, horn phantasmagoria. He had bagged them all—spiraled, lyre-shaped, ringed, triangular, corkscrew—but wished he'd never mounted just the heads. Those medallion things, he detested them; he might as well be some woman collecting plates. He was going to close off the damn head room.

There were eight rooms in all. Stumpp sometimes worried about the layout. Had a couple of okapi, the whole little family, weird ruminants. Moose, reindeer, should they be together? You could drive yourself crazy. The giraffes seemed to do well in corners, reaching out for twigs. Stumpp kept habitat replications to a minimum. Fake browse had no place here; he wanted to keep it dignified and simple. An atmosphere of limpid concordance. He gazed up at a giraffe. He had loved shooting them. There was nothing like the way they galloped and crashed, but as trophies they left something to be desired. They looked so mild and coquettish—those eyelashes!—and this one had been redesigned, with fourteen inches of tongue extended. To those of a moronic bent it might seem a little lewd. He didn't want people snickering at these animals and had directed his employees to throw the bastards out if they were caught at it. As well as wanting an attitude of limpid concordance emanating from the splendid corpses, Stumpp demanded a churchly respect, no matter how hypocritical, from the paying customer. He himself had never laughed at an animal's predicament, which had been, primarily, facing death at his hands. He'd never gotten a kick out of the deep death moans, the blood-choked sighs. On one safari he was driven almost to homicide by the habit of one of his companions, a urologist from Denver, who put his hand palm open on the side of his head, indicating "night-night, go to sleep" every time he brought an animal down. The urologist never, in an entire month, made a clean, instantaneous kill. At the end he was just potting hyenas to watch them tear out and gag down their own intestines. Stumpp later heard the stupid fart had been killed piloting an ultralight back home in the Mile High City. Night-night, thought Stumpp.

He had lost himself for a moment in the cinnamon-colored spots of his giraffe; there was true depth in those spots, they had in fact the potential of real sinkholes. He moved on to the elephant room. Here he'd gone to dramatic extremes, trying to do his best by the old girl who was his centerpiece and whom, he would admit to no one, he somewhat regretted having taken out. Matriarchs held the memory of the family, years and years of it in that small but heavily convoluted brain. The bulls were just all flesh and bluster; it was the succession of mothers and daughters who led the herd. The oldest cows knew time's history. They remembered Africa, the breadth of it, and were the sources of imparted knowledge. Once the guns erased them, the ones who remained could know only less, always less. There was that much less of Africa. The young ones knew—what? Boundaries, quibbling, quotas. Each one needed three hundred pounds of food a day and sixty gallons of water. Sixty gallons every day in a drought-plagued land! They had the capacity to solve problems. What did they think, how did they reason? "I'll cut back to forty, and perhaps I won't be culled"? "I mustn't get moody, or I'll be considered a rogue"? The youngsters now knew almost nothing in their shrunken Africa. Couldn't walk thirty miles without running into some piss-poor farmland from which they'd be excised like bugs. Agriculture—worst damn thing to ever happen to the human race. Hoeing and hoarding. Man lost a dimension. Lost all sympathy and sense of magic. Virgil, supposedly a sinless magician, referred to as such. Never cared for Virgil. Too rural, a farmer at heart. Plus a copycat. If Homer hadn't gone before, it would've never occurred to Virgil to be Virgil. Then farming brought all those little mouths to feed into the picture. Little mouths that weren't there before, not so many anyway, not construed as such.

He gazed at the great gone creature before him. Ears like sails, great trunk high. He'd had her redone three times, couldn't get her exactly right. Felt he owed that to her. He'd taken out an encyclopedia here. Still, there had been dozens of other hunters panting at his back, snapping at his heels, who would've done the same, the night-night urologist for instance. There had been a lot of unpleasantness in the bush, but if you were there to kill, some unpleasantness was necessary. It had taken years to put this all together, dozens of safaris. There were some trumpeting bulls and pretty youngsters, one positioned as though walking beneath its mother's belly as was the young ones' preference as long as they were able. It was an exceedingly remarkable setup. He didn't like people coming in here, actually, and often closed it off. The space was navelike, topped with a clerestory, a doxological space. There was a sound as though of the most beautiful music in here, but there wasn't any music; Stumpp had been told it was merely the proximity of the main air-conditioning system. Music an inadequate word in this case. Susurrus of celestial murmurings. How could such a sound be artificial? Many aspects to everything. World a mad orchestra.

Stumpp stood, half a century old, self-made. Had built himself from the ground up. Little Stumppie. Parents loving and good, tentative in all matters. Salt of the earth. Liked warmth and applesauce. Feared water in the cellar and tanks of oxygen on wheels. Dear ones, but never tutelaries. Not as many tutelaries in this world as should be. Nor tutors. The age distrusted instruction. Distrusted instinct. Instinct all atrophied. Adrift in the dark, no better off than a motherless calf. All souls lonely, but what did it matter? Couldn't matter less that all souls were lonely. Was in a soul's nature never to be satisfied until infusion was achieved with all. Price was obliteration, which was unacceptable. Though only on one level; on another level, perfectly okay. The stillness to which all returns, this is reality, objective reality being nothing. No wonder everything so nonsensical. In any case, all speculation and preparation was futile. But resistance was not. Push against those blocked doors, push, push, push. Had suffered share of pain. Broken back once, broken arm, leg, jaw. Scarred and stitched all over. Old war elephant who had never once been surprised by joy.

The air-conditioning continued to murmur away like God's own brook, unaware that it was a mere appliance, albeit a half-a-million-dollar one. Stumpp couldn't look at his elephants anymore. He didn't know why he came in here so much. Was coming in more and more. It hadn't been that long ago that there was meaning for him here, and now it meant less every time. Couldn't be good. He dimmed the lights and locked up, then followed the yellow footprints down the hall to the Wildebeest Lounge. Yellow footprints went to the lounge, blue to the exit, white to the water closet, green to the gift shop, red to the petting menagerie. Ridiculous idea though it had been his own, Stumpp being directionally challenged. No inner logic to the color code, no basis in anything. Still, of no import. Hadn't they gotten all the colors mixed up in some early translation of the *Tibetan Book of the Dead*? Now, there was a blunder. Someone working away on day seven after death or whatever day it was, working at following the red light and red wasn't the right light at all, took them straight to Hell.

Stumpp made another martini in the lounge, then went into the cafeteria and popped a bagel in the toaster oven. Onion, his least favorite. Only onion left. Old people had taken all the sugar packets again, kiddies had lightly unscrewed the tops of all the condiments. He ate his supper hurriedly, keeping all further thoughts at bay, rinsed his glass and plate, set all alarms, and walked out through the blueblack night to his blueblack limousine.

35

W
e went sailing today. It was a lovely day, you would've enjoyed it. A good brisk sail with a following sea."

"Darling?" Carter said.

"Yes?"

"That's impossible." He was going to stress this from now on in his dealings with Ginger.

She crossed one tanned leg over the other. "It was"—she paused—"a ketch. It was not a yawl. Won't ever mix those two up again. I remember asking you and asking you in the past and you never made the distinction clear. She was all polished and bright, and she had a lovely name. Her name was *Revelance*."

"Darling?" Carter said.

"Yes?"

"Don't you mean *Relevance*?"

"No, I do not mean *Relevance*, I mean *Revelance*."

"But she couldn't be named *Revelance*, darling. That would be a mistake. Now, it may very well be a mistake and your recollection quite accurate. The person who painted the name on the stern just got himself too close to the work. The fellow's laboring over one big letter at a time with the utmost care, and he loses, well, not perspective, but the sense of order, and an error is born. I'm trying to put myself in the poor man's shoes, darling."

"What are you talking about?" Ginger said with disgust. "You're not making any sense. You have no grasp of the situation at all. My best friend here is Cherity, are you going to dispute her name as well? You can't even picture this vessel, can you?"

"You said it was a ketch," Carter said dispiritedly. Scarcely out of the gate, and he'd faltered in his reserve.

"Try to picture the vessel with me, Carter."

"No," Carter said.

"Try to picture us all on board."

"No, no," Carter said.

She smiled at him in a friendly fashion, which was not like Ginger at all. The cordiality emanating from her felt almost sticky. She held the smile steadily aloft.

"Getting out on the, ah . . . water, certainly seems to agree with you," Carter said.

"You should come along next time. Always room for one more on the *Revelance*."

Carter winced. He simply could not stand the name. "I don't think I'd be welcome."

"Oh, you would, Carter, you would!" She bent toward him. "Why stay here? This is no place for you. Do you know that the desert is the loneliest land ever to come from God's hand?"

"No, I . . . why, that's very prettily put."

"He said that himself. Didn't know why he even bothered making the damn thing."

"Actually," Carter said, "on further reflection I'd have to disagree. I don't think it's any lonelier than anyplace else."

"You disagree?" Ginger said.

"That is only one of the sometimes many benefits of being alive, as opposed to being dead. When you're dead, as you are, Ginger, you don't have the option of expressing a conflicting point of view."

"You are actually disagreeing with—"

"Plus, when dead, I suppose you're more conscious of which side your bread is buttered on."

"I fail to appreciate the point you're making here, Carter."

She had recovered the use of phrasing, at least. They'd always been known for their educated quarrels. If overheard, people would say, "Well, at least it's an educated quarrel."

With a start, he realized it was daytime. Ginger was here at the pinnacle of healthful day, when the arrows of death flew unseen. This new development perturbed him. She had reached some new level of accomplishment or confidence. Daylight was streaming into the room as though to some promised jubilee.

Donald had suggested that Carter simply tell Ginger to *go away*, which just showed how little the wonderful boy knew about women, particularly a woman like Ginger. But Donald insisted that his mother had good luck with this back in Nantucket when there were silverfish in the drawers. *"Go away,"* she'd said firmly to the silverfish, not yelling, and they had. Another suggestion of Donald's, which he'd carried out surreptitiously, was to scatter salt in the corners of the bedroom, but that had not been effective either. He'd had an idea himself but had forgotten it. What had it been? An apathy had overtaken him in the last few days, a numbness, a peculiar weariness. A hair had sprouted from his ear, vigorously long and ugly. His headaches were adopting a schedule of sorts. His feet itched.

There was a knock on the door.

"I'm not leaving," Ginger said.

"Daddy?" Annabel called.

"What do you mean, you're not leaving?"

"I won't leave, and there's nothing you can do to make me, nothing at all. Your crucials are at hand," she added, alarmingly.

"Daddy!" Annabel cried. "A terrible thing has happened."

He flung open the door.

Annabel was holding a crumpled paper napkin in her hand. "She blew her nose in it!" she wailed.

Carter looked at it, dumbfounded. It did look used, not disgustingly so but definitely damp; a paper napkin, after all, fulfilling, perhaps, its destiny.

"I'm sorry," Alice called from somewhere.

"We were in my room," Annabel cried, "and I have this little thing for Mommy there that I've made."

"A thing for Mommy," Carter said. "What kind of thing for Mommy?"

"It wasn't like a *retablo* because I didn't have anything to be thankful for, but it was this little arrangement that helped me think about Mommy. It had this little napkin that was in her purse that night and a lipstick and then that little photo of us together—I cut you out of it,

Daddy, because this is for Mommy—and that silver hairbrush that had been on her bureau, it even had some of her hair in it—"

"Not my hair," Ginger mouthed, shaking her head.

"It was just something I could *dwell* on, and—"

"You shouldn't be dwelling on this, honey," Carter said.

"—they were these meaningful things I'd collected, and Alice knew that. She knew that! And we were in my room and she sneezed and then she grabbed the little napkin right off my arrangement."

"Honey, why don't you sit down while we talk." Carter gestured to the edge of the bed opposite to where Ginger had settled herself.

"I don't want to, Daddy. Daddy, what am I going to do?"

"I never carried paper napkins around in my purse," Ginger said. "What kind of person does she think I was?"

"I don't like it here, Daddy. I don't know what I'm doing here."

"Sit down, honey."

She looked directly at the place where Ginger was, he could swear she did.

"I don't want to sit down. What good would sitting down do?"

"Honey, what would you say if I told you Ginger visits me sometimes, that she comes right into this room. What would you say?"

"Poor Daddy," Annabel said.

Well, that's sensible, Carter thought.

"How do you make it happen, Daddy?"

"I don't know."

"Do you pretend?"

"God, no." Carter pointed. "She's right over there."

Annabel looked disconsolately through the empty space.

"She's developing your chin, Carter," Ginger said, "which is too bad. You could slice a roast with a chin like that."

"You have to be serious sometimes, Daddy."

He had never seen Ginger more incarnate. She was pulsating with an almost animal energy. No longer content with just existence after death, she had to be active as well. That day of sailing—but of course there couldn't have been a day of sailing. Even so, he could picture the good ship *Revelance* borne on the back of a great fish, though surely in Ginger's case the fish part was coincidence.

"Ginger," he said, "your daughter wants to think about you, to make contact, and you're being most inconsiderate, Ginger, by failing to respond. You were never as demonstrative toward Annabel as you could have been, and now's the time."

"Daddy," Annabel cried, wringing the napkin, "don't! You're scaring me."

"She's not very plucky, is she?" Ginger noted. "Not much spunk. Charge wasn't long on spunk either, as I learned to my disappointment."

"She has my chin," Carter said loudly. "You said so yourself."

"Daddy, Daddy," Annabel said.

"Honey, what would you like to say? Maybe this should be our approach."

"Mommy," Annabel said, "if you're there, I don't think you should be."

"That's very good," Carter said, brightening. "Very good, honey."

"Your opinions are laughable," Ginger said, then laughed. Annabel was gravitating toward her. *"Noli me tangere,"* Ginger warned.

"Oh, please," Carter said. "Isn't that overly dramatic?" Still, it probably wouldn't be helpful to actually touch . . . he tugged Annabel back.

"Must you involve everyone you know in our relationship?" Ginger complained. "This is between a man and a woman, you and me, two great antipodes of the universe. Why drag family into it? I'm asking for very little, only you." She made a dramlike space between two fingers, which triggered in Carter the desperate desire for a strong drink.

She was becoming so bold she was practically *thrumming*. She'd show up at his parties next. Surrounding himself with others would soon no longer help. She'd be leaping into his arms, and then no one need bother calling a physician, any coroner would do. And to think that chance had brought them together so many years before, sheer chance. Surely he hadn't been destined for this as a child, small for his age but then suddenly growing, thriving, at St. George's. The open window with its eight-over-eight lights. The huge sills dusted with crumbs for the sparrows. The coldness of his sheets. The clock tower overlooking his world of happy preparation. To persevere and grow! Their inquiries had been ontological in nature. Oh, happy happy years of preparation. But then the preparation stopped.

The phone rang. "Donald!" Carter said. "Listen, I can't talk just now, let me call you back." But after hanging up, he found himself alone. The air felt particularly worn out, depleted. He then recalled what his idea had been: he would abandon this room to Ginger! No more imaginative than throwing a bone to a beast, perhaps, but still. "Yes!" he shouted. He would leave this room, just shut the door and never enter it again. All his favored possessions were collected here, but it was also the place where Ginger and her horrors gathered and pooled. Donald's adjustments hadn't helped. So let Ginger have it, let her muss it up to her heart's content, take scissors to his fox-and-hound tie, scrawl obscenities in his books, smash his favorite whiskey glass into the whirlpool bath, scribble lipstick on his favorite pillow. . . .

Then he had a quick, keen vision of leaving the entire house behind, leaving the country and traveling for a year, maybe more, with Annabel and Donald. He saw the three of them on the cool verandas of mountain haciendas, chatting with other guests in the intoxicatingly dark nights, everyone attractive and world-weary, everyone quietly fascinated with the three of them and their story, which they would never disclose. They would rent villas and walk in the rain. Lease fine apartments filled with light and flowers. There was more than one way to resist, while accommodating, the temptations of a difficult time.

36

Emily was putting some words together. She wanted to protest a summer school excursion she'd been forced to take part in.

"Would you ride your bike down and get our burritos, Emily?" her mother said. "Just tell them to charge it to my account."

J.C. was sprawled on a cheap plastic reclining chair that Emily's mother had purchased especially for his comfort. He wore shorts this simmering day and spritzed himself occasionally with a water bottle her mother had also provided. On his feet he wore sandals from which his massive toes poked rudely.

"Watch this," he whispered to Emily's mother. "Hey, Pickless," he said, taking the key ring from his pocket and removing the smallest of the keys. "Stop by the post office and get my mail. It's Box Forty-two. It's to the left, one row up from the bottom, three over." He pressed the key into her palm.

Emily hadn't opened a post office box for weeks, not since the mother of her colleague Cedric had allowed her to open theirs. Cedric had never forgiven Emily for this and said he'd hate her for the rest of his life—a nasty, snotty, crappy hate, an icy hot hate mean as a hatchet, a fat white hate that would eat slowly at her like the worms in her grandmother's grave. But Emily was not alarmed, for she did not consider Cedric a worthy adversary.

"I knew that would tickle her," J.C. said to her mother. "A little kid's mind is a simple thing to figure."

"It's sad that as one grows older, one's pleasures become more complex," her mother said.

Emily gave her the startled, walleyed look of one unconscionably betrayed. She wondered if it was possible that in the future she and her mother would fail to recognize each other. She ran to her bicycle and rode quickly away, stopping at the post office first. The last time she'd been here, she saw a dachshund wearing a sun hat. Someone said to it, "You're very well turned out today, I see. You must've heard the weather report." But there was no one in the building this time except for a woman and two little girls, who were squabbling over whose turn it was to open their box. The boxes were bronze and ornate with a little square of glass. Emily piously looked at the children, who were whining and carrying on. The mother, or whoever she was, finally chose one and nudged the other back, and the one not selected sat down on the floor, put her head on her knees, and wept.

Emily found J.C.'s box, looked through the glass, and saw there was nothing in it.

The little girl who had inserted the tiny key and opened her box and drawn out some mail, lovely long envelopes and a magazine, looked at Emily smugly as she left, but Emily ignored her. The other girl was still crying bitterly. "There are more things to life than this," Emily would've told them if she spoke to children younger than herself, which she never did.

She picked up the burritos and pedaled home, hoping her mother and J.C. were not developing a desperate passion. Emily wished her mother would just settle down, but the world was just too full of distractions for her. In the last year she had joined the volunteer ambulance corps and taken up firearms instruction. She'd taken courses in bartending and blackjack dealing, all, Emily suspected, in the hope of meeting a desperate passion. Such dilatoriness was wasteful and improvident, Emily felt. You needed to know only one person in life, and that was yourself. You had to find that person and make friends with it if you could and hope it wouldn't turn on you before you had a chance to familiarize yourself with its habits and tear you limb from limb. She wished she could meet the person that was herself instead of all those distracting other people, but maybe that happened later and not when you were eight years old. Her mother said that she wanted to hurry things too much, that she had even hurried her own being born, appearing three weeks before she was supposed to. Emily never tired of hearing this story, which verified her belief that she'd been someone else from the get-go.

She had been born on a glass-bottom boat in the Gulf of California. "I just wanted to get one last little holiday in before my obligations," her mother recounted. Emily loved hearing the story of her appearance and didn't take offense at some of its meaner particulars, such as the demand by certain patrons for a refund, mostly an elderly contingent who undoubtedly saw in Emily's unexpected entry the writing on the wall. The vessel, which was named *The Bliss,* was scrapped shortly afterward, as underwater visibility had been declining for years. The crew was enthusiastic, perhaps even deluded, and kept the glass clean enough; but they were increasingly garrulous about an ecosystem in which the gulf no longer played a part. The paying customer saw not at all what had been promised or inferred, only a vague, grainy drift, an emptiness that with effort might suggest some previous thriving and striving, but all in all a disappointment.

Turning into the alley, Emily saw that something new had been added to the garbage-container vista, a neatly wrapped package that leaned against the great receptacle. It seemed a different caste from ordinary refuse. In many respects it was prerefuse. Emily stopped to look at this extremely inviting parcel. She put the kickstand of her bike down, went over, and picked it up. It was unaddressed and exceptionally light. The wrapping paper was beautifully creased and folded with geometric precision, tied and secured with string. She put it in the basket with the burritos.

J.C. was still taking his ease in the reclining chair.

"Where's my mom?" Emily asked.

"She's changing her dress for supper. You raised in a barn? You should dress nice for supper, even in your own home. Am I the only one who knows simple etiquette around here?"

Emily had the bag of burritos in one hand and the mystery parcel in the other.

"What the hell's that?" J.C. demanded. "You didn't get that out of my box."

"You didn't have anything in your box," Emily said. "I found this."

"You just go around picking up suspicious-looking parcels? If I've ever seen anything in my life that looked more suspicious, I don't know what it would be. You better stand back while I open it."

"Emily," her mother called, "come in and put this zipper back on its track for me."

"I think your mother's putting on a few pounds," J.C. said. "She doesn't want to put on too many more." He took the ring from his belt loop again and pulled out the blade of a knife with this thumbnail. Emily turned from him and walked toward the demands of a stuck zipper with small enthusiasm. She opened the screen door, and as it fell behind her on its coiled spring, almost clipping her heels as it always did, a concise explosion of demiurgical ambition occurred. Emily looked behind her, puzzled. Her mother ran past, her mouth freshly lipsticked, the wide-open back of her dress exposing the prominent vertebrae of her spine. Emily had always found her mother's spine terribly attractive.

The bomb had gone off compactly. J.C. was gripping his lap upon which, it appeared, a whole fistful of bright poppies had fallen. "Oh my God, it blew off Little Wonder," he said. "Holy frigging God."

A peculiar calm descended upon Emily. She stood just out of J.C.'s snatching reach—had he been interested in reaching for her, which was the furthest thing from his mind—and looked at him. It already seemed monotonous, though it had scarcely begun. Would this event lend itself to poetry? She didn't think so. She wasn't even actually sure what had happened.

J.C. peered between his outspread fingers and howled.

"Call the ambulance, Emily!" her mother screamed. "Call the emergency, call 911!" Then she said, "No, I'll do it." She looked at J.C. in an exasperated way and ran into the house.

Emily got a little dirt and sprinkled it on her head, rubbing it in good.

The ambulance arrived and the one who wasn't the driver greeted Emily's mother warmly. "What a coincidence," he said. "Didn't think we'd meet again like this." He pried J.C.'s fingers off his shredded shorts.

"My stuff, my stuff," J.C. mumbled.

"Be calm," the medic said. "We've encountered this before, I can assure you of that. If we can find the damn thing, the docs will be able to sew it back on."

"It's around here somewhere," J.C. whispered.

"That's what I'm saying," the medic said. "I'm sure it is. We'll just get you stabilized, then we'll start looking."

"Couldn't have flown far," J.C. said, his eyes rolling whitely.

The driver started canvassing the yard in a desultory manner, having no patience at all with victims of illegal fireworks. None. Damn thing shouldn't be so hard to find in this yard, which was very cruddily maintained.

"This your husband, Karen?" the medic asked Emily's mother.

"No, no. Just a friend." She smiled at the medic, then thought to reassure J.C. "We're going to start looking for it right now, J.C."

"Should I get a jar, Mom?" Emily said.

Her mother didn't answer. She and the medic were heading off to the ambulance with J.C. strapped to a gurney. The driver was standing meditatively at one of the corners where the fence met itself, then thought better of it. "You got a rest room I could use?" he asked Emily. She nodded and pointed toward the house. Alone, she struck out across the dilapidated terrain. She didn't know what the thing looked like, exactly. She guessed it had rings and was petaled sort of and squashed on top. She'd pieced this conception together from a number of sources. She would recognize it by its being there.

She saw the marble. There was the perfume bottle. Then she saw it, curled and winking on the dust by the lizard's hole. A pretty lizard lived in there, with a big purple fan at its throat. That had to be it, Emily surmised, though it couldn't be the whole thing. It didn't look like it was the whole of anything. Some ants were already investigating it in the way they investigated everything, by crawling all over it. She stuck out her foot and nudged it a little. It looked pretty unexemplary. She nudged it around, then tipped it into the hole and tapped it in. It seemed a little spongy and didn't want to go all the way in, so she ground it in.

Later that night, Emily sat at the foot of her mother's bed, eating from a can of pumpkin pie filling that Ruth the Neighbor, beside herself with excitement, had brought over.

"He was a good man. He was attracted to me. Sometimes we had fun together. Oh, I know it wasn't your fault, honey, I know. Knowing that is the only thing that's keeping me sane right now. The only thing that's keeping everything in perspective."

"It is?" Emily said.

"A bomb," her mother said. "I can't believe, a bomb." She was rubbing cold cream into her cheeks. Emily supposed that because of the seriousness of the exceptional event just past she wasn't using her Facial Flex, a bizarre device that she customarily placed in her mouth for five minutes just before retiring, to combat muscle sag. Emily could tell that her mother wanted more than anything to use it, but out of respect to J.C. and his first night in the hospital she wasn't.

"Do you want me to go away for a while?"

"What a thoughtful suggestion. Maybe. Not far."

"Mom!"

"Then don't say things you don't mean, Emily! I can't even think with you tormenting me like this. I thought you meant going to bed, to sleep. If you can sleep tonight, more power to you."

Both of them were silent, mother and daughter, neither of them thinking much about J.C. but instead of how stimulating and surprising life was. To Emily it felt a little like Christmas Eve.

"A bomb," her mother marveled. "The world has entered our lives." She screwed the lid back hard onto the cold cream. "I know you never thought he hung the moon, honey, but I have needs."

Though Emily wished that she herself had needs, all she could manage was colleagues, which, being as she didn't even want them, didn't come close to resembling needs.

"I'm just afraid that after this, people are going to think we're kind of unwholesome," her mother said. "This must not be made the centerpiece of our lives. I don't want you to think of yourself as being bad or peculiar."

"You mean strange?"

"We mustn't be discouraged, Emily. Did you get a chance to talk to that nice medic today? He's terribly nice. I met him in that class I took. He came in and gave a little slide show on the dangers of not knowing what to do in an emergency. Maybe when things settle down a bit, we'll all go to the movies together."

"I don't like the cinema, Mom, you know I don't."

"Well, then, he and I will just have to go by ourselves, won't we?" her mother said.

Emily finished the pie filling. Her mother continued to speak about the medic, who preferred to be referenced by his last name rather than his first. She said she liked this trait in a man.

Emily assumed that John Crimmins was in the past and was glad of it. Would she be required to send him a get-well card? Her mother looked tired and unhappy and confused but then she reached for the Facial Flex, which was in what she called her jewel box on the bedside table. There were no jewels within, but Emily knew that the device with its tiny rubber bands was special, slowing time's progress on a personal level, her mother having told her as much in a more carefree moment. Her mother slipped the thing into her mouth, arranged her jaws, and sighed.

37

The portion of the dresser that Annabel had made into a little memory square looked bereft now that the paper napkin had left it. That napkin had lent the scene some sincerity. Alice couldn't imagine where that violent sneeze had come from.

She was all right now. For a while she had saved, quite inappropriately, those stupid cigarette butts of Sherwin's. But when they started looking like everyone else's stupid cigarette butts, she threw them away. She couldn't have distinguished them from someone else's if her life depended upon it. Love was funny, the way it came and went. She gnawed her knuckles and looked at the orphaned items on Annabel's blueberry-colored bureau, which now, because of her, seemed unable to transcend their nature. The sad thing was that Annabel had really tried with this, the tackiest notion in the room. Everything else was so tasteful, so perfect, the result of serious, practically pathological consumer coding. This assemblage had perhaps been Annabel's first tentative clumsy baby step toward appreciating something larger—in this case, reductively, death, but with some work maybe something grander, like real life—and Alice had inadvertently, spontaneously messed it up.

Annabel returned and went directly to the bureau. Without a glance at its unevocative surface she pulled open a drawer and took out a beige cashmere sweater. She removed the one she was wearing, the gray one. Rather, it was shale. She didn't have gray. She didn't have beige either. God, *beige*. What were they thinking of back then? Ecru. It was ecru. Changing sweaters always soothed Annabel.

"Daddy thinks Mommy visits him in his room," she said. "He thinks she's in there now."

Alice was relieved she was still speaking to her. "Why doesn't your mother come in here?" she said. "Did you ask her to?"

"She won't see me. I mean, I guess she sees me, but she won't let me see her. I don't think Mommy ever liked me. She was in love with Daddy."

"You weren't one of those awful children who were always asking, 'Who do you love more? Me or Daddy? Me or Mommy?' were you?"

"Maybe," Annabel said. "Maybe I was." Though she had never truly dared. It would have been too horrible to know, and alarming either way.

"Well, you're paying for it now."

"You are incapable of empathy with another human being, aren't you, Alice? You must lack a gene. You're just kind of abnormal. You're like a fifth child or something."

Alice was not offended.

"Your desert is so creepy," Annabel went on. "I don't even like the clouds out here. I think they're creepy too. . . . This would never happen back home."

"The desert has a tradition of very fine clouds," Alice said. "I don't know what you're talking about."

"Why is she here and not here? It's not right. Have you noticed how much weight Daddy's lost? It's like he's being *drained*."

"Why can't your mother just stay around if she wants? What's so awful about that?"

"This is not Latin America," Annabel said coolly.

"What does Latin America have to do with it?"

"In Latin America these things happen, but not here. Didn't you ever have to read any of their novels in school? It's because their culture is oppressed or suppressed or something."

This sweater was coral. And this one was dusk. She had never thought dusk especially flattering, at least with her coloring.

"This is an interesting thing that's happening to you," Alice suggested.

"It's not happening to me at all. It's happening to my mother."

"How does she look?" Alice asked.

"You are so morbid."

"What does your father say? What does she do? Does she say anything? Can you remember what your mother's voice sounds like?"

"Her voice?"

"The last thing you forget is a person's voice. The next-to-last thing is the sound of their footsteps. Their tread."

"Tread? Nobody treads."

"The next-to-the-next last thing is . . ."

"You are not an expert on this, Alice. No one ever died for you. I don't mean died *for* you, of course, that would be preposterous. I mean died in your personal experience. You didn't even know your mother. You're not even entitled to discuss these matters with me, if you want to know the truth. The thing is, if my mother insists on staying here I'll never have my own destiny. What happens to me will still be part of my mother's destiny. That's not natural." Annabel stopped fluffing and stacking her sweaters and paused dramatically in thought, Alice assumed that's what it was, then began determinedly to pick apart the memory square. "Do you want this lipstick?" she asked.

Alice shook her head.

"I don't even think it's Mommy's hair in this brush. I'm remembering she used it to clean the backseat of the car. She hated the backseat and was always worrying about it, like who Daddy had given a ride to. He was always giving rides to all sorts of people, particularly in the rain. She used to spray the backseat with *poison,* practically. And photographs where somebody's cut out, that looks so dumb, you know? I never realized before how stupid that looks." Annabel dumped everything into a wicker wastebasket and placed a piece of stationery over it.

The room had its equilibrium back, its sterile calm.

"I have to find another way to grieve," Annabel said.

"I think you've passed through the grieving process," Alice said. "I think you're in the clear."

"Both of them are crazy, they always were."

"Who?" Alice said cautiously. "Mommy and Daddy?"

"Mommy and Daddy, right. I have to take a nap now. Come back later, okay, much later? You can come back later."

Alice walked a mile down to the intersection where the bus stop was. Annabel was one of those people who would say "We'll get in touch soonest" when they never wanted to see you again. Alice expected to hear those words any day now. She didn't know why she spent so much time at Annabel's house. The house meant something to her, she couldn't get enough of it. It was already like some stupid memory of a happier time, a time that she could look back on as belonging to someone who was not quite Alice yet. She had felt a beat off all summer—just an hour off her real life, a year or two, maybe a few hundred miles. She wished she could be *outside*, in the world, but not of it. Still, being outside was very much like being at the bus-stop intersection where the desert and its flitting birds had been transformed into four identical Jiffy Lubes, one on each corner, none seeming more popular or desirable in terms of patrons than another.

The bus bench was empty, but someone had left a portion of newspaper behind. VOLCANO BURIES 450 IN GUATEMALA, a smallish headline announced discreetly. Alongside the article was a large advertisement for a toenail fungus cure. Didn't people at the newspaper ever think of propriety and balance? Alice irritably stuffed the newspaper into a bulging trash receptacle.

She waited. After a moment or two she realized, realized fully, that she was waiting for the bus. This seemed to her the ugliest folly. She could always use Corvus's truck to visit Annabel, or indeed to go anywhere, but she wanted it available for Corvus. She fervently wished that her friend would want to use the truck, but she was in one of her sleep marathons, rising only to go to Green Palms. She slept lightly with her eyes open, causing Alice to suspect she wasn't sleeping at all but traveling somewhere terrible, following narrow, colored paths to multicolored lakes, all to the sound of jungles burning, waves crashing, mountains collapsing, horrible phenomena leaping out, frightful figures, masses of light—all Bardo bluff and all awful, with the added disadvantage that Corvus was alive while she was experiencing this, not only alive but just sixteen and a half years old. To experience Bardo normally, a person was supposed to be dead. Being dead would give a person some protection from this scary stuff, even though the whole point of the Bardo state, as Alice had struggled to understand it, was that it was just as illusory as life's little activities and memories were. Maybe Corvus was just trying to speed things up so that when she did die at a respectable age—thirty, say—she would've done all her Bardo time and could just slip into that thing that had no beginning and no end, which Alice couldn't grasp at all and didn't sound all that fabulous, either. She just wished she could keep Corvus from sleeping so much. When she got home she'd make her eat a Popsicle or something. A Popsicle at the very least.

A bus drew up to the curb, the door opened, and the driver called down, "You going to the Wildlife Museum?"

Alice shrank back. "I certainly am not!"

"It's Appreciate the Variety of World Wildlife Day. They're running special buses. The museum's the only place this baby goes. If you want to go someplace else, you'll have to wait another five minutes."

"I'd like to blow that place up!"

The driver grinned, then took a small camera from his pocket and snapped her picture. "I've received over one thousand dollars by providing the police with tips just on what I overhear on my route." He shut the door, waved, and passed through the light just as it changed from yellow to red.

To make matters worse, Alice had recognized the camera to be a disposable one.

By the time she got home, it was the news hour. Her granny and poppa had their snacks and seltzer arranged on their collapsible TV dinner tables, which had their own little rack to contain them slimly when not in use.

A large airliner had gone down in the Atlantic weeks ago, and they still hadn't found all the bodies. The entire glee club of a small southern college had perished, among others. It just went on and on, the search for bodies. The president was addressing the anxious relatives, and someone was screaming at him, "We want our bodies!"

"They're doing the best they can," Alice's poppa told the TV.

"I went to France with my glee club when I was your age, Alice," her granny said. "Did I ever tell you that?"

"It could've been you on that plane," her poppa said to her granny. "That airplane's destination was France."

Fury looked anxiously at the screen, his muzzle white, his eyes large. He was beginning to develop a distaste for the news. His stomach burbled, his paws hurt, he wanted to scratch and couldn't.

Alice went into the kitchen, removed two Popsicles from the freezer, and peeled back the papers on one, then the other. Both were a thin and watery yellow, a slim bullet shape. She gave one a quick lap and couldn't determine the flavor. Maybe the treats had been in the freezer too long along with the bagged remains of the birds Zipper had assassinated. Poppa was going to bury them when he was up to it, but he was becoming more and more preoccupied with the news, at all hours of the day. His handyman abilities were slowly atrophying. Overwhelming input and feeble output, he'd say, that's my problem now.

He called out, "They executed another of them at the state penitentiary. Strangled an old lady with her Christmas-tree lights. Shot a young mother square in the heart and left her triplets toddling around in her blood."

"Last words?" Alice called. Their last words were sometimes of interest.

"I think they drug them ahead of time to get some of those last words," her granny said. "Dope up that last piece of pie."

"There's that fellow again," her poppa said. "He's getting a lot of coverage."

We want our bodies!

Fury whined. It just came out. He was not one to whine as a rule.

"Don't eat alone in your room, Alice, come out here and eat with us," her granny said.

Corvus really had to return to the normal life of the household, Alice thought. Her granny and poppa had forgotten she was in the house with them.

Corvus is dreaming she's on the island where they'd lived one year. This island could be Heaven, with its wooden walls smelling of lemons, the rugusa roses and blueberry bushes pressing against the windows. There's a stone well outside with a pump handle and a raccoon who knows how to work the handle with his hands. There's a claw-footed tub in the yard filled with pansies. There are old blue bottles on the sills that fill themselves with light. The ponds are full of quahogs and the sea with fish and the sky with crying white birds. The house is on a hill, and old wooden steps morticed into the earth lead down to the beach, where begins a trail of silvered boards that wind through the witchgrass to a strip of hard sand. Then there is the cold, shadow-dappled sea.

Her parents are not there, but that's all right. Though she is still a child, there's no alarming explanation for their absence. If they were there, they might not permit Corvus to go off with the mail lady, and Corvus must, because this is the dream she is dreaming. This is the day she goes off with the mail lady on her rounds, a woman who looks every inch the man, with her khaki uniform, her black glasses, her black watch strap, her jeep. To accompany her is an honor, that's the thinking; she goes everywhere, knows everyone. Her big freckled hand slaps back the raised red flags of the mailboxes and reaches inside. She never looks at what she retrieves, just throws it in her sack, a slumped leather mouth beside her. She's neither happy nor unhappy, the mail lady. They are through picking up all the mail in just a few hours.

"Would you like to see my house?" the mail lady asks. "I have two red squirrels playing cards." Corvus pauses at such length that the woman is then forced to say, "I could give you something cold to drink. I could even make you a sandwich, I suppose, though normally I don't eat lunch."

"I'll look at the squirrels," Corvus says.

They arrive at the house. Seagulls stand one-legged on the roof, each with a drop of red on its bill by which each is known to its young.

There is one small room. A closed door leads elsewhere. Corvus looks at the squirrels, the cards wired clumsily to their long claws. She looks at a sanderling under a bell jar, at something suspended in a bottle. She declines the cold drink.

"I like animals," the mail lady says. "I like having them around me. I like to collect Victorian fantasy, but I don't snap up the truly freaky stuff like some collectors do, two-headed sheep and whatnot."

The mail lady doesn't have many people to talk to, Corvus decides. "Don't you have any real pets?" she asks.

"I don't have the personality for pets," the mail lady says. "I know a lot about myself, and I accept it."

Corvus doesn't believe she knows a thing about herself for she is in a dream and in costume and could go berserk at any instant, as people in dreams and costumes do. Or she could merely blur and fade away. Corvus scratches at a mosquito bite on her shoulder.

"What would you like to do?" the mail lady asks. She has taken off her shoes and belt; her brown shirt hangs over her brown trousers.

"I'd like to see the rest of your house." Corvus thinks the rooms are full of mail, hundreds of undelivered messages.

"There's just one other room," the mail lady says. "My mother's in there on her sickbed. She's very ill. This isn't an intermission, unfortunately. It's her final condition."

"How long has she been in there?"

"Three years."

The door is shut, there is no sound. There is some sort of object back there, Corvus thinks, an object with no meaning left. "Why do you keep her back there?"

"She's my mother. Never think your body's your friend. It's your enemy."

Corvus wets her finger and mops the bleeding bite with it.

"I'll see her if you want," Corvus says. "Do you want me to see her?"

"I didn't invite you here to see her. I invited you to see the squirrels, who I thought you'd enjoy." She appears to find the squirrels terribly congenial, prepared to provide hours of fun. "Look at this one! It can take our picture. I can put my camera between its paws and set the timer, and if we stand right here behind this line we'll be at just the right distance, there won't be parts of us missing."

Corvus can't see the line, which must be faint.

The mail lady is speaking faster and faster, as though she knows her time will soon be up. "There seem to be more girls around than ever," she says. "In my day, an abundance of boys being born meant a war coming. But an outbreak of girls, who knows what that means, something even worse perhaps. . . ."

There are a whirring sound and a blossom of light, but Corvus never sees the picture. It is Alice coming into the room, the sudden light the door's opening brings, and Corvus wakes up.

38

The summer nights were long. Stumpp left the museum shortly after eight one evening and to his astonishment saw a small child walking across the parking lot holding a sign. She had a narrow little face and wild hair and wore overalls, and she paced with the sign held rigidly in front of her.

POEM
Frightened
Unsafe
Grieving
In pursuit
Tracked down
Crying
Visiting
Hiding
They feel sad and unwanted

Emily Bliss Pickless   Grade 4

Stumpp smiled. "Are you Emily Bliss Pickles, Grade Four?"

"It's pronounced Pickless, not Pickles," the child snarled.

"What are you doing out here all by yourself? Where are your"—he hesitated—"guardians?"

She chuckled bitterly.

"Grade Four?" Stumpp went on. "Isn't that nice. And how old does that make you? Eight or nine?"

"A mature eight."

He came a little closer to her.

"Nine-one-one!" the creature screamed. She had the lung power of a diva.

"Oh, for heaven's sakes, I'm not going to harm you."

"You harmed *them*," she said, dipping the sign toward the building.

"You need a telephone to communicate with 911. You need an emergency, as well."

"This is an emergency, this place," the child said.

"The operator will wear you out with questions. She'll want to know your location and the situation. You not only have to know precisely what's occurring, you have to describe it as well. It's far more difficult than you'd think. Help isn't out there just for the asking, you know."

This was the exact moment of sundown and as scheduled, the lights went on in Stumpp's parking lot. "Let me drive you home," he said. "Where do you live?"

The child bared her tiny teeth, drew from the bib pocket of her overalls a pair of scissors, and pointed them at him.

"They're cutting-out scissors," Stumpp said. "They're for paper. They wouldn't do anything except to paper."

She stood no higher than a tabletop, and her hair was remarkably snaggy. Stumpp had never seen anything like it. He was surprised that geese or some damn thing didn't attempt to nest in it. Her eyes were too big for her face and her hands too large for her arms. He wondered if the future would show fast-forward visualizations of embryos, indicate how they'd turn out, their pluses and minuses as human beings, what they'd look like in eight years and so forth. Why not? They'd know everything they dared to know about embryos very shortly. Emily Bliss Pickless probably wouldn't have been given her chance at bat in more modern circumstances, not on the face of it anyway.

"You have a good hand," he said. "That's fine printing."

"I'm picketing this evil place," she said.

"Well, you should be out here during the day. The museum's closed, so your being here couldn't possibly have any effect." Stumpp had an impulse to give her a lifetime pass, she was such a funny little thing. Barnum in his heyday would've plucked her off the street and made her into an attraction.

She shook the sign and scissors at him.

"Do you have other poems?"

"This is what I have to say right here."

"But it's really not relevant to my museum," Stumpp said. "Whatever you're talking about sounds still alive to me. Maybe you were thinking of a zoo. Initially, your poem seems impressive, but upon further study it doesn't stand up. And this word 'visiting' is certainly not the word called for in this poem."

The child seemed unswayed by Stumpp's critical discourse. "I wish you were dead," she said. "How would *you* like to be stuffed?"

"No one would pay to look at me stuffed," Stump replied. "But my animals are beautiful. And you can get up very close to them, much closer than you could otherwise."

In fact, many of Stumpp's trophy animals had been shot at close range. They had seemed . . . disbelieving. That polar bear. Stumpp refused to muse overlong upon the polar bear. Whenever it shambled into his consciousness, it still had the power to mortify him. When you wanted to do a thing properly, that was just the moment when you wanted the process to be over with. You'll do the next one right, something in your mind whispered. There's always a next time, something in your mind said. What was desired, of course, was to hold on to the instant just before. But there was no holding on. Then you were just left with a carcass and a goddamn ringing in the ears.

"Why would I want to get up close to them? They're fake."

"They're not fake," Stumpp said indignantly. "What do you think fake is, anyway?"

"I like to get up close to things I know are there."

Like all of her gender she was semihysterical and somewhat illiterate. Still, there was something deeply irregular about her, and that hair. Did she live in a wind tunnel?

"Do you know Cedric?" Emily asked.

He'd known Cedrics. Mumblers. Sycophants. Vain about their ankles. Large wives. "Do you?" he demanded.

"Cedric's my colleague. He loves this place. He wants to be a sportsman and make conservation possible on a grand scale, just like you."

He certainly had swallowed the line about the museum hook, line, and sinker. It was disappointing when self-justification was so successful.

"Your arms must be getting tired," Stumpp said wearily.

"No, they're not," Emily said, "but I'm putting my scissors back into my pocket." She did so. "You should be ashamed of yourself, appealing to people like Cedric. He's not strong. He's just weak and clingy."

"How old is Cedric? Is he eight as well?"

"An immature eight."

"But little boys catch up," Stumpp said. "And then they leave little girls in the dust."

She seemed unperturbed by this judgment as well. "Cedric's always saying, 'The next time we go, I hope he has more of them.' 'We' as in our class, 'he' as in you, 'them' as in there."

"That's the kind of customer we like," Stumpp said distastefully. This little twit Cedric was uncomfortably familiar. So much in life was similar, remindful of something else. Wanted more more. Because nothing's there. No. Next to nothing, munificently robed. Even worse.

"I presume Cedric's not a friend of yours," Stumpp said.

"I don't have friends," Emily said.

"Ahhh," he said.

"I have to be careful concerning people I don't like. I didn't like someone and I wasn't even concentrating and something bad happened to him. I have to be extremely careful."

"Well, that's very responsible of you," Stumpp said. "Still, I guess I'd better watch out. In case you forget to forget your dislikes, as it were."

"You maybe better had," Emily said. "So do I have your assurance that you'll shut this place down?"

"Shut it down?" Stumpp looked at her tolerantly and shifted his shoulders inside his old oiled hunting jacket. The relationship with his animals was the only true connection he had ever known. He had been the instrument in a grave transaction. The primary instrument. Yet he hated the memories. Memory in man different, not so noble. First memory, first loss. All downhill thereafter. "I love my animals," he said. This felt to him somewhat inadequate.

Emily scowled at him.

"You'd better leave now," Stumpp said. "You're trespassing, you know." He pointed to a small pink bicycle flung down in the middle of the parking lot. It looked ridiculous and certainly seemed incongruous with the likes of Emily Bliss Pickless. "That must be yours."

"It is my vehicle of choice, yes, for the present anyway."

She really was an annoying little runt. Hers would not be a profitable or particularly satisfying life. "What's your favorite wild animal?" he asked. "What's the wildest animal you've ever seen?" He just wanted to needle her. She probably hadn't been anywhere or seen anything.

Emily twirled the sign and after a moment said, "A crow."

"A crow!" Stumpp laughed more loudly than he'd intended. He had shot so many crows, hundred and hundreds in his childhood alone. Ducks were no brighter than a knot of wood, but crows were sort of complex. Oh, those hecatomb days in the ragged swampy burnt-over woods of his youth! He seemed to possess a magic gun and could wander and kill at will in the dear old swamp next to his parents' simple home. And he had discovered something for himself in that lonely skeletal swamp: that it was more fun to wound a crow than to kill it, because then you could hear it calling out to the rest of the flock in an evangelical screech. Young Stumpp had been fascinated by the production an injured crow could make of its situation. Even now the sound remembered sent a lurchy thrill through his belly, the calls from the downed one and the answers from the rest of them, the still whole ones, beating heavily back and forth in the brown sulfurous emissions from the paper companies. He could almost taste the tang of that swampy air right here in his own desert parking lot and hear the calls of the heavily beating flock, sorrowing and apologizing and making plans for some other time. Time. He realized that crows had always reminded him of time, dark time. He gazed at the backs of his hands, at the plummy dark repellent veins.

"You're very misguided," Stumpp said.

"If you're kind to a crow, you'll receive a gift," the child said.

"I wouldn't want a gift from a crow," he said loudly. "God knows what you'd be getting. I'd say, 'No thanks, you black bugger.' "

"That's racist specieism," Emily said with some difficulty.

Stumpp looked at her, alarmed. "You've lost your childhood, haven't you? Smash-and-trash bastards have stolen it. Left-wing vegetarian freaks." Once more he was attacked by the impulse to snatch her up, take her under his wing as it were.

In his remembered swamp he once saw a flock of crows attack and kill one of their own. He didn't have his gun that day—it had been taken away as punishment for some failure on his part that he'd forgotten but that was undoubtedly hygienic or academic—and, idly wandering, he had come across the drama in some broken oaks. The attacked crow had submitted to them, hadn't tried to flee, and after not too long a time— young Stumpp being witness from start to finish—the torn, bloody, practically decapitated crow had fallen, and the muttering flock had vanished into the haze like black stones cast into water. What a judgment that had been! A judgment to fit a great crime, made by great mad wheeling clerics, a force, an incomprehensible damning intelligence. A formal sentencing made in the ruined air over a rotting landscape. His happy acts of extermination seemed but a happy game compared to this.

He looked at his old wattled hands and stuffed them into his pockets.

The child had walked over to the bicycle and was struggling to right it. "On further consideration, you shouldn't be permitted to just pedal off," Stumpp said. "It's getting dark, it's late."

"I've gone everywhere on this bicycle," Emily said, "though it's true I don't like it much. I'm not sentimental about it or anything. It's functional." She looked at it impassively. "Seven thousand miles," she said.

"Certainly not!" Stumpp exclaimed. "Impossible!"

"I've been around," Emily said.

"But I've never seen you around. And I know this city well. And I've never seen you in the museum, either, with your *colleagues*." Surely he would have remarked upon this phenomenon to himself, this phenomenon in passing.

"Do you have a mother?" Emily asked. She was on the bicycle, moving it forward a rotation or two, then backward, barely maintaining a balance. It made him nervous looking at her. She didn't look as though she knew how to ride at all.

"Of course I did," Stumpp said.

"Did she ever want you to pretend you were retarded so she could jump a line, say, at the bank or the grocery store?"

"What?"

"It's fun. You get to whirl, you get to gibber, I was just wondering if we had anything in common."

"She sounds unfit, your mother."

"She just doesn't like lines. Hates 'em."

A truck tore by on the road above them, its immense length rimmed in lights, with a cargo of acids or blood or veal calves. A cargo of caskets or pirated videos and perfumes, of those dolls that were the technological sensation of the coming season, that would spit at a child if their circuitry determined that not enough attention was being paid to it. The driver was smoking, tuned in to the libertarian station, half asleep.

"You'll be crushed out there," Stumpp said. "I'm driving you home tonight. Hate me if you wish." He grasped the handlebars and began towing her toward his limo. The sign almost clipped him on the head. That word "Visiting" really galled him. "Steady there," he said.

The doors floated softly open. Emily placed the sign inside and threw her faithful bicycle in without ceremony. "Where's the driver?"

"I like to drive it myself."

"These things are supposed to have drivers. That's why people have them. Does it have dual air bags?"

Poor tyke, Stumpp thought. Everything she was learning was beside the point, though everything anyone learned proved to be beside the point. How false and full of pretext is all that we accomplish. Little Pickless made him dwell on the undwellable.

"I've got air bags in here for twelve people." Car would float away like a zeppelin if they started to go off.

"Do you know twelve people?"

"I do not," Stumpp said.

"I didn't think so. I'm going to sit in the back."

"Lovely," Stumpp said.

"Can a person make tea back here?"

"They can, actually."

"This is very nice."

Gratitude flooded Stumpp's tired heart. Little precursor. Wee mahout. Form the mover of all things. Time mixed up, almost flew right past, the whole shebang. No need for time to be dark, could be bright, transcendent. Pickless, was it . . .

39

Alice," Carter said, "how much would you charge to kill Ginger for me?"

This was a strenuous request, and Alice was flattered. She would waive all fees for Mr. Vineyard, who'd been awfully nice to her. But Alice was a realist; murder, in this case was out of the question. "You want me to kill your wife?"

"It would be wonderful."

"I really think that's beyond me, Mr. Vineyard."

"You have the heart of an anarchist. I can't imagine where else to turn."

"But that would be awful, Mr. Vineyard. If you could kill a dead person, it would be like killing something really rare and special, like the first of its kind or something."

"Ginger is no unicorn, Alice."

"I wouldn't know where to begin, quite frankly, Mr. Vineyard."

"Please don't call me that," Carter said. "It has certain connotations for me, I'm afraid." He was so discouraged. He couldn't discuss Ginger with Donald anymore. Donald wanted to go on to other things, and Carter couldn't blame him. He was beginning to doze off when Carter went on about Ginger. He would just slip right off to sleep, the most innocent boy in the world. And there Carter would be, watching him, enchanted, still talking, talking interminably, uncontrollably, about the perverse, unholy demands of Ginger. Donald was becoming disenchanted with him in his sleepy, hospitable, uncomplicated way. Donald was beginning to think he was nuts.

"Think with me, Alice!" he cried. "Think with me! What can be done?

You're a thoughtful girl, a daring, irreverent girl. It would be a remarkable achievement."

"I could be Girl of the Year," Alice said gravely.

"At the very least!"

"It's against the laws of nature, Mr. V."

"People have done worse to nature, far worse. You of all people are aware of the perniciousness of humankind's presence on Earth."

Someone was listening to her! Or at least overhearing her as she wedged her warnings about ecological collapse into the most benign conversations. "The impending extinction spasm is going to produce a cataclysmic setback to life's abundance and diversity," she mumbled hopefully.

Carter looked at her blankly. There was a wafer of connection here. The dead are coming back. And it had to do with the diminishment of everything else. Like happiness. It was not just millennial thinking. It was Ginger. Perhaps there were other cases. The dead are coming back. Or not going away. Whatever.

"Your wife has got to be just in your mind," Alice said.

"Not my wife anymore," Carter protested. "Please, at the very least—"

"I mean, you don't even go into your room now, do you? I see you sleeping in the living room."

"Sometimes I go over to the Hilton," Carter admitted.

"The Hilton! They poison coyotes at the Hilton! They have the ones made of bronze in the lobby and then they kill the real ones on their stupid golf course!"

"I'll speak to them about it. Alice, dear, we're veering off track here." It was a lucent night, of a brilliance he was beginning to loathe. In fact, it was night *again;* the days just kept collapsing into one another. He had come back to pick up some shirts and see Annabel, but where was Annabel? He had estranged himself from Annabel with his . . . his instability. He had no idea where Donald was. He might be out on a *date* for all Carter knew. An immense encephalitic moon hung above them all, and it seemed an appropriate moment to plot the murder of someone dead, it just did. Weren't those stars up there dead? And they kept twinkling away, didn't even know it. There might be some foundation for Ginger's claim after all.

"Does she ever show up anywhere other than your room?" Alice asked.

"Never at the Hilton. I think the Hilton confuses her. They've got five hundred rooms over there, you know. Two hundred suites."

"Well, where is she now?"

"God knows," Carter shuddered.

"She's in your mind," Alice persisted.

"No, no, only to the extent that we're discussing her. You know how that works."

Alice didn't. Her own thoughts were like a masked, hoarsely babbling mob, speaking on the condition of anonymity.

"So what does she want from you?"

"She wants me to *die*! She wants me to share death with her!" She had always wanted to share her problems with him, her weight, her menses, the fading away of her menses, her crushes on men . . . now this. She was relentless.

"Everybody knows you can't share that," Alice said. "Maybe you only think she wants that. She probably wants something else."

"But what would that be? There isn't anything else."

"Some tiny thing, maybe," Alice said. "Microscopic. Infinitesimal." There was, of course, something horrible about the infinitesimal.

"No, no, she wants me to join her and go on as though nothing happened. She's getting more—maybe you're right in part. At first it was like motes, but—"

"Motes?"

"Yes, motes, they didn't add up at first. The first few nights she appeared, it was all sort of ambiguous." Maybe if he'd hired a band to play during the cremation; that's what the Buddhists did, according to Donald. But the crematorium was in an industrial park! And the undertaker said it would take three hours. No exceptions. It had always taken three hours, it would forever take three hours, which sort of ruled out a normal band. The undertaker, an unhappy man as he had never realized his dream of being a Navy SEAL, having an unreliable stomach, was not sensitive but nonetheless seemed to be functioning intuitively with the *three* business, for didn't three symbolize spiritual synthesis? Didn't it solve the problem posed by that infernal dualism? Three was a remarkable figure for the situation, Carter remembered thinking even at the time. He had never considered going to the industrial park as an observer for those three hours. He had passed the wretched plot on the highway many, many times; Ginger, too, for that matter. One building made velvet, another corrugated cardboard, another paint. One place had been busted for churning out fake military medals. Another, he thought he'd heard once, rendered horses. Oversized American flags flying, chained dogs everywhere, the hulk of bulldozed trees. Still, maybe if he'd had a band—a band might have been just the thing to occupy Ginger's mind during the difficult transition.

"But we're not talking motes anymore," Carter said. "This is far beyond motes. She's strong now. *Strong.* Sometimes I think she's about to *yank* me up out of here. She's just waiting for me to lose my balance, and then . . ." He trailed off. He wanted to get back to the Hilton, have a few drinks in the bar, take a piss in one of their splendid urinals filled with crushed ice. There was a world out there, a world where he could still be active. Donald said he should strive to make his mind buoyant and flexible, capable of addressing any situation. Yes, yes, he had only to convince this girl here, Alice, that she had what it took, had the potential, to murder his dead wife.

"Does she live in your room now that you don't?" Alice asked.

"Live there?" Alice didn't grasp the problem at all. "Why, no. That would be all right if she did, if she couldn't get out. That would be perfectly acceptable. But I'm afraid—let me tell you what I'm afraid of— that because I don't go into that room anymore, it gives her license to go everyplace else. I think I made a tactical error by abandoning the room, see, she was pretty much contained there. She hasn't come to the Hilton yet, but why wouldn't she, once she figures it out? Those key cards are hardly the ultimate in human ingenuity."

"Maybe it's her soul you're seeing," Alice proffered. This somewhat fit in with her more recent theory that the soul was something you acquired only after you were dead, and by then it was determined to pursue what was most important to it, no matter how misguided the pursuit was. Mr. V. was the treasure meant for Mrs. V. alone, which was having unfortunate consequences for Mr. V. Marriage sort of disturbed Alice; it seemed all aftermath.

"Her soul?" Carter shook his head and felt something pop and grind subversively. No, no, this was Ginger, a simple yet practically incomprehensible parallelism to Ginger. Clearly one couldn't murder a soul, or if one could it would be very bad, one of those inexcusable things. Still, he realized he was using Alice, or trying to, as cat's-paw. He should be ashamed of himself. "I'm sure it's not her soul. It looks just like her—I mean, just like she did."

"Just like she did when?" Alice asked, for there couldn't be just one moment that was you, could there? When you looked like yourself, the way you'd be remembered?

But Carter did not address this question. "She used to be rather languid, viperish certainly, but sort of indolent, the way vipers are when they're not trying to sink their fangs into you. But now she wants to sink in her fangs and she's coiled with intent. *Coiled.*"

Alice wanted to help Mr. V. out, he looked on the brink. "Let's take a look in your room again and see if she's there."

"I haven't been in there in a week," Carter said.

Alice had an alarmed instant of feeling they had to water Mrs. V. or something, a blurred glimpse of the soul as an animal, ignored if not forgotten, thirsting, its woeful paws curled beneath its famishing.

"Well, let's take a look," Alice urged.

He strode purposefully toward his bedroom door. He disliked the door; it was not a fine door and was even hollow. For an expensive house, much had been scamped. He turned the knob and pushed the door back.

Alice peered into the dark. "It's really quiet in there," she said.

He heard Ginger's laughter, which brought to mind the weekend they'd been Christmas shopping in New York, the evening they'd been drunk and run up the down escalator at Sak's—far more difficult and enjoyable than you'd think. He wrenched the light on so vigorously that the plastic dimmer switch came off in his hand.

Everything looked in terrible disarray.

"You've been robbed," Alice said. "Have you been robbed?"

Carter peered at the room. Initially, it didn't seem as if anything was missing except his little clock—no, it had been safely relocated, he kept it by the bar now. But he could hear it ticking, or something was ticking, a tocking rondo in his head.

"I don't think so," he said.

"But it looks as though the police have been here. What's that yellow 'Do not cross' tape?" The tape beribboned the room with festive authority.

"That's a joke," Carter said. "I put it up. Just a joke." There was *The Nature of Things*. It looked a little the worse for wear. Poor old Lucretius. A love philter had turned him mad. He reeled in the tape, winding it around his hand. "Do you feel a presence in here, Alice? Sort of a permeation?"

"No," Alice said.

He was afraid Ginger had gotten herself into everything: the broken pool pump; the shot exhaust manifold on the Corvette; the tax audit; the thickening muscle around his heart detected by the yearly exam (he *had* seen a little something on the X ray, a clinging succubus he knew was Ginger); the weevils in his favorite brand of instant scone mix; Donald's pulled groin muscle. Definitely Donald's groin muscle . . .

"Sherwin says that God permeates the whole world," Alice said, "and lives in everything as the purest spark."

"God!"

"Sherwin's saying that just popped into my head. I realize your wife— it's not the same thing at all—I realize that."

"Sherwin who? You can't possibly mean the piano player."

"Have you given any further consideration to the wildlife pool in this location?"

"Alice, I want to confide something to you. I don't think she's completely here anymore. I mean, we could bring in a wrecking ball but I don't think we'd get all of her now, if you see what I'm saying."

"There's nothing here, Mr. V."

"Exactly! Nothing can live anywhere! That's exactly what Ginger is doing."

"Do you two talk?"

"I shudder to say," Carter said. "We do."

"This is really sort of impressive, Mr. V. You two must've been exceptionally close."

Carter had been twisting the "Do not cross" tape around in his hands. He raised it to his mouth and bit down on it, looking at Alice dully.

"Mr. V.!" Alice said.

He lowered his hands.

"I don't feel any kind of presence at all in here." Alice hoped for his sake that she wasn't just having another no-kayak moment. Of course, she'd never even met this dame. She'd only heard Annabel's somewhat inconclusive stories about her, which she suspected were somewhat gilded.

"The problem is that she's not here now," Carter said.

Alice nodded. "I don't have anything to work with."

"But I could call on you again if necessary."

"Absolutely, Mr. V." She looked around the room a final time. A big no kayak.

Back in the living room, Carter seemed a little steadier. "Spending the night, are you, Alice? Keeping Annabel company?"

"Annabel's painting her nails, Mr. V. She has this new color called Needles in a Haystack. She's really happy with it."

"Why? It sounds gray."

"It's a complex gray. It has a whole world of sophisticated meaning for her. She wants to make herself over, but she's not considering reconstructive surgery."

"I would hope not," Carter interjected. Sometimes communiqués absolutely essential to being an informed parent were just thrown at a fellow. "I wouldn't acquiesce to anything like that." He had responsibilities toward his daughter, but they just made his mind fog over.

"She wants to perfect parts of herself by choosing patinas and little adornments and effects that are apparently recognized by people she wants to be recognized by, or so she says." Alice frowned.

"But that's so . . . so *common*, Alice. Annabel can't be obtaining her ethos through nail polish."

"It's so-called nail polish only to us. To Annabel it's something more. She's unhappy here. She needs a different set of acquaintances, I think. She's kind of mad at me."

"She's annoyed with me, too. I fear she finds my behavior erratic."

"That's okay, Mr. V., we understand. You've just lost your wife."

"If only I had," Carter said fervently. "Alice, I need to confess something to you. I wanted Corvus to speak with Ginger, and I wanted that because I find Corvus not quite there or even here, if you know what I—let me say it another way. A healthy, happy person wouldn't be able to talk sincerely with a dead person, particularly to someone as annoyed and annoying as Ginger. Now, God knows I'm not healthy or happy, but I'm not nearly as disillusioned or fatigued in spirit as Corvus, poor girl, *fine* girl, and I thought she could have a relationship with Ginger that would nullify her, blot Ginger right up, as it were, absorb Ginger's nada into her own. What was the harm, I thought. . . ."

He saw himself for an instant as a monster of the Russian persuasion, on a galloping sledge throwing an infant to the slavering wolves almost upon him. Then he saw himself as some idiot in a feathered loincloth throwing a virgin down a well—what were they called? Cenotes, of course. No, his might be a different mask in a new setting, but he shared the same withered atoms with the long-gone louts of a certain ilk. He'd do anything to get the job done.

"I'm actually quite appalled at myself for considering employing this troubled girl in such a way, but I thought afterwards she will be less troubled, because after Ginger's gone I will get the finest treatment for Corvus, the finest treatment for a fatigued and disillusioned spirit, available."

"You haven't looked into availability yet?" Alice said.

"I deserve your disgust and mistrust. I don't feel any better for having confessed this to you."

"I could have told you beforehand that you wouldn't."

"I can only say on my behalf that I did not approach her. She would have accepted, and I think it would have proved a terrifying experience for her."

"She shouldn't be occupied like that. It's beneath her brilliance. In many ways she can't be harmed. You couldn't have harmed her, so you shouldn't worry." Still, Alice was disappointed in him.

Carter was surprised that Alice saw her friend as such a model of stability, or perhaps she was just trying in her somewhat inefficient way to defend someone who was precious to her.

"When you go back to the Hilton," she added, "be sure to question them about their predator-control policy."

"Uhmm." He might forgo the Hilton and check into a Hyatt instead. He'd had the worst dream the night before. There were too many drapes on the windows, layers and layers of them; it was like coming to in a shroud. He couldn't remember the details, but like all dreams it seemed to partake of both death and life, something added to the first and subtracted from the latter in a foul union, most unpleasant.

"The coyotes," Alice reminded him. "Predators. Life needs predators to be in balance."

Carter asked Alice to return to the bedroom and retrieve his book. She reappeared to announce she hadn't seen it, which made Carter break into a pronounced sweat. Gone again? He was coming to the conclusion that nothing was easier than going insane.

In the Corvette, he misplaced the keys, finally locating them in his tightly clenched fist. He danced the car down the driveway, blowing a headlight just before he reached the road. Alice watched with concern. It sounded as though something metal was banging around under the hood. And that black smoke. Rings, she thought. She didn't know what rings were, though she'd heard the word spoken with assurance by those observing smoke pouring from a vehicle's pipes. It augured nothing good.

40

H is first and last canine had been a Border collie. Technically it was a triumph, but his client was upset because it didn't look as though "Jim" were herding anything. What's he got to herd now? the taxidermist said. He'd always been direct back then, believing only charlatans showed charm. He's got to be herding something or else he won't be happy, the client said. Then you need a surround to show him, the taxidermist said, "I ain't an interior decorator." But he knew he'd have to forfeit the bill, maybe even return the unrefundable deposit. The client was an old man, and a tear had run down to drop from the tip of his old man's nose. He felt in his bones that he'd arranged something terrible to be done to his Jim. I can't even bury him outside my window like I once could have, the old man said.

It had been an unfortunate moment even then.

The taxidermist scowled at the infant gorilla he'd been working on all morning. He was dissatisfied with its expression, it lacked hunger. He nudged it into his trash can and moved over to his broad wooden desk. He'd never heard of this wood before. Some new wood. Like the fish they were coming up with these days. Monkfish. What the hell was monkfish? Turbot. The same. He'd go home, and the wife would say, "I've got this lovely piece of monkfish from the new market," and he and the family would gather at the table beneath the cathedral ceiling in the house she'd insisted they purchase and eat it. The cathedral ceiling was ridiculous, the whole house was ridiculous, a Taj in the foothills for which they'd unwisely overextended themselves. Still, he was glad she was content. She'd been about to unravel back in Alaska. He'd enjoyed some prestige, having done all the bears in the Kodiak airport, but doing all the bears in the Kodiak airport didn't provide the kind of income one would expect and she'd had to take a job as a housekeeper in a hot springs resort where the Japanese honeymooners just about drove her crazy. The Japanese had invented the concept of the Alaskan honeymoon and came there in droves to do it. They didn't tip, they shed pubic hair like crazy, and they beamed, they were always beaming.

They'd gotten out of Alaska just before the short bitter days had come round again, the moose in the cesspit jokes, the grafitti on the snowbanks of the pissed-on frontier. The wife selected to bring nothing along but her old blue Samsonite filled with the tiny dresses of her babyhood. Just in case, she'd say, just in case, not that she was campaigning for another one, but if it happened and it was a girl, or if the boys had little girls when they started their own families—maybe the clothes could be used then. The thought that these rotting, stained, shrunken, incredibly delicate clothes worn by his wife when she was newly born would be imposed on the future, where naturally they would be entirely unwelcome, depressed him. Sometimes he didn't think his wife was well, that those goddamned cavorting Japanese had broken her spirit, that she'd lost the little something she had when he first met her that made it all seem worthwhile. Of course, she had her baby clothes back then, but they hadn't seemed so peculiar, so out of proportion to their lives; they hadn't reminded him, yellowing things, dark where they'd been folded, of the Momias de Guanajuato in Mexico, the Museum of the Mummies, where he'd gone when he was still single, when it was still weird and distasteful, before they'd cleaned it up and made it into a clean, well-lighted museum where you were funneled past the things through a narrow corridor so you couldn't linger to study them more closely, people pushing up behind you so you had to keep moving and before you knew it you were back outside where some pear-shaped amputee scooting around on a dolly was selling postcards of the *momias*, the baby *momias* dressed in their Sunday best, the embroidered smocks and bright blankets remarkably similar to the stuff his wife kept in that sinister blue Samsonite.

The taxidermist shook his head vigorously to free it of unwanted thoughts. He picked up the newspaper, leaned back in his chair, and propped his feet on the desk. He read that those goddamned Japanese had developed a prototype of a robotic cat. Those people needed to be given their own army again, get some realism back into their lives. A robotic cat, aimed at the elderly-widow market. This was what the future was: robots, artificial intelligences. There would be no sincerity, no art of the kind he'd devoted his life to. The future was a place where the dead looking alive would no longer be enough.

Abruptly, his door swung open and Emily Bliss Pickless entered carrying a cardboard box.

"Hey," the taxidermist said. "You knock first. You *knock*." He removed his feet from the desk.

"I need something," she said.

"Yeah, a brain." He loathed this kid.

Emily shrugged. People either wanted to worship her or snap her in half. So do the exceptional ones walk through this world. Though she was not vain.

The taxidermist peered into the box. A puddle of fur and blood and bone, impossibly breathing.

"You're not normal," he said. "Anybody ever tell you that?"

"I am distinguishing between life and death," she said, "which is more than anyone else in this place does."

"Don't quit your day job for that talent, missy." She was gazing around his workplace with maddening impunity. He'd smack her little fanny and push her out the door—this was his office, his workplace, his sanctum sanctorum—but he was uneasily aware that she enjoyed some special relationship with his employer. Maybe she was a niece, a grandniece. Unmarried oddballs like Stumpp always had nieces and nephews galore, and it was the taxidermist's opinion that these terms were code for abnormal or immoral relationships. The taxidermist had always felt this to be so. Say the word *niece* to him, and the red flag would go up right away.

"Pest," the taxidermist said.

"Why'd you throw this little gorilla away?"

"Get out of my trash, you!" He felt that he'd been hounded by this kid forever, though she'd showed up only a few weeks ago. Stumpp had given her one of the rooms at the museum for her animal "hospital." He'd had a carpenter build her some cages, and there was a tabletop full of dog and cat cages customarily used for airline travel. He'd bought her a refrigerator and a few heating pads and some pans and dishes and tow-els. Even told the chef in his café to provide the little freak with anything she required—salads, ground meats, fruit medleys—though the taxider-mist took pleasure in the fact that none of her "patients" had taken any nourishment before they croaked.

"You don't know how to do this anymore, do you?" she said. "You're just pretending."

The taxidermist stalked out of his office in search of Stumpp. He found him in the oasis room, where he seemed to be listening to the air conditioner.

"Hey boss," the taxidermist said, "that Pickless child? She's adorable but she's forever bothering me, wasting my time. You hired me as an artist, and she's always intruding on me, taking my needles, rummaging through my tooth and eye drawers—those things are organized, I tell her." He shivered, quite involuntarily, in the chilled air.

Stumpp looked at him irritably. Waves of an elusive melody had been bearing him outward, beyond the confines of this place wherein he had interred himself. This was one hell of an air conditioner. Airy-fairy flaky types, which the desert and these new millennial times seemed to pro-duce in abundance, would likely lose their wits after a session with this baby. You had to be a strong man to fiddle around with the kind of con-sciousness this unit inspired. This was ethereal business, and he resented being interrupted by this oaf. If he mentioned even once again in passing that he'd done all the bears in the Kodiak airport, Stumpp would punch him in his pink wet mouth—with a mouth that repulsive, hadn't he ever considered a beard?

"Pickless?" he finally said. "You came in here to complain about Pick-less?"

"People are going to be bringing her roadkill next. It's going to get out of hand. Your reputation will be wrecked. Besides, has she ever saved one of those things?"

"What do you mean, 'saved'?"

"Repaired it so she could let the damn thing go. No, the answer is no, she has not. Because everything she's got is missing something *which it needs*. If she wasn't eight years old, she'd realize this. Half those birds she's got in there go around in circles or tip over backwards because their backs are broken. You can't release a one-eyed hawk. Those poisoned things she gets, she's just torturing them. Their guts are moldering. Does she know the slightest thing about biology? About science? She should be playing with dolls. Or just getting over playing with dolls, though I'll admit I don't know how that works, I have two boys myself. Sons," he said for added emphasis.

Stumpp regarded him silently. "Let's move back to your office," he said.

En route, they passed Emily, hauling something heaving beneath a towel in a small red wagon. She opened the door to her section, struggled through with her charge, and shut the door behind her.

Stumpp grinned and shook his head with happiness. He was enchanted by Emily Bliss Pickless. Wry little elf singing, dancing to itself. Though not exactly. That always finds and never seeks . . . but that was sentimental doggerel. Pickless was more than that, made of sturdier stuff. Tyke had depths unplumbed—he'd bet his bonds on it. She kept a little diary, not the ordinary childish thing with a little lock and key but a sheaf of pages in a box with a screwed-down lid that required two different screwdrivers. He adored her.

In the taxidermist's office, Stumpp seated himself in the swivel chair behind the desk. "Why'd you throw this little gorilla away?" he asked.

"That kid probably pushed it in there," the taxidermist said.

"Needs considerable more work," Stumpp said. "Mouth in particular. Mouth looks like an omelet or something."

"That kid needs to know some boundaries," the taxidermist said. "Some rules need to be laid down. Whatever that little girl is doing—and God knows what it is—it doesn't coincide with my work at all. We don't complement one another one bit. It's a confusing situation. People come in here now, and they get confused."

"You're the best there is, aren't you?" Stumpp said. "The best in the business."

"Lucky is the creature that gets as far as me."

"How did you get into this business, anyway?" Stumpp inquired kindly.

"I've been doing it for twenty years," the taxidermist said, "since I was fifteen. I started out with bats, the only mammal that can fly. Loved doing bats, then kept moving up. I did all the bears in the Kodiak airport."

Stumpp reflected for a moment on his museum. It was nothing but a catacomb, a charnel house. "You're fired," he said.

The taxidermist felt the top of his head horripilating. "I have a contract."

"That contract's worthless," Stumpp said. "You should've had a lawyer look it over."

"I just bought a house here."

"You might have to think about giving it up. That house might not be yours after all."

The taxidermist wished it was fifteen minutes ago, before he'd opened his goddamned mouth. This profession was all he knew. The widowed skins. The winnowed skulls. This goneness, his clientele. "What'd I say, boss?" he said. "I didn't say anything. But I take it back." He'd picked up a large needle and worked it into the fat part of his own thumb. A thread was hanging out of his hand.

"I say, man, pull yourself together," Stumpp said. "I'll pay a year's salary, but I want you to leave immediately. Remove all personal effects." He pointed to a coffee mug upon which the likeness of the taxidermist's next of kin—a grimly smiling woman and two thuggish-looking boys— had been imposed upon the plastic.

Within the hour the removal of the taxidermist from the building had been accomplished, and by closing time Stumpp had quite forgotten the man existed.

"Pickless," Stumpp said, "I was thinking of shutting this whole operation down for a bit." They were sitting in the cafeteria, sharing a small stale cookie.

"Good," Emily said. "Then that's settled."

"Sick of the public's remarks. Sick of hearing them say, 'They'd be dead now anyway.' Catch my drift?"

"They say that all the time."

"Makes them feel better."

"No reason to make 'em feel better about this place."

"None," Stumpp agreed. He had to undo much, had to unknot the past, unknot it . . .

"Wish I hadn't eaten that cookie," Emily said.

"How's the work going?" Stumpp asked.

"Pretty much as expected." Emily thought she needed to go on a fact-finding tour. That was what life was, was it not? A fact-finding tour?

"Have to take you back soon," he sighed. "Back to your momma." Stupid woman, thought her child was enrolled in summer school. Demanding curriculum, involving nature, computers, sailing. Why not sailing? Could sell the woman anything. Parents these days remarkably lax.

"My momma," Emily said noncommittally.

Only fly in the ointment, this momma. "Do you want to meet my mother?" Pickless had inquired only yesterday. "Good God, no!" Stumpp had exclaimed. Terrible situation that would be. How to explain self? No way to do it. Didn't wish this woman any harm, just wished she were on another planet. Shuttled away on one of those great gaming ships wandering through space—free drinks, free food, free chips. Or, if she'd prefer it, a good sanitorium somewhere. White clothes, white bedding, white light, white noise. No expense spared for Momma's peace of mind. Pickless only eight, clearly a minor, but his own heart pure, would stand up to closest scrutiny. No heart ever purer. Thumping away in his chest, at last showing some commitment. He'd be elated to just sit on a rock in the sun with Pickless. Which was pretty much what he was doing, though they were perched on stools covered in dik-dik hide and bathed in halogen light.

"Do you believe in the story 'Two by Two'?" Emily inquired.

"Hate it," Stumpp said, surprising himself with his rancor. Pickless should be sufficient unto self. World leader, getting things done. Power of personality. Charisma. Blinded ordinary people into perceiving her as pipsqueak child. Book he liked by that fine African fellow, van der Post. *About Blady*. Blady the plow horse, discovered in a field by the right passerby, when rescued, becomes champion jumper. In the blood. Instinct, grace, like the tyke. Plus that propensity for fortuitous chance. Blady no nag, just waiting to be beheld in the proper light. Chance is what gets the damn thing done. The role accident assumes in life cannot be overestimated, and Pickless had the gift for accident. Now it was time to cut those corners, cut them. Had to crunch time now. Have to be unconscious, *pre*-conscious. That's when great feats were performed. All in the past. Stones of Henge, pyramids of Egypt, ziggurats of Sumer, temples of Teotihuacán. No fatigue or reflection, no doubt. Just action action action.

Emily felt a little sleepy. She was demanding of herself full and chaotic days that reflected neither rhyme nor motive.

Practically had the Dalai Lama on his hands here, but not in some airy-fairy sense. Nothing airy-fairy about Pickless. Nerves of steel. Would get over keeping those mangled things in boxes, just a phase. But no time for many more phases. Time running out. In a sense we're all already dead. We are. Shouldn't think so much. Thought supposed to be preferable to unconsciousness but develops its own problems. When thought first appeared, early thinkers believed they had to pluck out their eyes in order to do it properly. Shows how far we've gone, but further to go still. Something better than thought out there. Pickless had work ahead, no doubt about it. Must sense no limits. All things possible, otherwise why generation after generation? Still, wished they'd shared a bit of the past together. Wished she'd known Africa. Remembered the nights there, all nights the same then, all the creatures' eyes glinting visible in the meadow beyond the camp, in the meadow beyond. . . . Wasn't this wonderful, he'd be saying to her. . . .

Emily suppressed a yawn.

41

Corvus was in her sleeping bag in the corner. Both girls had sleeping bags that could maintain life's functions down to twenty degrees below zero, which Alice thought was excellent if unnecessary to present circumstances. They didn't cost any more than the ones that only worked down to zero, although Alice admired the kind of person who would risk one of those instead. When self-preservation became overly important, you were doomed. When you began making sacrifices toward security, you were lost, lost, lost.

Alice watched Corvus closely. It had been some time since Corvus had said anything. Her hair was dry and stuck up at odd angles.

"I think we should get out in the here and now," Alice said. "Drive around in your truck and *carpe diem*." Sherwin had told her that she gave the *carpe diem* concept a bad name. She'd been thrilled by this mis-judgment but was avoiding the piano player nonetheless. Mr. V. was giving a party tonight that she was also avoiding. From now on she would just step nimbly out of Sherwin's way at every opportunity. He could talk about the blackness of white to someone else. He could ask another to tub cuddle. She was no longer impressionable. Being in love had been interesting, but not exactly, and she wouldn't want it to happen again. As an inappropriate love object, Sherwin had been practically perfect, but she had to move on.

Corvus's eyes were open. She cleared her throat softly. "I . . ." she began.

Alice waited anxiously, encouraged. *I . . .* Who knew what it meant exactly, but it indicated that Corvus still knew how to disengage herself from the unconsciousness she preferred. She had inched out a bit from the sleeping bag's cocoon. These things were actually sort of malevolent-looking, Alice thought.

"I was in a tree," Corvus said, "between the branches of a tree, and this voice was saying 'I hold you lightly between two fingers, and if you disobey me I will drop you.'"

"Wow," Alice said. "Who . . . what does it say you're supposed to obey?"

"That wasn't clear. It pretty much stresses the holding lightly part." She cleared her throat again.

"I'm glad you're awake. You've been sleeping for *days*. Why don't we get out of here and camp in the Airstream for a while? We could hook it up to the truck and even go someplace."

"The Airstream's still here?"

"It's parked in the side yard," Alice said. Was it indeed in the side yard? Had the bad boys wearied of harvesting her granny and poppa's unkempt vegetation to supply the demanding clean urine market and decided to employ themselves more traditionally by simply stealing things?

"I haven't seen the Bubble for a while," Corvus said. "I'd kind of forgotten about it."

"Well, it's right outside," Alice said worriedly.

"I've been everywhere these last few days," Corvus said. "I never want to travel again."

"I just want to make sure it's there," Alice said. "I'll be right back."

Silence crept up on Corvus again, encircling her. She'd been dreaming too of a great racetrack enveloped in fog, a light on a great stanchion burning in but not through the fog. People thronged the course. A laconic voice said, *The field is in motion.* She was not of the race. She was alone, watching it. *Innumerable millions,* the voice said. She felt the fog lingering, dissolving on her face. Again she was weeping.

She crawled out of the sleeping bag and stood up, then walked unsteadily down the little hall to the bathroom. She wore a shirt of her father's. Fury gazed at her without moving. Everything had been scaring the soup out of him for days. Who was that now? He was too anxious to bark, and what was the use, anyway, what was the use of sounding the alarm?

Beyond the thin, aqueous-colored wall she heard Alice's poppa saying, "They don't use the word *used* anymore. With cars it's preowned. With books, preread. With clothes what would you say, preoccupied?" Around her on the shelves were the old people's innocent salves and potions, their eyewashes and aspirins and expectorants, their Q-tips and Vicks and Pond's, their flannel cloths and boxes of Endangered Species Band-Aids. The shower curtain hung before the tub on a crooked suction-cupped rod featuring grand, Rubenesque ladies gazing in a sultry manner out at the toilet, which had a puffy-lidded seat the color of charlotte russe.

It all was sadness, every bit of it, the purchasing and placing alike.

On the shelf was a little black comb, an old person's comb, sincere and ready to work, hardened dandruff high up in the tines. Corvus regarded it for some time. Then her eyes fell on a nail brush, and she ran water and used it to scrub the comb. Dark particles fell onto the sink's white surface, small particles, but not extremely small. The universe supposedly had come into being in the form of an extremely small particle containing space and time. Or through an event, was the newest theory, and, lacking form of any kind, contained the genesis for space and time though not, in the beginning, space and time itself. The elegance of the newest theory consisted in the admission that there was no beginning. This was debunked by more ambitious theoreticians.

The black flakes stopped falling. The comb now appeared a lovely shining thing. Ace, by name. A particle. An atom. A jot.

She would like to devote herself to such small, foolish good works, to have nothing, to labor in a job without honor, purposelessly, without contrition, for years. Each day the same though not the same, day after obsolete day in infinite vocation. The secretive thread of the weeks. She would labor unconjoined. She would not be remembered.

Corvus went barefoot down the hallway, past Alice's room, past the living room where Alice's poppa's face was bathed in the television's ashen glow. "Hello there," he called. Alice's granny was preparing snacks in the kitchen. "Who're you talking to, dear?" she said. He saw no one now. He'd been seeing more phantasms than usual of late. Maybe he should put a hold on those cheesy snacks of Ritz and cheddar, the most daring offering they made to one another these days, miniature Grim Reapers, little artery-wadding missives, Belial buttons on a chipped floral plate. But he liked them.

Outside, there was still some daylight not yet squandered, but the big crime lights on the concrete phone poles were shining regardless. The street was lined tightly with vehicles, though no car passed. Corvus's Dodge truck was at the curb fifty yards away. She softly passed the Airstream on her thin light feet. The door was open, and she glimpsed Alice moving about inside. It looked all jumbled up in there, a-tilt and a-scatter, and Alice was bent over a bowl, about to pick it up.

Corvus padded down the sidewalk. It was smooth and wide, and profane suggestions in both Spanish and English were etched on each square, the words in cramped unhurried script, as though copied from some holy guide instead of being its own screaming, shit-streaked cabala. She reached the truck. Someone had sideswiped the door and she couldn't open it, so she opened the passenger door and slid across the seat. She pulled out, shifting slowly, no thought arising, to Green Palms.

Nurse Daisy stood outside, smoking a cigarette and cooling her forehead with a moist baby wipe.

"*Catachresis* is the word of the day," she said to Corvus in greeting. "It was yesterday's word as well and, most probably, tomorrow's. It should be emblazoned on the pediments of this place. Catachrestic. Catachrestical. Catachrestically. The sound alone's enough to have one running for the exits. There's a rattle to it, a yeomanly phlegm. Its root means 'against what is necessary.' But try using it in a sentence. It won't fit. Resists the long thought. Nurse Cormac ran off with the exterminator. Those exterminators can talk rings around most people, and she fell for him hard."

She had drawn the cigarette right down to the filter and now placed it in a sand-filled urn among a good hundred others. "I sometimes think of freshening this up, raking the sand tidy with a fork, lightly sketching a pattern of wings in the Gnostic manner. I never will, of course, because I like it this way too. Not doing one thing is equal to not doing something else. Who said the following? 'Love, and do what you will.'"

Corvus cleared her throat but didn't speak. Corvus, barefoot, in her father's shirt, her hair unwashed.

"We have a new neighbor in my neighborhood." Nurse Daisy pulled out a fresh baby wipe from a packet and rubbed it over her temples. "It's a pet drop-off bin. People can drop off unwanted dogs and cats in specially marked bins. It's rather like a mail chute, which will accept animals up to fifty pounds. They drop down softly into a concrete chamber, which is checked and emptied once a day. They're kept for four days at the shelter, where they're offered the opportunity for another life in the form of a stranger coming in, though as you know there are never enough strangers. On the fifth day, bright and early, before the sun comes up, before the water dish has to be filled again, there's sodium Pentothal, quick-quick-quick. It's a humane alternative. There's disease out there, worms, blindness, mange, valley fever. There's neglect and random cruelty. There are designer poisons that take days to work their way through the system. How would you define," Nurse Daily asked, "the word *humane*?"

Two wraiths pottered out onto the balcony above them and dawdled, scratching their arms. Corvus could hear the rasp of their dry skin.

"I know how you got this far," Nurse Daisy said. "You figured out what you ought not to do, and you determined to do it. Against all advice. Not against the odds, however. The odds were always good. But to serve is not to love, you know. You could be washing old feet from now till doomsday, and there'll still be that hard dark little seed of doubt, that seed of awareness that isn't love."

The wraiths looked down on them with immense eyes. They scratched.

"I hope you don't think you've been chosen," Nurse Daisy said.

Corvus said nothing.

"I would rather speak five words with my understanding than ten thousand words in an unknown tongue, as the Good Book says. But you understand nothing, so you've decided to be dumb, and how long will this last, forever?" She looked out at Corvus from deep within her mismatched face. "Nurse Cormac was such a talker. My ears still ring from her prattle." She touched her tiny ears, which looked as though they'd been grafted on in some long-ago emergency operation by an inappropriate donor. "Winging her way to Kansas, she is, with her exterminator. Back to the seemingly endless plains where he was partly raised, back to the rats in the silos who were missing their master, missing his particular etiquette with them."

One of the wraiths was scratching his white arm with a card, an efficient scraping that sounded different from the other's ragged nails. Then the card tore free and fell like a dart at Corvus's feet. A Happy Birthday card with balloons on it, much thumbed and twisted. Inside, someone had written, "From all of us." The wraith leaned over the balcony railing, gesturing wildly, and commenced to cry. The other wraith began blubbering as well. "Hey!" Nurse Daisy screamed. They both fell silent and stared at Corvus resentfully.

"They can't see you, of course," the nurse said. "Most everyone in this residence has the dark water in their eyes, glaucoma. They only pretend to see you. It's much like life here, but it's not life and that's why you came back. Because you were going to leave us, weren't you? You were that close to leaving, but then—let me guess—you saw some cruddy thing that had within it all the importunate treasure of *being*, some cruddy thing that turned radiant in the light of your regard. So you've come back to wait without waiting, as one waits for the dead. You're not one of those signs-and-wonders girls; you'll have nothing to teach, you'll serve in silence, you'll get the dark water yourself, you'll labor undetected, they'll bury you out of this place like some failed old postulant."

The card beamed up at Corvus, its little back cracked. *From all of us!*

"That funny friend of yours," Nurse Daisy continued, "does she know about your decision? What a funny friend. She would've dissuaded you if she were able, but she's not able enough. Solitude is no refuge for the rebellious. She would never begin her search here. And if we're not what we will become, what are we, then?"

Corvus stood motionless. The evening's small moths dabbled around her.

"It's better to be dumb," the nurse said, "than to speak from a heart that's all darkness and distraction. I'm agreeing with you. I suppose we should go in. Are you ready to enter our little charnel community, not as docent or guide but as a living member? Do you vow to keep your wits among the witless? Do you commit yourself to pondering ceaselessly the uselessness of caring, the uselessness of love, that great reality for which all else must be abandoned?" She stood and seemed to lunge toward Corvus, but it was just one of the heels on her sensible shoes skidding, no harm done.

"I'm not glad you came," Nurse Daisy said. "If I were the wishing sort, I'd have wished otherwise, for your sake. But I haven't wished for anything for years and years."

CAUTION:

DOORS SWING OUTWARD

They passed the children's drawings on the wall. Pigs, cows, and bears. Wolves and butterflies. Birds, lots of birds.

"Scant comfort, the gullibility of children," Nurse Daisy remarked. "It's completely cynical, this continuous peddling of the natural world. It's not out there anymore! Even old-timers don't find anything familiar in this empty symbolizing, this feckless copycatting."

She looked at Corvus. "I'd wager that as a child you colored between the lines. And where has it gotten you?"

There was a newly empty room. In fact, an aide was still washing down the plastic sealing the mattress; some still bright flowers were tumbled in a cardboard carton along with rubber gloves and the menu for the week. "I want to go *hommmmmmme*," Nurse Daisy mimicked softly. "Thirty-one months, every waking minute, not one bloody, blessed other phrase."

Fluorescent brightness gnawed at the room. The aide swiped the mattress with a lavender sponge. There was a fuzzy slipper in the carton, a paper roll of pennies, not filled entirely, maybe thirty cents' worth. Corvus looked at all this from not far away, drifting, with the raven's eye.

The nurse scooped up the coin roll and dropped it into the pocket of her smock, which shone dully as though waxed. "It costs more to make pennies than they're worth, but the utterly useless exerts a sobering restraint upon society. If I have a penchant for anything, I believe it's for useless things."

The aide pressed fresh sheeting onto the bed and steered the carton into the hall with her foot. In the quiet, Nurse Daisy's breathing seemed to hiss a little. "Each room a palimpsest," she said. "I'm self-obliged to tell you, this place may not always be here for you. It's under investigation by the state. It's not just the dog meat, the trifecta tostadas, it's a number of things across the board. Records aren't being kept, bums aren't being scoured properly. Rat tails have been observed in the darndest places. Thus the exterminator's eventful arrival. As for the doctors, they're comically unqualified. Indeed, they're not even doctors, not even *vets;* they're handymen, gardeners. Death was once frequently portrayed as a gardener in serious verse. One of the problems with our technological age is that we can't picture death as a gardener anymore, or picture it as anything. A straight line on a screen is the best we can do. . . ."

She paused, and again Corvus could hear the rasping hitch in her breathing. She rubbed her mouth with the back of her hand. The horror of the orifice, its foolish greed, seemed apparent to her, its ardent deceptions and ambitions.

"You will make this your oratory," Nurse Daisy determined.

Corvus searched within herself. She had no intention of praying. But here she would hone her willingness to suffer, make it an ability, a feat no one would acknowledge or admire, least of all herself.

"You think you've found sanctuary here, but the whole place is closer than you think to being condemned, the whole kit and kaboodle. It will be turned into another desert spa. Loofah treatments, bikini waxes, energizing soaks. The quick will take it by privilege, storm it by entitlement. The new administrators will be utterly disapproving of your role. You'll be exiled once more, yet unable to wander like your funny friend. Of course she's doomed to wander, she has no choice. You'll grow further and further apart, you two, or perhaps it's closer and closer apart. Two halves of the same broken shell. Hell has no birds, it's one of its more alarming attributes. Do you believe me?"

She stared at Corvus. Her lopsided face narrowed and grew taut.

"You're a bit of deadwood, you are, a fruitless tree, fit only to be rooted up and cast into the fire." She smoothed her chalk-bright uniform, which she preferred to more casual attire. "I'd kiss you good night, but I don't want to frighten you."

"You don't frighten me," Corvus said.

42

S herwin was a great observer at parties. Never drinking himself, he had a great advantage, but the sound was beginning to get to him. It actually began to pain him, the sound of a party, the bedlam rattle and howl, the partygoers' faces opening and emptying and moist with excitement. Sherwin was becoming a little prim about it, and it was affecting his playing. He should do something else. Move to a metropolis or get another face-lift.

He moved from "I Get a Kick Out of You" to Haydn's Sonata in E-flat Major, which he played badly. "The underclass is menacing," a man said. "I don't care how well we seem to get along waiting in line at the Dairy Queen." Sherwin continued to softly crucify Haydn. "I mean, what are you *supposed* to get your mother after all these years? I got her a couple dung bunnies. They're little bunny figures made by Amish craftsmen from sanitized, deodorized, hundred percent cow manure. She can put them in her garden." Sherwin threw back his head and exaggerated his technique. "My wife's going to call Victoria and tell her she's letting me go. Victoria insisted that my wife make this call. She wants everything clear, she's a helluva girl." Sherwin started to play Haydn well, just because he could. "What happened to furniture? Don't they do furniture anymore, the Amish?" A woman approached the piano. Her lips were chapped beneath bright lipstick. She had a small black mole on her throat.

"Nice beauty mark," Sherwin said.

"You think so?" She nibbled at the lip of her champagne flute.

"Is it real?"

"Real?" She seemed genuinely puzzled by the inquiry, then drained the flute. "Who do you tell your troubles to?" she said. "I'm just curious.

I don't want to hear them myself, but I'd like to know. I tried to tell mine to my dog, and she growled at me. I lay down beside her and I put my arms around her neck and I snuggled up to her and cried in her fur and told her my troubles and she growled at me."

"What a *bitch,*" Sherwin said, pecking away at the Haydn. He cocked his head like a feckless little sparrow. Realizing he was overdoing it. One of these days he was going to get knocked on his ass by a broad like this.

"The hell with it," the woman said. "Nobody likes to hear your troubles, not even a goddamned dog from the pound who should be grateful for every breath she's allowed to draw."

"We should all be grateful," Sherwin said in his oiliest manner. "We are here to praise, to sing our little song of praise."

The woman regarded him. Her hands shook. She was really very drunk. "I know everybody in this room," she said. "And you know what I see when I look at them? I don't see anybody I know."

"What are your troubles, anyway, dear?" Sherwin asked.

"I'm a survivor," she said. "People dismiss me as a survivor. They say, 'That Adrianna, she's a survivor,' but they don't say it in a nice way. It has a lot of negative connotations the way they say it."

"You've been through a lot, have you, dear?" Sherwin had stopped playing, he couldn't quite recall when.

"Oh, fuck off," the woman said. She made a crooked way across the room on her battered high heels.

No way that mole was real, Sherwin thought. He was losing more and more of his already limited ability to extend himself to others. He should get an eye-lift, maybe, or go back to school, live in the city and study philosophy. Read Schopenhauer again. He loved Schopenhauer. There was a man who had the ability to extend himself to others. Hadn't people gathered each midday outside his favorite hotel to watch him eat? To him they were nothing, everything was nothing, but they were all crazy about him, even the women, who were forever approaching him, wanting to be seen with him, attempting to ingratiate themselves with his white poodle; there was always a white poodle, a succession of white poodles. The children of the neighborhood called the poodle "young Schopenhauer"—they had his number, yet everyone else adored him, not the complacent, egotistical, and cold man that was Schopenhauer but his thinking. His "the way of escape is not by the way of death" was the most delightful suggestion. To escape the fuss and pain and striving and confusion of trying to live, fully or interestingly or just at all, to escape all that through self-destruction, though not through the gate of death . . .

"How about playing 'Ghost Riders in the Sky'? You know 'Ghost Riders in the Sky'?" A young man wearing a squash blossom necklace the size of a softball was looking at him with shy concern. He wore soft pleated trousers and a muscle shirt.

"You want 'Ghost Riders in the Sky'?"

"I've been *asking*," the youth said.

"I love 'Ghost Riders in the Sky'," Sherwin said. "It just goes on and on."

The youth's friend materialized beside him. "Well, play the goddamn thing then," he said. The two of them could be twins, but this one was shaggier, coarser. Cute, Sherwin thought.

"I was just about to take a break," Sherwin said. "It's break time. I wouldn't want to play it when my heart wasn't in it."

"You should get a new personality," the rough one said. "Yours is just about worn out." He was looking pointedly at Sherwin's tuxedo jacket, which was, in fact, a little shabby. Sherwin had four of them, all in barely presentable condition.

"It's not that easy, pretty," the muffin one said. "You're very skilled at it, but most people wouldn't know where to begin getting a new personality." He put his hand on his lover's arm.

Sherwin sensed great animosity toward his person tonight. Perhaps his true self, usually so carefully concealed, had become visible, and instead of being remarkable resembled a little speckled stone that kept presenting itself to be kicked. People mostly left him alone. Or avoided him, whatever. But he was having a problem tonight. His friend Jasper, who was having a problem with brain lesions, who was dying, actually, had said, "Now, Win, when you've got a problem, don't think of it as such. Think of it as a mystery, then it's not a problem anymore but a lovely mystery."

Someone in the vicinity was saying, "If we can get enough people in that subdivision, there'll be enough effluent to support a golf course."

The rough darling was giving Sherwin a big murderous smile. His left incisor had been sharpened to quite a point. Sherwin missed being in love, the danger and stupidity of it. He walked outside and lit a cigarette. My self, he thought, a little speckled stone. Weren't there screaming stones somewhere? Probably in Celtic lands. They screamed when something bad was about to happen, some avoidable catastrophe poised to occur.

The woman with the rucked heels and sticker mole was lying on a chaise longue, her eyes closed and her hands folded over her stomach. Some people passed out like that, just had the knack of doing it in a formal fashion.

Sherwin walked around smoking. The party had reached that warbling keen, the trilling glossolalia he knew so well and detested. He saw what appeared to be a buzzard just before the curve in the driveway and flicked his cigarette at it. It dragged itself off a bit. A buzzard and something wrong with it to boot. He regretted throwing the cigarette. That had been unkind. He lit another and leaned on the haunch of a red Mercedes convertible whose bumper sticker declared, "My Friend Was Killed by a Drunk Driver." Person always had to have a certain kind of face on when driving that car. They must have another car they drove when they wanted to relax. Could this belong to the woman who'd passed out, the survivor who couldn't even get her dog to listen to her troubles? Did Schopenhauer tell his problems to his poodles? Maybe that's why he had a succession of them. *Let me just run this past you . . . Human life has no goal, nor could the goal be reached even if it existed. Sound right to you?*

That was the problem, the dilemma, Jasper was attempting to turn into such a delightful mystery at Green Palms. He had told Sherwin he was committed to conscious dying; he was sure he could make a go of it. You've got to go on a tour of unaccustomed thinking, Jasper said. If you're willing to take the tour, then . . . What? Sherwin had asked. What then? Anything can happen, Jasper said. That's all? Sherwin said. That's enough to make me laugh. Anything can happen? That's all you get for going on this tour? Jasper had never been congenial or hopeful, and now he was; it was terrible timing. His skin was sallow and his feet were bloated and gray, the long thick nails curving downward almost like a bird's talons. He couldn't bear the slightest pressure on his feet, not even a sheet; the breath of a door closing, a breeze, was agonizing beyond endurance. Sometimes the two of them would lose themselves for long moments, regarding Jasper's feet. Fissures would appear, exposing a slice of shining liquid, or a bruise, a black aureole, would be born. The feet seemed to want to possess a life independent of Jasper, who they possibly and quite rightly felt was going to quit them soon.

I'll be the first one to die consciously, Jasper assured him. Others have tried and failed, but I'm not going to fail. I think you have to start practicing for this moment at an early age, Sherwin said. Before I came here and was in the hospital there was this kid there, Jasper said. I never met him, he was in pediatrics and they wouldn't let me near pediatrics, but he was seven years old and he was going to die and his wish, his only wish, was to get into the *Guinness Book of World Records*. I didn't think that was even published anymore, Sherwin said. The record he was going for was to possess the largest collection of business cards by any individual on earth. Boxes were set up all over the hospital for people to drop their business cards in, to help this deluded kid meet his goal. I just wanted to find him and shake him, you know? That kid made me so angry, and the people who encouraged him in this . . . this *project* made me even angrier. They should've been helping him to die consciously. That might be hard for a little kid, Sherwin said. Yeah, to give him the benefit of the doubt, seven's a funny age, Jasper said. Even so, I just wanted to shake him; and that wasn't doing me any good, you know. Dying's like any other job, it's important to do it right. You've got to purify yourself. Maintain a schedule. With a schedule it doesn't seem so bad. On Jasper's schedule was a visit to the coast. He wanted cold seawater poured over his head, flattening his hair, chilling his scalp. He wanted the feel of that. They had to let him fly out to the coast, come back, it could be done, it wouldn't even take a day. This place is full of dying people, you know, this place I'm in, Jasper said, and none of them is going to die aware because they're so old and they don't have the strength for it. But I am because I'm young, Win, I'm young.

You're going to make me cry, baby, Sherwin said. But he didn't feel close to crying. He didn't even know why he came to visit Jasper. They'd had some good times once.

If you were me, I don't think I'd stay with you like this, Jasper said. It's awfully nice of you to visit me.

You wouldn't stay with me? Sherwin said, professing anguish.

I don't think so. I probably wouldn't, Jasper said. I don't like sick people.

Jasper faded in and out. He was struggling against it. He thought he was doing it in a new way.

I want to be *good* at this, Win. All these people here, they see with their memories. It's no good, Win.

I thought you were supposed to make nice memories, Sherwin said. I thought that was the point.

I asked my aunt to put my years and my months and my days on my marker, Jasper said. Do you think she'll do that?

I don't know from aunts.

They don't do it so much anymore, the months and the days. Jasper blinked his eyes several times. I'm going to change the subject. I'm announcing this so you'll know I'm doing it deliberately, that it's not like a weird mental convulsion I'm having. I'm doing this consciously. I don't think my voice sounds right. I've got to concentrate. Maybe you should go.

Sherwin undesirable even here at deathside; it was humiliating. Sherwin began feeling sorry for himself. No, I'm going to stay with you, baby.

Jasper looked upset, as though Sherwin were insisting on going into a party where people would think they were a couple.

Sherwin laughed. I know what you're thinking, baby.

Jasper raised his hand and smashed it all about in the air around his head. That's not possible, he said.

I'm loathsome, aren't I, Sherwin said, but didn't we have some good times together?

I'm not having a retrospective here. I don't want a retrospective. This is the tour now proceeding forward. I'm taking the tour by myself. Am I making sense? Is my voice all right? I don't want you. I never wanted you.

You're lovely and lucid, baby, Sherwin said. I never thought we were more than friends.

You'd like to exchange places with me, but you can't.

That's what I want, Sherwin said, to exchange places.

You'll die someday, Jasper said. Fuck up your own death, don't try to fuck up mine.

Spittle poured from the corners of Jasper's mouth. He fumbled for a tissue in his bathrobe pocket and mopped at it. It's the medication, he said.

Before Green Palms, when Jasper had been in the hospital, the doctors had opened up his head, looked inside, lay their scalpels down, and closed it up again. *We just lay our scalpels down, son.* For a while this phrasing had intrigued Jasper. He heard in it some obeisance to the mystery, the beautiful mystery that waited beyond the mere problem.

Sherwin smoked and thought of Jasper, who was probably dead by now, the aunt back in Alexandria thinking, But I don't want to put on the months and the days. That boy could be so affected sometimes. . . . For all Sherwin knew, Auntie might have been a figment of Jasper's lesions. The point was that Sherwin couldn't even have a conversation with a dying person without getting insulted. Wasn't being treated with insolence by the dying virtually impossible? And Jasper had been an insecure, unformed youth, still working on his languors and dislikes. They hadn't known each other to any true degree. Jasper knew nothing of Sherwin's suicide attempts, but then few did. Even Sherwin wondered how many could be counted as intentional. Sometimes he'd come up with six, sometimes eight, it depended on how inclusive he wanted to be. Do you count as one, for example, the thousand men who'd had you? He didn't usually count that. He'd thrown himself down a flight of stairs once; cut himself (embarrassing, that one, for they were clearly the cuts of a malingerer); smashed up a few cars (he didn't drive anymore, having lost confidence in that method); commenced to hang himself but then thought better of it. His most deliberate one was Seconal in the fine hotel: order some room service, masturbate to Pay-per-View, go out in a king-sized bed with a view of the Catalinas. But his vomiting had annoyed the people in the next room (a couple marking their thirtieth wedding anniversary) to such an extent that they called the front desk, and his efforts were thwarted by a pissed-off concierge. He'd never be allowed to play his parasuicide game in that establishment again. The fulfillment of one's most cherished desire can often founder on one's choice of means. He couldn't interest his body in helping him out. It was as though his body was saying, Wait a minute, we're not through with you just yet. We'll let you know when it's time. You have no idea what we have in store for you, you dabbler, you fabricator, you.

Sherwin no longer thought about his suicide stratagems in a responsible, straightforward fashion. He longed for an audience, an audience of one, namely Alice. Why Alice, he wasn't quite sure. He was a little annoyed with her for losing interest in him, obviously, but that in itself wasn't enough to propel him toward another attempt. He didn't construe his attempts as a reaction to anything, had never made even one in response to a particular, dispiriting event. He didn't want any connection to exist between occurrences in his flimsy life and the suicide act, should it occur. He wanted to deepen the gulf between what he was and the way he behaved. Still, he thought he'd probably been born a suicide, born with the little nothingness gene, the predilection to nothingness. Everyone must have it, it's just that Sherwin and his kind, or as he like to think of them, his *ilk*, nurtured and appreciated it and in fact would not be able to live without doting and dwelling on it. The thought of suicide was his passion, his pet, something he shared only with his own starved heart. The little nothingness gene—most people let it atrophy. Or they smothered it with the habit of living and self-interest. But Sherwin kept his in operating condition.

He wished he could get Alice interested. She didn't have to do it herself—he wasn't the kind of person who wanted company, exactly—but if she would just apply herself to conversation about it. Still, was there anything more boring than people talking? No, there was not.

He turned back toward the house, went into the kitchen, and ate, in rapid succession, a number of bread rounds topped with tiny, colorful, irrationally wedded and chic foodstuffs.

One of the caterers rapped his knuckles. "Hey, man, slow down. It took me half an hour to put that tray together. Eat some cashews or something."

"What's the occasion for this event, anyway?" Sherwin asked sulkily.

"Why should there be an occasion? People have parties." He shifted the tray out of Sherwin's reach. "Don't you have a job to do?"

Sherwin saw the host's daughter in the corner, flirting cautiously with one of the servers, a boy wearing his hair in a long ponytail.

"Hiya . . . Annabel," he said, her name coming to him.

She widened her eyes. The piano player looked so *morbid*. He was really the strangest person—the pitted skin, the too-black hair, the pale artificial-looking hands. When he wasn't playing the piano, they just hung there. He was really so ungainly and disturbing. "Jonathan and I were just talking about puns," she said, "about making puns. Whether that was middle-class or not."

"Middle-class," Sherwin pronounced.

"Every single thing you can probably classify whether it is or it isn't," Annabel said. "It's maybe a waste of time, but it's sort of fun, too, and could help you get organized and maybe save you some time eventually."

"Do you believe you're going to be resurrected or reincarnated?" Sherwin asked. "Quick, which?"

Annabel appeared frightened, but the boy looked at Sherwin and said softly, "Resurrected." She looked at him gratefully.

"But there are rules, the rules being, you've got to have all your own parts," Jonathan continued. "Can't have artificial organs, grafts, plates, implants, or someone else's blood in your body at the time of death. I intend to keep to the rules. If you don't abide by them, I honestly couldn't tell you what would happen, regardless of your beliefs." He looked at Sherwin appraisingly, as though to say, You're just fucked, man. . . .

Sherwin felt he was being toyed with.

"I'd like to come back as—" Annabel began.

"That's transmigration," Jonathan said, "not reincarnation."

"Oh . . ." she said.

"But both of those things are voodoo," the boy said. "Resurrection's the way to go."

"Middle-class," Sherwin opined.

"I've got to serve these salmon puffs," Jonathan confided to Annabel.

"So," Sherwin said after he'd left, "where's your friend tonight? That Alice person."

"She's either with Corvus or looking for her . . . whatever, like she usually is."

"I kind of hoped I might see her here."

"How old are you?" Annabel asked.

He'd forgotten for a moment what he'd told Alice. He usually told women that he was twenty-eight. He couldn't get away with that with men. "Twenty-eight," he said.

"How old *really*?"

"You're hurting my feelings," Sherwin said. In the other room, someone was playing the piano. He might as well not even be here tonight. It was a strange night, the kind of night where thoughts of the immeasurable greatness of the sea that none can cross kept intruding. He liked to keep such thoughts in their place. He didn't mind entertaining them amusingly while alone but found them formidably undesirable when they accosted him in public. In public, he preferred harboring thoughts of self-destruction, but not of the way-of-death variety.

One of the buttons of his shirt was cracked in half—therefore not qualifying as a button, right?—and Annabel could see his skin, which was watery white. He had to be forty years old, maybe even more. She shuddered. "Never mind," she said. "You don't have to tell me how old you are. You're only as old as you feel." What did that actually mean? Annabel wondered. She wished she hadn't said it.

"You don't want to know anything about me," Sherwin pouted.

"Oh, I don't," Annabel said with great feeling.

"Well, we're both great fans of Alice."

"We *are*?" Annabel said.

Sherwin laughed.

"Alice can be so mean," Annabel said. "Maybe you don't know her mean side. Once I said to her, 'You're such a septic, Alice,' and she was all over me because I said 'septic.' She's so vain about language. It was just a little mispronunciation, and she was all over me."

Sherwin laughed again.

"I don't think Alice will ever have fans." Annabel said. If Alice were here, she'd be having a fit about salmon being served. The whole thing about salmon *was* sort of pathetic. That need to return. And when they did succeed in returning to the place where they had been born or spawned or whatever, didn't they just rot? . . . like immediately . . .

"If you're not a fan by nature—I don't mean just a fan of Alice's, but a fan by nature—then you must be aware of the presence of God."

"Oh, I can't—I just can't talk like this." Annabel said.

"An awareness of the presence of God enables a person to resist the false values of mass communications, which create fans, enthusiasts, fantasists."

"I think mass communication is wonderful," Annabel said. "I think it's done an awful lot of good." She had turned quite pale.

"Hey, relax," Sherwin said. "I'm just kidding around."

The ponytail had returned to the kitchen, his platter of salmon puffs denuded.

"Jonathan!" she screamed.

"Will you tell Alice I'm sorry I missed her?" Sherwin said.

"Sorry you missed her," Annabel said. "Certainly." Is this what they did together, he and Alice? It was sick.

She picked up a little ceramic butter dish, took the top off, and then put it back on. The lid was in the shape of a little hen, and a chick was nestled in the hen's wing. She had bought it for her mother for Christmas one year and of course her mother had hated it, wanting nothing with the merest whiff of domesticity as a gift. Annabel took the top off again; it fit back only one way. How absorbing this little dish was . . . she wished Sherwin would leave. She glanced up and saw with relief that he actually was walking away, twitching and rolling his shoulders in the dark tuxedo. He was so odious and *incoherent*. Someone else was playing the piano anyway. Was he even necessary?

Sherwin passed through the kitchen and slowed but did not stop his passage into the great room, where the guests were still striving toward the party's high note, which it might not achieve. Madder music was required. He didn't look at the piano. By the door there was a table in the shape of an elephant. Indian, Sherwin thought. Right? They're the ones with the smaller ears, the longer face. On top of it was a glass of white wine with an hors d'oeuvre in it, looking for all the world like a turd in a toilet.

Outside, he moved away from the light of the party, down the length of the house. Below, cupped in the valley, the lights of the city trembled, and high up, in further darkness, a greenish wad of light burned solitary and bright—a mine reopened, working out its semiprecious stones. He stood and smoked. Sometimes we exist, he thought, and sometimes we pretend to exist, which takes considerably more effort. He walked to the end of the house. Metal animals were spiked into the decoratively inclined earth as one-dimensional entertainment. A troupe of quail. A life-sized javelina.

He hadn't realized how big a house it was. One wing angled off westward. The house, subtly, seemed to go on and on. Sherwin grinned and shook his head. It was like the classic dream where you dream there's one more room to your house—silly me, it's been there all the while, and what? I'd forgotten? A whole other room! Of course it wasn't his own house, it was his sometime employer's house, the man who signed the checks. He touched the handle on a glass door, and it slid back on its tracks with a dry whisper. He patted the wall for a light switch.

It was a bedroom, ornate as the rest of the house but tousled and cold. Cold as a meat locker. There were silk sheets on the bed of a dark rose color. Long mirrors, the kind you attached to the backs of doors, leaned against the walls. Drinking glasses and books scattered about, a few table lamps, the ones with shades as tall as a child. An overhead fan rotated slowly, making the room colder still. Now, this was a room you could go out in, a room that made no bones about it. This would be a room to introduce to Alice.

"'There shall be no sea, they say/On Nature's great coronation day/ when the Bridegroom comes to the Bride' dum dum dum dum." But what that meant, of course, was nullity, not the old in-and-out. Maybe he should make a few preparations and come back here to deal himself his blow. Clean his apartment, tell his few remaining acquaintances their failings, get a colonic irrigation. . . . He picked up the nearest reading material, *The Worst Journey in the World,* by one Apsley Cherry-Garrard. It had Carter's bookplate in it. Carter might be a bit of a goose, Sherwin thought.

The Worst Journey in the World was polar in nature, as the worst-journey genre tended to be, and concerned the doomed Antarctic explorer Scott, a figure for whom Sherwin had little empathy. Scott had made it clear in his diaries that although he and his little group (a fateful asymmetrical seven rather than the originally planned-for six) had the means to take their own lives in an emergency, they decided when the last fatal blizzard descended to die naturally. Sort of the let-the-body-deal-with-it-rather-than-the-mind attitude. But their decision to consciously freeze to death was sort of an ultrasuicide. They got foxed.

Sherwin put the book down. He was surprised there wasn't some porn or some other sign of innocent human diversion. The room eluded him, its destiny seeming a little vague. He couldn't even hear the party from here.

He switched on the VCR on top of the television set, and Africa bloomed. The veldt. People with remarkable cheekbones. A Land Rover tearing along.

"This is the part that's always supposed to bring a tear to your eye," a woman's voice said. "It's when they've left the lioness for a week and it's the rainy season and she isn't able to get anything to eat and she's half starved. But that's not the real Elsa there. That's her stand-in."

"Jesus! You startled me," Sherwin said. "My heart went skippety."

"I loathe that movie," the woman said. "It's been in there for a month." She smiled at him thinly, a hefty broad with sunken eyes wearing some sort of partygoing apparatus with gauzy overlays, the kind hefty broads ofttimes wore. She looked familiar, as though he'd seen her in a photograph somewhere, but a specific photograph, framed.

"So you slipped away from the party, too," Sherwin said.

"Some time ago," Ginger said. "Tell me, how did you find your way in here?"

"Yeah, I shouldn't be here," Sherwin said. "It's just one of those nights when I don't feel at home in my own skin. Whose room is this, anyway?"

"That boob Carter's."

"Yeah?" Sherwin said. "He likes Elsa the lioness?"

"If he were hip," Ginger said, "he'd have a sci fi, horror, and B-and-C flicks library, but Carter is as unhip as it gets."

She was hefty but rather remarkably bony, too. It sort of came and went.

"The mirrors are a kick."

"It's just one of his latest notions. He thinks they'll bother me, but they don't." She bent toward him. "Hi," she said.

He could see her breastbone, a bony wing. He had a quick recall of his sister, whom he hadn't thought about in years. After she was diagnosed, his mother insisted she'd caught cancer from eating dirt when she was little, making little cakes and pies out of dirt and pebbles and berries in her playhouse. She'd caught it and held it for ten years and then died when she was seventeen. His mother had kept bees. There was a saying: bees don't thrive unless they're told the news. She'd talked to her bees, he remembered, even more after his sister died. She was good with bees, his mother, which was another way of saying she wasn't all there.

"Whoa," Sherwin said. "I just thought about some people I hadn't thought about for a long time."

This did not engage her interest. "You know, I'm so curious about what people think—and then it's all so boring. Most of what people think aren't thoughts, anyway, they're memories. People treasure a good memory, but the thing you've got to realize is if you think about your dead daddy, it doesn't make him any less dead in his other life."

Sherwin listened intently.

"You may say, 'Well I don't have a dead daddy,' but many people do, and they think about that dead daddy and delude themselves into thinking they're keeping him alive somehow by the persistence of their memories. It's so ridiculous. That's just one example, I have others. People think memory grants an extension. Memory does not grant extensions."

Sherwin liked the way she talked. There was something wrong with her, he thought; maybe she'd had a stroke. What did they say the first overt sign of a stroke was? An odd look? She had that, all right. One taco short of a combination plate. "An extension?" He laughed. "An extension of what?"

"You've got bad teeth, you know that?" Ginger said. "You should be more discreet about laughing."

"I've got bad teeth?" Sherwin said. "Really?"

"I'm very conscious of teeth," she said. "You've got scoliosis too, it looks like."

"I hate talking health," Sherwin said. "You wanna talk about God?"

"Let me tell you something . . . how can I put this?"

"That's always the challenge."

"God sends you after something that isn't there."

Sherwin thought about this.

"I wouldn't smirk if I were you," she snapped.

"No, no, I like that. We're all bums on a scavenger hunt."

"I hate people who take something someone says, then say it in a different, far less interesting way and pretend it's better. I would never have said that. We are not all bums on a scavenger hunt."

"Cigarette?"

"Not yet," Ginger said.

There really was an odd smell in this room. It sort of soaked into you.

"You think I farted, don't you?" she said. "Well, I didn't."

"I don't for a moment think you farted," Sherwin said graciously.

"Carter believes I'm shooting breezers, and that's not it at all."

She was *big*. It was an odd sensation. He was, in this sensation, infinitesimally small.

"Why don't you go find Carter for me and bring him in here?" Ginger suggested. "Tell him that it's imperative that he come in here with you for a moment."

"What reason would I give?" Sherwin asked.

"Oh, just say it's an emergency. Say someone's hurt or something."

"Is someone hurt?" He grinned again, covering his mouth with his hand. He liked her, he didn't want to annoy her. Here was someone who could understand him completely.

"In a manner of speaking," Ginger said.

"Something could happen in here. I'm agreeing with you."

"Carter thinks I'm crude. Of course, he never found me welcoming or desirable before, either."

"He's a civilian. He's blind to greatness. You're a freak, baby. You're great."

"And you're the famous piano player, aren't you? The one with the little limp-dick death wish."

This summation of his situation in no way surprised him.

"You're the plenipotentiary, baby," Sherwin said. "You're my girl."

"Embrace me," Ginger said, "and I will be beautiful."

"Be beautiful and I will embrace you. That's a poem, isn't it? 'We argued for hours'? And 'it turns out to be life'? Is that the one? My mind's getting shaky."

She laughed. "No, no, that's not the one I'm thinking of. Give me a cigarette." She was laughing at him. Her teeth were great. Good strong teeth.

He shook a cigarette out of his pack, lit it, and held out his hand to present it to her, but she didn't move, so he took a step forward, then stumbled over something, losing his balance and pitching against one of the leaning mirrors. He turned, twisting, trying to recover, and fell hard against another one, falling harder than he could imagine possible, into the silvering, and felt it break into him, sliding its cool tongues into his hands and throat and heart. He lay on the floor among the glittering, his blood welling and then skimming down the slim nails of glass. He had almost heard the sound of the glass slipping into him, a sound like his father's shovels slicing into the ground. His father had called himself a tree surgeon, though in fact he had specialized in just cutting them down, taking them down to the stump. He had saws longer than his arms and called them his Bad Boys. Now look at this Bad Boy, he'd say. He kept his tools beautiful, his shovels so sharp a man could shave with them. No dead daddy, he was still alive, wearing out his fourth wife somewhere in the Texas hill country. Such a nice clean sound he'd first heard; but that was past now, replaced by a sloppier, more distracting one, a squeaking and gurgling. Death by mirrors. *Cave, Cave, Dominus videt* . . . and Sherwin was showing himself to be a mess.

43

Alice was walking. No place had yet received her, the world proving to be no solace. She had started out just past dawn while her granny and poppa were still murmuring in bed, having already brewed the coffee and fed Fury his applesauce from his favorite bowl, which had the image of a half-naked body builder on the bottom. The house was full of such odd bits of china, but this was clearly Fury's favorite, always shown to him empty, prior to being filled, so he could know he wasn't being deceived.

The heat was pure and light, hollow as a bone. She had been setting out each morning for a day of wandering but returned home to her granny and poppa each night. "No bird so wild but has its quiet nest," as Sherwin would have said, quoting another. Sherwin had been a big quoter. Alice had seen his pockmarked face and bottle-black hair materialize on certain boulders recently when the light was right or, more likely, wrong. It wasn't as though he'd died instantly, there had been some lag time. The county coroner, who had arrived with the ambulance, was not of the school that fed the foolish hope that a person could die instantly. Neither conciliatory nor compassionate, he had been educated by Jesuits and as such might as well have been raised by wolves. If you'd invited the coroner to imagine that such lag time served a purpose, perhaps by allowing the soon-to-be-deceased an opportunity to plead for nonforgetfulness and the remembrance of past lives in wherever was coming next, he would've laughed in your face. He was a regular on a local talk-show channel, and Alice's granny had described his laugh as *infectious.*

That elephant had died too, the same evening, the one who painted watercolors. Her keepers had shipped her to Phoenix and bred her there, and her unborn had slipped out of her womb into her abdomen, rupturing the uterine wall. They hadn't let her paint during pregnancy because they wanted her to focus on raising a calf, they'd denied her paints, brushes, the artist's life. Ruby was the name her managers had given her. And Ruby had spent her last hours all opened up on a pile of mattresses and inner tubes. She hadn't liked Phoenix anyway. Who would? Still, she'd had many mourners there. Cheap bouquets piled high against the zoo's gates. Plush toy elephants. Even a couple of old pianos, "Forgive us" painted on the keys. Candy, conversely, had not been pregnant at all, except hysterically. A combination of hypnotism and pharmaceutical mixing had untethered the imaginary child from her bitter and uncharismatic grasp.

Alice loped through washes and down the cracked beds of scalped rivers; she trotted through barren swales, past yellow earthmoving machines big as stables. Somewhere there was a hidden world, she hoped, closed to observation and obliteration. Closed to memory. Safe.

Annabel had written to her on one of those virtually weightless folds of blue paper where the letter was not enclosed but was the envelope itself. Annabel wrote that she'd had a facial in Paris, and the girl had discovered an imbedded, almost colorless blackhead on her cheek and she couldn't get it out and couldn't get it out and Annabel was half frantic with worry and the girl was just about to give up when she got it. Then she'd shouted, "Go, team!" and both of them wept with relief. "Go, team!" the French girl had said. Annabel had found herself quite adept at learning French, but what was the point if the French were learning dumb American phrases as fervently as they could? Annabel had just finished *The Stranger* in the original.

"Do you know how it begins, Alice?" she wrote. "*'Aujourd'hui, Maman est morte. Ou peut-être hier, je ne sais pas.'* I think there's a lot more to those first two sentences than most people think. At first I thought I couldn't go on, but then I whizzed right through it, the whole book. Daddy's very happy here, and so is Donald, who adores him, hangs on his every word, if you can believe it. He's forgotten all about Siddhartha. Daddy's going to buy Donald a vineyard, just a small one. Happiness is the most important thing there is. I've had two liaisons already and one *affaire de cœur. . . ."*

She had asked about Alice's new tooth but had not inquired after Corvus. There was more, written in the margins, but Alice didn't read it. She preferred not finishing something to having it end on its own terms.

She perched on a shelf of shale near a pack rat's impressive mound of cholla joints and stared down at Mr. V.'s vacated house. Mr. V. had practically teleported Annabel and Donald out of there after Sherwin's accident. "Sliced to ribbons" was the accepted phrase. By slicing himself to ribbons, Sherwin seemed to have provided a conduit of escape for the others, as though he'd been sacrificed or something. Still, it had worked out well enough. He wasn't living anyway, not really, and he had been tiresomely, peevishly aware of this for some time. But now that he was gone, he seemed more a strange thought she'd had than anything. He'd be the first to be amused by this, the first and maybe only. She could hear him say, *Why, Alice, you are empathetic.*

The house was empty, the pool drained. Everything had been auctioned off to benefit Mr. V.'s bill at the Hilton. He'd given the Corvette to the bartender, the piano to the suite's maid. Peeled of familiarity, the house looked a blind and formless thing. A realtor's sign glinted in the sun. Swaying on two little hooks beneath it was a cylinder that was supposed to provide information sheets, but there was nothing in it. Alice had looked. Now, from a distance, she gazed down at the house. Even the Indian was gone, and the chair he'd been placed in. At that very moment, some states and days removed from and unrealized by Alice, actual Indians were playing buffalo. They were making an attempt to dance the buffalo back into being—sticks shoved through their shoulder blades, bleeding, atoning, serving, pretending to be. A dance that hadn't been danced in a hundred years was now being rebroadcast. "Alicekins would enjoy this, wouldn't she?" her poppa was saying.

The emergency vehicles had certainly made a mess of the landscaping out here. On further reflection, Alice concluded it was cactus thieves who had struck. A large columnar cereus was just gone, off to a new decorating role in Palm Springs. Sophisticated burglars taking advantage of an ascendant retro surge had hit the place hard. There were holes everywhere.

Nothing stirred. Life was not obvious. The pack rat's spiny pile was festooned here and there with bottle caps and the blue plastic rings that had once ensured the purity of jugged water. The rat had to bear the burden of its incorrect name, for it was not genus *Rattus* at all although often slandered as such. Shy and misunderstood as it was, it must have been immensely pleased with the construction, which even included a tube of lipstick, Mrs. V.'s lipstick so recently enshrined by Annabel. Mrs. V. was stubborn—still being represented in this practically nowhere by this tube she had known, golden without, and within horribly crimson and waxily collapsed. Alice hoped Mr. V. had gone far enough away for happiness. And she hoped he wasn't eating veal over there, though this was unlikely, given the penchant of the French. They even ate horses. She should send him a little note, something fun, not too didactic: A HEART ATTACK IS GOD'S REVENGE FOR EATING HIS LITTLE FRIENDS. She didn't want to be informed that he'd had a heart attack, of course.

I shouldn't come out here after today, she thought. She felt a certain misalignment regarding herself and her life. A misalignment could make a big difference.

She had gone to Green Palms on the first of the days, and Nurse Daisy had appeared at the door.

"You look like you've got the flu," she said. "We can't expose our residents to random bugs that might carry them away sooner rather than later."

"I don't have the flu," Alice said.

"People deny, they conceal, they prevaricate. I've heard it all."

Inside, they were tossing a beach ball around a circle. Singing silly love songs. Getting their diapers changed.

"You've got something," Nurse Daisy said, "and it's not acceptable here. Go away, now. Shoo. Shoo!"

"I'm looking for Corvus."

"You always are. That's not her name anymore. She received a different name. What did you call your first little pets? Tyger? Domino? Don't you wish you were a little kid again?"

"Not really," Alice said.

"Your mind developing. You'd be two, then four. What a difference. People who cared would be thrilled at your progress. Those false-belief tests. You'd bring up your scores, eventually."

"What's a false-belief test?"

"Sally puts a chocolate in a box, then leaves the room. June comes in, takes the chocolate out of the box, puts it in a basket. Sally comes back. Where will Sally look for her chocolate? A two-year-old, a three-year-old will point at the basket, because that's where the chocolate *is*, but you won't. You'll be four. You'll point at the box. Theory of mind. Shows you're capable of simultaneously conceiving of and appreciating two alternative and contradictory models of reality. And it just gets better and better for a time when you're a little kid. The capacity to change nervous pathways—that is, to learn—seems unlimited. But then the changing slows, even stops. And all that's left is to get pig sick of things."

They were playing with their fruit cups on trays locked in place, the syrup too thick for their old throats. They were stroking the wheels of their chairs.

Alice could see them, dimly.

"You never long to be a little child again? Because look at you now, an odd one, one from whom love and participation are not particularly desired."

"You can't hold Corvus in here," Alice had said. "There are rules."

Nurse Daisy's jaw dropped. Rules, she mouthed. Alice almost turned to look behind her, for it seemed that the nurse was projecting to a distant, disbelieving audience.

"You must stop trying to impose yourself on that girl," Nurse Daisy said. "'*Sit in your cell, and your cell will tell you everything.*' That's something she's learned and you never will."

Inside, their names were posited in ink upon the collars of their clothes. Someone, something, was combing their old hair.

"This is not a nunnery," Alice said.

"It's a sexless place of contemplation. Don't pick nits."

"Corvus doesn't want to be in a nunnery."

"You'll never know. You are not her! Maybe you wouldn't score that nicely on the false-belief test. Maybe you'd keep going for that basket, much to everyone's disappointment."

Alice frowned. "Please," she said, "I want to see Corvus."

"Don't demean yourself with pleading," Nurse Daisy snapped. "Why do you always have to look at everything twice in order to see it? The short prayer penetrates Heaven, they say, but any fool can see this isn't

Heaven here. Your friend's disappointed you. Think of it that way if it will make you feel better."

"I'm a volunteer," Alice said. "I can come inside." Nurse Daisy firmly shut and locked the door.

Vexed, Alice had begun to walk, then run the four miles to the Wildlife Museum, with the vague intent of making a ruckus, of unroutine sabotage. But how could one sabotage death all doubled back upon itself, presenting itself so breathlessly intact? Still, she thought she'd knock some things over, rail at the paying customers, make them reflect on the transaction they were engaged in.

Then she had arrived, baffled, at the immense new wall encircling the place, to which small lettered signs in what looked to be a child's hand were attached at inconsistent intervals.

CLOSED FOR RECONSIDERATION

The cement smelled fresh. There was a smoldering smell, too. Maybe everything back there was getting an air burial. No, that was something different; pyres were not involved. With an air burial something had to come and get you. Something wild. There was no telling what. But you had to be carrion for air burial to be successful. And these objects weren't even dead. Rather, they had died but weren't dead now. It was like a church, this museum, a death dome full of fabrication and comfort and instruction and paradox. She hated it. She threw stones over the wall. Was there a vast pit back there then, tarred and lavender, offering final decease at last? She threw more stones. A limousine moved slowly past on the road above her, paused, and then proceeded on.

Stumpp and Pickless, driving with complacent aimlessness in the blue-black limousine, were each chewing on a piece of licorice. The child was in the front, and in the back there was something breathing in a box. A sweetish smell emanated. There was always something heaving in the rear in their rides together, depleted, partial, clinging to life, trying to flutter or crawl, still breathing. Something dumb, bewildered, in a weary-unto-death panic, covered in leather jackets or silken scarves, ringed with spilt dishes of water, pans of seed and crumbs. Emily liked driving purposelessly around with her charges; the motion and the little lights inside that looked like stars served to occupy their thoughts, she believed. She had put away the tea things and was gnawing on the licorice for Stumpp's sake. Stumpp had introduced her to it, both the red and the black. Licorice was very much an acquired taste, she suspected, pretty much like everything that lay ahead.

"Chucking rocks," Emily noted. A little thrill rose up in her, then subsided. She maintained a soft spot for irrational behavior. She turned to Stumpp and said somewhat fatuously, "I'm glad I'm not her." She was shocked she'd said such a thing, though it was neither true nor untrue. Lies, on the other hand, were more permissible, being nothing more than secrets.

"How could you be her?" Stumpp had finished his licorice. There was a last gummy node behind his molar. He left it there for the time being. Funny stuff, licorice. The root of the plant had been found packed in tombs in Egyptian lands. Had meant something once. Reduced to a confection now. The past was replete with lost guides.

"You can become something you're not," Emily said. She sensed, then, a whispering, a plunge and settle in the box of spilt offerings. She did not turn her head to confirm that for yet another, the intriguing passage had been breached.

Stumpp maneuvered the long car with incremental turnings of the wheel. Half-pint sutra, little Pickless. Unreaped whirlwind. The sun shone like oil upon the limousine's hood, which had been waxed to the shine of water. A futuristic ark with two unmateable souls within. As it should be. Into the future. Shouldn't even have a name, the future. Thing had died back there, whatever it was, whatever labors it had undertaken as a pup. Its time transpired. Knew she'd heard it go, little adept. Best *Homo sap* can do is perceive the penumbral. Yet not enough the penumbral. Not good enough for Pickless. Nothing too good for Pickless. Grateful he could see that so clearly. Scales all fallen away. For this was a rare confluence. Confluence to end all confluences, Stumpp and Pickless. Would never want materially, he'd make sure of that. All means must be put at her disposal. The rest up to her. For she was going to inherit the world. The world once more . . .

Was the last breath of a thing relevant? Emily wondered. She couldn't imagine why it would be.

Now this day was passing, the dreaminess of it. Alice Alive, she thought, running. Alice Endurance, Alice Errant, Alice the Dark. Alice the Alone. Dogs barked in the distance. Unseen traffic whined. The desert became pasture, then park. Permanent toilet facilities. Basketball courts. The former site of the Hohokam Drive-In Theatre, so recently torn down, where Corvus had taken Tommy to see the movies. There one day, gone the next, as ephemeral as the ephemerals it had, in its inception, replaced. Cars and trucks, separated by the now-speakerless pipes, still lined the slotted rows, drawn to this seedless waste as to the old memories of stories not their own. The occupant of each had something used for sale. Infants screamed. People were everywhere relaxing.

At the edge of the park, people milled about holding candles, each with a white, wax-catching skirt. There was a big box of candles. A boy was scooping them up and handing them out, a skinny, shirtless boy in brand-new dungarees, his hair white as glare. He reminded Alice of that boy the three of them had tied up, when there had been three of them. He looked just as eager and dumb, though he didn't have the same crookedness, and there was the hair of course. Still, he looked a lot like him. Everybody's got their double, it just wasn't good to see them. When Corvus had seen Sherwin's fetch it had certainly not done Sherwin any good. She heard the feign of him saying, "When the two shall be one and the without as the within and the male with the female neither male nor female, that's when the party begins."

"Hey there," the boy said, grinning at her. "You here for the vigil?"

"No," Alice said.

"First time, huh?"

"What's it for?"

"Tonight it's for the aquifer. Lots of people can't quite grasp the aquifer."

"Grasp it?"

"Understand how it works." He was so skinny his ribs showed.

She splayed her hand out before her. "Don't explain," she said.

"Last night it was the octopus. Would you have liked that better?"

She would not confess to this.

"Those big eyes, man. And, if they like you, they turn this rosy color. You know what its flesh feels like? Like the inside of your cheek. But things aren't looking up for the big mollusk. Richly deserving of a vigil, the octopus. Night before that, the Greenland ice sheet. You can't play favorites." He was efficiently handing out candles as he spoke. "To continue backwards. Wild horses on BLM land, fetuses, the earth in general, that synagogue from the thirties downtown they want to demolish, fetuses again. We try not to repeat in a month's time, but fetuses keep coming up. They're in demand. As a nonprofit, nonsectarian organization, we have no agenda. No long-term goal. We've got vigils *against* stuff, too. Nights against grafted cactus, technological entrancement, alternative fuels, the fur trim on those big ski parkas you see people wearing when it ain't even cold? That's German shepherd."

People were pushing against her, beginning to gather, gazing in earnest at the unlit candles, fingering and crimping the paper skirts. They had pictures of dusty foreign children pinned to their breasts. Pictures of beached whales. Human limbs in ditches. Humans without limbs in ditches.

"Caring doesn't have to be elitist. True compassion is wordless and hopeless of effecting change. You know what's nice? When we run out of candles on any given night. Then people come back earlier the next night. They want to be assured of a candle. To be without a candle is not a good thing."

People were chatting, smiling solemnly. Some had pictures of scenic highways hanging from eyeglass cords around their necks. These were the adopters—having adopted stretches of asphalt, library shelves, eroding beaches, grizzly bears, unique deadly microbes that nevertheless were singular life-forms and should not be exterminated.

"I've learned a lot since I started giving out candles. I'm going to start selling them soon, a nickel a pop, but for now they're free. I used to be so dumb you wouldn't believe it, but now I'm the Candleman. I'm smart and sane, living on the glow, the displacement in the air the flame makes. I could go anywhere with this routine. The world's my oyster."

"What does that mean?" Alice said.

"Another mollusk. Or are you referring to 'anywhere'? You don't know what anywhere is? You can live there when you don't know where else to go. You can make a living anywhere off the caring of others. Feel it! I can feel you feeling it. We're connected, you and I. I'm looking for a busker babe to work the crowds with, that could be you."

"You're kidding," Alice said, offended. She wasn't about to be someone who was in a place only because she wasn't anywhere else.

"You ever live in a pipe, a box, a Dumpster?" the Candleman said. You can be born without an enzyme, a brain, a sense of wonder. You can live like a rat, man, then *boom,* something better comes along. I've seen what comes next. Vigils. Concern is the new consumerism. A person's worth can be measured by the number and intensity of his concerns. Candles, lighting a candle, confers the kind of fulfillment that only empty ritual can bring. Empty ritual's important. It's coming back as a force in people's lives. Its role is being acknowledged. It's the keystone for tomorrow's dealings in an annexed and exploited world. And holding a candle, cradling a little flame with others holding their candle, cradling their little flame gives people the opportunity to experience something bigger than themselves without surrendering themselves to it. A single candle is the symbol of individuated as opposed to universal life. The latter scares people. They don't want any part of it. It's spooky, like primordial slime, man, it's not pretty. Still, a candle alone is nothing. The Candleman knows that. You know that. You'd feel stupid holding it, looking at it. But in the midst of innumerable strangers holding theirs, it works. It's absolving, it's reassuring. I'm down to two. Only two left. Take one."

But they were gone in a twinkling, the first claimed by a man, friend of the Salton Sea, the last by a woman, friend of the symphony.

"Concern for the aquifer isn't enough tonight," the Candleman said. "I've been detecting a softening around the edges for some time now.

Specificity isn't flying. Running out of candles is no longer going to be the exception but the rule."

"It seems kind of diluted out here," Alice said.

"Still ten minutes before shutdown and the lighting, and every bloody candle gone," the boy marveled.

A well-dressed gentleman in yellow trousers looked unhappily into the empty box. There was a Band-Aid on the bridge of his nose.

"Precancerous?" the Candleman asked solicitously.

Others came, looked into the empty box, departed wordlessly.

"The moment of silence is going to be the new desired thing," the Candleman said to Alice. "It's the appropriate response. There's a pertinence, a satisfaction, in respectfully acknowledging what's about to become history, whatever can't cope, can't adapt or relocate."

Two people walked past wearing straitjackets, their mouths covered with tape.

"Some, you know, their concerns are obscure, but they're all participating in a healthy outrage and sorrow. There's nothing like lighting your little candle when all around you others are lighting theirs. Nothing! Illumination. Extinguishment. Equilibrium. Then everybody goes home."

"I'm not going to be a part of this," Alice said.

"Not going to be a part!" He chuckled. "You've got to be a part. Don't you know anything about mathematics? The lost invariants of life can be found only through numbers and their relationships. You have a number, and what you think has happened to you has a number too. It's all numbers, man, just numbers. God talks in numbers, endless numbers." He gestured at the crowd. "This is nothing."

He really reminded her of that boy, that long-ago midsummer boy who had seemed so desperate to explain himself.

"You'll be a part of it, all right," the Candleman assured her. "You dream, don't you?"

Night was approaching in languorous measure. Alice didn't want to be here for it. And she didn't believe everything was numbers. Why would God bother to talk in numbers? This boy wasn't very convincing. She turned away from him without answering, away from the modest spectacle about to occur.

"You got no choice!" he shouted. "You'll see!" Oh, she thought she didn't dream, but one morning she was going to wake up, yes, she was, she would wake from the dream even the most reluctant and particular have but once, the one where four animals arrive to carry you off for the moment. You have never seen such animals as these who without a sound or a sign carry you off. You race with them across the long familiar ground that in that moment seems so glorious, so charged with beauty, strange. In their jaws you are carried so effortlessly, with such great care that you think it will never end, you long for it not to end, and then you wake and know that, indeed, they have not brought you back.